INVOLUTION & EVOLUTION

Joss Sheldon

www.joss-sheldon.com

Copyright © Joss Sheldon 2014

ISBN-13: 978-1789264906
ISBN-10: 1789264906

EDITION 1.0
Ingram Spark

First published in the UK in 2014.

Proofread by Jon Werbicki.

Cover design by Ahmad Priabudiman

FOR GRANDMA

INVOLUTION (noun) *in-voh-loo-shun*

1) Doing. **2)** Involvement in action. **3)** Involving one's body-mind-and-heart in new behaviour. **4)** Challenging one's limits.

EVOLUTION (noun) *eh-voh-loo-shun*

1) Becoming. **2)** A process of development. **3)** Improving one's nature-spirit-and-soul. **4)** Expanding one's limits.

SEE ALSO...

INVOLUTION AND EVOLUTION (expression)

1) The process through which a person-community-or-culture, by engaging in new actions, is able to achieve a new state of being. **2)** The use of one's body-mind-and-heart, to develop one's nature-spirit-and-soul. **3)** The descent of spirit into matter, and the ascent of matter into spirit.

1897

This is a story about understanding overcoming compulsion, love overcoming revulsion; and oneness overcoming abuse. About the rare sort of kind-geniality, and brave-morality; which we all possess but seldom use.

A story about detractors who will be defeated, challenges which will be completed; and principles which will be proclaimed. About acts of persecution, and threats of execution; which will all be constrained.

This is the beginning of Alfred Freeman's story, the beginning of a life full of glory; and the beginning of Alfred himself. Because Alfred is being born, in his human form; with peaceful-eyes and perfect-health.

The year is 1897.

An Italian Entrepreneur is sending the first ever seaborne wireless-message using his telegraph-machine, an Irish Schoolteacher is building the first ever engine-powered submarine; and an American Inventor is patenting his pencil-sharpener too. In India a famine is leaving the population angered, in Russia some politicians are adopting the gold-standard; and in America a marathon is being launched beneath skies which are blue. Whilst the British fight in Southern-Africa and Benin, where they hope to win; and stage a belligerent-coup.

But Alfred is only focussed on being born, serenaded by this raucous-storm; and this riotous-gale. This gale which is dazzling-deafening-and-dark, as it uproots those trees in that park; and covers them all in hail. As it sends forth this thunder which is frightening, and this lightning; which flashes on a supernatural-scale.

The animals in that barn are in a state of manic-dissatisfaction, manic-distraction; and manic-disarray. Owls cuddle to share their body-heat, a cat feeds her kittens some meat; and a horse begins to neigh. Sheep begin to hurry, chickens begin to scurry; and a donkey begins to bray.

A white-moon pierces a black-sky, as light pours down from up high; where Jupiter is in conjunction with Saturn. It reflects off this water-vapour, and that torn-newspaper; to create a celestial-pattern.

This pattern covers Alfred's Mother who is wearing two cotton-frocks, and two pairs of cotton-socks; with her hair in the pompadour-style. With braided-tresses which reach her waist, and a genteel-face; which features a genteel-smile.

She eats her way through this overripe-fig, cleans her teeth with this shredded-twig; and gets into her single-bed. She lies beneath these layered-sheets, and gazes out at those sodden-streets; with a pillow beneath her head.

Having already dreamt of angels who cloaked her in flowers, holy-spirits with magical-powers; and an elephant with a silver-trunk. This is the moment she has dreamt about, because her firstborn son is coming out; atop this silver-bunk.

She does not feel her contractions shake, her waters break; or her cervix become dilated. She just lies here feeling light, bright; secure-satisfied-and-sated.

So whilst outside there is stormy-pain, stormy-rain; and lightning which strikes the ground. In here there is peace, this sense of release; and this light which spreads around.

These curtains part after a few more seconds, this thunder beckons; and Alfred steps into the world. His Mother feels lighter than air, without a care; as Alfred is now unfurled.

As he acknowledges his cue, without much ado; and enters onto this stage. As he makes his debut-bow, with a soppy-brow; and begins his latest-age.

Without being coerced, he steps into the world feet-first; as if he is ready to walk through life. Unconscious of conventions, unaware of pretensions; and unaffected by earthly-strife.

Raindrops sparkle in the moonlit-sky, and perfumed-blossoms float on by; as this storm begins to die down. As that donkey goes to sleep, and those birds begin to cheep; with an angelic sort of sound.

All is now tranquil and all is now bright, all is now peaceful and all is now light; all is now clear-cool-and-calm. Alfred has been born without causing any strain, pain; hurt-horror-or-harm.

1899

As Alfred plays near those ticking-clocks, he starts to contract this bout of smallpox; which leaves him struggling in vain. This disease passes over his tongue, descends towards his lung; and ascends towards his brain. It covers him in pus-filled pimples, pus-filled dimples; and pus-filled pain.

Seeing Alfred like this makes his Mother start to panic, and become manic; so she takes him to see his Doctor. She takes him past this block of flats, this pack of rats; and that rather hairy Proctor.

The year is 1899.

A Norwegian Clerk is designing the modern paper-clip one afternoon, an American Astronomer is discovering Saturn's ninth moon; and a German Chemist is registering '*Aspirin*' as a trademark. In the Netherlands a treaty on war is being signed by diplomats in national-costumes, in America a new society is leaving bibles in hotel rooms; and in Australia a cyclone is spreading in the dark. Whilst the British travel to war in South Africa again, in a tram-truck-and-train; and a boat which looks like an ark.

But Alfred can only focus on his Doctor's crooked-lip, crooked-hip; and dusty-drug. Which his Doctor forces down, with water which looks brown; inside this dirty-mug.

Alfred's Mother carries him out of this surgery and along these paths, past those public-baths; and back home for a period of isolation. Because smallpox is rather egregious, and rather contagious; as it spreads its brand of damnation.

And so Alfred's Mother makes a fuss, cleans Alfred's pus; and helps him to flee from his disease. She changes his dressings, recites some blessings; and gives him some lumps of cheese.

She cares for Alfred all on her own, here in their family home; where they have both been confined. For Alfred's Father is a soldier who has gone to war, with his army-corps; and left them both behind.

His Father has left Alfred in this state of sickness-soreness-and-stillness, but Alfred fights his illness; and overcomes his ordeal. His pimples turn into thirty-two scars, these stigmata which look like stars; and will never fully heal.

These marks surround Alfred's eyes of smoky brown-quartz, and these three brown-warts; as Alfred's form takes shape all over. With cocoa-coloured hair, which flutters in the air; and these cheekbones which his Mother calls '*The White Cliffs Of Dover*'.

"These cliffs of yours will be attracting seagulls before too long, my little-soldier," she says as she picks this clover. "Look at me. There aren't any oceans which need a breakwater like this! There aren't any navies planning to invade your face, my wonderful-warrior. Oh, whatever shall I do with you and all your mischity, Alfred Freeman? I really don't know! I-don't-I-don't-I-don't."

Alfred's Mother is referring to Alfred's habit of stacking things up in piles, whilst he skips-shimmies-and-smiles; as his character also takes shape. As he scrambles up climbing-frames, plays infantile-games; and gets into many a scrape.

As the only child in a house without a dad, Alfred's presence stops his Mother from going mad; and so she coddles him more than is the norm. She takes him to the countryside, and to the seaside; when it is windy and when it is warm.

She makes him play-dough, and puts on a puppet-show; to give him stimulation. She reads to him, takes him to swim; and sings without cessation.

She takes Alfred to see these billowy-trees, who spend each winter losing their leaves; only to grow them back the summer after. And she rocks him on her knees, and gives his cheeks a squeeze; which leaves him in fits of childish-laughter.

So an appeal for '*Saturn and Jupiter's children*' in this feuilleton-section, inspires her to take Alfred in a whole new direction; past these Workmen with noisy-drills. Past this Boy who waves this stake, this loch-lagoon-and-lake; and those satanic-looking mills. This rabbit who is caught in a trap, this Goatherd who is taking a nap; and that row of giddy-hills.

They arrive at this farmhouse which is surrounded by brown-wheat, brown-peat; a brown-awning and a brown-deck. Where they meet this Receptionist who has rings on her fists, bangles on her wrists; and chains all around her neck.

"Do you know who I am?" She asks with a jiggle.

"Ye-ye-ye-yes," Alfred replies with a giggle. "You are Ācariya.

Ācariya! Teacher Ācariya."

The Receptionist closes her turquoise-eyes, lifts her chin towards the skies; and starts to glow. Alfred mirrors her movements, with his own improvements; and his own sort of natural-flow. Whilst his Mother becomes bemused, and confused; by this peculiar sort of show.

Until she is met by these three eastern Astrologers who are wearing regal-crowns, royal-gowns; and robes which look sublime. These men were inspired when Jupiter-and-Saturn aligned, to search and find; the children who were born at that time. So they take Alfred into this room, which contains this broom; and those dusty bottles of wine.

"We're going to show you two items together," this Tall Astrologer begins to chime. "All you have to do is point to the one which you prefer."

Alfred picks these prayer-beads in woody-tones, ahead of that necklace made from precious-stones; precious-gems and precious-pearls. He picks this ancient wooden-drum, ahead of that trumpet made from golden-crumb; golden-buttons and golden-curls. And he picks this ascetic's cane, ahead of that staff from a tyrant's reign; which was used to beat little-girls.

He puts the beads around his neck whilst he sucks his thumb, he creates a happy-beat on this ancient-drum, and he points this stick at the sun.

Before he chooses between battered-flasks, decorative-masks; and bronze-bells. Scented-soaps, woven-ropes; and seashells.

Without any obvious explanation, the Astrologers always respond with veneration; contented-eyes and contented-smiles. Until Alfred chooses one watch above another, when he is reunited with his Mother; who is unaware of these secretive-trials.

This Redheaded Astrologer gives her the gold which Alfred chose, whilst he brushed his clothes; and rejected some silver-coils. This Tall Astrologer gives her the frankincense which Alfred chose, whilst he scratched his nose; and rejected some scented-oils. And this Bald Astrologer gives her the myrrh which Alfred chose, whilst he smelled a rose; and rejected some stolen-spoils.

"You have a very special child," he says whilst he rubs his lumps, bumps; and boils. "He's destined to either become a mighty-soldier, who'll rule from north-to-south and east-to-west, or a great teacher who will enlighten humankind.

"If you allow him to walk his own path through life, he'll bring you untold joy-honour-and-glory. But if you stand in his way, he'll bring you untold sorrow-suffering-and-pain."

Alfred's Mother lifts her chin upwards, pulls her shoulders backwards; and blushes with maternal-pride. Before the Tall Astrologer gives her this garment, with this ancient-parchment; folded up inside...

A PROPHECY

First there was Owl, who was wise-and-old,
With understanding-and-knowledge too vast to be told.

The forest was Owl's, Owl was tough,
He ruled in a way which was viciously-rough.

Then came Dog, who was loyal-and-true,
With love-and-compassion all the way through.

Owl was old though, Dog was still young,
He outlived old Owl for many a sun.

Then came Boy, who was honest-and-pure,
With oneness-and-serenity which made him sure.

Dog needed companionship, Boy made him his own,
He mastered Dog gently, without needing a throne.

1901

After another two years of childhood, spent doing all the things which a young-boy should; Alfred is at home again. He is watching his Mother cry, sob-snivel-and-sigh; as if she is insane.

"God is dead!" She shouts out in pain. "God remains dead. And we've killed him, Alfred Freeman. We-have-we-have-we-have!"

Alfred's Father has died, so his Mother is teary-eyed; with teary-pain and teary-grief. Alfred is stroking her hair, with loving-care; and giving her relief.

The year is 1901.

An Australian Judge is inaugurating his nation's first ever parliament whilst wearing a cape, a German Pharmacist is inventing adhesive-tape; and an American Businessman is inventing disposable-razors. In China an anti-imperialist rebellion is being smashed, in America a stock-market has only just crashed; and in Sweden the first Nobel Prizes are being judged by appraisers. Whilst the British have been in Southern Africa for another two years, spreading trauma-torture-and-tears; dressed up in their khaki-blazers.

Alfred's Father was out there dressed up in his khaki-suits, khaki-boots; and khaki-shorts. He was a tall man who had a brown-nose, brown-clothes; and Alfred's eyes of smoky brown-quartz.

He was a proud man who had a perfectly straight back, a patriotic-tattoo which was perfectly black; and a family with proud military-traditions. His Great Granddad arrived at the Opium War by sea, his Granddad fought in New Zealand in 1850; and his Father fought in several African missions.

But Alfred cannot remember their days of paternal-union, before he was capable of communion; and before his Father left for war. He can only focus on his Mother who starts to trip, spin-stumble-and-slip; across this polished-floor.

She lands near this dogskin-glove which still has a label, this coffee-table; and that ivory-flute. These jars which are full of cooking-brandy, colourful-candy; and colourful-fruit.

She is thrown here by her uncontrollable-backbone, which has a mind of its own; and acts as her emotional-guide. It reveals her emotions with each whirl-wave-and-wiggle, jolt-jerk-and-jiggle; spin-shimmy-and-slide.

It whirls her to the left when she feels uneasy, waves her to the right when she feels queasy; and wiggles her around when she feels manic. It jolts her forth when she feels cool, jerks her back when she feels cruel; and jiggles her around when she begins to panic.

So in her heartbroken-condition, her spine bends Alfred's Mother into this foetal-position; as its top curls in towards its base. Vertebrae-kiss-vertebrae, and try to hide her away; out of this cold-hearted place.

"You must always act like the true child of your Father in heaven," she whimpers, and simpers; whilst tears roll down her face. "Look at me. He'll always be by your side, my little-soldier. He'll be with you wherever you go, my terrific-trooper. He-will-he-will-he-will. There. That is all."

"Wa-wa-wa-why Mother?" Alfred begins to stutter.

"Oh, you really are a beautiful boy," his Mother begins to mutter.

"Pa-pa-pa-please tell me! What's happened to Father?"

"And your cheekbones! They're just like the *White Cliffs Of Dover*!"

"Pa-pa-pa-please tell me! When is Father coming home? Pa-pa-pa-pretty please. Pretty please with a cherry on top."

"Oh, you'll be a mighty-officer, Alfred Freeman, just like he was. Somewhere-somewhen-somehow, you-shall-you-shall-you-shall!"

"Was, Mother?"

"Your Father is in heaven, Alfred, and he's looking down on everything you do. Oh, my wonderful-warrior, he-is-he-is-he-is."

"Why, Mother? What's happened to him? Please tell me. Please-please-please."

"Oh, how persistent you are, my fearless-fighter! I just don't know what I'm going to do with you and all your mischity. I-don't-I-don't-I-don't. But I suppose I really should explain."

So his Mother wipes these tears from her cheeks, before she speaks, shouts-squeals-and-shrieks.

"Look at me. 'Twer in South Africa, Alfred. Your Father had been there since the start of the war. He'd secured victory at the Tall Hill, enlisted child-soldiers in the Besieged Town, and led a breakthrough attack in the Dale.

"My notion, it's such a ghastly thing. It really is a thousand pities.

"Your Father was working in a concentration-camp, when a Zulu who had abandoned the British army, did attack him. Upon my senses! That savage struck your Father with a rock, crushed his brave-skull, and mushed his poor-brain.

"Look at me. Alfred, this is exactly why we need to fight in those countries. Oh, those brutes aren't civilised like we are. And we, as the guardians of civilisation, have a duty to tame them.

"Your Father was providing a service to mankind. He's dead, but his life wasn't wasted; he'll still be a glorious-example for us all to follow. And you, my terrific-trooper, *shall* follow in his footsteps. You shall be just like him! Somewhere-somewhen-somehow, you-shall-you-shall-you-shall!"

But despite his Mother's confidence Alfred still feels cold, because at just four-years-old; he has become the man of this house. So he cries like a fountain, sits still like a mountain; and is silent like a timid grey-mouse.

THE OWL

Once upon a time there was an Owl. A wise old Owl, with understanding-and-knowledge which was too vast to be told.

Owl understood every tree-animal-and-bird in his forest. He understood that the trees used their eyes to look for light, the animals used their noses to sniff for food, and the birds used their ears to listen for birdsong.

And Owl used his knowledge to control his forest, because knowledge is power, and Owl used his power to rule his fellow creatures.

He flew high in the sky, all day and all night, for many a day and many a night. And he blocked the sun with his wings.

"What do you think you're you doing?" Poplar protested.

"I'm controlling my light of course," Owl replied. "You might not be so civilised, relying on the sun for light, but I'm intelligent-respectable-and-strong. I can soar up high and swoop down low, fly over any tree on the planet, and hide the light whenever I like!"

Owl's words filled the trees with fear.

"We need that light to live," Poplar pleaded. "Please come down and rest on our comfortable branches."

"Only if you make me your king," Owl replied. "Only if you build palaces for me, hide my jewels, and become my servants."

The trees in Owl's forest were normally amicable folk, who wanted to be friends with all the forest's creatures. But Owl controlled their light, and so they had no choice but to obey him.

"Okay, okay," Poplar panted. "Our branches-leaves-and-roots are yours, all yours. You shall be our king."

This made Owl happy, it made Owl very happy, but he still wanted more. So he pestered the trees, all day and all night, for many a day and many a night. And he made them hide all the forest food beneath their roots.

"What do you think you're you doing?" Pig protested.

"I'm controlling my food of course," Owl replied. "You might not be so civilised, sniffing out your food one meal at a time, but I'm intelligent-respectable-and-strong. I can control the skies up high and the earth down low, govern any animal on the planet, and hide the food whenever I like!"

Owl's words filled the animals with fear.

"We need that food to live," Pig pleaded. "Please come down and ride on our sturdy-backs."

"Only if you make me your king," Owl replied. "Only if you build cities for me, guard my jewels, and become my soldiers."

The animals in Owl's forest were normally conscientious folk, who wanted to be equal with all the forest's creatures. But Owl controlled their food, and so they had no choice but to obey him.

"Okay, okay," Pig panted. "Our muscles-teeth-and-limbs are yours, all yours. You shall be our king."

This made Owl happy, it made Owl very happy, but he still wanted more. So he pestered the animals, all day and all night, for many a day and many a night. And he made them howl as loudly as they could.

"What do you think you're you doing?" Robin protested.

"I'm controlling my airwaves of course," Owl replied. "You might not be so civilised, unable to control the sounds which other creatures make, but I'm intelligent-respectable-and-strong. I can speak to the trees up high and the animals down low, deafen any bird on the planet, and drown out the airwaves whenever I like!"

Owl's words filled the birds with fear.

"We need those airwaves to live," Robin pleaded. "Please come down and listen to our beautiful-songs."

"Only if you make me your king," Owl replied. "Only if you build roads for me, search for jewels, and become my sentries."

The birds in Owl's forest were normally social folk, who wanted to work with all the forest's creatures. But Owl controlled their airwaves, and so they had no choice but to obey him.

"Okay, okay," Robin panted. "Our feathers-beaks-and-wings are yours, all yours. You shall be our king."

This made Owl happy, it made Owl very happy. He ruled the entire forest, and controlled every tree-animal-and-bird.

And so he made his subjects build him great-palaces, bring him resplendent-jewels, and protect him from insurrection.

No tree-animal-or-bird was ever brave enough to complain. Because Owl was intelligent-respectable-and-strong, and everyone knew it, since Owl told them so himself!

1902

With his Mother's bony-hands on his bony-shoulders, Alfred is being taken to learn the knowledge of his elders; here at this primary-school. He is wearing a flat-cap which is way too tight, long-socks which are way too bright; and grey-shorts which are way too small.

The year is 1902.

A Matron from New Zealand is becoming the first ever registered nurse as medical standards advance, a French Journalist is formulating his plans for the inaugural *Tour De France*; and an American Engineer is inventing electronic air-conditioning. In Egypt some workers are building a dam which makes their masters feel groovy, in France they are filming the first ever science-fiction movie; and in Cuba they are declaring independence after years of petitioning. Whilst the British are in Nigeria fighting a war, with a death-toll which is starting to soar; after weeks of military-positioning.

But Alfred's gaze is fixed solely on this rocky-wall, which surrounds this primary-school; which is housed in this rambling-building. This building which sits amidst this concrete-space, with jumbled-windows on its freckled-face; and a surfeit of grey-gilding.

He walks past these flowers which are in bloom, and this large-classroom; which doubles up as this school's main hall. He passes this dirty-broom, and arrives in this other classroom; which is tired-torpid-and-tall.

This room tastes of stale-ink, smells of eggy-drink; and sounds of stony-silence. It contains these slimy-slates, wobbly-crates; and items used for science.

Alfred finds this musty-classroom, which has so little light and so much gloom; so nauseating-nightmarish-and-new. Such that just being here makes Alfred feel dismayed, afraid; bleak-broody-and-blue.

He sits on the lowest-tier of seating in front of that stage, amongst the other boys his age; who are separated from the females. He sits at this desk which is full of creaky-hinges, splintered-fringes; and rusty-nails.

He shivers somewhat discreetly, and smiles somewhat sweetly;

because he is unused to this school's strange-ways. He is unused to the Authoritative Teacher's cane, which he swishes with disdain; and he is unused to his own Teacher's gaze.

His own Teacher tells Alfred that he is a 'Big boy', 'Don't play with that pencil as if it's a toy'; and 'You're expected to behave maturely'. So Alfred folds his arms when he is pressed, locks his hands at his Teacher's request; and sits here rather demurely. He feels shaky-scared-and-shy, so he is too timid to question 'why'; or challenge his Teacher prematurely.

But as Alfred gets older-and-older, he also gets bolder-and-bolder; and his timidity fades away. He talks to this Snotty Nosed Scamp who has a hairy-ear, and the Tallest Boy in his year; with whom he likes to play. And he talks to Bernie, his companion for childhood's journey; who he meets almost every day.

Bernie has been nicknamed '*Sun Head*', because his hair is bright-red; and a real beacon of fire-fuel-and-flame. His shoulders are too wide for his chest, his waist is too wide for his vest; and too wide for his gangly-frame.

Having been put together somewhat loosely, Bernie sweats profusely; and stumbles around with wobbly danger. He sways from right-to-left, with all his heft; as he searches for steady-behaviour.

Yet Bernie is not one of those awkward-boys, who cannot play with toys; and cannot play *Hopscotch*. He plays *Marbles* with aplomb, plays *Conkers* all night long; and excels at *Spinning Tops*.

He likes to play *Cricket*, using a lamppost for a wicket; as he bats with real ease. He likes to swim after school, in the public-pool; and he also likes to climb trees.

So Alfred and Bernie play *Noughts-And-Crosses*, exchanging wins-for-losses; almost every single break. They play *Hoops* in the dark, *Tag* in the park; and *Splash* in their local lake.

They run along pebbled-beaches and sandy-shores, through seas which are full of sponges-seaweed-and-spores; and through washed-up shipwrecks. They collect bible-cards, cigarette-cards, any old cards; and any old objects. They even enjoy the same academic-subjects. They enjoy swimming-lessons dressed in their school's bathing-clothes, classes on '*How to blow one's nose*'; and other vocational-projects.

But it is military-drill which fills Alfred with a real sense of pride, and makes him feel great inside; as if he is almighty. As if he is marching into action, indifferent to danger-distress-and-distraction; all in the name of Blighty.

Drill lessons were introduced to the school-curriculum because half the Boer War volunteers were considered to be too feeble to fight, whilst the other half could not impose Britain's might; which had made the government nervous. The government had feared that the population was undergoing a process of 'degeneration', so they listened to one of the National Service League's orations; which also demanded compulsory military-service.

And they made Alfred's school hold these drill-sessions, after Latin lessons; on this field which is bathed in sun. Where this Drill Sergeant who has hair which glimmers with gel, and a moustache which glimmers as well; holds a loaded-gun.

He calls for 'Attentions' whilst brushing his khaki-suit, he calls for 'Left Turns' whilst stamping his boot; and he calls for 'Forwards' whilst slapping his thigh. Alfred obeys for king-community-and-country, looks up at that gantry; and marches on by.

"My da-da-da-Daddy was a soldier," he says once this session has finished, with energy which is undiminished; and dust in his blinking-eye. "Did you know him? Pa-pa-pa-please tell me about him? Please-please-please."

This is a question which he often asks his Mother, who always avoids it in one way or another; which makes Alfred feel overlooked. It makes Alfred feel neglected, rejected; and crooked.

"Wa-wa-was my Daddy a real hero?" Alfred once tried.

"You really do love apples, my little-soldier," his Mother had replied.

"Di-di-di-did my Daddy have a big gun?"

"I've made your favourite, my wonderful-warrior; fish-and-chips."

"Pa-pa-pa-please tell me! Did my Daddy beat up lots of baddies?"

"Fish-chips-and-apples! The White Cliffs Of Dover! My fearless-fighter!"

"Pa-pa-pa-please tell me! Did my Daddy protect the weak? Pa-pa-pa-pretty please. Pretty please with a cherry on top."

"You'll be just like him, Alfred Freeman. Somewhere-somewhen-somehow, you-shall-you-shall-you-shall!"

But this Drill Sergeant is not nearly so evasive, abrasive; cagey-cunning-or-coy. He responds well, which puts Alfred under a spell; and fills him with gleeful-joy.

"Your Father led a raid on the Boers six years ago," he tells this boy. "He was on a mission bold, to capture an armoury, and make inroads into the gold-laden territory which lay beyond.

"But he was forced hard to retreat, to return to a nearby British province. Wasn't he! The sun had baked dry the land, water had forgotten to fall, and the natives were all athirst. Swarms of locusts had descended like a dark-cloud, eaten the natives' food, and starved them a bit. They were hungry, thirsty, and bursting out angry.

"Whereupon, needing someone to blame, they'd blamed the British. Those noble settlers who'd been civilizing the pagan natives, and making their country great.

"The natives had rebelled, killing dead over a hundred British citizens. Their Leader had told them they'd all be safe, that the bullets of the British settlers would turn into water, and our cannonballs would turn into eggs.

"Truth-be-told, the British settlers had barely any bullets or cannonballs to speak of. There was all but no standing-army, because it had gone to attack the Boer arsenal. And so the natives had run riot, without any resistance strong.

"Whereupon your Father was called to set the British settlers free, and return order to a land which had lost its way.

"So his troops marched smart across the veld, left-right-left, day-after-day. Didn't they! And before long every man in your Father's navvy-battalions, imperial-yeomanry and support-brigades, was all ate-up.

"It was no duff. The drought which had engulfed the British province had engulfed them too. The sun had baked them dry, and with no water left, they were soon athirst. They were beginning to fall-and-feint, desperate much for rain. It was real pear-shaped stuff; they hadn't a drop of water to drink. Sweet Fanny Adams!

"Whereupon, discipline in the ranks began to crumble horribly. It was a real scratch-force as it was, full of fresh-fish who were dog-tired and untrained. A real sorry-mix of old-army, new-army and territorials, all of whom did question your Father.

"'*Why*', they asked him. '*Did you bring us up out of Boer country, just to kill us and our animals with thirst?*'

"It was real tits-up stuff. A real soup-sandwich.

"Whereupon they came across a cliff, great-and-dry, with a boulder of rock at its base. From his travels, your Father knew that place well, and he knew what lay behind that boulder. Didn't he!

"So he called over some of the top-brass, who helped him to position a cannon.

"Whereupon your Father's war-brothers began murmuring with hostility. Hussars, skinny-berserkers and brawny-gunners, all talked vicious behind your Father's back; questioning his sanity a bit, and peppering the air with the sound of insults most horrible. Didn't they! But your Father paid no attention to their insubordination. He be not agreed with them at all.

"Together with the other ruperts, your Father loaded a sack of gunpowder into the cannon's mouth, rolled an iron-ball down its throat, and stuffed a chemical-charge up its nostril.

"He lit a match slow-burning.

"And BOOM!!!

"That cannonball flew quick along the cannon's chamber, whizzed through the air, and hit that boulder hard.

"That boulder crumbled asunder. Didn't it! Thousands of smaller rocks, none bigger than a melon, scattered this way and that.

"Whereupon your Father slapped his hands together, up-and-down, in recognition of a job well done. He threw the rubble aside, and created a gap of some size.

"'*Aah*', he said. And he motioned for his men to follow him into a hidden-cave. There was a lake magnificent inside. Wasn't there! The walls were covered in cave-water, and light glistened in every colour bright; in blurry shades of red-yellow-and-orange, and a hazy mix of greens-indigos-and-blues.

"There was enough water fresh for every footslogger and parlour-soldier there. It was clean, tasty, and real top-drawer stuff.

"So your Father's troops, thirsty, filled their bellies-bottles-and-beakers. And, fighting-fit once more, they returned to the British province.

"Stepping forth into the breach, they filled every kraal there with good old-fashioned British law-and-order, banished the wog insurgents to the hills, and left everything as you were.

"And a jolly good show it was too. Top notch!"

The Drill Sergeant strokes his khaki-suit, stamps his left-boot; and begins to exhale. He leaves Alfred wide-eyed with amazement, in awe of his statement; which he told like a fairytale.

Alfred feels glorious-gratified-and-glad, and proud of his long-lost Dad; who saved his men from the desert's heat. So he says 'thank-you' for the story, and feels hunky-dory; as he hops down this cobblestone-street.

As he skips down this grubby-lane, and jumps through this water-truck's spraying-rain; which dampens this dusty-road. As he runs past this flat-capped Road Sweeper, this honey-selling Beekeeper; and this donkey with a heavy-load.

He runs past this wild-dog and this wild-mouse, before he arrives back here at his house; and sits down by his Father's belt. For whilst no words have been said, or documents read; his Father's presence is still being felt.

Alfred's Mother still polishes Alfred's Father's army-boots, dusts his army-suits; and darns his army-costume. She still displays his medals on this fireplace, near that portrait of his face; and all around this living-room. And all around this man, who is chewing some spam; peach-pepper-and-prune.

This man has sideburns which reach his chin, scars which cover his skin; and boots which are covered in scrapes. He eats these chicken-legs, boiled-eggs; and sticky-grapes.

"Say 'hello' to this man, Alfred Freeman," his Mother says as she wipes these sticky-drapes. "Look at me. He's your new Stepfather. He-is-he-is-he-is. He's a carpenter. He's ever so respectable."

But Alfred believes that his Mother and himself, form a complete-family who do not need anyone else; and that he is the man of this house. Alfred cooks-cleans-and-clears, without tempers-tantrums-or-tears; and without his Mother's new spouse.

A new pension for war-widows was introduced last year, and his Mother has a new career; crocheting buttonholes into clothes. So they have food to eat, shoes to cover their feet; and socks to cover their toes.

Which means that this man's presence makes Alfred feel rejected, and dejected; as he starts to fall apart. As he starts to worry about their pension, with nervous-tension; and a broken-heart.

So Alfred ignores his Stepfather whenever he speaks, pinches his cheeks; or pats his hairy-head. He just stares at his Mother, whose clothes clash with each other; and are full of garish-thread.

"He isn't replacing your Father in heaven, you know?" She says with dread. "Look at me. Oh, I really don't know what to do with you and all your mischity, Alfred Freeman. You have two fathers now; one up in heaven, and one down here on earth. Oh, my terrific-trooper, you-do-you-do-you-do. It *is* respectable. There. That is all."

His Mother does not give in, because she is determined to win; and so she starts to whine. Whilst Alfred's Stepfather eats some evening-meals, jellied-eels; lamb-liver-and-lime.

His Mother's spine bends her back on each occasion, her lips produce gentle-words of kind-persuasion; and she keeps her posture humble. Whilst Alfred's Stepfather talks honestly, sits modestly; and blushes when his stomach starts to rumble.

"You're not my Fu-Fu-Fu-Father! No thanky-you!" Alfred shouts as his feet begin to stumble.

"No, I ain't," his Stepfather replies as he eats some apple-crumble.

Torrents of words break through this open-gate, and leave his Stepfather in a dizzy-state; before he gives Alfred these homemade-toys. Before he marries Alfred's Mother, under this church's cover; and amidst this background-noise. Before they move in here together, despite this stormy-weather; and despite those meddlesome Boys. Whilst Alfred beams with pride, with nothing to hide; and this peaceful sort of poise.

MISTER CONQUEROR

Owl was intelligent-respectable-and-strong, and everyone knew it, since Owl told them so himself. And he was powerful too; he controlled every tree-animal-and-bird in his forest.

This made Owl happy, it made Owl very happy, but he still wanted more.

For his forest was a green-and-pleasant land, full of gardens-grasslands-and-groves, lochs-lagoons-and-lakes, meadows-marshlands-and-meads. But he knew its boundaries well, and he knew that there were many other forests which he could rule; beyond his borders, across the oceans, and over the mountains.

So he sent his birds to spy on those forests.

The birds who spied on the nearby-forests found intelligent-respectable-and-strong leaders who ruled over every tree-animal-and-bird.

Whilst the birds who spied on distant-forests found organised-nations, civilisations with their own beliefs-and-traditions, but without any leaders like Owl. They found trees-animals-and-birds who were free.

Owl thought about this, all day and all night, for many a day and many a night.

"We'll conquer the distant-forests," he finally said. "We'll steal their resources, enslave their creatures, and impose our culture. We'll be richer and more powerful than you can ever imagine!"

Owl's subjects were nonviolent folk, who wanted peace. They wanted to talk with the foreign-trees, play with the foreign-animals, and sing with the foreign-birds. But Owl controlled their light-food-and-airwaves, so they had no choice but to obey him.

Owl's animals trained until they became stout-staunch-and-strong, Owl's trees armed them with spears-swords-and-shields, and Owl's birds supplied them with schemes-strategies-and-supplies.

When they were ready for war, an army of animals and an airforce of birds travelled beyond their forest's borders, across the oceans, and over the mountains. Until, after many days, they arrived at the distant-forests, where they attacked the foreign-creatures like Owl had attacked them.

Owl's birds hid the light from the foreign-trees, Owl's animals hid the food from the foreign-animals, and they worked together to hide the airwaves from the foreign-birds.

In this manner Owl colonised many forests, and built a mighty-empire. He posted viceroys to rule each forest, who harvested the foreign-trees, enslaved the foreign-animals, and used the foreign-birds as servants. They sent jewels-gems-and-gold, food-fuel-and-furniture, all the way back to Owl.

Owl used his newfound wealth to build a series of resplendent-palaces, grand-buildings and strong-barracks. He ate whatever he wanted, whenever he wanted, wherever he wanted. He wore a giant-crown, glorious-rings and exquisite-necklaces. And he gave just enough back to his subjects to stop them from rebelling.

This made Owl happy, it made Owl very happy. He ruled hundreds of forests, controlled millions of trees-animals-and-birds, and was richer than anyone else had ever been.

1905

After another three years, Alfred passes these Editors-Engravers-and-Engineers; and this bird who has a broken-wing. He passes this mouse-magpie-and-mule, and arrives at this Sunday School; whilst his Mother begins to sing. Whilst her spine stands her to attention, with a steely sort of tension; like a regal sort of king. She is wearing her Sunday best, Sunday vest; and Sunday bling.

The year is 1905.

A South African Miner is unearthing the largest diamond ever to be found, an American Child is inventing ice-lollies near his favourite playground; and a German Physicist is publishing the equation '$E=mc^2$'. In Norway-and-Sweden there is a process of dissolution, in Russia there is a process of revolution; and in Australia a new tennis grand-slam is being prepared. Whilst the British return from Tibet, where they have been a threat; and then call for conscription to be declared.

But Alfred is only focussed on this church, this silver-birch; and this litter of newly-born kittens. He is dressed in a tunic-tabard-and-tie, trousers which hug each thigh; and a pair of woollen-mittens.

He normally feels at home in his church where he sits near an engraved set of stones, a crucified Christ with protruding-bones; and some icons which hang down from the bleachers. Some gothic-gargoyles, which are covered in gothic-boils; and some columns which are covered in creepers. Some people in shiny-shoes, some shiny-pews; and some zealous Preachers.

He normally smiles at a Farmer's Daughter who reads a book, a Maid who stands in a crook; and a frowsy Dressmaker. A wheezy Choir Master, a sneezy Pastor; and a drowsy Caretaker.

But in a move which Alfred finds cruel, he is taken into this Sunday School; whilst this bird tweets and that Baby wails. He finds himself in this hollow church-hall, which is tawny-tarnished-and-tall; full of these ants and full of those snails. Where these wishbone-arches support that ceiling, this pale-paint is peeling; and this air smells of charity cake-sales.

He sits with Bernie and starts to pray, but he is not allowed to play; as he falls for this woman with kiwi-eyes. As he falls for her flowing-dress, her gentle-finesse; her slender-legs and her slender-thighs.

Alfred's infatuation with the Sunday School Teacher grows each week, but without the courage to speak; he has to imagine what she is really like. So he imagines a genial-gentle-and-gracious ideal, he imagines that she is his for real; and he imagines that they are alike.

When she calls him '*sweetie*' Alfred thinks that she finds him sweet, when she calls him '*love-bug*' that she loves him and is just being discreet; and when she calls him '*cutie-pie*' it makes him gleam. When she calls him '*angel*'-'*pumpkin*'-or-'*dovey*', '*cupcake*'-'*chicken*'-or-'*lovey*'; it encourages him to dream.

He dreams about her flirtatious-winking, unconscious-blinking; and dimple-making. Her foot-shuffling, hair-ruffling; and bottom-shaking.

He dreams about her slender-arms, pleasant-charms; and spangly-broaches. He dreams about her kiwi-eyes, and silky-thighs; as each new Sunday approaches.

As each new Sunday comes and each new Sunday goes, whilst Alfred gleams-glimmers-and-glows; during lessons which are full of honest-lies. Which are full of stories about a devil who sups with a long-spoon, a man who lives on the moon; and a heaven which is up in the skies.

His Sunday School Teacher is not deliberately-deceptive, deliberately-unreceptive; or deliberately-misleading. But she turns to fabrication, to compensate for her lack of education; and to make her lessons seem pleasing.

Alfred does not utter a single word, or any sound which can be heard; until today's lesson on the commandment '*Though shall not kill*'. When he finds his Teacher so radiant-righteous-and-right, brilliant-beautiful-and-bright; that he feels a colossal-thrill.

"If someone wants to kill you," she says whilst she starts dimple-making, and bottom-shaking; near that window-sill. "Let them! If they strike you on one cheek, offer them your other cheek too. And if they steal your coat, offer them your jumper. My darlings; you should love-and-pray for your enemies as if they're your very own bubbas!"

Alfred finds this lesson so ethereal, saintly-seraphic-and-surreal; that he questions his Father's wars in distant-forests and distant-lands. He thinks his Father would have defended himself from attack, and fought his enemies back; using his head-heart-and-hands. But he cannot be sure, because his Mother does not talk about his Father's time at war; when he followed his leader's commands.

"Was Da-Da-Da-Daddy very good at fighting?" Alfred once asked her.

"You really are growing positively quick, my little-soldier," his Mother had started to slur.

"Pa-pa-pa-please tell me! Did Da-Da-Da-Daddy ever hurt anyone?"

"You'll be just as tall as him, my wonderful-warrior. Oh, just look at how you've grown! Just look at the *White Cliffs Of Dover*!"

"Pa-pa-pa-please tell me! Did Daddy ever kill anyone else's daddy? Pa-pa-pa-pretty please. Pretty please with a cherry on top."

"Oh, you'll be just like him, my terrific-trooper. Somewhere-somewhen-somehow, you-shall-you-shall-you-shall!"

So with his affections undiminished, after this lesson has finished; Alfred finally approaches his beau. His brow turns wet, with salty-sweat; which makes his forehead glow.

"I lu-lu-lu-loved the lesson," he says with nerves which clearly show. "But I do have one question.

"Please tell me! If it's wrong to kill other people, and if we should love our enemies, does that mean that soldiers are ba-ba-ba-bad? Does that mean that my da-da-da-Daddy has gone to hell? I'd be ever so grateful if you'd tell me. I'd be very much obliged."

The Sunday School Teacher begins foot-shuffling, and hair-ruffling; before she takes a moment to think. Before she squats down to Alfred's height, flushes white; and flushes pink.

"I knew your Daddy," she says as she puts down her milky-drink. "He didn't strike me as someone who'd kill another person.

"Not all soldiers are killers, snuggle-bunny, they can secure peace-treaties and trade-agreements too. They can even liberate people, like your Daddy did in West Africa."

Alfred is keen to find out more, from this girl who he adores; acclaims-appreciates-and-admires. He wants to stay here, and be near; to this girl who he desires.

"Pa-pa-pa-please tell me more?" He asks whilst he perspires. "Please-please-please."

"Okay angel-face, you've got me!" His Sunday School Teacher replies without even thinking, amidst this cheeky-winking, and unconscious-blinking. "Well, your Daddy, it must have been about nine years ago now, was sent to civilise the Ashanti.

"Their Leader had been a naughty-boy; he'd forgotten to pay us a peace-tax, and he'd traded his nation's wealth for weapons. His army had become really strong, just like you Freddie-kins!

"Well, peanut, that didn't scare your Daddy one bit. He was happy to lead an expedition to the Ashanti capital, on a mission to win that nation over, bring it into the British Empire, and save it from the baddies who wanted to steal their gold.

"Now your Daddy knew that his troops could be more intelligent-respectable-and-strong than the Ashanti, but he also knew that they could get hurty-wurty. And he was keen to protect his bubbas, who were already suffering from yucky-illnesses because of the icky-sticky heat.

"So, sugar-plum, your Daddy's troops pitched their tents in the forests above the Ashanti capital, where they were hidden by coconut-palms, rubber-trees and colourful-orchids. And they made plans whilst they ate their din-dins.

"Once his friends were snug-and-snoring, your Daddy snuck off into the woods. He found every single hornets' nest in that forest, and carefully cut them all down. So soft was your Daddy's touch, that he didn't arouse a single one of those fluffy-wuffy bugs.

"Well sweetness, once his cart contained hundreds-of-nests and millions-of-hornets, your Daddy crept into the Ashanti capital. He attached his nests along the inside of the city-wall which was nearest to the British camp, smiled, and went to beddy-byes.

"The next morning the Ashanti capital was noisy-woisy. The heathen-temples rang out with their call-to-prayer, chook-chooks crowed, woof-woofs barked, and traders scurried off to market.

"Well poppet, those teeny-weeny hornets didn't like that noise at all; it made them crossy-wossy. So they left their nests, and they started to fly.

"But they found their new surroundings as odd-as-cod, because their forest had turned into a town, with rows of houses instead of rows of trees. So, with the city-wall blocking the way behind, they flew into the Ashanti capital itself.

"Well, honey-pie, when the townsfolk saw a swarm of hornets descending upon them, they were struck with fear and thrown into confusion. Those silly-billies, and all their moo-moos, neigh-neighs and baa-baas, ran right away. They left their capital completely empty!

"And, after searching high-and-low, your Daddy found the Ashanti's Leader, arrested him, and made him sign a treaty which brought the Ashanti lands into the British Empire.

"So you see sweet-cheeks, your Daddy was a real hero! He made our empire even greater than it was before, without ever breaking the sixth commandment, *'Though shall not kill'*. And he *'Loved his enemy'* too, because he improved the lives of the Ashanti people, by replacing the naughty Leader with a super-duper British Viceroy!"

Alfred starts to smile, because he is enraptured by the Sunday School Teacher's style; which he finds incredibly delicious. And he leaves this Sunday School, convinced that his Father was not cruel; mean-malevolent-or-malicious.

"Thank-you," he says as he becomes repetitious. "Thank-you, thank-you, thank-you! You're awesome! Awesome-awesome-awesome! You make me feel like I'm on top of the world! World-world-world!"

And as a result of the story he has just been told, Alfred's confidence increases fourfold; which encourages him to woo. He gives his Sunday School Teacher some blue-seashells, some bluebells; and this card which is pale-blue. He gives her some flapjacks made of oats, he brushes against her coats; and he writes her some love-notes too.

He writes that he *'loves her beautiful-smile'*, *'loves her beautiful-style'*; and *'loves her beautiful-feet'*. He blows her kisses during class, and strokes her arse; whenever they happen to meet.

At first his Sunday School Teacher finds this bonny-bewitching-and-bliss, then she considers it something to discard-disregard-and-dismiss, before she finally accepts that it is awry-abnormal-and-amiss.

And so she stops her flirtatious-winking, unconscious-blinking; and dimple-making. Her foot-shuffling, hair-ruffling; and bottom-shaking.

But Alfred believes that he is acting like his Stepfather when he courted his Mother, like one grown-up or any other; and so he continues on. He gives his Sunday School Teacher even more notes, brushes up against her coats; and sings her a romantic-song.

Until he meets this man who has a pair of red-socks which look like antiques, and a pair of red-cheeks; which make him look wild. This man snaps his forefinger-and-thumb, which turns Alfred dumb; like an introverted sort of child.

"I just so happen to be this Sunday School's Superintendent," he says in a voice which sounds disturbed, perturbed; and riled. "And I think you should know, that I just so happen to be your Sunday School Teacher's husband. I just so happen to be very protective of her."

As Alfred learns that his Sunday School Teacher is married, he becomes harried; with a shady case of the blues. This revelation stops his flirtation in its tracks, as he changes into his slacks; and into his everyday-shoes.

Before he walks with his Mother past these trees which are covered in plums, these slums; and that thicket. Those buzzing-bees, wobbly-trees; and amateur game of cricket.

This afternoon country-walk, and the Superintendent's talk; help Alfred to clear his mind. They help him to leave his childish-infatuation, and his childish-frustration; far behind.

And they help him to bounce back strong, as he skips along; and gets *involved* in a new school week. As he manages his inner-urges, and emotive-surges; which *evolve* towards a peak.

He sits with the Snotty Nosed Scamp who has a hairy-ear, and the Tallest Boy in his year; here in their new classroom. Where the Authoritative Teacher starts to whinge, cringe; and fume.

The Authoritative Teacher is wearing a studded-collar and a studded-shirt, a bowler-hat which is splattered with dirt; and a pair of laced-up boots. He has a penchant for swishing his rattan-wood cane, to inflict some pain; and end his countless disputes.

He loves to swish his rattan-wood cane, whilst he sometimes looks inane; and whilst he sometimes looks excited. Whilst he taunts *'You'll never use the test-tubes'*, *'Get away from those cubes'*; and *'Don't speak unless you've been invited'*.

He swishes the palm of any child who answers him back, whose posture is slack; or who arrives here slightly late. Before he makes them sit in the corridor alone, and sends a letter home; to spread his boundless-hate.

The Authoritative Teacher is ever so easily distracted, so he touches anything to which he is attracted; whilst he swishes his rattan-wood cane. He touches these clipboards, these dangling-cords; and that pot which is full of fresh-rain. This torn-up book, this curvy-hook; and that tinted window-pane.

Which is why he stops this class, fiddles with this glass; and swishes his rattan-wood cane. It is why he points at this map, and touches his cap; before he tries to explain.

"This is the empire on which the sun never sets!" He dictates from a book, with this baffled-look; which is insipid-imbecilic-and-inane. "A gift from God!

"It shows that we're what they call '*The Lord's Chosen People*'; fighting God's holy-wars, spreading his bible, civilising the heathens and so on. Replacing the queer cultures-religions-and-politics of idolatrous-savages with British ways. Intelligent-respectable-and-strong British ways!

"God is grateful for it. We're acting in his holy-name!

"God," he mutters. "Empire. Gift."

Alfred knows better than to debate-dispute-or-disagree, because he knows it would make his teacher angry; which would make him start to holler. The Authoritative Teacher is already jealous of the way Alfred amazed his elders last year, as if he was the real teacher here; and not just another scholar.

That event caused the Authoritative Teacher to fill with discontent, which inspired Alfred to dissent; riot-revolt-and-rebel. He shouted when he should not have been talking, he skipped when he should not have been walking; and he ignored his teachers as well.

So Alfred's angst-anxiety-and-agitation, fury-fretfulness-and-frustration; have all begun to swell. Whilst his teacher swishes his cane, mutters again; and fiddles with this bell.

"Heathens. Savages. Barbarians."

Alfred listens and wants to disagree, but he does not feel free; or in control. So he watches his teacher look away, fiddle with some hay; candy-cardboard-and-coal.

Alfred sneaks around this exposed piece of cable, runs towards his teacher's table; and grabs his teacher's book. He throws it into this fire, this flaming-pyre; and returns without a second look.

The Authoritative Teacher swishes his rattan-wood cane, fiddles with this model of a brain; and this piece of salted-bacon. He fiddles with this piece of chalk, and that piece of cork; before he sees that his book has been taken.

"What demn insolence!" He yowls like a bully.

"What ingratitude!" He yelps ungracefully.

"What sin!" He yells disdainfully. "Ye lot make my tooth ache. Don't ye think you'll get away with this, and so on. Ter dash it! Oh no-no-no-no-no! Ye Pharisees ought to be ashamed of yourselves. There's no more honour in ye than there is in a rotten-potato.

"Insolence," he mutters. "Ingratitude. Potatoes."

His narrow-teeth grind inside his narrow-head, which flashes rose-ruby-and-red; whilst his belly begins to quake. Whilst he fiddles with this chalk, this stalk; and that stake.

"Ye must act responsibly children," he cries, with furious-eyes; as his body begins to shake. "Ye must believe in personal-responsibility, and personal-everything. Because right now ye are as far from the right sort as one could imagine. The whole lot of ye!

"And ye shan't leave here until the culprit is found. My life upon it! Ye shan't play during break or leave for home until the blighter responsible for this abomination sallies forth. So sally forth now!

"Responsibility," he mutters. "Blighters. Home."

But no-one says a word, no sound is heard, and no comment is slurred.

"Very well then," the Authoritative Teacher says whilst he fiddles with this wall, this ball; and that curd. "I fancy I'll have to search each one of ye scrotes in turn, and so on. If ye must act all cat-lazy and dog-loyal, ye'll have to be treated like mangy-animals too.

"Cats," he mutters. "Dogs. Animals."

And with a facial-expression which looks fairly grotesque, the Authoritative Teacher goes from desk-to-desk; whilst he fiddles with these paper-dockets. Whilst he fiddles with this flag, empties each child's bag; and empties each child's trouser-pockets.

With just one place left to look, he walks past the fire and sees his book; which is ablaze-alight-and-aflame. His simmering-anger comes to a boil, he spits saliva which fizzes like oil; and he swishes his rattan-wood cane.

"Either own up to your crime," he yowls, and howls; as he turns insane. "Or sally forth with who committed it, and so on. Otherwise ye'll all be caned! Don't ye think ye're here for what they call a '*joy-day*'. There'll be no clipsing-and-colling in my classroom. How very dare ye! Your pigheadedness amazes me. Ye'll do nothing but make haycocks out of your lives by acting the fool.

"Tell me who ye suspect? I demand it! Speak out boys, speak up. One always suspects someone.

"Clipsing," he mutters. "Pigs. Haycocks."

Alfred is tempted to concede, as his friends start to bleed; at the hands of this rattan-wood cane. Which slices their skins, pierces their shins; and fills them with hellish-pain.

"It was Alfred, sir," the Snotty Nosed Scamp repeats again-and-again. "It was Alfred, sir. It was Alfred, sir. It was Alfred."

Alfred wishes that he had stood up to confess, as his friend becomes a teary-eyed mess; before his teacher beckons him forward. Before his teacher grabs Alfred's collar, and lifts his cane above his scholar; like a soldier with a sword.

The Authoritative Teacher flashes rose-ruby-and-red, as he grips hold of Alfred's head; bends Alfred over and canes Alfred's rear. Before he swishes his cane ten times, mutters '*carrots-criminals-crimes*'; and yanks at Alfred's left-ear.

He hits Alfred's palms with the sole of his shoe, which covers Alfred in blisters which are blue; and blood which is shiny-red. He starts to swear, as Alfred pants for air; and shakes his hairy-head.

Alfred would love to scream and he would love to shout, he would love to cry out; whoop-whimper-and-wail. But his mouth is being covered-compressed-and-choked, he is being poked; and he is turning pale.

So he can only manage this strangled-croak, as sweat covers him in a sticky-soak; and his body starts to jerk. As he is bent over this drum, and as he is caned on his bum; whilst his teacher goes berserk.

"This ought to be a lesson to ye!" The Authoritative Teacher groans, and moans; with this twisted sort of smirk. "To all of ye! Let it teach ye that the might of the British Empire is always right, and so on. Many a chap has put his prospects in others, like ye lot just did, and it never ends well. Never!

"Lesson," he mutters. "Empire. Prospects."

Each slap-slash-and-smack, during this vicious attack; make Alfred feel more bleak. But they help him to manage his inner-urges, and his emotive-surges; which *evolve* towards a peak. For Alfred is ready to grow, let his maturity show; and develop his physique. Just not here, anywhere near; or anytime this week.

REVOLUTION

Owl was intelligent-respectable-and-strong, and everyone knew it, since Owl told them so himself. He was powerful; he controlled every tree-animal-and-bird in his empire. And he was rich; he had more jewels-gems-and-gold than anyone else.

This made Owl happy, it made him very happy.

But the trees-animals-and-birds in Owl's distant-forests were not so happy. They wanted to be free from slavery, practice their own religions, and keep their jewels. They said they wanted a revolution, and they said they wanted to change the world.

Owl thought about this, all day and all night, for many a day and many a night.

"I'll deal with them myself," he finally said. "I'll show them just how intelligent-respectable-and-strong I am!"

So Owl flew across the oceans and over the mountains, before he landed in his distant-forests.

That was when the trees tried to overthrow Owl. They swung around and trapped him in a dome-shaped cage of platted-trunks, interlocked-branches and tangled-twigs.

"We'll keep you here without food until you've starved," Pine said. "And then we'll free this forest tree-by-tree."

"I think that's a grand idea," Owl replied. "But you can't just starve a king and then free his forest, the Gods won't allow it. You need to send a signal to the Gods if you want them to ordain your rule."

Owl's words made sense to Pine. The Gods, she supposed, would only signal her rule if she sent a signal to them.

So Pine removed all the feathers from Owl's torso and attached them to the other trees, as a sign to the Gods. But as she did this, Pine created a gap in her cage, and so Owl was able to fly away.

That was when the animals tried to overthrow Owl. Wolf pounced and grabbed Owl with his sharp-claws, strong-arms and spiky-teeth. He tore all the feathers off of Owl's right-wing.

"I'll keep you here and eat your flesh until you're just a pile of bones," Wolf said. "And then I'll free this forest animal-by-animal."

"I think that's a grand idea," Owl replied. "But you can't just eat a *king and then free his forest, the Gods won't allow it. You need to pray to the Gods if you want them to ordain your rule."*

Owl's words made sense to Wolf. The Gods, he supposed, would only glorify him if he glorified them.

So Wolf put his claws together and closed his eyes to pray. But as he did this, Wolf released Owl from his grip, and so Owl was able to fly away.

That was when the birds tried to overthrow Owl. They flew beneath Owl and created a blustery-wind, which blew Owl above the clouds. They blew all the feathers off of Owl's left-wing.

"We'll keep you here without air until you suffocate," Parrot said. "And then we'll free this forest bird-by-bird."

"I think that's a grand idea," Owl replied. "But you can't just suffocate a king and then free his forest, the Gods won't allow it. You need to guard the Gods if you want them to ordain your rule."

Owl's words made sense to Parrot. The Gods, she supposed, would only protect her if she protected them.

So Parrot took half of her birds to protect God's forest. But as she did this, she released Owl from her uplift, and so Owl was able to fly away.

The trees-animals-and-birds had all failed to overthrow Owl. Because Owl was intelligent-respectable-and-strong, and everyone knew it, since Owl told them so himself.

The birds who were still in the sky soon froze to death. So Owl took Swan's white-feathers, Sparrow's brown-feathers and Rook's black-feathers, which he attached to his body in the most regal pattern ever known.

Owl was rich, he was powerful, and he looked absolutely fabulous.

1907

Adolescence has broken through the yoke of youth, replaced Alfred's last ever baby-tooth; and given him a taste for exploration. So he climbs down from his favourite-oak, skips through this smoggy-smoke; and hops past this quiet train-station.

The year is 1907.

A French Engineer is piloting the first ever helicopter-flight despite feeling nervous, an Italian Entrepreneur is launching the first ever transatlantic wireless-service; and an American Janitor is building the first ever electronic vacuum-cleaner. On the Isle of Man a new motorbike-race is speeding around, in Jamaica a new earthquake is rocking the ground; and in America a new airforce is being launched by a man with a positive-demeanour. Whilst the British accrue a chunk of Persia in return for their diplomacy, and agree to fight with Russia globally; as they grow madder-mightier-and-meaner.

But in shoes which shine like polished-gold, and which have just re-soled; Alfred is unconcerned with such things. His ankles become muddy, his socks become cruddy; and his blazer flaps behind him like wings.

He runs down these smoggy-lanes, past these blocked-drains; this ryegrass-rosemary-and-rose. He turns and he twists, with his bony-ankles and his bony-wrists; inside his old school-clothes.

He runs past this Bobby-Buddleboy-and-Bookmaker, Usher-Umpire-and-Undertaker; and this Bummaree who has meat-juice dripping down his back. He runs without fear, fuelled by the free school-lunches which began last year; and a very sugary-snack.

"Hey there," an impoverished-voice calls from down that hidden-track. "I've got me a copy of *Boys' Own* 'ere if you want it. I've read it already, ya see. It's pretty *Robin Hood*!"

Alfred likes the puzzles of various-sorts, the various news-reports; and the various adventure-stories which the *Boys' Own Newspaper* contains. So without suspicion-scepticism-or-censure, he embarks on his own adventure; by entering this alley which is full of black-stains.

"He's just a kiddie," an anxious-voice soon complains.

Before this hand grabs Alfred's neck, throws him onto this stony-deck; and begins to attack. It turns Alfred around, drags him over this stony-ground; and along this stony-track. Towards this divide, which has bricks on either side; which are brittle-broken-and-black.

"See, he's got a scarf," this Dominant Assailant shouts back. "And an *Uncle Bert*. We could make a nice *Weepin' Willow* out of that."

This boy's sooty-clothes seem rather ragged, and his sooty-face seems rather jagged; whilst his hands move about in a hurry. Whilst they grind Alfred's face into this brick, as his feet begin to kick; which makes this Squat Assailant worry.

This Squat Assailant worries about this violence, as he stands here in silence; away from his partner in crime. Such that Alfred can only see that this boy is stumpy, frumpy; and covered in mucky-grime.

"'Ave yourself a *Butchers Hook* at that," the Dominant Assailant starts to chime.

He sticks his hand into Alfred's pocket, removes this dented-locket; and kicks this pile of dirt. He begins to laugh, steals Alfred's scarf; Alfred's blazer and Alfred's shirt.

"We can't just flee," the Squat Assailant begins to blurt. "Gawd knows this here boy will run after us. He'll shout very loudly, he will. People will hear. There ain't no safety in it. There ain't no safety in it at all!"

"We'll 'ave to break 'im some, methinks. Yeah!" The Dominant Assailant replies, and cries, with malice on his face and meanness in his eyes. "A bit of an *Unscheduled Meetin'* should do the job."

And so he kicks Alfred's midriff which makes Alfred groan, he stamps on Alfred's anklebone; and he drags Alfred over this uneven-floor. He kicks Alfred's chin, which makes Alfred spin; before he kicks Alfred's chest once more.

"Dat'll stop 'im runnin' too quick!" The Dominant Assailant says with a roar. "And this one will stop 'im from makin' a *Box Of Toys*! Now let's *Scapa Flow* before anyone sees."

These are the last words Alfred hears, before these assailants kick his ears; turn around and then leave. Before Alfred opens his battered-eyes, rubs his battered-thighs; and rubs his battered-sleeve. Whilst his face begins to ache, his body begins to shake; and his pain begins to seethe. Without the strength to get to his feet, walk towards the street; or breathe.

And through the smog which cloaks this town, Alfred sees this Priest in a long black gown, who wears a snooty-frown.

"Ha-ha-ha-help!" Alfred shouts down. "I've been beaten. Please help me sir. Please-please-please."

But this Priest does not seem to be aware, he does not seem to care; and he does not stop to help. He leaves Alfred in pain, as he begins to strain; yell-yowl-and-yelp.

And through this smog which cloaks the sky, Alfred sees this Professional in a suit and bow-tie, with a monocle in his eye.

"Ha-ha-ha-help!" Alfred begins to cry. "I've been beaten. Please help me sir. Please-please-please."

But this Professional does not seem to be aware, he does not seem to care; and he does not stop to help. He leaves Alfred in pain, as he begins to strain; yell-yowl-and-yelp.

And through the smog which cloaks this town, Alfred sees this man in brown; who looks a little bit spooky. His trousers are tucked into his boots, his hair is red at its roots; and his oily-cape looks kooky.

"Ha-ha-ha-help!" Alfred shouts as he becomes hazy, crazy; and loopy. "I've been beaten. Please help me sir. Please-please-please."

This Good German looks down this lane, where Alfred is wriggling around in pain, near this pile of rubbish and that flooded-drain.

"I'm at the end of this alley," he shouts out again. "Please help me sir. Please-please-please."

The Good German assesses the scene, before he rubs Alfred clean; with this alcohol which starts to sting. Alfred wants to shout 'No', or 'Go slow'; but he does not say a single thing.

"Poor boy," the Good German begins to sing. "Vot a cruel vorld vee live in today."

The Good German bandages Alfred's ankle with a piece of his shirt, removes this piece of dirt; and carries Alfred to this inn. He calls a Doctor to this room, fans that fire to reduce the gloom; and wraps Alfred's arm in this sling.

The Good German sits on this wobbly-stool, and holds himself tall; with a straight-back and a pointy-knee. He says that he works as a greengrocer here, and moved somewhere near; after he left his own country.

"I left my homeland some time ago," he says as he sips his tea. "My Farzer, you see, was a Mennonite priest; a man who prayed so hard for me to be born, zat it struck him dumb for veeks on end!

"Vell, he'd been owed money by a layman, yah. Ziss layman, to escape his debt, had crept up behind my Farzer ven he was deep in prayer, ant slit his throat. My Farzer lay slain on zee cold stone-floor, between zee temple ant zee altar, viz blood bubblink ziss vay ant zat.

"As for me, I left on a mission to become a man of zee Vorld; to escape zee pain of my Farzer's murder, ant to affoid conscription, vich was beink introduced into Germany at zat time.

"I vent through Syria-Iraq-ant-Iran, before I arrived in India. I visited zare temples ant conversed viz zare priests. I learnt zare stories, studied zare animals, ant practiced zare diets.

"Effentually I found peace, ant set off for America with my fellow Mennonites. Only I fell in love viz ziss part of zee Vorld en-route, ant have remained here effer since.

"Vell, dear Alfie, I'd like to zink zat my trip taught me a thing or two. Perhaps I'll tell you about it someday. It vood save you a journey, yah!"

The Good German's eyes are puffy with compassion, his hair is slightly ashen; and his face is slightly strong. Alfred gives him an easy-glance, falls into a sleepy-trance; and is snoring before too long. So the Good German pays, gives Alfred a loving-gaze; and smiles as he moves along.

"Take care of him," he says to this Innkeeper who is dressed in a shirt, a skirt; and a sarong. "Vot-effer you spend beyond ziss, I vill repay ven I return."

Alfred sleeps-snoozes-and-shakes, before he rolls over and wakes; when the morning eventually comes. When he rides this tram which is covered in wires, with rubber-tires; which are covered in rubber-crumbs.

From its window he sees this Lavender Lady with an exposed-naval, who carries her Baby in a wicker-cradle; and sings '*My sweet-lavender will help you to strive!*' He sees this donkey who has a rickety-heart, who pulls a clickety-cart; whilst this Orange Man sings '*Five fah a penny - just a penny fah five!*'

And he sees this Gypsy's caravan, near this Organ Grinder Man; who pulls his music-machine. Whilst his monkey doffs her cap for coins, swings her apish-loins; and makes an apish-scene.

Alfred returns home where he passes his Father's army-washrag, army-bag; and army-paraphernalia. For like a cobwebbed-mausoleum, or a stuffy-museum; this place is full of his Father's regalia.

Here is his Father's sleigh, his Father's beret; and his Father's gun. His flags, his tags; his medals and his drum.

Stood amidst it all Alfred's Mother is full of fright, because she has been worrying about Alfred all night; which has made her a bit insane. But she brings Alfred some cocoa in a brown-mug, and a brown-drug; as soon as Alfred starts to explain.

In a little under a week Alfred is just about able to talk, and just about able to walk; so he goes to look for the man who came to his salvation. He looks in valleys, he looks in alleys; and he looks in this new fire-station.

He searches down roads with names like 'Lepers Lane', he sees names like 'Rotten Row' time-and-again; and he sees roads named 'Sewer Street'. He passes houses which stand to attention, joined at their shoulders with concrete-tension; and joined at their concrete-feet.

He passes these Teachers who are riding their peddle-bikes, these hansom-cabs which are full of spikes; and these horse-drawn buses which have wonky-wheels. These carts whose covers are starting to unravel, these motorcars which are churning the gravel; and these Ladies who are wearing high-heels.

Before he stops outside this greengrocery, in front of this pile of rosemary; and this awning which is lined with blue-cables. Beneath which these tangerines, and these curly-beans; are displayed on these outside-tables.

"Hello Alfie, my dear boy," the Good German says as he writes on these white price-labels.

He stands upright, and holds himself tight; dressed in an apron which keeps his clothes clean. Which protects his suits, and protects his boots; which have a glossy-sheen.

"You are better, yah?" He asks in a voice which sounds serene.

"Yes-yes-yes," Alfred replies in a voice which sounds keen. "Thank-you for asking. Thank-you, thank-you, thank-you. You're tremendous! You really are top-drawer!

"My ah-ah-ah-ankle is healing, my rib will mend given time, and I've even got a heart-shaped bruise on my chest!"

"You're very brafe, Alfie. I am grateful to you, my dear boy," the Good German replies.

"Not at all, sir," Alfred cries. "I'm grateful to *you*. I was left for dead and you saved me. You're a hero sir! You're a superstar! When I grow up, I want to be just like you."

"Nonsense, dear boy! Vair I come from, helpink zose close to you is a duty, yah. *'Much of a muchness'*, as I zink you say. But helpink a stranger is a priffilege, a real honour, yah.

"You've given me ziss great honour, ant I'm zankful to *you* for it."

Alfred starts to feel dazzled, flustered-flabbergasted-and-frazzled; so he shakes his hairy-head. Before the Good German sits Alfred down, starts to frown; and starts to turn dark-red.

"Are you familiar viz zee story of zee *Two Dining Rooms*, Alfie?" He asks with his arms outspread. "Ziss may help you, yah.

"You see, zare was once a brainy-boy, a bit like yourself, dear Alfie. Vell, one day he went for dinner in a restaurant viz two dining-rooms.

"In zee first dining-room, he saw rows of long-tables vich verr covered viz platters of sumptuous-food. But zee people at zose tables verr starvink-emaciated-ant-moanink. Zare spoons verr full, but zare arms verr set straight in splints, yah. No matter how hard zey tried, zose people could not bend zare elbows, ant so zey verr unable to feed zemselves.

"Zee second dining-room was also full of tables covered viz platters of sumptuous-food. But zee people in zare verr content-talkink-ant-full. Zare arms verr also set straight in splints, but instead of feedink zemselves, zey verr feedink zee people opposite zem. Ant zee people opposite zem verr feedink zem back!

"Feeling excited, zee brainy-boy returned to zee first dining-room. *'Feed zee person opposite you'*, he told zee people in zare. *'Zey'll feed you too! You'll all get to eat!'*

"Ant zey all got to eat!"

Alfred finds this story so cool, that he no longer climbs his favourite-tree after school; and visits the Good German here instead. He arrives here today, with his hair all astray; on both sides of his oval-head.

"I fa-fa-fa-found three juicy-apples, sir," he says with cheeks which are ruby-red. "And I gave them to three strangers. I just wanted to be nice, like the people in the second dining-room. I wanted to be like you!

"But the first-stranger refused to take her apple, the second-stranger threw his in the bin, and the third-stranger just ignored me.

"Please sir! Tu-tu-tu-tell me what this means? I'd be ever so grateful. I'd be very much obliged."

"Vie do you zink zare is a hidden-message, dear child?" The Good German replies. "Ziss is real life, yah. It's not a fable; zare is not alvays a lesson to be learned."

"Oh, thank-you," Alfred says with dejection.

"Let me tell you a story, dear Alfie," the Good German says with affection. "About a village vich was struck by famine-ant-drought, yah. Food had forgotten to grow zare, ant zee rains had forgotten to fall. Zee villagers had no seeds to sow, nor any water eizzer.

"Until two bruzzers returned home after many months of vork.

"Zee Tall Bruzzer returned viz seeds-ant-water, yah. Zee villagers celebrated; zey heaped praise upon zat boy, ant planted his seeds in an open-field vich faced zare village.

"But zee Short Bruzzer was modest. He told efferyone zat he'd invested zee money vich he'd earned. Ant so zee villagers ignored zat boy, like zee three strangers ignored you. Zey even ignored him ven he returned viz seeds-ant-water of his own. He had to plant zose seeds himself, in a field vich was hidden by trees.

"Zen came zee rains! Zee skies opened, ant all zee vater vich had forgotten to fall poured down. Down onto zee village, down onto zee villagers, ant down onto zee villager's fields.

"Vell, zee field in vich zee Tall Bruzzer's seeds verr planted was open, proudly displayink itself to zee village, viz no protection from zee rain. So zee vater flooded zat field, ant washed zee Tall Bruzzer's seeds avay.

"But zee field in vich zee Short Bruzzer's seeds verr planted was hidden avay from zee village. It was protected from zee elements by zee trees, yah. Ant so zee rains fed zee seeds zare, vich produced enough food to feed zee entire village.

"Zee villagers verr elated. But zey had no-one to zank, because zee Short Bruzzer had remained silent, yah. Ant so zey celebrated together, ant heaped each uzzer viz praise."

Stood near the carrots-cabbages-and-courgettes on this slanted-table, Alfred likes this fable; which he thinks he understands. He thinks he understands all his mentor's tales, which he listens to whilst he chews his nails; and waves his childish-hands.

"I get it!" He says as he hops past these potatoes, tomatoes; and cans. "I get it! I get it! I get it! It doesn't matter how others respond to the good which you do, or if they abuse-ignore-and-mistreat you. It's enough that you do good. Yes-yes-yes! That's just it!"

So Alfred is inspired by the Good German's fables-folktales-and-facts, compassionate-acts; and passionate-zeal. He is inspired to perform good-deeds, for people with needs; and for people who have a raw-deal.

He helps paupers with limited-wealth, and paupers with limited-health; almost every single day. Until the old Alfred of Sunday School crushes, and Primary School head-rushes; completely fades away.

He writes some jokes for the dejected, some compliments for the disaffected; and some proverbs for the morose. He puts them in pockets-packets-and-purses, and gives them to nannies-navvies-and-nurses; without ever starting to boast. He hides them in books, and he hangs them on hooks; without getting caught despite coming close.

Which brings him to these woods on this balmy-afternoon, where Bernie is climbing trees like a wobbly-baboon; who is clearly in his element. Although with shoulders which are too wide for his chest, and a waist which is too wide for his vest; he does look a little inelegant.

He engraves this tree, '*Alfred and Bernie - friends for ever - A. B. See*'; before he rolls up both of his sleeves. Before they stop to speak, play '*Hide and Seek*'; and throw these autumn-leaves. Before they blow into pine-needles, catch some beetles; and play '*Cops And Thieves*'.

And before Alfred climbs this majestic-willow and finds this metal-trap, in which these pieces of leather-strap; divide two separate compartments. One contains berries which entice birds in, whilst the other contains twelve birds who are thin; and pressed into these metal-

vents.

Alfred sets eleven birds free, and watches them flee; whilst they sing-shriek-and-squeal. But this poorly-thing, has a broken-wing; and so Alfred wants to help her to heal.

"You can't do that," Bernie begins to appeal. "How rum! Have you gone mad? Bonkers? Doolally? Cuckoo? Those birds belong to the trapper. Good god man! What on earth do you think you're playing at?"

"But these ba-ba-ba-birds were free before they were caught," Alfred replies. "Which means they belong to nature, not the trapper. Please understand! Please-please-please."

"Not really, no, not at all," Bernie argues. "Things change; hunters eat the animals they capture, fishermen keep their catch, and nations rule over the lands they conquer. It's precisely the same thing! Stuff only belongs to nature before men take it."

Alfred pauses to think, takes a swig of his drink, and turns pale-pink.

"Bernie," he says with a wink. "You'll always be number one in my book. But please understand! Fu-fu-fu-friends live side-by-side and enemies live apart. Rabbits live with worms but flee from foxes, robins live with sparrows but fly from cats, and voles live with mice but hide from hawks.

"Well, whoever owns this trap is this bird's enemy, because he meant this bird harm. So this bird shouldn't have to live with him. But I wish to heal her, which makes me her friend. So she should come to live with me. Yes-yes-yes. Yes thanky-you!"

Bernie can only shrug-sneeze-and-sigh, because he is unable to reply; or respond. So he talks about comics, with histrionics; whilst they walk around this pond.

Before Alfred walks back to his family's home, on his own; and gets mud all over his boots. Whilst he looks in these shops which sell fishing-tackles, metal-shackles; and frilly bathing-suits. And this café which is full of colourful-dust, colourful-rust; and colourful-fruits.

He gazes into this drapery which is full of colourful-fabric, colourful-plastic; and colourful-dye. Before he sees this fishmonger, when his belly begins to hunger; and his eyes begin to spy.

His eyes spy on the fillets which get smoked inside, the fishes which get fried; and this alley which is hidden next-door. Where he finds scraps-slivers-and-skins, in these big blue-bins; and in the crates which cover this floor.

Alfred sneaks behind this pretty-promenade, and skips from yard-to-yard; on top of these yellow-brick walls. He sneaks past these shops which sell lemonade, sheets of suede; and bags of bouncy-balls.

Before he spies on this bakery which is full of rice-cakes stuffed with berries, shortbread topped with cherries; and bread made from sourdough. Where he finds crusts-cookies-and-crumbs, inside these wooden-drums; which are arranged in a wonky-row.

He finds food outside factories which have machines, schools which have canteens; and the homes of the wealthy. And amongst the scraps, cores-crumbs-and-caps; he finds some food which is actually healthy.

He finds pies-puddings-and-potatoes, tuna-trout-and-tomatoes; beef-bacon-and-brisket. Lentils-lettuce-and-lamb, seeds-swedes-and-spam; beans-broccoli-and-biscuit.

Before he finds this orphanage which is made of collapsing-walls, crumbling-halls; creaking-doors and cracking-windows. And he is rendered tender-hearted with pity, for these Orphans who are just so gritty; with gritty-fingers and gritty-toes. They sit on these gritty-stairs, and in these gritty-chairs; wearing these gritty-clothes.

They are wearing shirts which need to be mended, and trousers which are far from splendid; with bare-arms and bare-feet. Some of them are hawking, some of them are talking; and others are sweeping this street.

This Malnourished Child lies in a gutter, this Maimed Child lies behind a shutter; and this Teenager lies beneath a tree. Alfred feels a connection, so he fills with loving-affection; and passionate-loyalty.

He sneaks in through this building's back door, tiptoes down this corridor; and slinks into this pantry which looks like a shed. Its shelves are completely bare, apart from two fishes just there; and five loaves of stale-bread.

"Please can I bu-bu-bu-borrow your trolley sir?" Alfred asks the Good German tonight, whilst he stands by this light; and shakes his hairy-head. "Please-please-please."

The Good German is slightly confused, slightly bemused, and

slightly amused.

'Vie?' He asks, and laughs; because he is slightly intrigued.

"Well, sir," Alfred replies, and sighs; because he is slightly fatigued. "I'd be hu-hu-hu-happy to tell you. But, please tell me, have you ever heard the story of *The Two Brothers*? About how it's better to do good things, than it is to talk about them."

The Good German chuckles, clicks two of his knuckles; and agrees. Before Alfred pushes this trolley, with childish-folly; and springy-knees.

He pushes it to the fishmonger in a hurry, and he begins to scurry; as he heads to the bakers in a buoyant-mood. He takes these fish-heads and fish-fins, and all the bread in these bins; as he fills his trolley with food.

Before he sneaks inside this orphanage with nervous-trepidation, and a fear of damnation; which builds as he enters this pantry. Where his heart begins to thump, and his knees begin to bump; as he fills this empty-gantry.

He fills it until his bread covers every inch of this store, his fish covers every inch of this floor; and there is food on all of these racks. So that where there was a stack of dishes, five loaves and two fishes; there is food piled up in stacks.

Alfred leaves and hides behind this car, which allows him to spy from afar; as these Orphans sit down on that peat. As they kneel, marvel at their meal; praise the heavens and begin to eat.

Alfred runs away beneath these smoggy-skies, before he returns each week with the new supplies; which he finds all around this town. He returns with vegetables which are green, meat which is lean; and tuna which is brown. With berries from a vine, pots of brine; and fruit which has fallen down.

He starts to find the Good German's trolley full of berries, carrots-courgettes-and-cherries; peppers-pumpkins-and-peas. Perhaps it is because the Good German likes what he hears, with his ears; or because he likes what he sees. He would not be the first person to spot Alfred as he sneaks around, without a sound; before he turns and flees.

"Get back 'ere you besmirched little-scoundrel," the Fishmonger often starts to wheeze. "I see what you've been a-doing, a-fiddling with my fish!"

And this Chef who eats more food than he serves, also fills Alfred with nerves; and also lets him go. Perhaps he turns a blind-eye, or perhaps he prefers not to pry; Alfred does not know.

But neither this Fishmonger with his noisy-screaming, nor this chubby Chef with his busy-scheming; can curb Alfred's taste for mischief. He continues for a hundred weeks in all, and brings five-thousand meals down this crumbling-hall; which brings these Orphans relief.

He also carries bags for every pregnant-lady he meets, helps old-dears across the streets; and helps people with diseases. He helps people in this poor-neighbourhood, with deeds which are good; whenever he pleases.

It is here that he approaches this Daughter who is covered in greasy-mud, spurting-blood; and purple-bumps. She is a similar age to Alfred, with freckles on her head; and her hair in tangled-clumps.

She sits with her Mum who seems stressed, panicked-petrified-and-possessed; and in distress. As her wig falls over her face, these strips of purple-lace; and this tatty purple-dress.

"Wu-wu-wu-what's happened?" Alfred asks because he is unable to guess.

"This!" The Daughter says with as she wipes away this blood, this mud; and this mess. "Oh, I am sorry, I didn't mean to make you worry. It's just that I've been bleeding for twelve hours now. I can't afford a doctor, I'm ever so poor, and no-one will help me. I'm ever so sorry. I haven't offended you, have I? Oh, what shall I do? Whatever shall I do?"

As he listens Alfred realises that he had once bled like this Daughter, and pled like this Daughter; before the Good German saved him when no-one else would. So he spots an opportunity, to serve his community; to do the same and truly come good.

The Good German had put Alfred's arm a sling, tied his ankle with pieces of string; and bandaged him with his own shirt. So Alfred uses the fringe of his cloak to stem the Daughter's bleeding, and finds himself succeeding; as he reduces her torturous-hurt.

The Good German had taken Alfred to an inn, wiped Alfred's chin; and carried Alfred in his own arms. So Alfred carries the Daughter, gives her some water; and comforts her with his charms.

And the Good German had taken Alfred to a hotel-room, fanned a fire to illuminate the gloom; and paid for a doctor with his own money. So Alfred takes the Daughter to this Pharmacist, who can assist; and pays for a coagulant to stop her blood from staying so runny.

His *involvement* helps the childish Alfred who was plagued by Sunday School crushes, and Primary School head-rushes; to *evolve* into a man. Matured by the adult company which being a single-child brings, the presence of his Father's things; and the Good German.

He continues his random acts of kindness without suspension, and *involves* himself in too many mention; which totally *evolves* his behaviour. He evolves from mended to mender, from defended to defender; and from saved to saviour.

He does not care for tradition, custom-culture-or-condition; or any sort of convention. He does not hold a grudge, judge; or act with any pretension. Without getting distracted, he becomes pro-active; and pays very close attention. He continues to learn, acts with concern; and real comprehension.

EVERYONE IS GUILTY

Owl was intelligent-respectable-and-strong, and everyone knew it, since Owl told them so himself. He was powerful; he controlled every tree-animal-and-bird in his empire. He was rich; he had more jewels-gems-and-gold than anyone else. And he was magnificent; no creature could overthrow him.

This made Owl happy, it made Owl very happy, but he still wanted more.

For his forest was a green-and-pleasant land, full of gardens-grasslands-and-groves, lochs-lagoons-and-lakes, meadows-marshlands-and-meads. But he knew its boundaries well, and he knew that there were many other forests which he could rule.

Those forests, however, had all been conquered by creatures like Eagle, who were almost as powerful-rich-and-magnificent as Owl himself.

Owl was jealous of Eagle, and Eagle was jealous of Owl. They both wanted to impose their own intelligent system of rule on the other, prove that they were the most respectable creature, and display their strength.

And so they went to war.

Owl thought it would be a short-and-glorious affair which would be over by Christmas. He thought that Eagle's subjects would rejoice when he set them free.

But Eagle was also intelligent-respectable-and-strong. He also took the light from Owl's trees, the food from Owl's animals, and the airwaves from Owl's birds. He met each of Owl's attacks with raids of his own.

So Owl-and-Eagle's resplendent-palaces, grand-buildings and strong-barracks, all began to crumble. Their jewels-gems-and-gold were spent on weapons, their supplies dwindled, and they both became fatigued.

Owl-and-Eagle could not dream, could not sleep, could not even see. They could not breathe, could not weep, could not even speak.

The animals in their forests died, and the animals in their distant-forests died. Their birds died, and their trees died too.

And, with no armies left, Owl-and-Eagle were overthrown by their *remaining subjects. They had both been defeated.*

Owl was still intelligent-respectable-and-strong, and everyone knew it, since Owl told them so himself. But he was no longer powerful-rich-or-magnificent, and he never would be again.

1909

Alfred's legs grow upwards, and his chest grows outwards; as he develops his manners-morals-and-mind. As his classmates enter the wider-community, leave school at the first opportunity; and leave him far behind. Alfred wants to join them and earn an honest-crust, but his Mother insists *'Your education is a must'*; which puts him in a bind.

The year is 1909.

A German Physicist is developing a cure to syphilis whilst he wears a blazer made of flannel, a French Engineer is piloting the first ever plane to cross the English Channel; and a Belgian Chemist is unveiling synthetic-plastic. In Antarctica the first ever steps are being made on the Magnetic South Pole, in America the first ever radio-show is being broadcast whole; and in Israel the first ever kibbutz is being built by some people who are enthusiastic. Whilst the British sign a treaty to accrue some Malaysian land, which makes them feel grand; famous-fabulous-and-fantastic.

"My notion!" Alfred's Mother starts to coax, having washed her hair with the raw egg-yokes; which she keeps near that elastic. "I really don't know what to do with you, Alfred Freeman. I-don't-I-don't-I-don't. You're just not respectable.

"Your future depends upon an education. Look at me. Lawyers-accountants-and-bankers are educated. Politicians are educated too. Education is respectable. It-is-it-is-it-is!

"Really, you make an old-woman all a-quiver. You and your mischity; tramping around in all weathers, like a pair of young-lovers or a stray-dog. If only you were more like your Father in heaven. If only you were more like Bernie. Now there's a boy I'd be proud to call my son.

"Alfred! If you want to be a well-paid and well-respected member of society, you really should stay on at school. You-should-you-should-you-should. There. That is all."

But Alfred is not interested in any of the professions which his Mother has listed, because they remind him of the Professional who had left him twisted; after he was mugged in an alley full of dirt. The Good German was not so respected, but was compassionate to be affected;

and so wrapped Alfred's wounds in his shirt.

"But what if I du-du-du-don't want to be a banker?" Alfred begins blurt.

"You'd be fantastic in the army, my little-soldier," his Mother begins to flirt.

"Pa-pa-pa-please! What if I don't want to join the army?"

"You'll be a splendid-soldier! A mighty-musketeer!"

"Pa-pa-pa-please! What if I don't want to be a soldier? Pa-pa-pa-pretty please. Pretty please with a cherry on top."

"Top-notch! You'll be a first-class officer. Somewhere-somewhen-somehow, you-shall-you-shall-you-shall."

As his Mother speaks Alfred is moved by her frenzied-state, and the way she tries to debate; with all these impassioned-emotions. She strokes Alfred's arm at a manic-pace, with concern on her face; and she mirrors Alfred's motions.

But this does not assuage Alfred's guilt, because he knows his Mother will have to work to the hilt; whilst he studies geology-geometry-and-Greek. His Mother finds her seamstress-work fairly dour, and only earns six pence an hour; so works for sixty hours each week.

Therefore whilst Bernie has a cupboard full of games, and a collection of toy-trains; which have been passed down from sister-to-brother. Alfred's family substitute chicory-dust for tea, water down their curry; and rely on his Stepfather and Mother.

His parents keep their pennies close to their chest, and they stay at home to rest; they do not go out or entertain. Alfred believes that if he could earn some money, his parents could afford to buy some honey; or visit some places by train. That they could afford to get a barber to cut their hair, go to a country-fair; or drink some pink-champagne.

"I just want to cu-cu-cu-contribute," he tries to explain. "You shouldn't have to struggle away just to feed-and-clothe me. Please let me help you. Please-please-please."

Alfred's Mother hobbles past these seven-penny novels, these military-models; and this potted-fern. She stumbles past this paraffin-lamp, and this postage-stamp; because she is moved by Alfred's concern.

"You know, your Father in heaven once served in a particularly queer engagement over in Benin?" She says as she speaks of Alfred's Father for the first ever time, with a vibrating-spine; which makes her twist-and-turn. "Look at me. This was back in 1897; you were just a babe in my arms back then. My wonderful-warrior; you were no bigger than a small bag of carrots!

"Now Benin was a rich country; full of palm-oil, rubber and ivory. But by gum it was a frightful place. It had dealt in slavery, and it had dealt in human-sacrifice. 'Twer a closed country.

"The British had tried for many years to open up that small city-state; they had sent peace-envoy after peace-envoy to talk to their King. Oh, how they had tried to foster trade! Oh, how they had tried to negotiate an end to their god-awful barbarity!

"Alas, I'm afraid to say, that it had been to no avail.

"Look at me. The envoy sent in afore your Father's had come to a sticky-end. It was perfectly-awful Alfred; a real deuce. Benin's King believed that our men were planning to attack him, and so he'd sent his troops to ambush us. Just two of our soldiers survived, as the green-forest turned red with rivers of British blood. Oh, it just wasn't respectable. Our soldiers were positively astir!

"'*This is our inheritance*', they thought to themselves. '*We shall return and utterly destroy those savages. We shall teach them that their actions are sinful!*'

"This was the mood amongst the troops. Their friends had been left in seas of blood and mountains of sorrow. They considered it unjust-improper-and-unfair. Oh, my fearless-fighter, how they considered it unfair!

"Now Alfred, your Father in heaven knew that his mission was dangerous. He-did-he-did-he-did. He knew that he could be ambushed at any time.

"But your Father in heaven was stouthearted; he was a different pair of shoes. He was happy to lead his unit through the gnarled-trees, tangled-undergrowth and poisoned-shrubs, which filled that forest. He was happy to lead his men along paths which were normally only navigated, single-file, by barefooted-natives.

"Your Father in heaven didn't see a single adversary during his blind-march forward, but he oft heard them, each forenoon and each afternoon. Their yells would howl, their calls would cry, and their bullets would burst. Oh Alfred! All your Father could do was fire back into the thicket.

"Look at me. Your Father in heaven knew that despite the strength of his enemies, and the challenges posed by the forest, his own men could be triumphant. For they were intelligent-respectable-and-strong.

"But he knew there would be bloodshed, and he was keen to protect his men. You shall be the same one day. Oh Alfred, you-shall-you-shall-you-shall!

"So, on arriving near Benin's capital, your Father in heaven sent a decoy to distract their enemy, before he climbed the cliffs which surrounded that city. Oh Alfred! He dug a whole series of tributaries up there, and re-routed the rivers towards the cliffs' edges, where he blocked them all with tree-trunks.

"Once many tributaries had been dug, your Father in heaven stretched forth his hand. He signalled for his men to break down those barriers, and let the water flow. I shouldn't wonder that it was one hell of a sight.

"The natives fled from the oncoming-waters, and were overthrown in the midst of the sea which descended upon them. Those waters covered their monuments, crushed their palaces, and corroded their pagan-art. They flushed every member of the old-regime away.

"And, as a result of your Father's actions, Benin was liberated from the savages, trade made that nation great, and your Father's men returned unharmed. They-did-they-did-they-did. Oh Alfred! If only you could have been there; it was ever so respectable.

"My notion! We cannot know what dangers we'll have to face, or what sacrifices we'll have to make, during our own blind-march forward. But we'll overcome every obstacle too, just like your Father in heaven. You shall be just like him! Somewhere-somewhen-somehow, you-shall-you-shall-you-shall!

"Enough of your mischity! Enough of your tramping! Oh Alfred Freeman; I know exactly what I shall do with you. I shall house-feed-and-clothe you, and you *shall* stay on in education, my terrific-trooper. You shall become respectable, and you shall become a mighty-soldier, who'll rule from north-to-south and east-to-west. There. That is all."

Alfred's Mother becomes soppy-shivery-and-sweaty, as she collapses into the arms of this grey-settee; exhausted with mental-strain. But Alfred is excited, dreamy-delirious-and-delighted; hoping his Mother will speak about his Father again. For he is tired of relying on stories from people like the Drill Sergeant, and things like this garment; so would love to pick her brain.

He is tired of having to feed off little-scraps, and fill in the gaps; with help from books like '*The Battle Of Dorking*'. With help from books like '*The Riddle Of Men*', and the '*Invasion Of 1910*'; which he reads when he is not walking.

So hearing his Mother speak, hearing her shriek; and hearing her slur. After so many years, and so many tears; shows what this means to her.

"Okay," Alfred starts to concur. "I ah-ah-ah-understand. Thank-you for telling me about Father. I hope you speak about him again. Thank-you, thank-you, thank-you. You're better than chocolate! You're better than sunshine! You're the best Mother a boy could have!"

So Alfred enrols with Bernie at this brand new school, with this brand new hall; and these brand new Teachers who are always interfering. Whilst they teach these new lessons in biology, zoology; and engineering.

Unlike his old school where the cane was inescapable, this new school provides free education for the most capable; thanks to a new regime. So Alfred writes with new inky-pens, makes new friends; and plays for a new football team.

And because he still wants to work, and does not want to shirk; Alfred also helps with his Stepfather's carpentry. They draft-design-and-draw, shape-strike-and-saw; which improves their relationship markedly.

They make a desk for a weather-forecaster, a stage for a news-broadcaster; and some boxes for a dance-troupe. They make some pews for a church-pastor, benches for a stationmaster; and tables for a youth-group. Whilst they chew some beef-jerky, munch some turkey; and slurp some mushroom-soup.

This work means their income increases, and their poverty deceases; so they go to the football and they go to play pool. Alfred's Stepfather starts to shoot, his Mother buys a flute; and they go to the music-hall.

His Stepfather has friends over to play some outlandish-games, and make some outlandish-claims; whilst they sing-shout-and-smoke. His Mother attends a dance-class, has some picnics on the grass; and rows boats which are made of oak. Whilst Alfred does good-deeds, helps people with needs; and helps people who are broke.

Alfred stopped taking the Fishmonger's fish when he changed schools, but remembers seeing that man clean his tools; outside his fishy-shop. He was serving some fish with a spoon, sweeping his floor with a broom; and wiping his tiles with a fishy-mop.

"I don't 'ardly know where I are!" He told a friend whilst Alfred had started to skip, slip; and hop. "My son is evva so poorly. He's precious 'ard, but I'm up to my eyeballs 'is in doctor's fees, and I owe four pounds in taxes. I can't be a-paying that kinda money nohow; 'tis three weeks income! Demn, desh, and darn it!"

Alfred considers the Fishmonger's debt to be a worthy one, accrued in an attempt to save his son; like he was once saved from smallpox. And having taken so much fish from his big blue-can, Alfred feels a debt to that man; who wears discoloured-socks.

So he approaches the Good German who is dressed in a waistcoat, which reaches his throat; with his back held perfectly-straight. And he waits as his mentor locks this door, sweeps this floor; and unpacks that wooden-crate.

"Can I bu-bu-bu-borrow four pounds please?" Alfred asks as he locks this wooden-gate. "Please-please-please."

"How are you goink to repay me Alfie, dear boy?" The Good German asks his mate.

Alfred is unable to reply, or look the Good German in his eye; so he looks down at his size-five feet. He looks down at these melons, leeks-lentils-and-lemons; and this sack of durum-wheat.

"You could vork for me on Saturdays, perhaps?" The Good German suggests, whilst he rests; on this yellow-seat. "To earn back zee money, yah."

And so Alfred smiles with glee, taps his knee, and nods to agree.

Because this arrangement means that he can listen to the Good German's tales, whilst he weighs fruit on these scales; which are tied together with thread. It means that he can listen to his mentor quip, whilst he scrapes coins along this strip; to see if they are forgeries which are coated in lead. And it means that he can listen to his mentor's fables, whilst he arranges these tables; which have just been painted red.

So Alfred finds himself hired, with the four gold-sovereigns which he desired; before he leaves this place in a dash. He puts his coins on this fish's tongue, and puts this hook through its gum; to lead the Fishmonger to his new cash.

And with a head full of grizzled-hair, and opaque-eyes which glare; here this Fishmonger stands. He stamps his fishy-feet, to create this fishy-beat; and he waves his fishy-hands.

"Get back 'ere you besmirched little-scoundrel," he commands. "I see what you've been a-doing; a-fiddling with my fish!"

The Fishmonger gives chase, begins to race, and ups the pace.

He forces Alfred to flee past this coughing Typist, this hiccupping Cyclist; and this burping Nun. This greasy Mechanic, this lisping Hispanic; and this Nit Nurse's Son.

He forces Alfred to run across these paving-stones, which jangle his bones; as he dodges to the right. As he dodges around these Walkers, Haberdashers-Housekeepers-and-Hawkers; before he dives out of sight.

Before he dives into good-deeds for the obese-ordinary-and-old, creaky-crusty-and-cold; ugly-unfed-and-unwell. He helps the wobbly-woozy-and-weak, and this Mute Boy who cannot speak; and cannot hear that well.

This Mute Boy has a ghastly-stare, fluffy orange-hair; and gnashing orange-teeth. He is grabbed by this Carer who throws him through this mire, this fire; and this weed-ridden heath.

"Wu-wu-wu-whatever makes your boy angry," Alfred suggests, and protests; because he is horrified beyond belief. "This'll only make him worse. Pa-pa-pa-please let him go. Please-please-please."

Alfred's challenge makes the Carer agitated, irked-irate-and-irritated; and it makes him turn dark-red. As if to query why Alfred was ever born, he glares at Alfred with spiteful-scorn; and shakes his clean-shaven head.

"It's outwith ye remit!" He bellows with dread. "Aye! Ye dinna ken what I've done for this here wee laddie. Aye! How I've stood fa' his madness; his turns, his bitin' and his stramash; his punchin', kickin', pushin' an' a tearin'. He's no' muckle use to anyone. Aye!

"Losh man! By dod, I've tried to destroy him. Aye! I've bared him. Aye! I've tried to heal him. Aye! But nothin' will work. He's possessed by a foul-spirit I tell ye. He's a bampot. Aye! A reet screwball.

"I'm just tryin' to calm him, get him ca' canny, so I can take him to the asylum. Aye! I dinna want nay stushie, I've had my fill. Aye! I've done all that can be doon."

Alfred looks up at the skies, whilst the Mute Boy's cries, with crystalline-tears in his sallow-eyes.

"We shouldn't cu-cu-cu-cast him out," Alfred replies. "He can be healed. Please believe it! Anything is possible if you believe in it enough."

And as the Carer looks around, Alfred grabs the Mute Boy without a sound; and carries him down this street. He carries him down these smoky-lanes, past these smoky-trains; and past this smoky-meat. Past this Baby in a blue-crib, this Baby in a blue-bib; and this Baby who sucks a blue-sweet. Before they arrive at this orphanage which is full of ill-fitting bricks, wooden-sticks; and cracked-concrete.

"Good-day ma'am," Alfred begins to tweet. "This Mute Boy was being abused by his cu-cu-cu-Carer. Please can you house him? Please-please-please? I'd be ever so grateful. I'd be very much obliged."

This Matron with grey-hair looks far from impressed, as if she is ready to reject Alfred's request; repel-rebuff-and-refuse. She does not have any beds, any bedspreads; or any bed-sheets for the Mute Boy to use.

But the Chef walks over here, and whispers in her ear; which make her change her mind. She begins to grin, and lifts her chin; which makes her look caring-compassionate-and-kind.

"Okay-okay-okay," she says as her teeth begin to grind. "We'll give him a go and see if he settles. Settles-settles-settles. But I'll make no promises. No guarantees. Just you wait-and-see. See-see-see."

Alfred turns around and retreats, down these narrow-streets; whilst the Mute Boy stays behind. He goes to school when he should, does deeds which are good; and deeds which are kind. Whilst his work at the greengrocery, and his work with carpentry; make him more refined. As he grows upwards, grows outwards; and develops his youthful-mind.

THE DOG

Once upon a time there was a Dog. A loyal young Dog, with love-and-compassion running all the way through.

Dog loved every tree-animal-and-bird in her forest. She loved Willow who shaded her, Beaver who played with her, and Thrush who sang with her each day.

And Dog used her love to enjoy her forest, because love is life, and Dog used her life to become friends with all her fellow creatures.

Owl, meanwhile, was still intelligent-respectable-and-strong. But he was no longer intelligent enough to outmanoeuvre the trees, respectable enough to outfox the animals, or strong enough to outwit the birds. He was no longer powerful-rich-or-magnificent.

Without a penny to his name, he lived in a rickety-hut, and had to use a rope-trap to catch his food.

And so, on one sunny-afternoon, he used that trap to catch Dog, who was left dangling from Willow's branch, next to her favourite lake.

"This is Owl's doing," Thrush said. "If we don't do something soon, he'll come back and eat Dog!"

This upset Willow and Beaver, who both loved Dog a lot.

"Owl is more intelligent-respectable-and-strong than us," Willow said. "We know that, because he tells us so himself. But we're more loving than Owl. So we should use our love to save Dog."

"Beaver," Thrush continued. "Use your powerful-teeth to bite through that rope. Willow; use your sturdy-branches to cradle Dog. And I'll use my nimble-wings to delay Owl."

Thrush flew away and found Owl, who was leaving his hut with a big-bag. So Thrush flew straight at Owl, and hit his head with her beak. It left Owl so dazzled, that he had to lie down in his hut to recover.

After a while, Owl left for a second time, carrying a big-sword. So Thrush flew at Owl from behind, and hit him in the back of his head. It left Owl so dazzled, that he had to lie down again.

And, after a while, Owl left for a third time, wearing a big-helmet. There was nothing Thrush could do, so she flew back to warn her friends.

"Owl will be here any minute," she told Beaver.

This news encouraged Beaver to bite faster than he had ever bitten *before. He bit all the way through the rope around Dog's leg, and Dog fell to the floor just as Owl arrived.*

Dog ran into the forest, Thrush flew into the sky, and Willow stood still in the ground. But Beaver was so exhausted that he could not move. So Owl put him in his big-bag, closed it with a knot, and tied it to Willow's branch.

Dog knew that she could flee from Owl, who was very old. But she knew that if she ran away, Owl would eat Beaver. And that upset Dog, who loved Beaver a lot.

So Dog appeared in front of Owl, and feigned a limp. She was so convincing that Owl believed Dog was an easy-target, and followed her through the forest.

But Dog kept her distance, and upped her pace whenever Owl got too close. She led Owl past so many trees-animals-and-birds, that he became completely lost.

Dog turned, laughed at Owl, and ran back to her favourite lake. She left Owl so dazzled, that he had to lie down to recover. And she released Beaver from Owl's sack, like Beaver had released her from Owl's rope.

Because Dog was loving-loyal-and-passionate, and everyone knew it, since Dog showed them so herself!

1910

Alfred's muscles have grown rather strong, and his hair has grown rather long; after another frenetic-year. During which time he has done more good-deeds, at high-speeds; and worked away in top-gear. Meeting new people at his workshop, at his bus-stop; and at home just here.

The year is 1910.

An American Physicist is publishing the first ever infrared-photographs in a scientific-publication, a Chinese Politician is ending slavery in his nation; and a French Actress is becoming the first female to hold a pilot's licence. In France the first ever neon-lights are being displayed, in America instant-coffee is starting to trade; and in Korea a whole country is being annexed in silence. Whilst the British elect 177 politicians who support the *National Service League's* stance, call for conscription to be given a chance; and call for more violence.

Alfred reads about this whilst his Stepfather greases his boots with some fresh pig-fat, adjusts his Gibus hat; and falls asleep in his favourite chair. Whilst his Mother washes these clothes with some *Sunlight Soap*, and mends this rope; near this Retired Captain who has white-hair.

This Retired Captain talks about breeding dogs, and carving logs; as he smokes his mermaid-shaped pipe. He talks about spotting trains, and exploring remains; with a lively sort of hype. And he talks about collecting stamps, and making lamps; of every imaginable type.

He is here because Alfred's Mother has become far less reserved, with a spine which is far less curved; since she spoke of the Beninese war. Which is why she welcomes this man, who drinks from this can; and why she removes a watch from that drawer.

"I'd like you to have this, my little-soldier," she tells Alfred as she closes this door. "Look at me. Be respectable!

"This belonged to your Father in heaven. He bought its ivory-strap back from Africa, but the watch itself has been in your family for many generations. It's been passed down from father-to-son, man-to-boy, and soldier-to-soldier. It-has-it-has-it-has.

"Now, my wonderful-warrior, it's yours. All yours! Because you shall be a mighty-soldier too. You'll rule from north-to-south and east-to-west. Somewhere-somewhen-somehow, you-shall-you-shall-you-shall!"

"But weren't elephants ku-ku-ku-killed to get this ivory?" Alfred questions.

"Oh, how it suits you Alfred!" His Mother mentions.

"Pa-pa-pa-please tell me! Isn't killing elephants cruel?"

"Oh, how it brings out the *White Cliffs Of Dover*! Oh, how it brings out your love-loyalty-and-passion!"

"Pa-pa-pa-please tell me about the elephants? Pa-pa-pa-pretty please. Pretty please with a cherry on top."

"Oh, what a handsome boy you're growing into, my fearless-fighter. Oh, what a handsome-soldier you'll become. Just like good old Bernie."

Alfred does not know what has caused his Mother's transformation, which has made her treat soldiers with veneration; affection-adoration-and-adulation. He does not know what has made his Mother attend army-events dressed in khaki-sweaters, re-read his Father's old army-letters; and agree with this man's narration.

She usually only invites her sisters into their family-home, to sit on these seats which are stuffed with foam; where they always start their yawning. Before they start their soggy cheek-wetting, gentle hair-petting; and overbearing-fawning.

'Gollys! He's going to be a brave 'un, I can see it presently. Just look at how he walks around as if he owns the place,' a Drooling Aunt once said whilst she ate like a glutton.

'He's a fine laddie! He'll grow into a strong-soldier; I'd bet my last ha'penny on it,' a Fidgety Aunt once said whilst she played with a button.

'Right you are! He has his Father's long-legs, and his Grandfather's muscled-arms,' a Restless Aunt once said whilst she chewed some mutton.

But with the freedom which retirement grants, this Retired Captain is older than those aunts; with hair on his ears and lines on his chin. With glasses which fall down his nose, patches on his clothes; hair on his hands and lines on his skin.

"I was a bit of a father-figure to your Pa, even if I don't say so myself!" He begins to sing. "Well, I was at first. I can't help thinking that he became *my* teacher in the end. He was a dashed good sort, and a mighty fine soldier. He was intelligent-respectable-and-strong, with an ability to pull off the impossible. Fine-o!"

The Retired Captain begins to choke, coughs up some smoke; and smiles at his own conclusion. Before Alfred's Mother's makes a forward-sway, and backs away; in a dizzy state of confusion.

"I've some things to see to, my terrific-trooper. I-do-I-do-I-do," she says as she leads Alfred's Stepfather past these books, these hooks, and this chessboard which is covered in regents-rectangles-and-rooks. "I'll leave you two soldiers alone."

She leaves them alone whilst the Retired Captain adjusts his glasses, fills his pipe with fresh-molasses; and lights this lamp which glows. Before he speaks about the wars he has won, in Burma-Sudan-and-Afghanistan; and about crushing all of his foes.

"But I guess you want to hear about your Father," he sings as he taps his toes. "You're tarrying for the juicy-bits? Right-o!"

Alfred nods, looks up to the gods, and down at these fishing-rods.

"Well, my son, your Pa was one of the many thousands of men sent to South Africa, just a few months into the offensive there," he continues in a joyous-tone, which shakes his nasal-bone, with the brassiness of a tenor-trombone. "We journeyed to that distant-land together, as it just so happens. Sure-o! For our country! For our country!

"This was back in 1900, when you were just three years old. Your Pa had left you and your Ma with a heavy-heart. He was perfectly obsessed with you. Surely to goodness, he was infatuated with his little lad!

"Well, the Boers had been at odds with the British for many years. Those uneducated-fools, who had pea-soup for brains, didn't take kindly to our banishment of slavery. Those buffoons, whose hearts were awry with their heads, had refused to bestow voting-rights on the decent British citizens who'd been mining for gold-and-diamonds.

"A deuce of a row was brewing, and war broke out in 1899. True-o!

"After many battles and many sieges, after many losses on both sides, and after starvation which saw surrounded-towns turn to dog-meat and horse-meat for nourishment, your Pa rode in to save the day.

"My son; he was a knight in shining-armour, your Pa. He vanquished the enemy, stood up for law-and-order, and protected the good British folk. It was a splendid thing. Fine-o!

"But 'twer not all plain-sailing. No-o! South Africa wasn't exactly a go as you please sort of a place. Far from it! Most fights were as broad as they were long. The Boers knew the terrain well; they were skilled-marksmen who were accustomed to stalking game in the bush, with a never say die attitude which proved to be an almighty-nuisance. Tricky-o!

"So we won battles as well as lost them, and there was no such thing as an easy victory. Not against the Boers, not in South Africa. My word, it was a darned slop, even if I don't say so myself.

"Well, my son, one such battle was still in its first day. Fighting had started at dawn, and the British Commander was keen for it to end by dusk. Guns had been fired, bullets had rained down from the skies, and the earth had shaken beneath our feet. Offensives-and-counteroffensives had ebbed-and-flowed. My lord, it was a frightful kick-up. A real ding-dong affair. Nasty-o!

"The battle had eventually turned in our favour. Our higher position, greater numbers and advanced weaponry, had all begun to tell. But dusk was throwing its dark-cloak over the arena of war, time was running out, and your Pa had to think fast to save the day.

"So, as cool as a cucumber, he gathered up his soldier's pocket-mirrors, the serving-trays in the canteen, and the cutlery in the pantry; double-quick.

"And with help from his men, he deedily attached the mirrors to his unit's steeds, using company-rope and his soldiers' darning-kits. He affixed the trays to the army's mules, and the cutlery to a herd of mountain-goats. It was all rather tip-top and Bristol fashion, even if I don't say so myself. Fine-o!

"My son; he lined those noble-steeds, strong-mules and grazing-goats, in regimented army order; head-to-heel and heel-to-head, in long-lines which stretched across the hillside. For his country! For his country!

"The goats were at the front, the mules rose up behind them, and the steeds were up top. The Boers hadn't an earthly what was going on. They just stood there as a big mass of glossy-mirrors, sparkling-trays and polished-cutlery, formed a metal-wall before them. Shiny-o!

"And, angled betwixt the setting-sun and the enemy below, that wall reflected every ray of light back down onto the Boers, and blinded them all. Bright-o!

"The sun stood still in the heavens, whilst the moon was made to wait. And your Pa's men picked off their foe one-by-one. It was a real knock-out! A real blood bath! A blooming good show! Top notch! Good-o!

"No day hath been extended like that afore or since. My son; only your Pa could have made it happen. And your Pa, he fought for Britain. For his country! For his country! This land of hope-and-glory."

The Retired Captain looks at Alfred with eyes which seem fresh, as if he believes that Alfred is made from his own army-flesh; and his own army-blood. His glasses fall off of his face, his smoke fills this place; and his heart begins to thud.

But the thought of picking-off humans '*one-by-one*', and killing them dead with a British gun; does not fill Alfred with glory. It makes Alfred feel sad, it makes him feel mad; and it makes him dislike this story.

For whilst Alfred is still keen to listen to his Father's stories, learn about his glories; and unravel his hidden mysteries. The Retired Captain's tale makes Alfred doubt the virtue of soldiers' corps, the veneration of their wars; and the value of their victories.

So instead of being swayed by the Retired Captain's narration, he looks to the Good German for inspiration; afflatus-assistance-and-advice. He walks towards his mentor, passes this shopping-centre; and this Iceman who is selling white-ice.

He arrives at this greengrocery where he sees the Good German counting his rosary-beads, at varying-speeds; with tranquillity on his face. But these red-rubies with magenta-twirls, and these perfectly-spherical aqua-pearls; do look a bit out of place. Unlike the wooden beads which Alfred is used to, these are beryl-bronze-and-blue; with a gentle sort of grace.

"Zey're from India, yah," the Good German says as he cuts to the chase.

"They use ru-ru-ru-rosaries in India sir?" Alfred asks with confusion, and disillusion; whilst he stares into empty-space.

"Oh yah," the Good German continues as he puts his beads back into their case. "Zey have monks who wear similar robes to our priests, ant who take zee same vows of pofferty-chastity-ant-obedience. In India people giff offerinks, like we do here, ant zey have holy-pictures viz auras which are just like zee halos you see on Christian paintinks too."

"Oh," Alfred replies. "Do they have ba-ba-ba-baptisms in India? Please tell me, sir. Please-please-please. My baptism is next week."

"Oh yah Alfie! Zey fully submerge zemselves in zee Riffer Ganges, to vash avay zare sins. To 'valk in a newness of life', as I zink you say?

"Just vait here, dear boy."

The Good German scuttles across this rickety-floor, scampers through that swinging-door; and scurries up to his flat. He returns with this murky-liquid, whose smell is somewhat vivid; and then he begins to chat.

"I vant you to have ziss," he says whilst the clouds begin to part, above that cart; that dove and that cat. "It's holy vater from zee Riffer Ganges, yah. Dear child, you can use it durink your baptism!

"You're like a son to me, Alfie. Viz you, I am vell pleased!"

Alfred uses this holy-water, during a joint-baptism with a Tailor's Daughter; before he walks towards the seaside. He walks along these rocky-drags, and past those rocky-crags; which are damp from the last high-tide.

These trawlers come-and-go, and these Anglers to-and-fro; amidst torrents of noisy-speech. Whilst these Traders stack, these dogs yap; and the sea laps over that beach.

But in the blink of an eye, waves jump up towards the sky; hit by rain and hit by hail. Like when Alfred was born, so begins this storm; and so begins this feisty-gale. These skies turn dark, as does that park; whilst lightning strikes that whale.

This salt-water sea spits out with disgust, as these Fisherman are rocked by this gust; and rocked by this windy-storm. These waves shrug their watery-shoulders, and crash boats into boulders; with windy-derision and windy-scorn. Whilst here on dry-land, these people offer a hand; without becoming forlorn.

Here is this formal Auctioneer, this shady Racketeer; and this Newspaper Seller. This passing Shopper, this off-duty Copper; and this

Fortune Teller.

Alfred joins them near this port, offers his moral-support; and pulls these trawlers aground. He pulls these Fishermen ashore, until his hands are sore; and his body is totally browned. When he finds them a place to doze, some clothes; and some blankets to pass around.

Alfred rebukes the wind-water-and-waves, blesses everyone he saves; and calms the effects of this storm. He does not stop, and he does not drop; until these Fishermen feel well-welcome-and-warm.

His actions earn Alfred love-loyalty-and-passion, in a friendly-fashion; from the all the men who he saves. So they take him to sea, train him like a new draftee; and teach him about the waves.

They teach him about the burbot-bream-and-bass, ray-roach-and-wrasse; bluefish-boarfish-and-brill. About where to cast his net, how to avoid the wet; and which fish not to kill.

"Cast your net on the other side," he says after they fail to catch a fish one day, whilst he points away; towards that distant-hill. "Please-please-please. I think you'll do mu-mu-mu-much better over there."

The Fishermen take a chance on this suggestion, catch too many fish to mention; and struggle to pull them all on board. They catch so many codlings, and so many rocklings; that they need help with this massive-hoard.

They sail away, across this bay; and reach this sunny-land. Where they nod, barbeque cod; and dance on this sunny-sand.

"Please can you apprentice my fu-fu-fu-friend?" Alfred asks as he gets up to stand. "Please-please-please. I'd be ever so grateful. I'd be very much obliged."

The Fishermen agree, and smile with glee; before they employ the Mute Boy as a deckhand. Which makes Alfred feel delighted, excited; glad-gleeful-and-grand.

FREEDOM

Owl was still intelligent-respectable-and-strong, and he still coveted power-riches-and-magnificence. So he visited a muddy-pool where he approached Frog, Water Snake, and some fishes.

"Hello," Frog said. "What brings you here?"

"Well," Owl replied. "I was thinking about what a hard life you must have, trapped in this dirty-pond without much food. You know, there's a beautiful-lagoon which is full of yummy-grubs and clear-water, just beyond those trees?"

The pond-animals were unsure why Owl was gloating about another lake. They knew their pool was dirty-and-small, but it was the only home they had.

"I could fly you through the skies and drop you in that lake, if you like," Owl explained.

"Why would you do that?" Water Snake challenged. "I think you just want to eat us!"

"No! No! No!" Owl replied. "I'm a reformed character these days; I'm trying to atone for my sins. I'd never eat you. Please let me take one of you to check out the lagoon; they'll confirm everything I've said. I promise."

The pond-animals argued amongst themselves, before they finally agreed that they needed a new home. And so they nominated Bream, who Owl carried across to Dog's favourite lake.

Bream investigated every rock-reed-and-root, crook-crevice-and-cranny, in that beautiful-lagoon. And he returned to answer his friends' questions.

"Is it really full of yummy-grubs?" The other fishes quizzed.

"Oh yes," Bream replied. "It's full of weeds-winkles-and-worms."

"Is it really full of clear-water?" Frog quizzed.

"Oh yes," Bream replied. "The water is clear-crisp-and-clean."

"Is it really big?" Water Snake quizzed.

"Oh yes," Bream replied. "It's ever so wide-deep-and-long."

The pond-animals were happy with Bream's answers, so they allowed Owl to carry them to the beautiful-lagoon, like motherless-children who were a long way from home.

But Owl landed short, wedged the pond-animals between Willow's branches, removed their skins and ate their flesh.

After eating all the fishes, and after eating Frog, Owl carried Water Snake to Dog's favourite lake, where he wedged her between Willow's branches.

But Water Snake was strong, she was bold, and she could breathe out of water. So Water Snake slithered free.

Owl could not control himself. He flew after Water Snake, and dived at her headfirst.

When Water Snake saw Owl hurtling towards her, she opened her mouth as wide as it would go, and swallowed Owl whole! Owl's head slid through Water Snake's jaws, and down into her long-body, whilst Owl's feet waggled away in the air.

That was when Dog arrived.

"Stop! Stop! Stop!" She shouted. And she pulled Owl's legs with all her might.

But Water Snake pulled back, because she could see her friends' bones, and was determined to get revenge.

"Beaver," Dog called. "Help me!"

Beaver was scared of Owl, who had tied him in a bag. But Dog's love-loyalty-and-passion overpowered Beaver's fear. And so Beaver joined Dog, and pulled at Owl's legs. Until, after much huffing-and-puffing, they finally freed Owl, who was covered in a layer of sticky-bile.

Water Snake slithered off into the lake, Beaver ran off into the forest, and Owl started to shiver. He looked completely bewildered.

"Why did you save me?" He asked. "I'm your enemy, not your friend."

"Love-loyalty-and-passion," Dog replied. "Because love can overcome intelligence, loyalty can overcome respectability, and passion can overcome strength."

1911

Alfred has a grocery job which pays, a carpentry job on weekdays; and an education on which his mind likes to feast. And as a result, he has become an adult; in his own eyes at least.

But his Mother considers Alfred to be his Father's son, a boy who was born to carry a gun; and her first husband's double. A soldier in the making, and a cure for her aching; who has his Father's brown-stubble.

So she is inspired by the Retired Captain's words, these singing birds; and the prophecies which ring in her ears. As she pushes Alfred through this door, towards this cadet-corps; to enlist with those Volunteers.

The year is 1911.

An American Engineer is giving away the secrets of air-conditioning without selectivity, a Dutch Scientist is discovering superconductivity; and a Frenchman is winning the first ever *Monte Carlo Rally* with a roar. In Libya the Italians are becoming the first ever nation to drop bombs from the sky, in Peru a lost city is emerging up high; and in France a beloved-painting is being stolen through a door. Whilst the British sit on some leather-seating, at a secretive-meeting; and formulate plans for a European war.

But Alfred is only concerned with his own society, with its every tavern-townhouse-and-tree; so he does not get distracted. He focuses on his own nation, on its every shop-school-and-station; and on this park to which his Mother is being attracted.

His Mother drags Alfred past this creepy Stalker, who pursues that Seafood Hawker; who sells cups which are full of squid-shrimp-and-stones. Past this group of Amateur Musicians, who sit on that bandstand in different positions; and play music in different tones. And past this Italian, who wears a medallion; and sells ice-cream in wafer-cones.

She drags Alfred past these Picnickers who eat bowls of lumpy-custard, roast-beef sarnies which are smothered in mustard; and lashings of cold-brawn. And past these Ladies who look flustered, these Students who have clustered; and these puppies who have just been born.

Past all this razzmatazz, towards these Cadets who march with pizzazz; beneath this sunny-sky. These Cadets march with pride, as the Retired Captain calls from one side; in his khaki-suit and khaki-tie.

"Attention! Left turn! Forward march!" He starts to cry, as these Cadets march by, with their backs held straight and their chins held high.

Alfred is made to shoot arrows whilst under observation, watch a first-aid demonstration; and comply with regulations. Which makes him feel weak-weary-and-wild, like a restless-child; who is overwhelmed by his Mother's expectations. He wishes this session would cease, looks around for release; and shakes in his foundations.

So whilst Bernie finds balance hunched over his gun, with his blazing-hair reflecting the blazing-sun; as he enjoys every single activity. Alfred feels weak in each limb, because his Mother's presence embarrasses him; and fills him with passivity.

Alfred has the natural-skill, the ability to run-ride-and-wrestle come to him at will; but he finds this place unseemly-unproductive-and-uncool. Because the passion he had for drill when he was aged just five, has taken a dive; after endless repetition at school.

"What do you think son?" The Retired Captain asks in his joyous-drool.

Alfred does not know what to say, because he does not want to cause this man dismay, so he stays silent and he looks away.

"Come, come," the Retired Captain prods in his jovial-way. "You can tell me; we're practically family, you-and-I, even if I don't say so myself. True-o!"

"I fu-fu-fu-found it uncomfortable, I'm afraid," Alfred replies, as he almost cries, with tears in his teenage-eyes. "I found the uniformity a bit soul-destroying, the blind acceptance of commands a bit unbecoming, and the bows-and-arrows a bit outdated too.

"It's not you, it's me. I do enjoy spending time with you. You have a great personality! I just don't fit in here. No thanky-you. It's just not for me."

Alfred can see that his words have made the Retired Captain feel hassled-harassed-and-hurt, because he runs his toe through the dirt; and looks a little bit frightened. So Alfred does not add that he opposes the army's brutality, that blindly following orders lacks morality; or that he finds this place unenlightened.

The Retired Captain places his index-finger on his lower-lip, nudges his glasses when they start to slip; and ruffles through his sack. He gives Alfred this copy of '*The Great British Army*', and looks a bit smarmy; whilst he pats Alfred's sweaty back.

"Have a gander," he says whilst they walk down this track. "'Tis a grand thing, the British Army; a real merit to God. Real first-rate stuff, my son, even if I don't say so myself. Only a whimsical-nincompoop or an industrial-innocent would disagree. Right-o!

"What you see here is just child's play; I can see that you're bigger than it, just like your Pa. But don't dismiss it son; 'tis an honourable start. Stick with it and you'll be a brick in the wall of our empire in just a jiffy. Biff! Bizz! Curtain! Real quick-sharpish! Sure-o!"

Alfred does not say anything more, because he does not want to disgrace his Mother who he does still adore; and he does not want to disgrace this soldier. So as his Mother sits down to eat a snack, Alfred and this man walk down this track; and sit down on this greenstone-boulder.

"You know, your Pa and I were in Zanzibar together?" The Retired Captain says as he closes this folder. "For our country! For our country! It was just after the Good Sultan had passed on.

"The Good Sultan had been a great leader; a thundering-good sort who'd signed trade-agreements which brought new wealth to his people. He was a smashing chap, plumb honest. He'd even opposed the slave-trade. Free-o!

"But a Bad Sultan, a ghastly fellow, had killed the Good Sultan and taken his throne. He was not a great leader, even if I don't say so myself. He was callow, half-baked, and easily enticed by the insular-folk who wanted to stop foreign-trade. And he was most wrong-headed; he was lured by the slave-traders' bribes. He hadn't the faintest notion of right-and-wrong. He was a real frozen-faced dago, with less sense than God gives to geese. Bad-o!

"We were all jolly miffed. My son; if only there were only more brains in this poor old muddle of a world!

"Our General, he had brains. A good set of them too! So he sent a message to the Bad Sultan on the first day, beseeching him to step down, and allow a better sort of person to rule. A gent. Good-o!

"But the Bad Sultan jibbed at the notion. He said '*no*'!

"And so our General sent another message to the Bad Sultan on the second day, again beseeching him to step down.

"And again the Bad Sultan said '*no*'.

"The General sent messages to the Bad Sultan on the third-fourth-fifth-and-sixth days too, each beseeching him to step aside.

"And the Bad Sultan said '*no*'-'*no*'-'*no*'-and-'*no*' each time. He didn't believe that the British would act. He didn't believe that we'd stand up for the enslaved, or fight for the trade of nations. He reckoned we were full of hot-air. He reckoned our words were just bluff-and-bluster.

"Of course he was mistaken. The British, as we know, are the saviours of freedom, the protectors of liberty, and the guardians of goodness. We're jolly good eggs as a rule, even if I don't say so myself. Fine-o!

"So your Pa went on a reconnaissance-mission. For his country! For his country! He tramped around the Bad Sultan's complex once an hour, every hour, for six long hours in all.

"And he found a wooden-wall which surrounded the Bad Sultan's palace, a temple whence he prayed, and a harem whence he played. Before he returned to the General, who he told that the wall was weak, and would be easy to breach.

"So your Pa was bestowed with seven men, who he led around the compound seven times. My son; they buried rams' horns stuffed with dynamite every few metres. For their country! For their country! And, under the cover of cannon-fire, with the sound of bellows-and-blasts ringing out like screeching-cats, your Pa detonated it all. Bang-o!

"Hark! Such was their might, that the rams' horns made a loud trumpet-sound as they exploded, and the walls surrounding the compound fell completely flat. They fell flat upon the palace-temple-and-harem, and those buildings collapsed in on themselves too. It was a real deuce of a scene. It was full of guts-grizzle-and-gore. Death-o!

"Your Pa's bombs destroyed everything in that city; the palace's servants and the harem's girls, the fighting-soldiers and the praying-priests, the ox-sheep-and-ass. Biff! Five-hundred people fell on the side of the Bad Sultan that day.

"But, thanks to you Pa, the British didn't lose a single soul. It was some smash. We beat them to a frazzle!

"My dear son! My dear boy! It was such a boohoo; a big success. A blood bath! Jolly-o! Rule Britannia!

"The war lasted just eight-and-thirty minutes. 'Twer the shortest conflict in the whole of military-history. And your Pa was declared a hero. He freed tens-of-thousands of people from slavery.

"Tens-of-thousands, my son! Tens-of-thousands!"

Whilst Alfred can see that the Retired Captain is sincere, and genuinely enthusiastic about his military-career; he considers his story to be wrong. Habituated to war, the Retired Captain seems proud of the horrors it holds in store; as if he finds them intelligent-respectable-and-strong.

But Alfred believes that the massacre of innocent-people can never be right, that to fight for trade can never be alright; and that to fight with dynamite can never be brave. It makes him question the way the British military, his government's war-ministry; and people like his Father behave.

He realises that when his Father blasted a Southern African boulder to find water, it enabled his men to start a mass-slaughter; of the insurgents who had made a stand. And that when his Father placed some hornets inside an Ashanti wall, he only did so to impose British rule; and steal the Ashanti's land.

He realises that when his Father had flooded Benin, he had drowned people's kith-kinfolk-and-kin; and destroyed their shanties-sanctuaries-and-spaces. And that when his Father illuminated the South African sky, it had allowed his troops' bullets to fly; and kill the Boers who were defending their birthplaces.

So like when the Authoritative Teacher dictated from a book, Alfred's respect for his Father is shook; shaken-smashed-and-shattered. He now considers his Father to be a human, all too human; tyrannical-tasteless-and-tattered.

Alfred listens to the Retired Captain and wants to disagree, but he does not feel free; or in control. So he waits until the Retired Captain walks away, past that hay; pond-plant-and-pole.

Alfred then walks past this Muffin Man who rings a bell, this Gypsy who casts a spell; and that Woodsman who is selling some wood. This delivery-van, this Rag-And-Bone Man; and that Stonemason who is wearing a hood.

He skips past his outside-lavatory, and hops past his scullery; with a burst of new confidence. He runs past these chairs, and ascends these stairs; in search of a new source of evidence.

He passes this bin-bureau-and-broom, enters his Mother's bedroom; and unearths this mahogany-box. He finds a key near this award, and a key near this board; which he uses to open its locks.

And whenever the coast is clear, he returns to read about his Father in here; using these letters as his guide. He learns about barracks-battalions-and-baiting, wars-walks-and-waiting; and all the people who died. He learns that his Father was no better than a carpenter, or his Stepfather; and was easy to deride.

But it is this collection of newspaper-pieces, which are covered in cuts-crinkles-and-creases; which fill Alfred with real malignment. Hidden beneath these postage-stamps, entitled '*THE CONCENTRATION CAMPS*'; they expose his Father's last assignment.

They reveal that his Father's troops had slaughtered whole herds of the Boer's livestock, burnt their farmland until it was just ashen-rock; and burnt their farmhouses to the ground. Before the Lord of War starved his enemies into conceding, by taking Boer farmers from the soldiers they had been feeding; and putting them in a compound. For an army marches on its stomach as well as its horses, and a hungry-army could never match the British forces; who killed without a sound.

So the Lord Of War's concentration-camps squeezed thousands of civilians into cramped-conditions, in tangled-positions; in tents made of tattered-scraps. In tents which were covered in ties, a layer of dead-flies; and a layer of moth-eaten wraps.

Those tents leaked whenever it rained, whilst rats were left unconstrained; to spread their deadly-diseases. Whilst dry-air filled each street, with burning-heat; dust-clouds and sandy-breezes.

Less than a third of the prisoners were given food, whilst excrement accrued; and freedoms were denied. Whilst crimes were allowed to abound, diseases spread around; and twenty-six-thousand died. Whilst barbed-wire, a spire; and Alfred's Father kept people inside.

As Alfred reads about his Father's role in that place his views adjust, he fills with disgust; and he feels red-raw. He feels that his Father was cruel, like the Authoritative Teacher at school; and his new cadet-corps.

But Alfred still attends the cadets for his Mother, because he does not have the courage to speak out against her; or make any sort of a scene. His beliefs do not behove a soldier's son, and so he fears what might be done; by the army's military-machine.

Which means that meetings come and meetings go, whilst Alfred's feelings continue to grow; and he fills with a sense of dismay. Before his corps avoid the rain outside, by choosing to hide; here in this church-hall today.

These wishbone-arches still support a distant-ceiling, this pale-paint is still peeling; and this air still smells of cake-sales. It still smells of the Sunday School Teacher's perfume, as weapons fill this room; and these Merchants sell uniforms with tails. As they take fees before this session can start, offer credit for cadets to take part; and weigh bullets on these scales.

Alfred sees this church-hall abuzz with noisy-conviction, alive with animalistic-friction; and awash with bloody-space. He sees his Vicar turn a blind-eye, take his rent without being shy; and hand over this godly-place.

And so after all these weeks, Alfred finds the courage he seeks; to oppose these slaughterhouse-tactics. He simmers with dissatisfaction, as he is called into action; to oppose these militant-antics.

He runs past these Strangers, toward these Moneychangers; and he overturns their chairs as he passes. He overturns their tables, which are covered in labels; guns-grenades-and-glasses.

Charts-chairs-and-coins scatter across this glossy-floor, and roll towards that glossy-door; before this room fills with stony-silence. Before Alfred holds this split-ended rope to increase the tension, wins everyone's attention; and speaks out against their violence.

"You've tu-tu-tu-turned this hu-hu-hu-house of pa-pa-pa-prayer into a da-da-da-den of thieves," he begins to utter, with a manic-stutter; whilst he struggles to breathe. It is as if the air in his lungs has become concrete, will not retreat; and will not leave.

Air should not be solid! It should not be stolid! It should not be squalid!

It is as if a belt has been tied around Alfred's chest, his lungs and his breast; at an impossibly tight-setting. He gasps for the air which has disappeared, and been cleared; whilst he starts shaking-shivering-and-sweating.

"Va-va-va-this is meant to be God's house; a house for all nations. But you've turned it into a house of slaughter, and filled it with abominations. There shouldn't be any guns, bullets, or vessels of blood in here.

"Yu-yu-yu-you've turned this go-go-go-godly place into a trainee slaughterhouse! Pa-pa-pa-please put away your animalistic sacrifice of men. Please keep yourself from blood. Please-please-please.

"Bu-bu-bu-be aware of worshipping this army which steals distant-forests, distant-seas and distant-lands. Be aware of their acts of cruelty. Be aware of their ill-gotten spoils of war. Pa-pa-pa-pretty please. Pretty please with a cherry on top.

"Pa-pa-pa-please put down your weapons and repent. Please cease your evil, stop your worship of war, and ignore the army's laws. Please act with love, worship peace, and fulfil the law of the Lord. Please-please-please!

"Lu-lu-lu-leave this darkness and follow me into the light. Pa-pa-pa-pretty please. Pretty please with a cherry on top."

As Alfred runs out of words to utter, with this crazy-stutter, these Moneychangers all murmur-mumble-and-mutter.

They murmur; "It doesn't do! It just doesn't do! Is he possessed?"

They mumble; "He can't be British like us. He can't be blessed."

And they mutter; "He's mad. I should've guessed."

So Alfred leaves this cadet-corps, and walks next door; into this ancient-church. His audience all swallow, but they do not follow; they just leave him in the lurch.

Because whilst Alfred might still become the great teacher, and the great preacher; which Astrologers once predicted. This was Alfred's debut-speech, his first step into the breach; and he was a bit constricted. These Moneychangers, and those Strangers; all thought he was afflicted.

Alfred has grown upwards, grown outwards; and developed his childish-mind. He has carved wood, done deeds which were good; and deeds which were kind.

But respect is hard to earn and easy to lose, his good-deeds have never made the news; and so these people consider him awry. Like a crownless-king he does not have a throne, and like a diamond in a rock he is left alone; as these people all pass him by.

He wanders absently-aimlessly-and-alone, and avoids his childhood-home; where his Mother will be full of fury. He passes this Peasant who screams, this Sleeper who dreams; and this deliberating jury.

Without a single ally, days pass him by; as he wanders on his own. As his fingers shake, and his toes all quake; whilst he wanders on alone.

"Have you gone mad?" Bernie finally begins to moan. "Bonkers? Doolally? Cuckoo? Have you any idea how rum you've been? Good god man! What on earth do you think you've been playing at?"

"I know, I know," Alfred begins to exclaim, before he tries to explain, aware of his best friend's pain. "I know what you must be fu-fu-fu-feeling.

"Well, it's just that all this military-stuff, this aggression-and-plunder, is really not for me. I'm more into kindness than violence. I find drill a bit silly and blind-obedience absurd. Please understand! Please-please-please."

Bernie knows that Alfred has a strange-singular-and-subversive side, which he does not try to hide; cloak-cover-or-conceal. He knows that Alfred gallivants round town on secretive-sprees, works without fees; and talks with passionate-zeal. But he cannot accept the way that Alfred speaks so shamelessly, and so gracelessly; despite how others might feel.

"Not really, no, not at all," he replies whilst he stamps his heel. "Britain is God's nation; our soldiers are brave-angels protecting heaven's gates. How dare you take truck with them? You didn't ought to do what you did. Acting like that dishonours your Father, the state which protects you, and the school which educates you too."

"At least I'll never be a mu-mu-mu-murderer," Alfred accuses.

"No you won't. You'll be a coward!" Bernie muses.

"I'd rather be a coward than a cu-cu-cu-clone."

"A clone? You're mad! Bonkers! Doolally! Cuckoo! You belong in an asylum."

"I'd rather be in an ah-ah-ah-asylum than in the army. I'd rather be ma-ma-ma-mad, than be a brave-brave-brave butcher like you!"

Bernie's wide-waist and narrow-hips cause him to wobble, hop-hurtle-and-hobble; with shoulders which are slightly tilted. He avoids Alfred for a week, during which time they do not speak; which makes Alfred feel slightly jilted.

It makes Alfred feel absent-aimless-and-alone, when he returns to his childhood-home; after he passes this cotton-mill. After he passes this pile of snow, this crow; and this hill.

"Don't you be standing hither looking all deedy!" His Mother begins to drill. "Look at me. Don't you think I don't know all about your mischity, you dotty little-boy.

"Oh, it's just not respectable. Deserting the army! Defecting! Mutinying!

"My notion! I could cry out with shame. I just don't know what to do with you, Alfred Freeman. You should be ashamed of yourself, you-should-you-should-you-should!

"Your destiny, as prophesised by three wise Astrologers, to be a great-solider like your Father, the only man I've ever loved, is broken. Why-oh-why can't you be more like your Father in heaven? Why-oh-why can't you be more like Bernie? Oh-why-oh-why-oh-why?"

Alfred's Mother takes a moment to think, before she takes a gluttonous-gulp of her fruity-drink; and switches the blame to herself. Her spine swings her from left-to-right, from ill-ease to restless-blight; as she stumbles past this shelf.

"Oh, it's all my fault, my little-soldier. I should've spoken more about your Father afore.

"Your Father in heaven, he was more like Bernie than you; a hearty-patriot and an honest old blood-and-bones nationalist. He was respectable! Respectable!

"Oh, I beseech you to give the cadets another try. You'll see the error of your ways, my wonderful-warrior. Look at me. No, I shan't have you shirking. I-shan't-I-shan't-I-shan't. Look at me.

"We could go to a different unit. We could even go to the sea-corps if you want to. Oh, you like the sea, my fearless-fighter, you-do-you-do-you-do. Yes, that's a proper good notion! That'd be respectable. You could be a glorious naval-officer one day, if you like, if it makes you happy. Oh, I only want to make you happy."

"Please!" Alfred replies. "I'd only be hu-hu-hu-happy if I never went near the armed-forces again. Please let me walk my own path through life. Please-please-please. I'd be ever so grateful. I'd be very much obliged."

"But you could be great, Alfred. Really great! By gum, you could be heroic! You could be respectable! There's a fine soldier within you, the army's in your blood. Like your Father afore you, your Grandfather afore him, and your Great-Grandfather afore us all. Oh, you'll see. Somewhere-somewhen-somehow, you-shall-you-shall-you-shall!"

And now there is respite, now there is fright, and now there is fight.

"Turncoat," his Mother begins as she tears at her cuff.

"Wu-wu-wu-wierdo," Alfred begins to huff.

"Traitor!"

"Warmaker!"

"Terrorist!"

"Warlord!"

"Tasteless!"

"Wicked!"

"Tender!"

"Wild!"

"Tramp!"

"Witch!"

A sigh. A cry.

A wheeze. A sneeze.

Some grief. Some relief.

This confusion. And this conclusion.

"I don't know what's come over you of late, Alfred Freeman, I really don't. I-don't-I-don't-I-don't," his Mother says. "You ain't fit to be your Father's son. Oh, if only you were more like Bernie. You're certainly no son of mine! There. That is all."

These words break Alfred's heart, encourage him to depart; and encourage him to visit the Good German. Who is standing near these fruits, with his trousers inside his boots; and his head inside that turban.

"I ju-ju-ju-just don't know what to do, sir," Alfred confesses, and stresses; whilst his mentor drinks some bourbon. "Please help me sir? Please-please-please."

"Hmm," the Good German says whilst he drinks, thinks; and muses. Whilst he scratches his chin, his skin; and his bruises.

"Dear child, zare was once a Burly Boy, who was a bit like yourself, yah. Only ziss Burly Boy had lived his whole life trapped inside a cave, viz just his siblinks for company. Zare heads had been fixed firmly in place, facink zee far-wall. Behind zem was a fire, ant behind zat was a lane.

"Venn-effer an animal valked down zat lane, zee fire vood cast zare shadows onto zee far-wall, ant zare voices vood echo all around zee cave. Zee Burly Boy ant his siblinks believed zat zose shadows-ant-echoes verr real, because zey had neffer seen zee animals zemselves.

"Zey'd even test each uzzer on zee shadows-ant-echoes, yah. Who-effer did zee best was considered to be zee most intelligent siblink. Zee uzzer siblinks believed vott-effer zey said. Ant who-effer did zee vorst was ignored. Zey verr considered to be stupid.

"Vell, one day zee Burly Boy was set free. But zee daylight hurt his eyes, because he was accustomed to zee darkness of zee cave.

"Effentually he acclimatised, yah. He saw zee animals, heard zare voices, ant realised zat zey verr real. He realised zat zare shadows-ant-echoes verr just illusions.

"Feeling excited, he freed his siblinks ant showed zem vot he'd discovered. But his siblinks verr blinded by zee light, ant so zey ran straight back into zare cave.

"'*Your eyes have been corrupted*', zey told zee Burly Boy. '*You cannot see vot is real anymore*'.

"To prove zare point, zey tested him. Ant zee Burly Boy did poorly, because his eyes had adjusted to zee light. So his siblinks concluded zat he was stupid, ant refused to believe anyzink he said.

"Zee Burly Boy vent to live in zee light. He was sad at first, but he soon made friends viz zee animals, yah. He played viz zem in zee sunshine effery day, ant he lived in zare homes at night.

"He still visited his siblinks, ant his Big Sister even came to live viz him in zee end. She was grateful to zee Burly Boy for showink her zee light, vich made zee Burly Boy very happy indeed!"

"So," Alfred concludes with a smile on his face, a heart which begins to race, and feet which begin to pace. "If you've su-su-su-seen the light, and you know that you're right, you shouldn't be swayed by others? For their good, not just for yours?"

"Perhaps," the Good German says. "But, dear boy, can you alvays know zat you're right? You must be modest, yah. You must be humble."

"Thank-you sir," Alfred replies. "Thank-you, thank-you, thank-you! You're wonderful! You're the cat's pyjamas! You're the kitten's mittens! You're the bee's knees!"

Alfred stays behind to serve some friendly-folk, and repair some things which are broke; until he is covered in a layer of fresh-sweat. He works for stories like these, and to earn some pennies; now he has repaid his original debt.

Which means that along with some drafts-directives-and-dockets, there is now some cash in Alfred's pockets; and it is more than he feels he needs. He is far too young to smoke, far too shy to elope; and far too busy with his good-deeds.

So Alfred laughs without force, and takes this frothy-mouthed horse; out on his delivery-rounds. This horse moves without any directions, or any corrections; because he is familiar with all his surrounds.

This horse trots past that brook, whilst Alfred reads this book; with these reins placed over his knees. Before he looks out at this traffic-jam, this tram; and those trees.

He sees the Sick in this hospital-ward, and the Poor who work hard without reward; whilst they stress-struggle-and-strain. He sees the Elderly who are ageing, and these Mourners who are raging; with a ghastly sort of pain.

He sees this corpse who owned a gold-chain, and a gold-cane; when he took his final breath. This corpse who owned a gold-thing, and a gold-ring; but could not escape from death.

And he sees this Monk without any possessions, who wears the most content of expressions; without being vexed-vapid-or-vain. He realises that to hunger for material-things, when paupers can be happier than kings; verges on the insane.

So he walks around his town, he walks up and he walks down; for quite some distance. Before he finds these beeches, these peaches; and this Councillor who needs assistance.

Here in the town-square with a paper on his lap, this downhearted-chap; has a face which reveals his years. He has a jacket which is full of dark-thread, a beard which is dark-red; and eyes which are full of dark-tears.

"My Girl, *cough*, is the best thing that's ever happened to me," he sneers. "She's my whole life-heart-soul-being-and-world, the apple of my eye, and a blessing who's brought me untold joy-jubilance-jollity-jauntiness-and-jubilation. She, *sneeze*, turns me from weak-to-strong. She's given me more, *hiccup*, than I've ever given to her.

"But, *burp*, she's getting espoused this weekend, and I can't even afford the wine. After all she's been to me, *yawn*, it puts me in a right jargoggle. It makes me feel, *sniff*, like the most wretched-weak-woebegone-woeful-and-worthless excuse of a father there ever was; a regular fish out of water."

"My friend, you are doing all you can," his Companion consoles. "At all events, you are helping with the celebrations. You love your Girl, and she loves you back. It's enough. All the rest isn't worth a straw. You do a fearful lot for others, and it's no secret that you're not well to do. Why I do declare, you're doing a smashing job, dear boy. You'll put on a jolly fine show!"

The Councillor accepts that his friend is right, even though it does not improve his plight, or make him feel alright.

"I'll, *cough*, provide water-juice-biscuits-bread-and-fruit," he sighs, whilst he rolls his eyes; and feels contrite. "I can, *hiccup*, just about afford that. Isn't it something chronic?"

But Alfred is in no mind to let this stand, so he has a new mission at hand; as he walks past this busy church-service. But he makes up with Bernie first, with lips which are pursed; and a voice which is slightly nervous.

"Please-please-please! We shouldn't let su-su-su-silly things like the cadets get between us," he tells his friend. "Our friendship should be worth more than our opinions."

"Friends forever," Bernie replies. "For better-and-worse, richer-and-poorer, in sickness-and-health, till death makes us part!"

Alfred has also reconciled with his Mother, and their relationship has started to recover; without any further grief. Because whilst they are still ashamed of each other, they are attached to one another; much to their mutual-relief.

So Alfred is able to discover that his Mother used to babysit for the Groom, when he was fresh from the womb; and has been invited to his wedding. Which means that Alfred can read his Mother's invitation, and leave without hesitation; now he knows where he is heading.

He soon arrives at this town-hall which is full of sloping-brickwork, rambling-turrets which seem to smirk; and merlons like those on a castle. With gothic-lines above purple-paint, wooden-panels with a varnished-taint; and curtains which each have a tassel.

There are very few decorations, for the upcoming celebrations; but everything fits like a glove. These water-pots are neat, this food is discrete; and that balcony is hidden above.

Alfred carries these water-pots into this lane, pours this water down that drain; and spills it all over his thumb. He fills these jugs with the wine he bought with his money, whilst his stomach feels funny; and his heart beats away like a drum.

Boom-bosh-bash! Crack-clash-crash! Snap-smack-smash!

This wine pours more slowly than Alfred thought it would, this process takes more effort than he thought it could; and he feels like this is a crime. The wedding is now ending, people's arrival here is impending; and those church-bells all begin to chime.

One-jug, two-jugs, three-jugs; four. Nine jugs are filled to the brim, and these people make a din; as they open that heavy-door.

This last jug is still half-empty, but Alfred has already done plenty; so he flees down this shady-street. He flees past this Coalman who is delivering some coal, this red-and-white pole; and these cats who are all in heat.

"My notion; 'twer such a joyous wedding," his Mother says the next day, whilst she starts to sway; and tap her restless-feet. "Look at me. 'Twer a real good show, my terrific-trooper. 'Twer fuelled by the nicest wine anyone had ever tasted.

"The Councillor was having a right lark; wiggle-woggling around, blessed with merriment. He kept on saying '*I can't believe my luck*'.

"I've never met anyone with such *joie de vive*. I must say we got on rather well, we-did-we-did-we-did. Oh, I'm sure the two of you will hit it off; he's all about the '*community*' too. A very respectable man!"

STRANGE FRUIT

Owl went to visit Dog, because he wanted to learn more about Dog's love-loyalty-and-passion, without which he would have died.

And, after he had flown over the forest, Owl found Dog near her favourite lake. She was eating the juiciest-apples, plumpest-berries and sweetest-honey, that Owl had ever seen.

"In all my years in power," Owl said. "Whilst I ruled many apple-trees, berry-bushes and honeybees, I never had a feast like yours. How could you accrue such a meal without any power-riches-or-magnificence?"

Dog looked at Owl and smiled.

"Come with me," she said, before she led Owl through the forest, carrying a bucket of water in her mouth.

Eventually they reached Apple Tree, who was so bent-bony-and-bumpy, that everyone else had ignored her.

"Out of love I water Apple Tree, to nurse her back to health," Dog said as she emptied her bucket of water over Apple Tree's roots. "And out of love she gives me her apples."

Owl plucked an apple from Apple Tree's scrawny-branches. It was the tastiest apple he had ever eaten.

Dog looked at Owl and smiled.

"Come with me," she said, before she led Owl through the forest, carrying a trowel in her mouth.

Eventually they reached Berry Bush, who was so scruffy-scraggly-and-straggly, that everyone else had ignored him.

"Out of love I plant Berry Bush's seeds, to help him to have children," Dog said as she dug some holes with her trowel. "And out of love he gives me his berries."

Owl plucked some berries from Berry Bush's thorny-vines. They were the tastiest berries he had ever eaten.

Dog looked at Owl and smiled.

"Come with me," she said, before she led Owl through the forest, carrying some flowers in her mouth.

Eventually they reached Poplar, the tree who had protested when Owl hid the light with his wings. Hanging from her branches was a hive which was full of delicious-honey.

Owl could not control himself. He dived at that hive headfirst! His head slid through its wall, and down into its honeycomb-belly, whilst his feet waggled away in the air.

Owl ate so much honey that the hive wrapped itself around his body, and he was left hanging there like a strange sort of fruit, with bulging-eyes and a twisted-mouth.

"Help! Help! Help!" He screamed. "Help me! I'm trapped!"

"Out of love I bring pollen for the Bees in this hive, to help them to prosper," Dog said. "And out of love they give me their honey.

"But you took their honey without offering them anything in return. This is why you're trapped."

Owl understood what Dog was saying, because Owl was intelligent-respectable-and-strong.

"How can I escape?" He asked.

"All you need is love," Dog replied. "If you love Poplar, she'll set you free."

So Owl tried to be loving. He sung Poplar a lullaby, massaged Poplar's branches, and gave her Dog's flowers. He recited poetry, hummed a tune, and said kind things. But it was not love, and so Poplar did not let him go.

Owl could not think of a single thing to do. And after many moments of thought, he finally gave in. He hung his head in shame, looked down into his chest, and deeper down into his heart.

No longer relying on his intelligence-respectability-or-strength, Owl used his emotions instead of his intellect, and his heart instead of his head. He bit through his shoulders and removed his wings.

"Poplar," he said. "You are a beautiful-tree, who selflessly houses these bees in your branches. And yet I enslaved you, using these wings to hide your light. Please take them, so I can never be so cruel again."

Poplar's branches curled upwards to form a dendroid-smile. She took Owl's wings, attached them to her branches, and set Owl free.

Owl's belly was full, his body was free, and his lesson was truly learnt.

1912

Alfred has developed an adult's physique, grown wiser each week; and done good-deed after good-deed. But right now he can only focus on this Daughter, who runs past that pool of water; with spryness-swiftness-and-speed.

The year is 1912.

A Belgian Chocolatier is inventing praline-centred chocolates whilst he eats a meal, a German Physicist is patenting a new form of stainless-steel; and a French Historian is inventing the modern-pentathlon after weeks of thinking. In the Netherlands an international-consensus on drug control is starting to form, in China a new republic is being born; and in the Atlantic Ocean an unsinkable-ship is now sinking. Whilst the British get ready for war, by forming the '*Royal Flying Corps*'; which they celebrate with copious amounts of drinking.

But Alfred only has eyes for this Daughter who he first met five years ago when she was covered in greasy-mud, spurting-blood; and purple-bumps. He had helped her when she was bleeding, but he cannot now stop her from receding; as she jogs-jinks-and-jumps.

As she darts-dashes-and-dives, jolts-jostles-and-jives; to escape from the stones which whizz past her head. As this Shopkeeper throws stones into green-hedges, green-ledges; a green-bench and a green-shed.

"Who do you think you are, fu-fu-fu-throwing stones at helpless-girls?" Alfred asks as he stops the Shopkeeper from moving ahead.

"She blundered right on in and damn stoled a pan from my shop, she did!" The Shopkeeper replies with dread. "I caughted her in the act!"

As he yells this defence, the Shopkeeper pushes Alfred into this fence; with his hands on Alfred's breast. But Alfred stands firm, which makes the Shopkeeper squirm; become manic and become possessed.

"Who's she to be taking my things?" The Shopkeeper says as he becomes demented, discontented; and stressed. "Dash and plunge! Stealing is stealing, and it's our duty to make sure her type don't never get away with it. You listening to me boy?"

"Re-re-re-really?" Alfred asks as he taps his shoe, whilst the

Daughter disappears from view, and that cow begins to moo. "Are you really without sin yourself?

"If so, please, be my guest. Please throw the first stone. Please-please-please. Throw as many stones as you like. But if you've ever sinned, then you're no different to her. No-no-no. No thanky-you! And you should take a long-hard-look at yourself."

The Shopkeeper's face flushes with red-splodges, because he is angry at the way Alfred counters his dodges; and blocks his retribution. But he cannot do anything about the Daughter's theft, because she has already left; and cannot be seen from this institution.

So Alfred walks past this Coachman who flicks his reins, this Motorist who greases his chains; and this Driver who puts his car in gear. Before he rests his feet, on the very same seat; from which he spied on the Councillor last year.

"Sorry," the Daughter says as she approaches Alfred here. "Oh, I am so very sorry. So very-very sorry.

"My name is Cleo, by the way."

Cleo is as delicate as a flickering-flame, both slight in figure and slight in frame; with a pair of eyebrows which rise like the morning-sun. Her face is covered in freckles which her Mum called '*My solar system*', as she pointed at dots as if to christen; before she pointed at Cleo's tongue.

"That's oh-oh-oh-okay," Alfred replies with this warm-inflection.

"You saved me before, you know?" Cleo says with affection. "Most people would condemn me; I'm so awfully naughty. I hope you don't consider me wrong. Oh damnation! I suppose I am a bad girl, a damn bad girl. I was born bad, I've lived bad, and I'll die bad in all probability. But upon my lost soul, I won't ever be bad near you again."

"It's not for me to condemn," Alfred replies as his heart caves in.

"Let me repay you," Cleo says with a giggle, jiggle; and grin. "Oh, you will let me cook for you won't you? It's only fair. Oh, I am sorry for suggesting it."

"I'd love that!"Alfred replies. "Yes-yes-yes. Yes thanky-you!"

Alfred says '*Goodbye*' and goes to work, but he still sees Cleo's freckled-smirk; which is the only thing on his mind. He desires their attachment, with a passion which verges on harassment; and leaves him feeling resigned. So he walks with this restless-action, and looks for a distraction; of any imaginable kind.

He walks past this Cats' Meat Man who is pushing horseflesh onto a skewer, this Dredger is working in a sewer; and this Farmer who is working on his land. This Farmer who milks his cow, and guides his plough; through soil-shoots-and-sand.

Alfred watches on as this crumbly-earth gets turned, these slimy-worms get churned; and their bodies get cut into slivers. He watches a robin eat the worms' remains, before a hawk carries that robin over these plains; and over those gushing-rivers.

Alfred realises that all actions have reactions, all creatures are united by alliances-associations-and-attractions; and all things are connected. So his plan has succeeded, his obsession with Cleo has receded; but the worms' pain has left him feeling dejected.

He decides that he will never cause any living-creature pain, that he will never eat meat again; and that he will tell the Good German what he just saw. So he tells the Good German about the Farmer's furrowed-cheek, the robin's wormy-beak; and the hawk's spiky-claw.

"Please to-tu-tu-tell me, sir!" He asks his mentor. "Why are you a vegetarian?"

"Vell, dear boy," the Good German replies as he closes this door. "Let me tell you about a friendly Priest.

"Ziss Priest once saw a Merchant carryink a cage of birds to market. Zee birds verr miserable, yah. Zey vanted to fly free.

"'*Vie have you imprisoned zeez birds?*' Zee Priest asked zat Merchant.

"'*To earn money*', zee Merchant replied. '*So zat I can buy food for my family*'.

"Vell, dear Alfie, zee Priest listened patiently, like you are now.

"'*If someone stronger zan yourself,*' she replied. '*Verr to capture your family, lock zem away ant sell zem as slaves, vood you be happy?*'

"Zee Merchant shook his head.

"'*Vell, aren't zeez birds also alive?*' Zee Priest continued. '*Doesn't zat make zem members of your family too?*'

"Dear boy, anyone can make an argument like ziss. But zee Priest made her case vell, yah. Zee Merchant marvelled at her words. He started to make vicker-baskets, ant over time zey became so profitable zat he stopped selling zee birds."

"But this mu-mu-mu-Merchant, was he a vegetarian?" Alfred disputes.

"Maybe he was, maybe he wasn't," the Good German hoots. "But he made a change for zee better. It was hard for him, yah. It took him time. But it was vorth it in zee end. Ziss, I zink, is zee message."

It is a message which Alfred takes to heart, as he waits for his date with Cleo to start; and practices his new diet. Whilst stars shine their lights, days become nights; and this town becomes eerily quiet.

Alfred gets tear-like rain on his homburg-hat, before he finally arrives at Cleo's one-room flat; where he removes his shoes-and-socks. Cleo falls to her knees just there, and cleans Alfred's shoes with a cloth made of hair; which she keeps in an alabaster-box.

As she does this Alfred notices how dark it is in here, he sees these mice who are slow to approach but quick to disappear; and these flies who have tiny-faces. This straw-mattress which is propped against that wall, this stove which is tall; and this box which is full of shoelaces.

He sees these drawers which are covered in tiny-hairs, and this pair of broken-chairs; which are covered in tiny-cracks. This tub of *Cadbury's Cocoa* which Cleo stole from an inn, this battered-tin; and this pile of hessian-sacks.

Alfred can see why Cleo stole that pot, because it is the only one she has got; and it is the only piece of cookware in here. She uses it to cook a stew with some bread on the side, before she blushes with pride; with a smile which reaches her ear.

"Do you like it?" She asks in an attempt to endear. "I do hope you like it. I am sorry if you don't."

"It's de-de-de-delicious, thank-you," Alfred replies. "Thank-you, thank-you, thank-you. It reminds me of my Mother's cooking. You've done a stand up job! You're awesome! You're great! You're super-duper!"

They continue to eat whilst Alfred talks about his folks-friends-and-family, before Cleo uses her pan to make some fresh tea; which she gives a hearty stir. She leaves it to simmer on this coal-fuelled hob, before she starts to sob; when she says that her Dad beat her.

"Not out of spite," she adds with a slur. "No, oh no, Alfred! Oh no! I'm sorry if I've portrayed him as some sort of a brute. Please don't judge him. He did care.

"It's just that when he became unemployed and was sent to the workhouse, where they made him break granite for twelve hours every day, he let his anger out on me. That's all. Oh, I am sorry for mentioning it."

Alfred can see that those beatings have decorated Cleo's skin, and Cleo's chin; with these marks which look like henna-tattoos. With this lotus-leaf near her thumb, this butterfly near her bum; and this bullfinch down near her shoes.

"Whenever Dad beat me, I'd bleed for hours on end," she continues. "Like when you first met me. Dad had kicked me, punched me, and slapped me that day; he'd started the bleeding which you stopped.

"Well, that had turned Mum crazy, and convinced us both to run away.

"Eventually we found this place. It wasn't much, but it was ours, and that was all that mattered. We set up a laundry-service for the middle-classes, and washed clothes by hand using lukewarm-water, carbolic-soap and washing-soda. We were happy too, until Mum died of tuberculosis last year.

"She was only five-and-thirty, but I suppose it was for the best. Oh, I am sorry. That does make me sound awfully horrible, doesn't it just? But she had the most chronic cough. She was always choking up blood, shaking, and shivering with cold-sweats.

"Oh my! Oh, I am sorry for rattling on about such ghastly-things. I haven't disgusted you, have I? I hope I haven't disgusted you. Aren't I terrible?"

Cleo grinds her freckled-jaws, which leads to this pregnant-pause; which is the first silent moment tonight. Alfred cannot think of any words which would be receptive, perceptive; or right.

"Why did you save me when I was being so awfully naughty?" Cleo asks in a manner which is forthright. "You'd already rescued me once before. Oh, I am sorry for putting you out. I didn't inconvenience you, did I? How very ghastly!"

"Please tell me!" Alfred replies with this grin, which covers his chin, as he speaks in the manner which the Good German speaks to him. "When you see someone du-du-du-drowning at sea, do you ask if they're a bad person who deserves to drown? Or do you do whatever you can to save them?"

"You try to save them, I suppose," Cleo replies. "Do you try and save them? Oh, I hope I've said the right thing. I am sorry if I haven't."

"Yes-yes-yes," Alfred continues. "And so when I saw the Shopkeeper chasing you, I didn't ask if you deserved to be chased. No-no-no! I simply saw that you were in choppy-waters and dived in to save you. And we're here as a result, so I'm pretty grateful for it really.

"Anyway, that Shopkeeper isn't so perfect himself. He's always lusting after women and pining over cars. He's rich, but he's not content. In his heart, if not his body, he steals with every breath. But you only steal out of necessity, and we'd all do that if we had to. Yes thanky-you!"

These words heal Cleo of her seven-demons, and pave the way for the coming seasons; during which time she meets Alfred each week. They scamper along the beach when the sea is still, they scurry up this town's tallest hill; and they sit in the town-square to speak.

They walk past this Luthier-Lorimer-and-Librarian, and Cleo becomes a vegetarian; within a few short weeks. And in the summer, Alfred tells Cleo he loves her; and smiles whilst he speaks.

"You make me fuzzy-wuzzy inside," he says with bulging-cheeks. "Well. Err. What I mean is. You know. I kinda. I think. No, I know. Yes, I know! I lu-lu-lu-love you Cleo!"

Alfred struggles to speak because whilst he has had childish-flings before, and given gifts to each new amour, he has never said anything more.

He has given a Red Headed Girl with a triangular-face, and some wonky-teeth in a wonky-brace; a bouquet of flowers in bloom. He has given a Spotty Girl with a chubby-smile, an awkward-walk and awkward-style; a homemade wooden-spoon. And he has given a Busty Girl with a crooked-nose, and crooked-clothes; a bottle of cheap-perfume.

But such gifts do not seem enough, they seem ribald-rugged-and-rough; without any calibre-charisma-or-charm. So Alfred removes his watch this afternoon, and straps this family-heirloom; to Cleo's left-arm.

"It's too much," she says with alarm. "Oh, it's very kind of you, but do I deserve this? I am sorry, but it's too much for a ghastly girl like me. Oh my!"

"I insist," Alfred replies. "Please-please-please. You mean more to me than anyone else in the world. I think you're great. A top-banana! The cream of the crop! And I want a small part of me to be by your side you forever more. Yes-yes-yes. Yes thanky-you!"

Cleo touches her nose, bounces on her toes; and turns bright-red. She flushes, she blushes; and she nods her freckled-head.

"I want to be more like you," she tells Alfred. "Wouldn't that be nice? I'm a good girl really, aren't I? But I do want to be kinder, I'm not nearly kind enough. I am sorry for it, truly I am. Please show me how to be good?"

Cleo asks this question because she knows about Alfred's good-deeds, and about how he helps people with needs; since he has saved her twice before. And although this is the first time Alfred has been asked for this sort of advice, he does not think twice; before he leads Cleo out through this door.

They soon arrive at this orphanage which is full of collapsing-walls, crumbling-halls; cracking-furniture and creaking-doors. Where Cleo is rendered tender-hearted with pity, for these Orphans who are just so gritty; sat down on these gritty-floors. Near the Chef who is counting some food, in a sleepy-mood; inside these empty-stores.

"Long time no see!" He says as he closes these empty-drawers.

"Time flies," Alfred roars. "This is Cleo. She'd like to vu-vu-vu-volunteer here. She'd be ever so grateful. She'd be very much obliged."

And so Cleo starts to wash these Orphans' laundry, clean their pantry; and serve their tea. She wipes this Orphan's nose, darns his clothes; and smiles with cheeky-glee.

But it is this Matron with wispy grey-hair, and this crooked-stare; who inspires Cleo the most. She teaches Cleo how to treat chills, administer pills; and bandage wounds which are gross.

Cleo loves this nursing-work, and so she starts to smirk; when she talks about the cutest-babies she has ever known. About goofy-tots who look so sweet, naughty-toddlers with grubby-feet; and the sick-children who she treats alone.

Cleo's energy is so carefree-cheerful-and-contagious, that it makes Alfred find this town outrageous; wherever he goes to roam. He falls in love with the places, streets-structures-and-spaces; which surround his childhood-home.

He sees vigour wherever he goes to sneak, even though strikes are at a peak; with forty-million days being lost to industrial-action. Even though twenty percent of the population, live in poverty in this nation; without any satisfaction.

Alfred sees Chimney Sweeps work for Gentlemen who are dressed in silk, Milkmen who deliver their milk; and Salesmen who shout until they are sore. He sees this Painter paint these loos, this Cobbler fix these shoes; and this Handyman fix this door.

He sees these Women in their allotments who work on their knees, make homemade-chutneys; and bake homemade-bread which is brown. And he sees these Women who cook-clean-and-care, sew-stitch-and-share; before they go to shop in town.

So he feels proud-privileged-and-patriotic, regal-refined-and-rhapsodic; as he walks down this market's paths. As he walks past these stalls which sell white-wheat, white-meat; white-sinks and white-baths.

He skips all the way to these bustling-docks, which sit beneath these tumbling-rocks; and above this tumbling-ocean. This ocean which is full of gudgeon-grindylow-and-globsters, lusca-leviathans-and-lobsters; who all swim with a wonky-motion.

His friends are out in the bay, on a sea which starts to sway; as this wind grips hold of their sail. As this wind creates a crescendo, with this mighty-blow; which sends forth this icy-hail.

This gust pummels their trawler starboard-bound, and lifts the Mute Boy off the ground; along with this other debris. It carries him through the air, above that chair; and then dumps him into the sea.

His ship moves right on the breaking-swell, and the Mute Boy drifts left as well; on top of these frothy-waves. He floats away, across this bay; towards that row of caves.

So Alfred throws his clothes down onto this scree, and runs straight into this sea; without even stopping to think. Without leaving anything to spare, he exposes this hair; and this skin which is pale-pink. He bashes these waves into place, with a serene-face; and feet which are both in sync.

Alfred's feet keep him stable-steady-and-strong, as they propel him along; with a melodic sort of grace. Such that Alfred appears to elevate, to levitate; and walk on this water's surface. Before these Fishermen fill with fear, grab anything near; and ignore the pleas in this place.

Which shout; "Please don't think we're making a fuss."

Which scream; "Please hu-hu-hu-help us."

Which ask; "What's to discuss?"

Alfred swims alongside the Fishermen's ship, with the Mute Boy in his grip; inside his muscled-arms. But overcome with confusion, the Fishermen think that he is an illusion; and that his calls are false-alarms.

"An evil spirit is calling from the heart of the storm," a Rugged Fisherman begins to shout.

"Ignore her, she'll gobble youse down whole!" A Ragged Fisherman blurts out.

Before this bucket falls from its hook and hits his head, which makes him fall over with his arms outspread; and roll across this soggy-deck. He rolls towards where Alfred is yelling, with skin which is swelling; around his soggy-neck.

And now there is restoration, there is liberation, and there is salvation.

This Fisherman holds out his soggy-arm, catches Alfred in his soggy-palm; and lifts Alfred up high. These winds now cease, these waves now decrease; and these rains now begin to dry. This thunder lightens, this lightning quietens; and this storm begins to die.

This crew escape death, so they catch their breath; and they guffaw. They snicker, they snigger; and they roll across this sodden-floor.

"Alfred! Ye truly are something else," these Fishermen start to yowl, howl; and roar. Before the Mute Boy shrieks, with a smile on his cheeks; and Alfred speaks once more.

"Oh ye of little faith! Thank-you, thank-you, thank-you! Did you ever du-du-du-doubt me?"

ALONE AGAIN OR

Owl went to visit Dog, because he wanted to learn more about Dog's love-loyalty-and-passion, without which he would have been trapped.

And, after he had walked through the forest, Owl found Dog sat next to her favourite lake. She was building a beautiful-kennel; chopping-sanding-and-hammering like a carpenter.

"In all my years in power," Owl said. "Whilst I ruled many woody-trees, sandy-beaches and metal-mines, I never had a home like yours. How could you build such a palace without any power-riches-or-magnificence?"

Dog looked at Owl and smiled.

"Come with me," she said, before she led Owl through a dense-forest, over a row of giant-hills, and along a gushing-river.

Owl had never experienced anything like it. He was used to flying, but he had to walk because he had given his wings to Poplar. And so his muscles became stiff, his feet began to blister, and his head grew light. Until, after many days and many nights, they eventually reached a mountain which was taller than the clouds and wider than the sky.

"At the summit of that mountain," Dog said. "Is passion."

Owl was tired, but he was determined to show that he could be intelligent-respectable-and-strong. So he continued to climb with Dog until they saw Pig, the animal who protested when Owl hid the forest-food. Pig was slumped on the ground, exhausted, and unable to move.

"I'll save you," Dog said. And she put Pig on her back, turned around, and started to carry Pig home.

But Owl began to protest.

"What do you think you're doing?" He squealed. "We can't go back now, we've almost reached the top!"

Owl could not control himself. He dived at the mountain's summit headfirst. His head slid through its snow, and down into its icy-belly, whilst his feet waggled away in the air.

He was stuck there, buried beneath the snow, for many minutes before Dog finally arrived. Dog had followed Owl to protect him from harm, but had been walking very slowly because she was carrying Pig.

"How have you managed to stay so warm?" Owl asked her, frozen beneath a layer of ice.

"Through passion," Dog replied. "It was my passion which compelled me to carry Pig, and it was Pig's body-heat which kept me warm.

"Just as it was not the wood-sand-or-metal which made my kennel so splendid, but the passion with which I built it. Passion adds all the vibrancy you'll ever need, and it's all you'll need to escape from this snow-and-ice."

But Owl could not carry Pig himself, because he was frozen stiff.

Owl could not think of a single thing to do. And after many moments of thought, he finally gave in. He hung his head in shame, looked down into his chest, and deeper down into his heart.

No longer relying on his intelligence-respectability-or-strength, Owl used his emotions instead of his intellect, and his heart instead of his head. He thrashed his ankles on a rock, and removed his feet.

"Pig," he said. "You are a beautiful animal, who has heated Dog with your belly. And yet I enslaved you, using these feet to hide your food. Please take them, so I can never be so cruel again."

Pig's tail curled upwards to form a suilline-smile. He took Owl's feet, gobbled them down, and recovered his health. He was so grateful for the food, that he carried Owl down the mountain himself.

"You know," Owl said to Dog. "I think you could be in love with almost everyone. You think that life is the greatest fun! But I will be alone again tonight."

1913

With that long brown-beard just there, and this long brown-hair; Alfred has become a man. He controls his emotions, has moral-notions; and does all the good that he can. But he is not yet political, or critical; like this Suffragist who speaks with élan.

The year is 1913.

An American Socialite is inventing the modern-bra using a silk-hanky and a metal-clip, a Swedish Engineer is inventing the modern-zip; and a German Chemist is inventing *MDMA*. In Russia the first ever loop-the-loop is being performed, in Australia a capital-city is being formed; and in Ireland some protests are culminating in a *Bloody Sunday*. Whilst the British ensure the Ottoman Empire is diminished, now the Balkan War has finished; and they can finally have their say.

Alfred thinks about these things as Cleo holds his arm, and they walk past this farm; whilst spring begins to bloom. Whilst birds return to British ground, and fluffy-lambs skip all around; beneath this smoggy-gloom. Before this Suffragist speaks to these people, near this steeple; and near this crumbling tomb.

Here is this unshaven Optician, this cloaked Physician; and this Widow who shakes as she weeps. This Bus Conductor, this Drill Instructor; and this Dog who farts as he sleeps.

The Suffragist leads this *University Of The Street*, where these people have come to meet; with passion in her voice. She starts to lecture, and forms conjecture; as these student's professor of choice.

With a banner which demands '*Votes For Women*' tied up behind, she seems weak in body if not in mind; with sickly-skin and sickly-eyes. She wears this old-fashioned shirt, and this old-fashioned skirt; which are part of this spinster's disguise.

"One is here to send a message to everyone responsible for today's rejection of '*The Women's Suffrage Bill!*'" She starts to roar, as if she is at war; and recruiting new allies. "My message is a simple one; that we live in an uncivilised-society!

"Because only when you make males-and-females equal in law, so that men do not rule over women and women do not rule over men, so that female-eyes are considered equal to male-eyes, female-hands are considered equal to male-hands, and female-feet are considered equal to male-feet, can you call our society '*civil*'!

"Women now hold positions of responsibility on school-boards, as councillors, and as doctors. Doesn't this show that we can be responsible enough to vote?

"Boys-and-girls all receive an equal education. Shouldn't it give them an equal ability to select a government?

"Men-and women are all made to pay taxes. Shouldn't we all be able to influence how those taxes are spent?

"Shouldn't we treat all the players the same, play on a level playing field, and play by the same rules?

"Of course we should! We should secure equality of liberties-status-and-opportunities between all men-and-women, rich-and-poor, young-and-old. And we should do it now!"

The longer the Suffragist speaks for the louder she becomes, to overcome these heckles which boom like drums; and screech like violins. Until this Man Mountain with a double-chin, yells so loudly she is forced to give in; as soon as his heckling begins.

"What infernal nonsense!" He sings "The bill was only defeated because of your arson-abuses-and-antics. You're just a posh bunch of terrorists, and everyone here knows it!"

The Man Mountain wears a rolled-up balaclava, and spits phlegm like molten-lava; as he talks of the '*suffragettes*'. A militant-faction, who are intent on violent-action; and act without regrets.

That feminist splinter-group has set churches on fire, strapped themselves to the King's palace with wire; and destroyed shopfronts. They have attacked politicians in taxis, refused to pay their taxes; and used force during most of their stunts.

"Don't judge the whole of womankind by the actions of a militant few," the Suffragist replies, calls-cheers-and-cries, with fire in her belly and fire in her eyes. "You only have to look at our army to see that men can be savage too. And it's a little harsh, is it not, to expect women to obey laws which they've had no say in making?

"So make no mistake! When women are involved in the process of lawmaking, the suffragettes will stop their acts of law-breaking; there's no hidden agenda here. But until then, the government's laws will remain men's laws, without a mandate to rule over women.

"And so you can sling as much mud as you like, but it's not going to stick. Because we're the political heavyweights now, we hold the moral high-ground, and we're here to stay. You can bet your final farthing on it!"

Alfred smiles at the Suffragist, who pumps her fist, whilst these heckles still persist.

"What blasphemy!" This Hunchback yells through the mist. "What rot! What claptrap!

"The bill was a disgrace! A constitutional-outrage! The electorate hasn't ever demanded votes for women, and no election has ever been won in its name. How crusty-and-queer you are."

The Hunchback continues to cry, as these missiles start to fly; and whizz through this chilly-air. As these bloody-bandages, and those soggy-sandwiches; land just over there.

Before a stone like the one which killed Alfred's Dad, is thrown by this Drunken Lad; who is amongst that gang of Teens. It hits the Suffragist's face with a wallop, and spills her blood by the dollop; whilst her shoulder gets pelted with beans. But she stands still without even flinching, whilst this Policeman prevents a lynching; by leading the gang past those streams.

"The electorate only represents half the population," the Suffragist screams. "Across the full population, there's a clear majority who support female-suffrage.

"It's the system which is the outrage, it's just not fit for purpose. One wouldn't touch it with tongs, oneself. The system is broken, it ignores the will of the people, and one is throwing one's hat in the ring to fix it.

"Because now is the time for democracy! Now is the time for equality! And now is the time for majority-rule!

"We mustn't let another generation of women waste their lives begging for the vote. This isn't some sort of passing whimsy that can be kicked into the long-grass; this is a tipping point. The political landscape *is* about to change!"

As soon as she finishes speaking the young Labourer who is stood over there, with a head of cropped-hair, shouts across this busy town-square.

"Do bear up woman, for God's sake!" He begins to blare. "You must think us noodles, what with all this theatrical-poppycock.

"Poison merchant! If you get what you say you want, we'll end up with women in parliament. They'll want to send men to wars in which they'll never fight. It's un-British! It's unbecoming.

"Women will never be able to understand the mechanics of politics; they belong in the kitchen, not in the Commons. So don't you be getting too big for your boots, you rascal. This society wasn't built on equality, it was built on people knowing their place!"

"Okay! Okay!" The Policeman says to cut the Labourer short, as he scratches a wart, and starts to snort. "*Pffft! Snrrk! Gumph!* Methinks we've all seen enough, we have. And anyways, I make it time for dinner, I do.

"Yes-oh-yes, 'tis definitely home-time. Off you all go. Much obliged. Much obliged."

The Policeman resembles the Grim Reaper today, with a scathe-like baton which starts to sway; beneath his cloak-like coat. With a hood-like helmet above his face, and skeletal-fingers which wag with pace; beneath his skeletal-throat.

Alfred knows this friendly Policeman from their many talks, during Alfred's many walks; when they have met on many a street. Alfred has seen the Policeman direct traffic with a baton, light lamps with a cap on; and wave from his bicycle's seat.

"Don't you come causing trouble on my patch no more young missy!" He begins to bleat. "I don't never want the pleasure of your company again, I don't. I shall arrest you in an instant for '*breaching the peace*', I shall. You can consider yourself lucky not to be on your way to the cells presently. It'd certainly behove this situation, it would."

But the Suffragist is far too tough, and far too gruff; to accept this Policeman's dark-charity. With her eyes wide-open, and her spirits unbroken; she sees things with perfect clarity.

"Say, what about my bloody-brow?" She asks in search of parity. "What about the gang who assaulted me? Where do they fit into the grand scheme of things? Honestly! You distress me, officer, with such inconcinnity. Shouldn't you be charging them with *'breaching the peace'*?"

"I don't see me a gang, I don't," the Policeman concludes with this glare, as he starts to stare, around this grassy-square. "I know your type, I do. I suspect you inflicted this bleeding upon yourself, you did. Always after attention, you suffragettes. A bunch of rotters, the lot of you! So I've heard, anyways.

"Now off you trot. Get off my land!"

But because of the Suffragist's passionate-persuasion, Alfred ignores the Policeman's strong-dissuasion; and basks beneath these skies. This square soon clears, this crowd disappears; and the Policeman rolls his eyes.

He pivots and turns around, walk across this grassy-ground; and leaves. He rides his bike, past that dyke; and gets mud all over his sleeves.

Alfred unties the Suffragist's big white-banner, whilst Cleo nurses the Suffragist in a professional manner; and stitches her bloody-cheek. For Cleo's nursing has improved beyond recognition, since she started to work for a clinician; in a hospital which cares for the meek.

"Oh darling child, please excuse my appearance," the Suffragist starts to speak. "One will be in cigarettes-and-shorts, with painted lips-and-nails, before too long."

"Please!" Alfred replies. "Appearances are one thing, but hu-hu-hu-health is another. Are you sure you're okay?"

"No!" The Suffragist admits. "Not at all! Today was my first speech since hunger-striking in prison, and one did feel a bit light-headed up there. Malnourishment has a horrible habit of causing one temporary-blindness.

"But one will be fighting-fit and punching above one's weight before you know it. One has a vision for the future, and one will battle for it against all the odds, no matter one's condition.

"Say, one shall be imprisoned again under the *'Cat And Mouse Act'* whatever one does. They only ever set one free when force-feeding one with a food-tube doesn't work. They don't want a martyr on their hands, you see.

"But they'll arrest me as soon as I'm better. They've released-and-arrested me four times already; it's the politics of control, so to speak. The last time one was released, one was re-arrested just four weeks later, when one booed the Prime Minister.

"But it's a marathon, not a sprint, and these disguises do help."

"How ghastly!" Cleo gasps. "Oh, I am sorry!"

"No really, it's okay, one's fine with it," the Suffragist says with this nervous-laugh, with one bony-hand on her skinny-calf, whilst the other grips her scarf. "At the end of the day, whatever happens will hit the government. If one gets away they will be laughed at, and if one is arrested then the people will be roused. The fools hurt themselves every time! They don't seem to know their own minds about it."

The Suffragist talks about the *Workers' Suffrage Federation*, which inspires Alfred to make his first political affiliation; as he joins her socialist sect. He considers the Suffragist's campaign for equality, to be a good-deed for the community; and he believes that her views are correct.

So these friends continue their conversing, and Cleo tells the Suffragist all about her nursing; her travails-treatments-and-training. About twelve hour shifts which quickly pass, and her nursing-class; which often leaves her straining.

The Suffragist speaks about the magazine she writes, which keeps her up at nights; whilst she dreams of starting a charity. Whilst she dreams of employing the unemployed, and assisting the socially-destroyed; who have been forced act with austerity. And feeding the famished, and welcoming the banished; with acts of real dexterity.

"Say, one does believe that we can overcome our own problems, by losing ourselves in other people's troubles," she says with clarity. "One feels that one ought not to be too comfortable, snug and well-fed, whilst other people are starving.

"And so one is on a charm-offensive to make a real difference! One is winning over the floating-voters! And one can feel the winds of change which one is stirring!"

They bid farewell but Alfred visits the Suffragist whenever she is in prison, on a hunger-strike which affects her vision; and makes her stumble around. He talks about the golf-clubhouses across the land, the cricket-pavilions and the racecourse-stand; which the suffragettes have burnt to the ground.

He builds an affinity with the Suffragist, whilst he becomes quite the artist; at work with his Stepfather. Where he wears that man's old monkey-suits, and old work-boots; whilst he works with real ardour.

Whilst he saws-sands-and-shaves, etches-enamels-and-engraves; almost every single day. Whilst his Stepfather gorges on tinned-sardines, baked-beans; and bowls full of pink-soufflé.

Their earnings go into a household-kitty, but Alfred is allowed to make some toys which are pretty; as long as he does not spend a dime. So he makes these picture-frames, gizmos-gadgets-and-games; which he gives to children at Christmas time.

"I don't know whither all the wood goes, my little-soldier," his Mother begins to whinge, cringe; and whine. "My notion. Someone's been getting up to mischity, they-have-they-have-they-have. Oh, it's just not respectable."

But his Mother cannot stop Alfred from making twelve pots for the town-square which he arranges in a loop, a spoon which he uses to serve the needy with soup, and a sign for Cleo's hospital which he hangs on this hoop.

Before he walks down this hospital corridor, and sees suffering across this floor; which makes him feel rather ashen. He sees patients in broken-chairs, and patients on broken-stairs; who all fill him with compassion.

He sees patients who are full of pains, and patients who are full of strains; spread along these endless-aisles. He sees patients with pneumonia, dystonia; pox-plague-and-piles.

But it is this ever-present poverty which Alfred finds so gut-wrenching, soul-drenching; and morose. He sees people who could be saved, who are not being treated because they have not paid; and he finds it utterly gross.

He sees this Rheumatic with a fever, who flashes red like an angry-beaver; and white like a waterfall. He sees this Paralytic with palsy, who drops her cup of tea; as she drags herself down this hall. And he sees this Blind Man who cannot see, who bumps his knee; on the side of this whitewashed-wall.

So Alfred walks through this waiting-room, and searches the

Groom; who now works in medical-supplies. He walks past these lanes, and past these trains; which puff steam into those skies.

He walks past this robin-rabbit-and-rat, before he arrives at the Groom's new flat; which is spacious but unfurnished. There is nothing in this scullery, apart from this celery; and this coal-hole which still looks burnished.

"I'll make you a bed, a kitchen table, and some ch-ch-ch-chairs," Alfred says to cut a deal, as he taps his heel, and kicks this orange-peel. "And I don't want a ha'penny in return. No-no-no. No thanky you!

"Please! I'd just like a pair of glasses, a wheelchair, and some medicine for a fever. Don't ask any questions, and we'll have ourselves a deal. I'd be ever so grateful. I'd be very much obliged."

"I do like a mystery," the Groom replies, as he rubs his eyes, and prods these cherry-pies. "I'm all for a mystery. All for it! Wine once magically appeared at my wedding. So I'm all for the unexplained. All for it! And we could certainly do with the furniture."

With a youthful-face which does not feature a single wrinkle, dot-dent-or-dimple; the Groom shakes hands to seal this deal. And in just a few days, without delays; Alfred gets the things he asked for in his appeal.

So he walks with this wheelchair under his shoulder-socket, this medicine in his pocket; and these glasses in his hand. He walks past this hospital-gate, this iron-grate; and this pile of builder's sand.

This mouse scurries, and that fox hurries; so Alfred's starts to sweat. This vehicle toots, and that Owl hoots; so Alfred starts to fret.

Because even after many years of sneaking about, strange-noises still fill Alfred with doubt; and cover his brow with crinkles. His pulse accelerates, his heart palpitates; and his skin gets covered in pimples.

So when this Janitor bursts into this hospital-ward, looking blasé-bedevilled-and-bored; Alfred hides behind this door. He hides from this Insomniac with a broken-hip, and this Sleep Walker with a split-lip; beneath this open-drawer.

He hides inside this cupboard where no-one else will follow, within this hidden-hollow; and behind this bright white-screen. He hides from these Porters with tired-demeanours, and these Cleaners; who clear-cleanse-and-clean.

These nocturnal-workers are an inconvenient challenge for Alfred at first, but he soon sprints past them with an energetic-burst; as his confidence starts to improve. He leaves the medicine for the Rheumatic so she can return to her family, the glasses for the Blind Man so he can see; and the wheelchair for the Paralytic so she can move.

Unheard-unseen-and-unfelt, Alfred's good-deeds have been dealt; as he walks into another new year. As the sun shines bright, and spreads its light; before darker-times appear.

SKINNY LOVE

Owl went to visit Dog, because he wanted to learn more about Dog's love-loyalty-and-passion, without which he would have frozen.

And, after he had rolled through the forest, Owl found Dog sat next to her favourite lake. She was playing with Cat-and-Mouse; swimming-swinging-and-singing like an innocent-child.

"In all my years in power," Owl said. "Whilst I ruled many swimming-lakes, swinging-branches and singing-birds, I never had any friends like yours. How could you build such alliances without any power-riches-or-magnificence?"

Dog looked at Owl and smiled.

"Come with me," she said, before she introduced Owl to Cat-and-Mouse.

"When I first met Cat I wanted to be friends with her," she explained. "But Cat was scared of me. So I caught her a fish every day for a month, to show her how loyal I could be, and eventually we became friends.

"And when I met Mouse, I wanted to be friends with him as well. But he was also scared of me. So I protected Mouse from Cat, and in time we became friends."

Owl saw that Dog's love-loyalty-and-passion had helped her to make friends, whilst his intelligence-respectability-and-strength had only ever brought him enemies.

"You need to be patient," Dog concluded. "You need to be fine, you need to be balanced, and you need to be kind."

So Owl rolled through the forest, because he had given his wings to Poplar and his feet to Pig. And he came across some birds. Owl wanted to play with those birds, but they were scared of him. So Owl gave them a feather each, to show them how loyal he could be, and he soon became bald.

Eventually Owl reached Robin, the bird who protested when Owl hid the airwaves. Owl wanted to befriend Robin more than any other bird in his forest, but he did not have any feathers left.

Owl could not think of a single thing to do. And after many moments of thought, he finally gave in. He hung his head in shame, *looked down into his chest, and deeper down into his heart.*

No longer relying on his intelligence-respectability-or-strength, Owl used his emotions instead of his intellect, and his heart instead of his head. He butted his face against a tree and removed his beak.

"Robin," he said. "You are a beautiful-bird, who entertains everyone with your songs. And yet I enslaved you, using this beak to hide your airwaves. Please take it, so I can never be so cruel again."

Robin's cheeks curled upwards to form an avian-smile. She took Owl's beak, and she attached it to her face.

Robin was so grateful for Owl's apology, that she carried Owl to a beautiful-cliff, made him a comfortable-nest, and visited him there every day. She made Owl feel more valued than he had ever felt before.

1914

Alfred's life has been bright, lively-laudable-and-light; full of geniality-generosity-and-goodness. He works in a greengrocery, he works with carpentry; and he performs random acts of kindness.

But Europe's chessboard is set with the pawns in their grooves, as the warmakers make their opening-moves; and their war gets ready to start. So Alfred faces months full of pain, as the warmakers play their game; and pressure him to play a part.

The year is 1914.

A Belgian Doctor is performing the first ever non-direct transfusion of blood using a sanitised-flask, an American Handyman is patenting a revolutionary gas-mask; and an Italian Cardinal is being elected as Pope. In America some performers are debuting the *Foxtrot* dance, in Panama the construction of a canal is starting to advance; and in Germany a group of churches are uniting with hope. Whilst the British vote on home rule for the Irish, and annex Cyprus along with its fish; roads-railways-and-rope.

But as black-and-white pieces take their positions on Europe's chequered-board, Alfred feels abhorred; full of dejection-despondency-and-despair. It starts during a procession past a Serbian hall, where Austria-Hungary's black-knight is the first piece to fall; after he is assassinated without a prayer. Germany's black-bishops slide to Russia where they try to seduce, and propose a truce; before her rooks attack there. Before European civilisation commits suicide, as nations pick their side; and sacrifice pieces on every square.

So invited by a flyer which reads '*Don't be a soldier – Be a man*', influenced by the *Neutrality Committee*'s plan; and inspired by the *Neutrality League*'s flair. These events propel Cleo-and-Alfred, to march ahead; towards an anti-war protest in the Big City square.

They march past shops which are full of knickknacks, bric-a-bracs; and dusty-gubbins. Saltshakers, newspapers; and rusty-nubbins.

They march past this row of smoking-chimneys, these carts full of cheese; and these carts full of meat. These red-brick houses, these Ladies in blouses; and these Men breaking stones in the street.

Alfred has already rebelled against cadet-meetings, and stories of army-beatings; in a series of experiences which have brought him here. So he feels at home amongst these Butter Makers, Bankers-Builders-and-Bakers; who have all begin to cheer.

With attentive-eyes, these peacemakers wear trousers-tuxedos-and-ties; and white-hats which are looped by black-laces. With open-ears, they wear calico-skirts which are free from smears; and flat-caps which shade their faces.

Here is this gangly Lamplighter, this muscly Firefighter; and this Lime Burner who is dressed in white. This Boiler Fitter, this Babysitter; and that Student who seems up for a fight.

And above them all in front of that phallic-column, is this Scottish Socialist who looks slightly solemn; as he takes in all these sights. With a face which looks hearty, this man was the first ever leader of the *British Labour Party*; and believes in women's rights.

His formal three-piece suit is just as dark, and just as stark; as the mine he worked down as a child. His face is almost square, with a head of white-hair; and a beard which is neatly-styled.

The Suffragist looks at him with passionate-love, camouflaged by this dirty-glove; and these glasses which hide her eyes. This brush-broom-and-buffer, doily-dustpan-and-duster; which form a housemaid's disguise.

"Say, that's my man, so to speak," she cries. "One does hope he does a stand up job. This war malarkey is so awfully immature; it reminds one of two tots squabbling over a silly little-toy."

And now this man opens his beak, puffs one cheek, and starts to speak.

"Welcome to the streets, for this, the biggest protest in two-thousand years of British history!" He starts to shriek. "When I walked hither today, people were stood shoulder-to-shoulder, packed in wall-to-wall, and lined up from end-to-end of every street!"

The Scottish Socialist pauses as this crowd bellow, before their cheers mellow; and then recede. He takes a deep-breath, looks up afresh; and then begins to proceed.

"There are those who've said, '*You must speak up on the issue of Germany and Austria-Hungary*'. But this is wrong!

"'Tis wrong because there can only be one standard by which we judge nations; there cannot be a double-standard. If we denounce one country for attacking another country, then we must denounce all countries who attack other countries.

"The Prime Minister says that he's worried about marauding-armies marching across Europe. Well he's in charge of a nation whose army has marched across more countries-and-continents than any other in history! A nation which has inspired Germany to behave in the manner she is behaving."

The Scottish Socialist pauses to take in these peacemaker's lifted-hats, noisy-claps; and boundless-adulation. '*Neutrality for all*' is howled, '*Down with the war*' is yowled; and '*Not in our name*' is growled with exultation.

"We can take pride in the fact that this protest is like a microcosm of Great Britain," the Scottish Socialist continues with elation. "People of all ages-classes-nationalities-and-religions have united hither on these streets. We should be proud to be marching together.

"But can we be proud of our Prime Minister? Can we examine the record of this man? Has this man who is about to send our brothers-sons-and-lovers to their deaths ever been to war himself? No he has not!

"This creature is a coward; he's spent his entire career behind a desk. And yet he has the gall to send our men away to die. What effrontery!

"He expects us to take the lives of tens-of-thousands of innocent German men-women-and-children. Whatever for? In the name of a madman who killed a Duke in some far-away province? I don't think so!"

This Bagman shouts '*toot-toot*', and this Restorer shouts '*hoot-hoot*'; whilst that Boy climbs up a crane. Whilst that Clergyman chats to a Miller, this Loafer leans on a pillar; and this Girl climbs up a drain.

"Who complained about the Kaiser when he built a railway to our oil in Persia? Who complained whilst we collaborated with him in East Africa? The warmakers speaking against the Kaiser presently, didn't give a damn about him when he allied with us against Russia in the Balkans last year.

"So don't give me any hypocrisy from the Prime Minister about his concern for human-rights. Wars only ever lead to a blatant disregard for human-rights. They only ever make the poor poorer, and condemn the poorest to tragic-impotence.

"The warmakers are no example! We must set the example! We, the peacemakers, must take the lead. We, the workers of the world, must unite. For together we can conquer the militarists, we can conquer the imperialists, and we can let the warmakers know that their days of plunder-and-butchery are over. We can send a message of peace-and-fraternity to everyone with less liberty than ourselves.

"Down with the rule of the upper-classes! Down with the rule of brute-force! Down with mass-slaughter! And down with the war!

"Not by our hands! Not by our mouths! Not by our hearts! And not in our name!"

As he shouts this conclusion, these peacemakers celebrate with inclusion, passion-pleasure-and-profusion.

'*Neutral! Neutral! Neutral!*' They chant as they punch the air.

'*Peace! Peace! Peace!*' They shout across this square.

'*Love! Love! Love!*' They blare.

Alfred walks past people who are small, people who are tall; and people who are all full of peaceful-emotions. He falls in love with their tumultuous-applause, riotous-roars; and peaceful-notions.

But this anti-war protest, is far from a success; it is just a placebo for the people. These peacemakers feel so satisfied, gratified; gay-gallant-and-gleeful. But they do not achieve anything acceptable, perceptible; or peaceful.

For whilst the grey-haired and split-chinned Prime Minister, was not at all sinister; when he spoke of improved relations with Germany last week. When he said that Britain should be no more than a spectator in this conflict, sounded strict; and sounded sleek.

And whilst he does not want to commit, his coalition-cabinet is split; and the Labour Leader is pro-peace too. The warmakers are up for a fight, so they hold a cabinet-meeting tonight; at which they cry out anew.

Germany's black-pawns march into Belgium, where they are not welcome; before they outflank France's white-defence. Before Luxembourg is captured by the black-queen, and starts to scream; as the hostilities all commence.

As empires are sucked in by secret-contracts, and secret-pacts; which tie Britain-to-France and France-to-Russia too. They tie Russia-to-Serbia, across cities-countryside-and-suburbia; which puts Europe into a stew. When Serbia is invaded by Austria-Hungary, who are allied to Germany-and-Italy; and the warmakers stage their coup.

British knights neigh in parliament, and overpower their government; with bloodlust in their bloodshot-eyes. Before the peacemakers fall on their swords, in the Commons and in the Lords; rather than compromise.

So Britain descends from a nervous sort of peace, into a state of war which does not want to cease; and which wants to be adored. Warmakers mobilize and anticipate glory, citizens celebrate and feel hunky-dory; whilst Alfred feels abhorred.

He walks through this street-party, where this Road Sweeper seems hearty; as does this out of work Actor. This potential-killer, this inebriated Distiller; and this intoxicated Contractor.

These people start to shout-scream-and-sing, skip-shimmy-and-swing; as they all come together. As their spirits are lifted by this glowing-sunshine, flowing-wine; and hedonistic-weather. Which encourage them to lose their individuality, and their sense of morality; near that purple-heather.

Where they contract a contagious bout of optimism, which infects them with its populism; with symptoms which include eagerness-enthusiasm-and-expectation. This disease spreads undiagnosed, to infect teeth-tummies-and-toes; all across this war-crazed nation.

And because of this optimism-epidemic, this blind-faith pandemic; no-one notices the cat beneath their feet. Only Cleo sees this skinny-feline, only Cleo hears her whine; and only Cleo dives towards the street. She dives through this mob, is kicked in her gob; grabs the cat and begins to retreat.

Cleo gives this cat a loving-glance, which puts her into a sleepy-trance; and makes her begin to purr. Before Alfred forms a cradle in his shirt, which reduces this cat's hurt; and helps to support her.

Cleo wraps this cat in an orange-sweater, and nurses her till she is better; when Alfred gives her to a widow who would like a pet. Before he goes to see Bernie who looks more dejected, and more neglected; than the last time these friends both met.

"It's bonkers Alfred! Doolally! Cuckoo!" He starts to fret. "I've lost my job. Good God man! I just don't know what to do."

Bernie had been a commuter, who worked for an international food-producer; for whom he dealt with purchase-orders. He loved doing office-chores, putting files into drawers; and sending food across national-borders.

But the British navy has taken to the high-seas, and launched a blockade to bring Germany to her knees; as hostilities continue to grow. That blockade is stopping weapons from reaching their enemy's hands, resources from reaching their rivals' lands; and food from reaching their foe. Such that thousands of German civilians are taking their final-breath, and German children are starving to death; without any drugs-drink-or-dough.

It is not good news for international-companies, or any of their employees; who need foreign-trade to thrive. And it is not good news for people in Bernie's situation, who need a new vocation; in order to survive.

"It's a God-awful-slop I'm in!" He continues with a jive. "My income is falling and prices are rising, unemployment is high and opportunities are low. No-one's going to employ me. Not really, no, not at all!

"Most companies are even using child labour. Good God man! Some of them are even employing women. I don't know what they think they're playing at. They can't do that! What chance does it leave the rest of us? Corr blimey it's rum. My heart and my liver, it ain't half-bad."

These words fill Alfred with empathy, sorrow-sadness-and-sympathy; but he does not know how to reply. So he takes Bernie out, past this Sailor-Shoemaker-and-Scout; and this Girl with a wandering-eye.

He brings him to this music-hall, where cigarette-smoke reaches each wall; and these people all slurp their drinks. Whilst these floorboards squeak, and these people speak; near that model-sphinx.

Alfred-and-Bernie watch this amateur Ventriloquist, this athletic Trampolinist; and this Magician. This dog-show, this puppet-show; and this Musician.

They watch these Actresses, who wear extravagant-dresses; as they act with frivolity. And these Bell Ringers, who precede these Singers; who sing with very little quality.

They sing '*Sergeant Solomon Isaacstein*', about a Jew who trades in a trench full of grime; and lends money at ninety percent. And '*It's a long way to Tipperary*', about an Irishman who becomes contrary; when his illiteracy causes him torment.

Before this group of bubbly Brunettes, who are dressed in these khaki-sets; sing songs to unite the nation. They dance a soldier's march, with a boyish-arch; which earns them this ovation.

> *'We must all stick together, all stick together,*
> *And the clouds will soon roll by.*
> *We must all stick together, all stick together,*
> *Never mind the old school tie.*
> *United we shall stand, whatever may befall,*
> *The richest in the land, the poorest of us all.*
> *We must all stick together, birds of a feather,*
> *And the clouds will soon roll by!'*

This haggard Strumpet, who is dressed up like a hot piece of crumpet; sings songs to encourage enlistment. She dances on tiptoes, and strikes a pose; to secure this crowd's commitment.

> *'We don't want to lose you, but we think you ought to go,*
> *For your King and your country do need you so.*
> *We shall want you, and we shall miss you,*
> *But with all our might-and-main.*
> *We shall cheer you, thank you, kiss you,*
> *When you come home again!'*

And this group of Blonde Bombshells, who are dressed in short-skirts and low-cut lapels; sing songs to seduce the youth. They dance with swinging-hips, and kissing-lips; which they use to disguise the truth.

> *'I didn't like you much before you joined the army John,*
> *But I do like you cockie, now you've got your khaki on.*
> *I do feel proud of you, I do honour bright,*
> *I do want to give you a special time tonight!'*

The performance has finished, but this Blonde Bombshell's energy is undiminished; so she stays on this wooden-stage. Where she exposes her breasts which are shaped like eggs, bends a knee to open her legs; and strokes her slender-ribcage. Before she gives her buttocks a jiggle, gives her belly a wiggle; and then begins to engage.

"Now I know that there is a bunch of mighty fine gentleman in here tonight, and I love you one-and-all," she says as she blows this kiss, winks with bliss, and starts to hiss. "But I'll only be yours, all yours to hold, if you fight in wars, in wars be bold.

"For sure, for sure, it must be told. For you, for you, I want to hold!

"I want to see every young man in front of me, every last one of you beauties, up here on this stage right away; signing up for your King, for your country, and for me. 'Cos you're all my boys, my dear-dear boys, and I'm just waiting for you to come and get me!"

As she let out this frisky-giggle, and this flirty-jiggle; Alfred's ears are bombarded by those brass-bands. And his eyes are blinded by these standing-ovations, hypnotic-gyrations; and clapping-hands.

So Alfred cannot see this music-hall transform, rotate-revolve-and-reform; whilst this audience begins to yowl. Before these Merchants sell sheet-music to earn a wage, and these Warmakers register men on stage; who all begin to howl.

"I wanna see blood-and-gore-and-guts in my teeth!" A Carter shouts as if he has no choice.

"I wanna kill!" A Bailiff shouts as if he is in love with the sound of his voice.

"Kill! Kill! Kill!" A Draper shouts as if to rejoice.

Alfred is caught off balance, beneath this curtain's valance; as he is pushed on into this queue. As he is punched by these fists, and slapped by these wrists; until his face turns blue.

"I'm going to sign on," Bernie begins to coo.

"What?" Alfred replies as he loses a shoe.

"'Pon my sammy; they pay! Good God man, they pay. They pay good money. They house you, feed you, clothe you, and pay you a shilling a day. Oh Alfred! I was in doubting-ditch before you brought me here, but now I'm in certainty-castle!"

"But you're only su-su-su-seventeen."

"Good God man! They'll take anyone, they're desperate. They're even taking fourteen year olds."

"Bu-bu-bu-but they'll ask you to kill! Please don't do it. Please-please-please."

"I'll get the girls. I don't have a girl like you; this is my chance!"

"Girls? Money?" Alfred pauses. "You're going to war for lu-lu-lu-lust and filthy-lucre? Really? Really, Bernie?"

And now it is Bernie who twiddles his thumb, because he is struck dumb; and unable to reply. He just shrugs with resignation, sighs with frustration; and tries not to cry.

"Please don't ku-ku-ku-kill anyone," Alfred says whilst he looks frustrated, agitated; and awry. "Please-please-please. Not even to save yourself. Please don't kill anyone. I'd be ever so grateful. I'd be very much obliged."

But Bernie cannot reply because he is pushed along this queue, and shoved in his shoulders too; before he is lifted onstage to enlist. Whilst Alfred heads for safer-lands, and avoids these slapping-hands; this swinging-bat and that swinging-fist.

And after a night of broken-sleep which leaves him yawning, Alfred searches for peace at church this morning; inspired by the Pope's call for neutrality. Dressed in his priestly-attire, that man has demanded a cease-fire; a truce and a dose of sanity.

So Alfred runs down this street, through this sleet; and sits amongst these people who are wearing their suits. They are wearing their formal-frocks, black-socks; polished-shoes and polished-boots.

Alfred feels at home near this engraved set of stones, this crucified Christ with protruding-bones; and these icons which hang from the bleachers. These gothic-gargoyles, which are covered in gothic-boils; and these columns which are covered in creepers.

So he prays through the *Apostle's Creed* and the *Lord's Prayer*, he meditates on benedictions with religious-flair; and he muses over some psalms. He sings '*A Lost And Sinful World*' like a pious-knave, and '*Eternal Father Strong To Save*'; with open-eyes and open-arms. Before he settles into his seat, as the Vicar gets to his feet; with sweaty-toes and sweaty-palms.

Judging by his busty-boobs and his bulging-belly, which wobbles around like a plate of fruit-jelly; this Vicar must love to eat. A smirk usurps his chin, which is far from thin; and his lips which look like meat.

"Heavenly Father," he begins to bleat. "We bow in your presence. May your word be our rule, your spirit our teacher, and your glory our supreme concern.

"Ladies-and-gentlemen, boys-and-girls; let us remember the thirty-nine articles on which our church is built. Let us remember the article which tells us that the King and his government, as the chief powers in this holy-empire, are ordained to rule on all matters, ecclesiastical-and-civil, as judge-jury-and-executioner.

"And let us remember article thirty-seven, which tells us that 'tis not only lawful, under the command of the authorities, to serve our country in battle, but 'tis honourable-reverent-and-chivalrous too.

"Because those of us who are able, have a divine-duty to fight; for King, for country, and for Jesus Christ our Lord!"

Alfred feels that this Vicar's speech crushes free communion with the scriptures' law, free love with dogmatic-awe; and free association with bureaucracy. That his Vicar prefers the text of an earthly King to the spirit of a celestial God, to push-pressure-and-prod; like a man who carries a boat when he is not near the sea.

"Let us remember Matthew chapter ten," the Vicar continues his plea. "This tells us that Jesus did not come to earth to bring peace. Oh no! He came carrying a sword, on a mission to turn fathers-against-sons, mothers-against-daughters, and brothers-against-sisters too. He came to make enemies of us all!

"My congregation, we are pupils, and a pupil can never be above his teacher. Our Lord, our teacher in heaven, has put a sword in our hands, taught us how to use it, and expects us to fight.

"So we must fight our German fathers, Austrian mothers and Ottoman brothers. We must fight them in the name of the Lord!"

As he speaks the Vicar's arms fly outspread, and his face turns red; which makes him look fairly gory. His words pour forth with tub-thumping, heart-pumping; and goose-bump inducing glory.

He starts to wave and he starts to nod, but the God he is talking of is not Alfred's God; it is an interloper who has been invented by human-pride. Like a statue made from rotting-wood disguised by beautiful-stones, or a beautiful-tomb filled with rotting-bones; it is an attractive God which is ugly inside.

"For those brave men amongst us who are ready to defend their nation, their community, and their religion; we salute you!" The Vicar says whilst he stands here narrow-eyed. "Your sacrifice on the battlefield shall be like Christ's upon the cross; a martyrdom which shall save us all.

"Because we must stop these heathen-hordes! We must stop these godless-goons! We must stop these pagan Germans from bringing a curse to our land!

"These pagans who chop off the hands of babies, are not the children of God!

"These pagans who crucify their enemies and drink their blood, are not the children of God!

"These pagans who hang monks from the rods in their own church-bells, and ring them until those monks die, are not the children of God!

"To kill a German, to kill one of these sub-humans, is not like killing one of us. Their blood is not like ours, their minds are not like ours, and their souls are not like ours.

"Killing these heathens is a divine-service, done in the name of truth-and-justice, intelligence-respectability-and-strength. It must be done so that good can conquer evil, purity can reign, and civilisation as we know it can survive.

"Because this war is a crusade; a holy-war ordained by God, a war for Christianity against the antichrist, and a war for the bible itself. This is a war for those who respect the weak, honour treaties, and stand shoulder-to-shoulder beneath the Lord.

"And so, to every man of fighting age sat here today, I tell you this. Sign up! Sign up today! Sign up forthwith!

"This is your once in a lifetime opportunity to act with holy-patriotism, sacred-honour and divine-duty. So serve in this glorious battle! Sign up! Sign up today! Sign up forthwith!"

The Vicar's huff-puffery fills Alfred with angry-indignation, angry-irritation; and angry-disbelief. His body is overcome by numbness, his mouth is overcome by dumbness; and his mind is full of grief.

He cannot believe the way the Vicar binds burdens which are hard to bear, without a qualm and without a care; as he threatens his congregation's health. The Vicar reminds Alfred of a rabbi who refused to save a life on the Sabbath day, but called for compassion anyway;

since he calls for war but avoids it himself.

And Alfred is overcome by a mixture of bothersome-pain, bothersome-shame; and bothersome-gore. As the Vicar attacks those who are unwilling, to join in with the killing; and go to fight in the war.

"Don't think you'd be doing anything but evil by shirking your duties in the name of so called '*pacifism*' or '*peace*'!" He begins to roar. "Every man who is content to labour in our chosen-nation, must be prepared to fight for it too. Those who aren't, should forfeit their right to work here!

"Every man who is content to consume food grown on our green-and-pleasant lands, must be prepared to fight for them too. Those who aren't, should forfeit their right to eat here!

"And every man who is content to reside under our heavenly-skies, must be prepared to fight for them too. Those who aren't, should forfeit their right to live here. They should be taken to the place which gets bombed the most!

"May God be with you. In the name of the Son, the Father, and the Holy Ghost. Amen."

"Amen," the congregation reply before they exult the commandments carved into these stones, and this crucified Christ with protruding-bones; who gazes towards the heavens. They open their books and they sing along, to validate their Vicar with this greedy-song; which lusts for wealth-wagons-and-weapons:

'Bring me my bow of burning gold,
Bring me my arrows of desire.
Bring me my spear, o clouds unfold,
Bring me my chariot of fire!'

But Alfred refuses to bow down to this effigy of Christ which is rather hairy, this grandiose-statue of the Mother Mary; or this garish-painting of Saint Paul. He rises above the temptations in this den of thieves, where these people worship false-gods as they please; whilst they chant-croon-and-call. He rises above this incense, this bloody-altar and that bloody-fence; these idols which are short and those idols which are tall.

He gets up from his dark polished-pew, passes this Chauffeur and that Rector too; before he leaves this wayward-church. He leaves his

Sunday School Teacher, his Mother and that Preacher; behind him and in the lurch.

Alfred blames himself for coming here when he had felt disrupted, to seek solace from a Vicar he knew had been corrupted; when he accepted the Retired Captain's gold-pieces. But he resists these clawing-clutching-and-clasping hands, which try to pull him into their hellish-lands; as the pressure to fight increases.

He backs himself to overcome the propaganda on cinema-stages, and newspaper-pages; which has become omnipresent-overbearing-and-oppressive. As copies of the Prime Minister's speeches are handed to the youth, and the '*Defence of the Realm Act*' censors the truth; in a manner which is aggressive.

Censors examine every substance which is sent in the mail, smear crayon-marks across private-letters on a massive-scale; and confiscate pamphlets too. Whilst posters proclaim '*Remember Belgium - Our Ally*', '*No Price Is Too High*'; and '*Your Country Needs You*'.

People are misled by this deception, which breeds false-perception; which two-hundred-thousand citizens a month cannot withstand. As gleaners-gardeners-and-goons, lepers-layabouts-and-loons; sign on across the land.

A quarter the size of its French-and-German equivalents, the British army acts without diligence; to recruit somewhat cleverly. They recruit people on anti-depressants, unshaven-adolescents; the erratic-epileptic-and-elderly.

They recruit unemployed-people who are desperate for remuneration, poets who are desperate for inspiration; and bachelors who are desperate for wives. Students who want a gap-year at war, and peasants with nothing to fight for; who flee from their hollow-lives.

So Alfred watches this crowd, become lairy-loutish-and-loud; as they cheer those Recruits off to war. He counts '*One murderer*', '*Two murderers*'; '*Three murderers*' and '*Four*'.

But there are plenty of peacemakers who are refusing to be thrown, so Alfred is not alone; and he does have some other comrades. The Good German is amongst their number, but he is a victim of the poison-prejudice-and-plunder; which was started by a tabloid's tirades.

That paper has inspired people to refuse service from German waiters, loot German shops whilst they call Germans '*Traitors*'; and call them '*Dirty spies*'. It has inspired people to boycott the Good German's store, accuse him of starting the war; and accuse him of spreading lies. Which means that his cucumbers are now covered in wrinkles, his corn is now covered in pimples; and his fruit is now covered in flies.

Whilst German Measles become '*Liberty Measles*' in a wave of translations, which sees German Shepherds become '*Alsatians*'; all because of this new teutophobia. Orchestras no longer play music composed by German musicians, and children no longer study Germany's artistic traditions; all because of this new xenophobia.

Serials depict Germans as spies disguised as publicans-plutocrats-and-prostitutes, who work in infirmaries-institutions-and-institutes; and so spy-fever starts to grow. It is fuelled by films like the '*The Kaiser's Spies*' which screen for a small-fee, and films like '*The Huns of the North Sea*'; which draw crowds wherever they show.

Germans are accused of sending smoke-signals to zeppelins, obstructing the production of weapons; and burning down the docks. They are accused of infecting cavalry-horses of every size, sabotaging medical-supplies; and poisoning the water-stocks.

But only nine Germans have been found to be spies, and they were mostly amateurish-guys; who were arrested at the outbreak of war. So people write to the police, call for their efforts to increase; and call for more arrests than ever before.

This encourages the police to arrest Germans all the time, without any reason-rationale-or-rhyme; as they react to the public's rancour. They arrest an army-officer for reporting to his constabulary, a bureaucrat for his stilted-vocabulary; and a naval-architect for designing a tanker.

It is within this culture of public-appeasement, that the Policeman visits the Good German in search of an agreement; discourse-discussion-and-deal. A lantern hangs from the frame of his bike, a truncheon hangs from his belt-buckle's spike; and a leaf hangs off of his heel.

"You are the Good German, you are?" He inquires.

"I am he, yah," the Good German says as he puts down his pliers.

But before the Policeman can respond he trips over this sack of seeds, and this stack of swedes; which crash-clatter-and-crack. He starts grunting-groaning-and-gasping, rocking-rolling-and-rasping; whilst he holds his battered-back. Before he gets to his feet, and starts to repeat; in an attempt to get back on track.

"You are the Good German, you are?" He asks in pain.

"Yah," the Good German says again. "I have told you zat is me. Here I am!"

"Good, good. Anyways, I'd like you to come to the station for a friendly-chat, I would. Just to be friendly, ever so friendly."

In a state of stress, Alfred thinks that this is an arrest; which is disguised as an invitation. So he grabs this knife, overcome by strife; and overcome by a vicious-sensation.

"Put it avay, Alfie, dear boy," the Good German says without hesitation. "Ziss nation has been good to me, yah. I'm happy to drink from its cup.

"Don't ever turn to violence for me, dear boy."

Alfred laughs with humility-humbleness-and-humiliation, before he follows his mentor to this police-station; where he waits beneath this clock. He waits until the Good German emerges from that room, which reduces Alfred's gloom; and reduces Alfred's shock.

"I'd like a word, I would," the Policeman says as he adjusts his cotton-sock. "Tell me what do you know about this German? You won't be false with me, you won't!"

"I know that he's a gu-gu-gu-good man, full of love-loyalty-and-passion," Alfred answers. "I know that he's a peaceful man; a Mennonite opposed to militarism-conscription-and-war. And I know that he loves this country more than his own.

"Please don't hurt him. Please-please-please."

"I see, I see. But we live in grave times, we do. Your friend is going to find life a queer old business, he will. 'Tis nice of you stand up for him, but 'tis rash. It'll bring you face-to-face with danger, so it will.

"Anyways, I only say this because I care, I do. I've suggested that your friend wears English clobber, speaks with an English accent, and displays a Union Jack. His German nature is inciting the townsfolk, so it is.

"And anyways, methinks he can take care of himself, he can. So I'd be much obliged if you'd spend a little less time worrying about him, and worried a bit more about yourself. You've enough battles of your own, so I've heard. And the more battles you fight, the more you'll lose, so you will."

Alfred leaves and walks past this Fettler-Fewterer-and-Fishmonger, before he climbs the oak he loved when he was younger; pleased with the Policeman's sermon. And as he gazes out at this twisted-elm, he returns to his childhood-realm; to a time before he met the Good German.

With feet which swing in his boots, like leaves or dangling-fruits; Alfred must look ridiculous to these Carters-Caulkers-and-Cooks. But as he escapes from his society's condemnation, he does not care about his presentation; or about his looks.

He breathes in the air which blows off this aqua-sea, and gazes out at this scenery; which makes him feel esteemed. He sees carnelian-rays in the skies, and golden-towers arise; which makes him feel redeemed.

He sees clouds full of white-pearls, which float above streets full of sapphire-swirls; and he fills with glee. He sees rhodonite-leaves, which flutter in this breeze; and he feels free.

This is Alfred's Britain! This Britain which gives his soul release.

This is Alfred's Britain! This Britain which will never cease.

This is Alfred's Britain! This Britain at peace.

But Alfred cannot stay here on his own, because he is needed at home; where his work still needs to be done. He has vegetables to sell, and carpentry as well; he needs to see Cleo and he needs to see his mum.

Which is why he returns to the Good German's greengrocery, which is full of this rocket-rhubarb-and-rosemary; peach-potato-and-pear. A Union Jack faces the street, British boots are on the Good German's feet; and a British hat is on that chair. Whilst British idioms fill the air.

With some '*Jam on the brakes*', '*Pieces of cakes*'; and '*Let sleeping dogs lie*'. A '*Caught in the middle*', an '*As fit as a fiddle*'; and an '*Other fishes to fry*'.

But the only customers they see today are this teeth-grinding Housekeeper, this eye-rolling Street Sweeper; and this foot-tapping Gleaner. This Statistician, this Physician; and this Cleaner.

And this man who looks like the Dominant Assailant who attacked

Alfred as a child, who looks riled; wiry-warped-and-wet. He still has a face which is rather jagged, clothes which are rather ragged; and this smell of stale-sweat. Whilst his accomplice is still fairly stumpy, and fairly frumpy; like the Squat Assailant was when they first met.

"Long time no see, yah," the Good German says in a voice which sounds muddled, befuddled; and upset.

"Dat's 'cos I prefer to avoid Krauts myself," the Dominant Assailant says as he starts to twiddle, fiddle; and fret. "To buy British. To give my 'ard earned wonga to the good British folk dat toil 'ard for this 'ere green an' pleasant land.

"I'm what they call a '*Super Patriot*'. I'm 'ardly gonna waste my *Bratwurst And Mash* on a Rhine-monkey like you, am I now?"

"And I'm a racist," the Squat Assailant adds with a lurch, as he starts to besmirch, inspired by a sermon he heard in his church. "Gawd knows it! I hate the dirty Jews, I hate the dirty Irish, and I especially hate you dirty Germans. You here militant, child-eating, blood-drinking, monk-killing, filthy Hun."

The Good German looks serene, cool-civil-and-clean; calm-composed-and-collected. Alfred finds his good-grace, so out of place; that it makes him feel dejected.

"But a plague 'as sprung up on our 'ere fields green," the Dominant Assailant says, with this gaze; as he continues on unaffected. "A fire of a plague, lit by a dirty sauerkraut, dat leaves me no choice but to visit this 'ere *lollipop*."

The fire he is referring to burnt down a naval radio-mast, with flames which were vast; and flames which were heated. Fireman could not contain that fire, and so the locals have filled with ire; and feel incredibly cheated.

"We know dat you done it," he continues in a manner which is victorious, vainglorious; and conceited. "We know dat you was taken to the ol' *Bucket and Pail* just last week, 'cos you're a dirty-criminal who needs some good ol' fashioned British justice."

The Dominant Assailant puts some vegetables into his sack, along with this Union Jack; and this German book. Before these Ruffians with dirty-footwear, and dirty-hair; enter and give Alfred a dirty-look.

"You're comin' with us," the Dominant Assailant starts to roar, as he throws the Good German onto the floor; near that hidden-crook.

Before his Ruffians drag the Good German over these stony-streets, past those splintered-seats; and through these muddy-squares. Where stones spike him, pebbles pierce him; and gravel covers his clothes in tears.

The Good German's recent call to non-violence, keeps Alfred in a state of silence; as he walks ten metres behind. As he passes this market-stall, before he enters this music-hall; which is full of humankind.

Which is full of people like this Hop Picker, this Vicar; and this Milkman who downs his beer. This brawny Shoe Shiner, this skinny Miner; and this Grinder who scratches his ear. This Irish Water Carrier, this Belgian Farrier; and this Welsh Cabbie who starts to cheer.

These people watch on as the Ruffians drag the Good German through this lobby, become gobby; and storm this shiny-stage. Where they start to glare, slap-shout-and-swear; with a malicious sort of rage.

The Dominant Assailant gives the Blonde Bombshell a sloppy-kiss, spits at this Impressionist; and slaps that timid Musician. The Musician starts to cry, whilst the Impressionist starts to dry; and the Blond Bombshell shakes with inhibition.

But the Good German looks calm-composed-and-collected, so even though Alfred feels dejected; he stays at the back of this music-hall. He stares into the Squat Assailant's eyes, whilst his shaky-thighs; pin him into this shaky-wall.

The Squat Assailant puffs his chest, like a man possessed; and expels these satanic-chuckles. He wails, inhales; licks his lips and cracks his knuckles.

"Ladies-and-gentlemen," he sings as he grips his buckles. "Well ain't you all very lucky, very-very lucky indeed! Cos we've got a very-very special treat for you all today!

"You see, the test of loyalty in times like these, ladies-and-gentlemen, is whether or not a man acts with wholehearted support for the war. Whether or not he'll do anything for king-and-country. Which means that the Germans must denounce Germany, and wholeheartedly embrace Britannia, ladies-and-gentlemen."

A few spectators start to tap, cheer-chant-and-clap; lift their hands and lift their hats. Alfred finds this so disturbing, and so perturbing; that he almost falls onto those mats.

"Now," the Dominant Assailant chats. "Repeat after me; I swear by God and this oath, dat the leader of the *Great British Empire* and the *Great British People*, the King, is the supreme commander!"

Unaffected by the Dominant Assailant's oration, the Good German is happy to repeat his dictation, with ease-equilibrium-and-elation.

"Louder you mutt! I shall render unconditional obedience," the Dominant Assailant bleats.

"I shall render unconditional obedience," the Good German repeats.

"I shall be a brave soldier, prepared to give ma *Nelly Duff* for this oath a' any time.

"To 'ell with the Kaiser!

"To 'ell with the 'un!

"To 'ell with Germany!"

The Good German repeats each line, which encourages this crowd to whoop-whale-and-whine; whilst they down their brandy-bourbon-and-beer. Whilst these Ruffians grin, and down some gin; which fills Alfred with frenzied-fear.

"Kiss this here flag!" The Squat Assailant begins to jeer, clap-chant-and-cheer; whilst his arms now fly asunder. Whilst he holds the Union Jack near this ledge, and the Good German makes this pledge; which fills Alfred with boundless wonder.

"Not like that Jerry. Gawd knows I ain't asking you to kiss your mother on her square-headed cheek. Where's the energy? The intensity? The sensitivity?

"Use your tongue you slutty-kraut!"

He sticks his finger through the flag and into the Good German's beak, circles it around inside the Good German's cheek, and then he begins to speak.

"Please don't consider us very-very cruel, ladies-and-gentlemen," he begins to shriek. "Gawd knows we're only doing our patriotic duty; wiping away disloyal elements in this here godly-nation. Putting the fear of God into the hearts of those very foreign people who live among us, and eat our very tasty food, when they ain't even very British themselves."

Some of this crowd shout '*hear-hear*', some of this crowd cheer; and some of this crowd stays silent. Before the Rude Ruffian who is standing in that nook, takes the German book; and gives it to the Squat Assailant.

"Burn it Fritz! Burn it now!" He begins to shout, with cheeks which pout, and legs which stomp about.

"Certainly," the Good German replies whilst he holds his hand out. "Please may I have a lighter, yah?"

"*Please may I have a lighter*?" The Squat Assailant teases like a child, with eyes which look riled, wicked-wolfish-and-wild. "Whatever happened to the lighter you used to burn down our mast, strudel-fucker?"

The Good German maintains a dignified-silence, as the Squat Assailant turns to violence; with angry-indignation. He throws this book across the stage, and begins to rage; with angry-irritation.

"Good British citizens," the Dominant Assailant says with angry-exasperation. "There are those who say dat the Germans livin' 'ere amongst us ought to be taken out and shot, and I agree dat we'd all benefit from a few 'angings, for sure; most of these *Rainbow Trouts* would be better off *Brown Bread*. But I'm a kind and gentle bein' me, I prefer song to bullets, don't you know?

"Now what d'ya say we make this Helga sing?

"Sing! Sing the national anthem you stiff piece of bratwurst. Sing!"

The Good German trips over words like '*glorious*', and words like '*victorious*'; as he stumbles through the well-known verses. Before he follows the Dominant Assailant's dictation, which earns him an ovation; whilst this Ruffian swears and that Ruffian curses.

> '*Lord, grant that every raid,*
> *May by thy mighty-aid,*
> *Victory bring!*
> *May he sedition hush,*
> *And like a torrent rush,*
> *Rebellious Hun to crush,*
> *God save the King!*
>
> -
>
> *From Germans and Pretender,*

Great Britain defend her,
Foes let them fall!
From foreign slavery,
Priests and their knavery,
And popish reverie,
God save us all!'

Alfred is relieved that this ordeal is over, but he is worried that these Ruffians may not have achieved closure; as they stomp their heavy-feet. As they drag the Good German down this aisle, spit phlegm at him just to be vile; and then drag him down this street.

They drag him past this pharmacy which is full of sanitary-masks, and colourful-flasks; which are full of colourful-liquids. They drag him past this bakery which is full of cakes of every size, homemade-pies; and homemade-biscuits. And past this butchers which is full of fresh-ham, fresh-lamb; and fresh-briskets.

Before they arrive in this grassy town-square, with these Children here and those Adults there; who are drinking soda-squash-and-soup. Who are watching the sun leave the sky, as Alfred waits nearby; near these Teens who are sat in a group.

"Dump the Prussian," the Dominant Assailant begins to whoop. "Grab some tar from those there road repairs, and some feathers from that butchers. We're gonna 'ave ourselves a fine *Tommy Tucker* tonight!"

The remaining Ruffians attach their belts to form a cord, lift the Good German from where he is floored; and strap him to this tree. The Squat Assailant clicks his knuckles, the Dominant Assailant chuckles; and these Ruffians smile with glee.

And as soon as this Ribald Ruffian returns with this tar, which is blacker than char; they spread it over the Good German's skin. They spread it over his bulbous-nose, tidy-clothes; and hairless-chin.

These Picnickers become manic, these Dog Walkers panic; and those dogs begin to shriek. The Good German stays formal, and Alfred stutters more than normal; as he finally begins to speak.

"He's a gu-gu-gu-good man! A bu-bu-bu-British pu-pu-pu-patriot! Haven't you done enough? Pu-pu-pu-please stop! Please-please-please."

"Don't you be getting shirty, little boy," the Squat Assailant replies. "Do you really think that if there was nothing wrong with this here scummy Hun, we'd be treating him like this? Come on! How very-very silly of you.

"The very fact that good British folk would do these nasty things, should show you what a dirty scumbag this here sausage-muncher is.

"Now we've been very-very kind to you; we ain't touched a hair on your chinny-chin-chin. But you really should scuttle away very-very quickly if you don't want to be blacked-up like this here traitor. Gawd knows you'd deserve a nasty beating!"

Alfred is soothed by the Good German's perseverance, his serene-appearance; and the peace in his eyes. So he leaves and walks past these Belgian Grannies, Belgian Nannies; and Belgian Guys.

This Ragged Ruffian soon takes his place, presses some feathers into the tar on the Good German's face; and pours some feathers over his head. So that the Good German's cheeks are now covered in a mixture of feathery-quills, and feathery-frills; in many shades of red.

"There ain't no magical power in you," the Squat Assailant begins to natter, as he steals this brown-platter; which is full of brown-bread.

Before he begins to fiddle, as he cuts this platter down the middle; and splits it into two. Before he removes the Good German's coat, attaches this platter to his throat; and fills it with vegetables too.

"There ain't no miracle gonna save you from this, pretzel-lover. Gawd knows it ain't very lawful for you to be here, and we ain't gonna stand for your dastardly presence no more!

"Ladies-and-gentlemen," he continues with theatrical-flair, as he turns to face this square, waving his hand through the air. "I give you the head of a German on this here shiny-platter! Look at the chick-chick-chicken. Listen to him cluck! Hear him cock-a-doodle-doo! Ain't it very-very funny? Ain't it very-very seemly?"

These Ruffians flap their arms like wings, and mock their beheaded-prisoner like subordinate-kings; before Alfred and the Policeman appear. When without any interference, the Policeman's very appearance; encourages them to flee in fear.

"You better buy some war bonds, you better pack your bags!" They shout as they retreat, down that street; before they disappear.

Before Alfred unties the Good German's straps, gives him some apple-schnapps; and wipes his feathered-face. He removes this shiny-platter, which causes these vegetables scatter; all over this grassy-place.

"I knew it'd all vork out okay. You've been most kind, yah," the Good German says as he cuts to the chase.

"Well then, this is all sorted, it is," the Policeman says with a smile on his face.

"Va-va-va-those thugs need to be brought to justice," Alfred protests without any grace. "Please do something. You're such a good Policeman! You're a pillar of society! I'd be ever so grateful. I'd be very much obliged."

But the Policeman's work has already been multiplied by the *Defence Of The Realm Act's* new measures, which means that he now works overtime without extra pay-profit-or-pleasures; or any extra leave. So Alfred's naivety makes him shake his head, turn bright-red; and wipe his brow on his sleeve.

"What folly!" He replies because he is unsure what an investigation would achieve. "Goodness gracious me! You really think a magistrate would prosecute a British citizen for attacking a German, you do? What with things the way they are? How very queer! It'd offend the whole community, it would."

These words rattle around Alfred's brain, and cause him no end of pain; despair-discomfort-and-dejection. But he understands the Policeman's view, and respects it too; so he does not make an objection.

"Do you ru-ru-ru-remember when I was mugged as a child?" He asks after a moment of introspection. "Well, it was today's assailants who did it. I'm sure of it! You could prosecute them for that without offending the community. Please give it a go. Please-please-please."

"I see, I do," the Policeman replies. "That could work, it could."

The Policeman goes one way whilst Alfred goes the other, and cares for the Good German like a friendly big brother; as he fixes his mentor's hip. As he fixes his mentor's bruised-thigh, black-eye; and split-lip.

"Vee have four new belts now," the Good German begins to quip. "But I do zink zee time has come for me to move on, yah. I love ziss country more zan you vill effer know, but it does not appear to love me back."

"I understand, sir," Alfred replies with resignation, frustration, and vexation. "I'll miss you, but I'll never forget you; I'll think of you wu-wu-

wu-whenever I re-tell one of your stories, or follow one of your lessons. You've made me the man I've become. You've done a stand up job! Top notch! Champion! Crackerjack! Thank-you, thank-you, thank-you."

But as he says this Alfred starts to feel forlorn, touched-troubled-and-torn; sad-sombre-and-stirred. So these friends stand face-to-face, and embrace; before the Good German has the last word.

"I'd like you to have zee shop ant zee flat, Alfie," he says as he rolls Alfred's palm around these keys, and gives his hand a squeeze; stood near that singing bird.

And so after all these years, Alfred's face floods with tears; and his hands begin to shake. As a brave new world is born, and Alfred walks into a brave new dawn; with feet which begin to quake.

Canada adds her pawns as the bloodshed increases, Turkey adds her shiny black-pieces; and Japan's black-knight lifts her sword. Britain wins a checkmate in black Basra, Austria defends against white Russia; and black-and-white bombs flood the board.

Whilst down near England's south-coast, this retired Admiral butters his toast; and shakes his furry white-head. With his men away in distant-lands, the Admiral needs recruits to follow commands; and help his rule to spread.

So he mobilizes these Ladies to embark on a mission, with white-feathers as their ammunition; and rouge on their seductive-cheeks. With a variety of ages-attitudes-and-appearances, these Ladies are ready for a variety of interferences; so they listen as he speaks.

"Aha! I've just read this novel, '*The Four Feathers*', about a Private who deserted his unit as soon as it was sent to war. The coward! The wimp! The weakling!

"Aha! Four of his comrades plucked a white-feather from the arse of a beaten fighting-cock, which they gave to that Private. Aha! It shamed him so much that he went off to fight, and became a real British hero. Spying! Brawling! Fighting! Killing!

"Aha! The Private returned his four feathers to his comrades, with his head held high. The little blighter just needed a second chance!"

The Admiral walks down this path, and begins to laugh, like a demented-psychopath.

'Oh-hoho! Ah-haha! Ee-heehee!'

"You see, the British are a race apart. Aha! There's a soldier in every Brit, whether they know it or not. Gunners! Belligerents! Fighters! The lot!

"But some citizens, like the Private in this book, do need some help to see it. Aha! You, with your feathers, can help them. Assist! Aid! Pressure! Serve!

"So give your feathers to every young slacker, deaf-or-indifferent to their country's needs, who you find loafing about the leas. Aha! Let them know that soldiers are fighting-and-dying for them, humiliate them, and march them off to enlist. Enrol! Sign-up! Volunteer! Aha!"

These words inspire chauvinistic-harassment, and shameful-embarrassment; to spread across this land. As ladies with pigtails, perfumed-necks and painted-nails; pass feathers from hand-to-hand.

Indifferent to the capabilities of the men they hunt, they send the infirm-injured-and-indisposed to the *Western Front*; to kill men in distant-fields. They take the discharged to re-enlist, they separate fathers from children as their efforts persist; and they send boys to act as bomb-blocking shields.

Alfred's Mother joins them and hands out feathers on trams-trawlers-and-trains, up busy-roads and down country-lanes; with putridity-prejudice-and-pride. She hands out feathers in stores-saloons-and-cinemas, bars-banks-and-bazaars; in town and the countryside.

Before she sits down by the cups which hang on these hooks, and this complete set of *Punch's Pocket Books*; from where she watches as Alfred enters. She has just made these rock-cakes using something runny, some amber-honey; and some rocky-raisins with seedless-centres.

"Take one, my little-soldier," she says as she holds this feather by its quill, whilst her spine moves her past that sill, towards this coal-powered grill. "Oh, they're just scrumptious Alfred. They-are-they-are-they-are."

"I'm good, thank-you," Alfred replies. "Man does not live by bu-bu-bu-bread alone."

"Oh no, they live because they have brave-soldiers protecting them, people like Bernie. Oh-why-oh-why-oh-why can't you be more like Bernie? Why-oh-why can't you be more like your Father in heaven? Oh, I just don't know what to do with you Alfred Freeman, you're just not respectable."

Alfred's Mother takes a deep-breath and pulls herself together, before she gives Alfred this beautiful white-feather; which she holds by its beautiful white-quill. Hundreds of barbs jut out from its shaft, thousands of barbules jut out with craft; and millions of hooklets link up in a grille. Alfred finds it sumptuous, scrumptious; and still.

"You really should fight, my wonderful-warrior," his Mother says as she bends over this pepper-mill. "You-should-you-should-you-should. This is your once in a lifetime opportunity to fulfil your destiny, and become a mighty-soldier who'll rule from north-to-south and east-to-west. It-is-it-is-it-is! Don't you reckon you ought to fight?"

"You know I don't," Alfred replies as he becomes stressed, pins this feather to his breast, and speaks out with real zest. "There's no goodness in war, Mother. There's no goodness in death-and-destruction, murder-and-malice, bullets-and-bombs.

"But there is goodness in the army Alfred. There-is-there-is-there-is!" His Mother starts to confer, with a slur, before she passes Alfred his gold-frankincense-and-myrrh. "Look at me. Oh do take your chattels."

"Give the gu-gu-gu-gold to charity," Alfred replies. "I'll take the frankincense-and-myrrh for Cleo, but I'll never fight. No-no-no. No thanky-you!"

"What irresponsibility! Who'll protect our nation if you don't, my fearless-fighter? Look at me. You could be bathing yourself in honour-and-glory; somewhere-somewhen-somehow. And yet here you are giving yourself airs-and-graces, like an uppity moral-snob, or some sort of pathetic do-gooder. 'Tis positively foolish. I fear can't tell you how it hampers me so.

"Our relations shall reject you, Alfred Freeman. They'll abandon you! You'll become the black-sheep of the family. Don't you give a straw? Oh, it's perfectly awful. I just don't know what to do with you. I-don't-I-don't-I-don't."

Alfred shrugs his shoulders, looks at these saucepan-holders, and this pile of paper-folders.

"Think of your Father in heaven; he'd be the first in line to fight, just like Bernie, and you know it. Do it for him, and do it for the Belgians.

Look at me. Their country is in a right funk. My notion! People are saying it's been raped. Raped! Raped, my terrific-trooper. Raped!"

Alfred's Mother shakes her head, turns bright-red, and stares ahead.

"The Belgians?" Alfred replies with frustration, agitation; and dread. "The Belgians, Mother? Please! The same Belgians who've spent the last forty years raping the Congo? The same Belgians who've been enslaving the Congolese natives, severing their penises, and severing their breasts? The same Belgians who've been flogging the Congolese people with whips, torturing them with burning-copal, and chopping off their hands? The same Belgians who've slaughtered ten-million innocent Congolese natives already? The Belgians, Mother? That secret society of murderers? That slave-driving nation? Really? Really, Mother?

"We're not fighting because the Belgians are innocent-victims, Mother; we're fighting because they sell us cheap-rubber. We're fighting to make a profit, to accrue land-oil-and-gold, and impose our ideologies-politics-and-religions on everyone else. We're fighting to break up the German-and-Ottoman empires, so we can control their land-workforce-and-capital. And we're fighting to stop Germany from overtaking us as the world's leading naval power. It's ridiculous! Britain fighting Germany? It's like an owl fighting an eagle."

This rant drives a wedge between Alfred and his Mother, who sways one way and then sways the other; before she tumbles from side-to-side. Which means Alfred has lost the Good German who was abused before, Bernie who has gone to war; and his Mother who has too much pride. So his heart begins to ache, and his body begins to shake; whilst he cringes deep down inside.

"The Belgians? The Belgians, Mother?

"What about the bu-bu-bu-Boers, Mother? What about the zu-zu-zu-Zulus? What about the Ashanti, the Zanzibaris and the Beninese? What about when Father '*raped*' them, Mother? I've heard all his stories, don't you worry about that!

"I've heard about how we invaded their independent nu-nu-nu-nations, Mother. How we plundered their wealth, sold their people as slaves, and destroyed their cultures-and-religions.

"So don't you judge Germany for having a speck of sawdust in her eye, when we have a whole plank of wood in ours. And don't you tell me about countries raping other countries, when we've been doing it for years.

"Really? Really, Mother?

"Do you really want me to kill the ju-ju-ju-Germans, now they're acting like my own Father once acted. Really? Really, Mother? Will that make you proud? Will that make the community proud? Will that make the nation proud? Really? Really, Mother?

"Because if it does, if mu-mu-mu-murder make you proud, then I don't want anything to do with you again. No-no-no. No thanky-you!

"I love you Mother, I really do, I think you're the best. I think you're like a spring-flower; beautiful-and-vivacious. But this really is the limit. I don't need you anymore. No-no-no. I'll live in the flat above my greengrocery, and I'll never come near you again!"

This tirade leaves Alfred breathless as he begins to retreat, and walks down this street; past this Vagabond. Past this Jobber-Janitor-and-Jailor, Tinker-Tobacconist-and-Tailor; park-puddle-and-pond.

He returns home before he walks over here, near these Drunks who eat warm-eels and drink warm-beer; beneath these cloudy-skies. Where he sees the Blonde Bombshell who smells a bit fruity, as she flaunts her beauty; and flashes her seductive-thighs.

"Hi, hi, cherry-pie," she sings, whilst she flashes her rings; and flutters her come-hither eyes.

Alfred lusts after her slender-legs and silky pink-skin, but he tells himself not to give in; as he flushes with this skittish-smile. He tells himself that the Blonde Bombshell's beauty will wilt like a flower, that only true love has real power; and any real style.

"This is for you, my pet, to show the world that you're a coward," she continues with guile.

She winks with her emerald-eye, flashes her silky pink-thigh; and passes Alfred this beautiful white-feather. She is no more aware of the barbs on its shaft, or its barbules' craft; than she is of next week's weather.

"You'd look pretty wonderful in khaki, Alfie-kins. Oh yes darling! I don't think I'd be able to keep my hands off a dear creature like you, if you were in a uniform. Oh no I wouldn't! I just couldn't!"

The Blonde Bombshell turns to walk away, now she has said what she came here to say; and pinned her colours to Alfred's mast. But Alfred blocks this track, and talks right back; with speech which is manically-fast.

"Thank-you, thank-you, thank-you," he says as he stops the Blonde Bombshell from moving past. "I really am very grateful for this fu-fu-fu-feather. You're most kind! You have ten of the best fingers I've ever seen.

"But I'm afraid to say that you've given it to the wrong man; I'm no coward, I'm one of the bravest people around. Yes-yes-yes. Yes thanky-you!"

"Brave? Brave? Brave, you nasty-man? If you were brave you'd be knee-deep in French mud, alongside those heroic-beauties who, indifferent to their own health, are risking life-and-limb to keep you safe.

"But you're not. You're doing nothing for your King, nothing for your country, and nothing for me. How dare you call yourself brave? You're not brave, you're the lowest of the low! You, Alfred Freeman, are indeed a coward. A gargantuan coward. A lily-livered, callow and fainthearted coward!"

As she speaks Alfred rolls this feather around his finger, allows this meditation to linger; and allows it to set him free. Like when the Good German was neglected, Alfred is calm-composed-and-collected; for everyone here to see.

"Your '*heroes*' aren't ru-ru-ru-risking their '*lives-or-limbs*' for me," he replies as they walk past this tree. "And they're not brave either. They're the cowards! Soldiers are cowards! All the warmakers are cowards!

"They're cowards because, overcome by fear, they turn their backs on morality. They act in response to a fear of being invaded, a fear of the Germans-Austrians-and-Turkish, and a fear of the foreign-unknown-and-unusual. A fear which makes them brutal-barbaric-and-bloodthirsty.

"And since only cowards respond to fear, without the courage to overcome it, soldiers must be cowards.

"But my actions aren't guided by fear. I laugh at fear! I don't fear being invaded, the Germans-Austrians-or-Turkish, the foreign-unknown-or-unusual. I haven't become brutal-barbaric-or-bloodthirsty.

"And since only brave people can overcome fear, I must be brave!"

The Blonde Bombshell taps her feet, walks down that street; and swishes her golden-hair. She walks off in that direction, with bilious-dejection; and bilious-despair. Whilst Alfred walks past this bar, this spa; and this square.

He walks past this group of Boys who are attracted to that group of Girls, who wear fake-pearls; and are attracted to them as well. But neither group approaches the other, they just stand with one another; whilst they yap-yack-and-yell.

He walks past this Mother with her Baby, who she rocks on her knee; whilst she dreams about what he could become. He walks past this Old Man who thinks about his childhood, and all that is good; whilst he sucks on his wrinkled-thumb.

And he reaches the tallest hill in his town, where this Moneychanger is wearing a gown; with her hair in the Flapper fashion. With a face covered in shiny-veins, a neck covered in shiny-chains; and a voice which is full of passion.

"Hello there. I see you haven't joined the ranks of the intelligent-respectable-and-strong. It doesn't do! It just doesn't do!

"Well this is your lucky day, good sir. Come with the Retired Captain and me to the enrolment office. We'll take good care of you. The army will lift you up; it'll fill your pockets with pounds-shillings-and-pence. Everyone will love-and-respect you. The whole world will be yours! All yours!"

"But what shall it profit a man," Alfred replies. "If he gains the world but loses his soul?

"You can sh-sh-sh-shoot your words at me. Please do! Please-please-please. But I'll never worship your war. No-no-no!"

"Shoot words at you? I can shoot words at you?" The Moneychanger bribes. "But the Germans don't shoot words, they shoot bullets. And if people like you don't fight them, they'd march across Europe unopposed. It wouldn't do! It just wouldn't do!"

"Not at all!" Alfred replies. "You're ever so kind to talk to me. You're ever so dashing. But please understand! Wars will su-su-su-cease when men refuse to fight in them. If *'People like me didn't fight'* there'd never be a war again!"

"That's all very well in theory, but in practice it doesn't do. It just doesn't do! Germans *are* fighting, and they're doing the most heinous things. Shouldn't you be avenging them?"

"I ain't got no quarrel with the Germans," Alfred answers. "No German ever called me a '*Fainthearted-coward*'.

"And anyway, forgiveness is the greatest ru-ru-ru-revenge. It can make us the superior-nation, win us a worthier-victory, and help us to triumph in a nobler-war. Yes-yes-yes!"

"Forgiveness is the greatest-revenge? Forgiveness is revenge?" The Moneychanger mutters, near those flooded-gutters, and corrugated-shutter.

She removes this feather from her purse, starts to curse; and shoves it up Alfred's nose. She twists it around, and begins to pound; until blood drenches Alfred's clothes.

Frustrated by Alfred's stubborn-firmness, serenity-straightness-and-sternness; she turns and she runs away. She mutters '*Selfish shirker*' and begins to spit, she mutters '*Innocent halfwit*'; and she heads towards the bay.

And with three white-feathers to his name, three weeks pass without acclaim; or any sort of reaction. Before Alfred sees his Sunday School Teacher, this bottom-shaking creature; who is seeking satisfaction.

"Alfred! Cuddle bunny!" She sings as she dives into action. "Aren't you going to join our boys in khaki, my muffin?"

"Oh no thank-you," Alfred answers. "I couldn't ever go to war, having heard you speak about loving your enemy and turning your other ch-ch-ch-cheek. No thanky-you!"

"But you wouldn't be fighting your enemy, sweetie-pie," she replies amidst this foot-shuffling, hair-ruffling, and scuffling. "You'd be fighting your nation's enemy. It's not at all the same.

"We have a holy-empire to defend. To go to war will bring you power-and-glory in this lifetime, and eternal-life in the next. It's time for you to take up your Daddy's throne, sugar. It's time for you to rise to the top!"

But Alfred has already made his choice, he has chosen to use his voice; as a pro-peace teacher. Rather than rule from north-to-south, he has chosen to use his mouth; as a pro-peace preacher. He has chosen to free the chained, and soothe the strained; with love for every creature.

"Do you remember when you tu-tu-tu-told me to overcome temptation, and follow the Lord?" He asks the Sunday School Teacher. "It was good advice. Thank-you, thank-you, thank-you! I was ever so grateful. You were as sweet as a bucket of bonbons; I could've swallowed you whole!

"Well, I listened! And so I won't be tempted by power, I won't be tempted by glory, and I won't be tempted by eternal-life. No-no-no. No way! Not today, not tomorrow, not ever. Never-ever-ever!"

And so just like the Private in the Admiral's book, this rebuttal earns Alfred this condescending-look; and this fourth white-feather. But unlike the Private who was swayed by his mate, Alfred has not been tempted by food-fornication-fame-or-fate; he has kept himself together. He has protected his substance-senses-spirit-and-soul, from the ladies who have tried to swallow him whole; dressed up in lace-linen-and-leather.

He receives many more feathers in the post, but cherishes these first four the most; since they inspire him to confront the warmakers. They inspire him to preach on the street, wherever people meet; near a bailiffs-butchers-and-bakers. They inspire him to get off the shelf, stand up for himself; and all the other peacemakers...

SUFFERING AND SMILING

Without any feet-feathers-or-wings, Owl sat on his cliff, all day and all night, for many a day and many a night. And from that spot he saw that Rabbit was about to eat her own Kittens, just to stay alive.

"You've taught me love-loyalty-and-passion," Owl told Dog. "I love Rabbit, I'm loyal to her family, and I'm passionate about her wellbeing.

"But I'm old, weak, and unable to help her. Please can you find her some food?"

Dog was honoured by the changes which she had inspired in Owl. And so she went in search of grains-grasses-and-greens. She travelled over borders, across oceans, and up mountains. But she could not find any food, and so she returned to Owl's nest with her tail between her legs.

When she arrived she saw that Owl's nest was completely empty. Owl was nowhere to be seen!

Feeling confused, Dog took a seat and looked down at the forest below. She saw rocks-roads-and-rubble, woods-willows-and-weeds, ponds-puddles-and-pools. And she saw Rabbit, who seemed to be healthy.

"Rabbit," Dog shouted. "You were starving, but now you're full. What happened?"

"It was a miracle!" Rabbit replied. "The torso of a great Owl fell from the sky. We ate its meat and recovered our health."

Dog smiled. She was happy to see that Rabbit was alive, and she was proud of Owl for sacrificing himself in order to save Rabbit's life.

And Dog suffered. She was sad to see that Owl was dead, and she was upset that they would never speak again.

Dog suffered for the world. Suffering-and-smiling, her tail became limp, her appetite vanished, and her energy faded away.

She was still loving-loyal-and-passionate, and everyone knew it, because Dog showed them so herself. But she was no longer loving enough to fall for the trees, loyal enough to visit the animals, or passionate enough to sing with the birds. She did not have any sort of oneness-serenity-or-peace.

1915

Alfred had felt dejected-depressed-and-downhearted, after Bernie had departed; and the Good German had been left in the lurch. After propaganda had usurped his nation, his family had left him in isolation; and he was abandoned by his church.

But enough is enough! Alfred is becoming tough! He is becoming rough!

The sun gets reborn in the sky, teary-eyes begin to dry; and a phoenix begins to rise. Lawbreakers get driven, wrongdoers get forgiven; and the peacemakers fight the lies.

Their fight back starts today! Alfred enters the fray! He has his say!

It begins in private across this British nation, in many a hushed-conversation; in many a darkened-room. As peacemakers take up all the seating, at many a protest-meeting; whilst conscription begins to loom.

Peacemakers mobilise against officers with pennants, authoritative-lieutenants; and privates alike. They give the silent a voice, the enslaved a choice; and the workers a chance to strike. They wage a war on wars, and spread news of the peace-cause; by bus-boat-and-bike.

The year is 1915.

An Indian Lawyer is returning home to lead his nation out of colonial-captivity, a German Physicist is publishing his 'Theory Of Relativity'; and an American Cartoonist is patenting the Raggedy Ann Doll which makes him feel elated. In Lithuania the Jews are being expelled despite all they have achieved, in France the first ever transatlantic telephone-message is being received; and in America the first ever space-agency is being created. Whilst the British annex two archipelagos in the Pacific Ocean, to expand their empire in slow-motion; with greed which is still unsated.

Alfred hears about this and he hears about the peacemakers in his nation, who sign up to the Fellowship of Reconciliation; a hundred-thousand at a time. He hears about the Independent Labour Party, and the Socialist Party; who both take a pro-peace party-line.

He hears about the Slave Emancipator, the Union Of Democratic Control's leader; who leads the way. He hears about the Philosopher

King, who travels around this spring; to lecture away.

And he hears that despite the overbearing-censorship of 'Dora' (as the 'Defence of the Realm Act' has become known), clandestine-publications still help the truth to be shown; and unite peacemakers from shore-to-shore. The Tribunal-Leader-and-Friend all have a say, and issue ten-thousand copies every single day; which all oppose the war.

So Alfred knows he is not alone, when Cleo moves into his brand new home; and sits down by these condiment-packets. Before the Suffragist sits down by this picture-frame, this broken board-game; and these wooden tennis-rackets. This candle-snuffer which is slightly warm, this brass shoe-horn; and some of the Good German's old jackets. Where they some drink tea, and laugh with glee; near that row of unused gas-brackets.

The Suffragist has avoided the Cat And Mouse treatment, after the suffragettes and the government came to an agreement; and so she now looks rather active. In this veil-visor-and-vest, she is certainly well dressed; although she is too plain to be called 'attractive'.

For the suffragettes have fought for their country like they fought for the vote, and called for conscription from the pit of their throat; with militant-pride and militant-zeal. They have handed out feathers and they have acted smarmy, they have called for women soldiers in the British army; and they have run a war-bond appeal. But the suffragists have opposed their assaults, because they consider their violence to have its faults; and so they have called for a peaceful-deal.

The Suffragist has formed the Women's Peace Army, joined the Women's Peace Party; and the Women's Peace Crusade. She has been stopped on her way to a European peace-conference, amidst shouts of 'Nark'-'Nefarious'-and-'Nonsense'; from the pro-war brigade.

"Oh darling child, it's okay," she says in a style which is spunky, punky; and unafraid. "Really, it's fine. One has faced far worse before.

"And there were one-and-a-half-thousand women there, who were all singing from the same hymn sheet! One-and-a-half-thousand ladies of all ages-and-backgrounds, from all over Europe and the States. One-and-a-half-thousand ladies who were all trying to clear up this male-made mess, so to speak; demanding peace, an end to the bloodshed, and an international organisation to arbitrate against future wars.

"Say, at the end of the day, it really does lift one's spirits to hear of people travelling so far-and-wide to express their beliefs."

The Suffragist shakes her knees, whilst Cleo pours the teas, and Alfred agrees.

"I'm pleased to say that we're gaining support on the home front too," he cheers, with his hair tucked behind his ears, as his stutter fades away after all these years. "The Home Secretary and the Chancellor are standing firm-firm-firm against the threat of conscription, and the Lancastrian is fighting for peace in parliament too. Yes thanky-you!"

But most of the pro-peace politicians have already left the government, to act for their country's betterment; dressed up in their formal-suits. They are opposing the underhand nature of treaty-making, and the cheapness of life-taking; whilst calling for a *League of United Nations* to prevent disputes. They are standing with cooperatives which are intent on communion, many a trade-union; and lots of women's groups.

"Peacemakers are writing in to my paper, *'The Workers' Dreadnought'*, from all around the country," the Suffragist says as she eats these fruits. "There's no north-south divide on this one!

"There're protests against military-displays in the north, strikes in ammunitions-factories all across Scotland, and mass demonstrations up-and-down the land. We're encouraging soldiers to mutiny in every single region!

"We're up-and-running, we've set the ball rolling, and we've put the wheels in motion. There really is nothing quite as powerful as an idea whose time has come!"

This squadron clink their mugs in celebration, and as they make this triumphant-gyration; Cleo drops this stolen ball of twine. Because unaware of what she is achieving, Cleo has an unconscious habit of thieving; and regularly steals wigs-whisky-and-wine.

Last year she stole a bearded-gnome which pushed a wheelbarrow, a female-gnome which held a sparrow; and a model of an eagle which had a broken-head. Without making her feel small, Alfred made Cleo return them all; as he took her by her hand and led her ahead.

But he has not been able to stop Cleo from stealing bent-cigars, broken-guitars; or clockwork toy-cars. Cleo has even stolen the

Neighbour's dog, a porcelain-frog; and a box of jam-jars.

"I'll return it," Alfred says as he takes the twine.

"What can we do to help?" Cleo asks as she returns back in line. "Oh, I do hope we can do something to help. Wouldn't that be grand? I'm very sorry for not having done more already."

There is still a lotus-leaf on Cleo's thumb, and a butterfly on her bum; which both look like henna-tattoos. A nymph can be seen near her frock, a mermaid near her smock; and a bullfinch down near her shoes.

"Say, whatever you do will be dangerous," the Suffragist begins to muse. "You'll be like a sheep amongst wolves!"

"Oh, I am very sorry, but you really should know that I'm prepared to face the bullets for this cause," Cleo shoots back. "I'm prepared to serve my class-and-caste, gender-and-generation, with quintessentially British resistance. I really ought to suffer for my conscience, oughtn't I? Oh, I am sorry for my passion, but I really do care."

"Hear-hear," the Suffragist replies. "Oh darling child, that's just it! How bang on the spot you are. Quite so, quite so.

"It's that sort of British patriotism will help us reclaim the streets! It'll help us to crush all the warmakers; the politicians who wage wars, the arms-dealers who fuel wars, and the soldiers who fight wars."

"Our government, thanks to *Dora*, won't even allow you to erect a flagpole these days," Alfred agrees. "Not without arresting you for it. We need to make a stand for freedom. Yes please. Please-please-please. We need to make a stand for Great Britain!"

These friends lift their mugs and give them a clink, they continue to drink; and they continue to natter. They natter about their dreams, their schemes; and the issues which really matter.

"The truth is," Alfred continues to chatter. "That we don't know what dangers we will have to face. We need to be as wise as serpents, and as innocent as baby doves.

"Please! The warmakers' sticks-and-stones will never break our spirits, but our resistance will break-break-break their resolve!"

"That's just it!" The Suffragist agrees. "We shall stop all this breaking of bones, this mangling of men, and this making of widows. We shall not flag-or-fail; we shall go on to the end. We shall take our war-on-war to the streets, with growing confidence-and-strength, to defend our island whatever the cost. We shall protest on the beaches, we shall protest in the fields, and we shall protest in the hills. We shall not rest, subjugated-and-starving as we become, until we've won back our basic British liberties!

"Because I have a dream today!

"I have a dream that this Britain, which uses wars to spread injustice-oppression-and-greed, will be transformed into an oasis of freedom-and-justice.

"I have a dream today!

"I have a dream that our children will not be judged by their nationality, but by the content of their character.

"I have a dream today!

"I have a dream that one day, here in Europe, little British boys-and-girls will be able to join hands with little German boys-and-girls, as sisters-and-brothers."

"Yes-yes-yes," Alfred concludes. "We'll go far-and-wide. We'll enlighten the lost-sheep, cleanse the lepers, and expel the demonic-soldiers.

"Please! Let us live in peace, stand for peace, and dream of peace. Let us give peace to this war-crazed world, without ever being troubled-or-afraid. Yes thanky-you!"

So these three peacemakers mobilise and set off to war, they convert the rich and they preach to the poor; wherever they happen to tread. They print fliers which say 'Life not death is the source of all goodness', 'Act with kindness'; and 'Don't help this war to spread'. Which say 'Stand for love not hate', 'Resist the bait'; and 'Abstain from all the bloodshed'.

They sprinkle in a 'Noble cause', a 'Sacrifice for conscience not for wars'; and a 'Glorious heartstrings'. They report on abuses, overcome the warmakers' excuses; and promote their pro-peace meetings.

They trawl streets-squares-and-stores, to combat support for wars; by accosting loafers-laymen-and-lords. They post flyers through doors, hide flyers in drawers; and stick flyers to notice-boards.

But to print-publish-and-post this propaganda, is not easy because of a governmental-memoranda; which has reduced their freedom of speech. Peacemakers are getting arrested for the things they say, their houses are being raided each day; and they are threatened whenever they preach.

Nonetheless, Alfred-and-Cleo use this *Labour Printing Press*; in this den run by volunteers. Where these pressers press, these printers progress; and these machines pass through their gears. Where metal-threads dangle, metal-frames jangle; and deafen everyone's ears. With these noisy-bumps, noisy-pumps; noisy-jeers and noisy-cheers.

This place enables the peacemakers to get out and preach, stand up for the freedom of speech; and send posters across the nation. It battles the censors on behalf of every dad-dowager-and-daughter, saves the people from mass-slaughter; and immunises the population. It fights the optimism-epidemic, that blind-faith pandemic; with many a note-notice-and-notification. It truly is the beating-heart of the pro-peace operation.

It prints away whilst Japan gobbles up China again, Russia gobbles up the Ukraine; and Italy deserts the *Triple Alliance*. With some poison-gas and some zeppelin-bombs, a genocide of a million Armenians; some hatred and some violence.

It forms an offensive against the ladies who join the *Women's Naval Force*, the *Women's Air Force*; and the *Women's Auxiliary Corps*. It opposes the mothers who dress their children in military-attire, sell war-bonds to any buyer; and take men's jobs like never before. And it opposes the women who wear shorter-skirts, smoke like flirts; and profit from the war.

"Feminist sisters!" The Suffragist says with a roar. "We've already stood for womankind. Now we must stand for humankind! We, the people, must be blind to nationality, just as we've asked others to be blind to our gender.

"Humanity before nationality!"

Her recruiting-spree frees Alfred-and-Cleo to continue their pro-peace campaign, so they graffiti this tannery-tenement-and-train; using black pen-paint-and-pencils. They graffiti a tank firing balloons towards some towers, and a soldier launching a grenade made of flowers; using these cardboard-stencils.

They paint aeroplanes with gnashing-teeth and beady-eyes, soldiers refusing to compromise; and fields which are full of white-gravestones. They paint a dove of peace in bulletproof-vest, a khaki-clad rat in barbed-wire nest; and a politician gorging on bones.

This earns them a number of enemies, such as this Vigilante with protruding-knees; who chases them down this street. Who chases them through this mist, and waves his fist; whilst he throws this muddy-peat.

Alfred-and-Cleo flee from this attack, down this leafy-track; with legs which start to pace. With pimples on their arms, sweat on their palms; and pulses which start to race.

"I'll kill you when I catch you! Skunks!" The Vigilante shouts his first profanity.

"Death would be too good for you! Shirkers!" He shouts with insanity.

"You live like Germans and deserve to die like them too! Sloths!" He shouts with vanity. "Ever so painfully! Ever so, ever so painfully!"

Alfred-and-Cleo run past this Cabinet Maker, this Belgian Undertaker; and this Yeoman who eats his own crumpet. This Hotel Porter, this bookish Reporter; and this Musician who blows his own trumpet.

But Cleo's pace starts to slow, with her fatigue on show; and the Vigilante is about to attack. So Alfred turns around, returns along this leafy-ground; and along this leafy-track.

"Shouldn't we all be free to air our opinions?" He says as he drops his pack. "If not, then what on earth are your soldiers fighting for? Please tell me! Please-please-please."

But the Vigilante just throws these stones, which hit Alfred's bones; neck-nose-and-knee. The Vigilante swings his fist, but Alfred does not resist; which allows Cleo to run free.

"You deserve this rough-housing, you dirty peace-crank!" The Vigilante growls with glee. "From a superior Brit; an upstanding citizen who's courageous enough to fight. Ever so courageous! Ever so, ever so courageous!"

The Vigilante stops speaking as he drags Alfred through this scree, past this gawky Postman and past that gawky-tree, before he throws him in this canal which is full of algae.

"My son is dead," he continues his repartee. "Ever so dead! Ever so, ever so dead! He'll never walk this earth again.

"He was brave. Ever so brave! Ever so, ever so brave!

"He was gallant. Ever so gallant! Ever so, ever so gallant!

"And now he's dead. Ever so dead! Ever so, ever so dead!

"He died for you! So don't you tell me about the horrors of war. I know more about them than a slacker like you ever could."

Alfred floats away in the breeze, towards those gnarly-trees; whilst the Vigilante throws a stone. Alfred floats with jumpy-thighs, and jumpy-eyes; whilst the Vigilante starts to groan.

"Please use your pain for good," Alfred replies as he floats off alone. "Please-please-please. I can see you're a good man; I bet you were the best father there ever was.

"But just think of all the other sons you could save, and all the other fathers who could benefit from your intervention, if you became a peacemaker. No-one should lose a son like you have. This is your chance to do something about it!"

The Vigilante begins to chuckle, as his legs begin to buckle; because he is confused by a mix of emotions. He begins to sway, turns away; and then gestures with random motions.

But Alfred's hands have begun to flick, and his legs have begun to kick; as he swims to the opposite shore. Before he rides this tram away, and talks of his treatment today; stood here on his kitchen's floor. Near this piece of cable, his kitchen table; and his kitchen door.

"Oh, that's nothing!" The Suffragist begins to roar. "A howling-mob burnt an effigy of me last night. One must admit that it was rather impressive, with a wig which looked exactly like my hair. It burned so brightly, stuffed with dry-straw, that one did look rather regal."

"How ghastly! How can you quip about such things?" Cleo asks. " Oh, do ignore me. I am sorry; do go on."

"Darling child, one gets accustomed to the abuse, it comes with the terrain; the courage of your convictions gets you through. And if it saves just one life, then it will all be worth it. Our efforts are taking effect!"

Their efforts are swelling the ranks of the *UDC* without detection, as new devotees go forth in each direction; to preach two-by-two. They earn respect for their puritanical nerve, and religious verve; as they push the peace-cause through.

They gain support from their comrades, unwilling soldiers in different brigades; and the unenthusiastic majority. Who after lots of cost-counting, and lots of self-doubting; have started to question authority.

And they gain support from this Deserter who is big-headed, and bow-legged; with this scar across his cheek. This paradox of a man is both exacerbated-and-effervescent, aged-and-adolescent; weighty-and-weak.

"'Pon my word, I just can't understand those wi' war fever," he begins to speak. "Ye'd 'ave to be mad to enjoy it. The people who talk about '*glory*' can't never 'ave been to war themselves."

The Deserter talks about rains which brought trench-foot in seas of mud, cat-sized rats who gorged on human-blood; and diseases like nephritis. About everlasting-days and eternal-nights, shots-shells-and-shrapnel which gave grown-men the frights; and diseases like bronchitis.

He talks about the plates of horse-meat which fuelled the killing, the hours of repetitive army-drilling; and the dirty army-beds. The body-parts which flew through the air, the blood which got in his hair; and the corpses without any heads.

He talks about a teenage-soldier who howled like a fox, hid in a box; and meowed like a timid-kitten. And about the guns which growled, the Germans who howled; and the drunks who sang for Great Britain.

"I even met the Hun at Christmas!" He says, with this friendly-gaze; which makes him look a bit smitten. "Yeah! We lined candles up along the tops of our trenches, illu'minating the darkness, and joined in wi' their hymns. We sung ''Ark The 'Erald Angels Sing' for peace on earth and mercy mild, '*God Rest Ye Merry Gentleman*' for tidings o' comfort-and-joy, and '*Silent Night 'Oly Night*' for all to be calm and all to be bright.

"The Germans stood arm-in-arm wi' us in *No Man's Land*. I even visited their trench and saw their Christmas trees. Yeah! I gave a German my whisky, and 'e gave me 'is chocolate. We shared a Christmas sermon and Christian prayers.

"We even played football with them, using a woolly-hat stuffed with straw for a ball. They beat us by three goals to two. The buggers! But it ain't as if their national team will ever beat ours. We'll always 'ave that, I s'pose."

Alfred chortles without refrain, as it starts to pour with rain, before the Deserter speaks again.

"Things wasn't never the same after that; I just didn't have the heart to kill those kind men.

"Fort'nately I got this 'ere gammy-leg before too long, which gave me an excuse to get out o' there. A friend o' mine, a Miner, weren't so lucky. 'E was already s'ffering from shellshock, because he'd seen 'is brother get blown clean in two. So meeting the Germans proper finished 'im orf. 'E didn't never follow an order again.

"Only the Miner weren't a cripple like me; 'is injuries was only mental. So 'e faced a court-martial without a single lawyer and, under order 585's principal o' *'Guilty unless proven innocent'*, 'e was sentenced to death.

"Yeah! 'Is commander made a right example out of 'im. He was worried that the other soldiers might cause trouble if he was lenient. They was like that, the officers. I even saw one of them shoot a cat for treason once. That scruffy little fur-ball 'ad made friends with the Germans as well as us Brits, and 'ad carried messages between the trenches in 'er collar. Our officers didn't take kindly that sort of fraternity, so they shot the little kitty dead.

"Anyway, the Miner was given so much rum, 'e fair well passed out. 'E 'ad to be carried to his execution, tied up from 'ead to toe like a string of sausages, wi' a bag placed over 'is 'ead.

"We didn't wanna shoot 'im. Imagine being made to do that! I aimed wide. But someone must 'ave shot on target, 'cos the Miner copped one in 'is 'ead.

"The little laddie was only sixteen years old!"

Seeing the Deserter return to the light, and refuse to fight; reminds Alfred of one of the Good German's old proverbs. About a shepherd who loved the lost sheep who returned to him teary-eyed, more than the ninety-nine others who stayed by his side; eating hay-heather-and-herbs. It gives him the confidence to speak out in this square, near this tree and that fair; these Belgians and those Serbs.

Near this Curiosity Shop Man, this old Gentleman; and this dusty Wood Cutter. This Grandson, this Nun; and that Tramp who is sat in a gutter.

He waits as this striking Tram Man curses the thirty-two percent increase in food-prices last year, which encourages this crowd to cheer;

growl-gurgle-and-grunt. And he waits as this Flapper with curly-hair, waves her hand through the air; whilst she raises funds for the front.

The three men who heckled the Suffragist's speech allow Alfred to pass, so he walks across the grass; which covers this *No Man's Land*. He passes ladies in coats-cardigans-and-caps, men in hoods-headbands-and-hats; and this pile of golden-sand.

"Hello! And thank-you for taking the time to listen," he says as he takes to the stand. "Thank-you, thank-you, thank-you. You're glorious! You're splendid! You're the sugar on my cereal!

"But as we stand here today, ugly-ugly-ugly news is reaching us. Because one-hundred-thousand innocent German civilians have now died as a result of our naval-blockade. Famished without food, frozen without fuel, and diseased without drugs. Slain by our swords!

"And they're sure to retaliate. It won't be long before the Germans are blockading British ports and bombing British buildings. It won't be long before our own wives-mothers-and-daughters are dying here at home.

"Is this what we want?

"Because I'll tell you this; you reap-reap-reap what you sow-sow-sow! If you condemn the Germans you'll be condemned by them, if you judge them they'll judge you back, and if you live by the sword you'll die by the sword whilst the meek inherit the earth. The first will be last, and the last will be first; it's a karmic necessity!

"Because of our wars we're at war, because of our blockades we'll be blockaded, and because of our bombs we'll be bombed.

"Please! Is this what we want? Is this what we signed up to? Is this what we're supporting?"

Alfred pauses as his crowd shout '*We do*', '*Let's kill their babies too*'; and '*Anything to hurt the Hun*'. As this bird begins to tweet, this cat licks her feet; and this moth flies towards the sun.

"What infernal nonsense!" The Man Mountain booms like a drum. "You, skunk, are a neuter. You're a dewy-eyed girl in a man's body. You're the opposite of a soldier; selfish rather than sacrificing, sin-begotten rather than righteous, and cowardly rather than brave. Everyone here knows it!"

"I'm not opposed to selflessness-righteousness-or-bravery," Alfred replies. "No-no-no. No thanky-you! I embody these virtues myself!"

Alfred pauses for suspense, before the Councillor comes to his defence, with a voice which is tough-tolerant-and-tense.

"Let the lad parley," he scolds from behind that fence. "I, *sneeze*, implore you to be merciful-magnanimous-moderate-meek-mellow-and-mild. We've, *burp*, heard enough from t'other side. This one's only providing some, *sniff*, evenness-equilibrium-parity-and-proportion."

The Councillor defends Alfred because he tolerates Alfred's point-of-view, he respects it too; and he respects Alfred for speaking out here. Because his son-in-law returned from war with an injured-thigh, and an injured-eye; at the end of last year. The Groom's skin had melted near his nipples, to form undulating-ripples; which reach as far as his ear.

"This man," Alfred resumes with cheer. "Shows what a great-great-great nation we all live in. Thank the Lord for this man! And thank the Lord for this nation. What a wonderful place it is. On a scale of one-to-ten, I'd give it eleven. Let's show this great-nation to the world!

"Please! Let us live at peace with all men.

"Please! Let us bless the Germans who persecute us, without cursing them back.

"Please! Let us feed the Germans when they're hungry, and give them water when they're athirst.

"For everyone's blood is red, and everyone's tears are salty. The Germans and the Brits all feel pleasure-and-pain, faith-and-fear, delight-and-despair. So it's wrong to separate us into nations, which create false-divisions between us, and it's wrong to fight people on the basis of those false-divisions.

"Therefore I ask you to think of the Germans in the same way that you think of yourself. Only give them the things which you'd like to receive, only serve them as you'd like to be served, and only treat them as you'd like to be treated.

"Only shoot at the Germans if you want to be shot at by them, only stab them with bayonets if you want to be stabbed yourself, and only blockade their land if you want your own friends-and-families to starve to death here in Britain.

"Because the Germans will only be merciful if we're merciful, they'll only forgive us if we forgive them, and they'll only stop fighting if we stop fighting too.

"Until then we'll all be made to suffer, and we'll all be made to strain. Because you cannot beat hate with hate, you can only beat hate with love. And peace will only be achieved through peaceful means. Yes-yes-yes. Yes thanky-you!"

A grenade of mud pelts Alfred's belly, as does this plate of meaty-jelly; and this plate of meaty-stew. He gets hit by these mouldy-pantaloons, mouldy-mushrooms; mouldy-sock and mouldy-shoe.

"What blasphemy!" The Hunchback begins to coo. "What rot! What claptrap! How dare a shirker, a dandy, and a mad-scoundrel like you, speak like this whilst our brave-and-manly soldiers are dying abroad? How crusty-and-queer you are!"

"I say to you, kind sir," Alfred replies as he wags his fist, through this mist, with the assurance of the Suffragist. "That soldiers aren't brave-or-manly; they are not even good men. Far from it! A good soldier is a bad man!

"A good soldier is a blind-and-heartless machine. At the word of command, he'll shoot the bravest-or-noblest person that ever lived. He respects neither the grey-hair of age, nor the weakness of infancy. He's unmoved by tears, by prayers, or by argument. He's indifferent to human-thought and human-feeling.

"Please understand! Virtue cannot be found in an army-uniform, purity cannot be found down the barrel of a gun, and merit cannot be found at war. No-no-no! Feeding the hungry, comforting the troubled, and helping the needy will bring you far greater glory than fighting ever will.

"For real men serve their country with random acts of kindness, not vicious acts of violence. And real soldiers have one duty, and one duty only; they have a duty to mutiny!

"So don't give yourselves to men who despise you; who enslave you, regiment your lives, tell you what to do, what to think and what to feel. Who drill you, diet you, treat you like cattle, and use you as cannon-fodder. Don't give yourselves to these machine-men with machine-minds and machine-hearts. You are not machines! You are not cattle! You are men! You have the love of humanity in your hearts!

"So don't fight for slavery. Stand for liberty! Campaign to free the world; to do away with national barriers, greed-hate-and-intolerance.

"Don't fight! Unite!

"Don't murder! Love!

"And don't be a soldier! Be a man!"

But Alfred's words do not conquer this crowd, who become lairy-loutish-and-loud, pompous-prejudiced-and-proud.

"Do bear up man, for God's sake!" The Labourer cries, with angry-eyes; as he continues on unbowed. "You must think us noodles, what with all this theatrical-poppycock.

"Poison merchant! If you get what you say you want, we'll end up having to speak German. It's un-British! It's unbecoming! You should know your place, you rascal; you should be fighting.

"Tell me, crackpot, what would you do to stop the Hun?"

"What would I do?" Alfred replies as this crowd approach, and encroach, ready to push-punch-and-poach. "I'd refrain from violence, I'd refrain from slander, and I'd be content with my lot. I'd withstand the warmakers, I'd withstand temptation, and I'd be strong-strong-strong. I wouldn't resist evil people. No-no-no! I'd call for a *League Of United Nations* to prevent future wars, I'd call for soldiers to mutiny, and I'd make a stand for good old-fashioned British values.

"Because I'm not un-British or against Great Britain. I'm not here to condemn the British or the Germans. I'm here to save both nations!

"I mean, our government, thanks to *Dora*, won't even allow us to buy a pint after half-past-nine these days. They won't even allow us to buy a pair of binoculars. Not without arresting us for it. Is this the Britain you know-and-love?

"Please! It's not the Britain I know-and-love. It's neither loving-loyal-nor-passionate. No-no-no! It's a phony Britain which is full of hate-hostility-and-horror, it's a fake Britain which is destroying the Britain we love, and it's a nasty Britain which needs to be put back in its place.

"For no blood-offering will wash away our sins, the shedding of German lives won't purge our consciences, and a violent-war won't bring about peace! How could it?

"Please! We must walk uprightly, love mercifully, and do justly.

"Please! We must act peacefully, live in peace, and be the peace we want to see in the world. For blessed are the pure at heart; they shall see a purer world. And blessed are the peacemakers; they shall be called the children of God!"

Alfred's voice is drowned out by these shrieks, these squeaks; and these pro-war songs. These nasty-jibes, vindictive-vibes; and artful-tongues.

So he makes a quick-retreat, down this shaded-street; towards his comrades who are stood by these tracks. Because he recalls the abuses at similar rallies, where soldiers beat women down dingy-alleys; and beat the speakers with an axe. The police had arrested the peacemakers, but not the warmakers; who carried out those nasty-attacks.

"I'm a soldier now," this Fisherman soon yaps. "And verily proud I am too! I'm back off to the front tomorrow, as it happens.

"So I loathe your audacity, but I also love your passion. I loathe your conduct, but I love your actions. And I loathe your beliefs, but I love your courage.

"It makes me right hearty to know there are folk like you who call this place their home. Garn! That's why this country is worth fighting for. Stick it to 'em Alfred! Stick it to 'em my son!"

This is not the first time Alfred has earned support for his stand, from soldiers who have experienced the war first-hand, in many a distant-land.

A Snazzy Soldier once told him; '*Keep the peace-cause churning*'.

A Sneezy Soldier once told him; '*Keep the home fires burning*'.

And a Sassy Soldier once told him; '*Keep your lust for learning*'.

So although today's foray was Alfred's first speech in the name of peace, his offensives begin to increase; as he opposes spite-savagery-and-sins. As he speaks in auditoriums-amphitheatres-and-arenas, markets-meadows-and-marinas; jails-junkyards-and-gyms.

Alfred continues this conversing, whilst Cleo improves her nursing; with skills which improve all the time. But with the warmakers prevailing, her life is not plain-sailing; and so she struggles to stay in line.

"My hands are so awfully small compared to all the suffering around me," she begins to whine. "It does make me sorry. I am doing a good job though, aren't I? I am a good girl, aren't I? Oh my. My giddy-aunt!"

Cleo cries-cusses-and-curses, when she sees that most of her fellow nurses; seem happy to support the war. They fix the soldiers who fill every bed, so they can return to war and kill people dead; whilst civilians are left on the floor.

But Cleo is determined to help the people who need her the most, so she withstands the pressure to desert her post; on these posters which are glued to that granite. Which plead *'Carry our soldiers back into the light'*, depict crucified nurses shouting *'Fight'*; and call nurses *'The Best Mums On The Planet'*.

And so she turns to the Suffragist in search of clarity, and finds this politico at work with the charity; which she opened at the end of last year. Her charity now runs a cost-price restaurant to feed the famished, and a factory to employ the banished; whom it offers a new career. And it has just converted *'The Gunmaker's Arms'* pub, into *'The Mother's Arms'* maternity-hub; which is due to open here.

"Say, it's wrong for our nurses to treat soldiers," she agrees, as she scratches her knees; and her ear. "Whilst one-in-eight babies are dying in infancy.

"In the time it took seventy-five-thousand soldiers to die in France last year, a hundred-thousand children died here in Britain. So it's clear to see that we need our nurses here. We need to get our priorities straight!

"Children are our future, and love-and-freedom is vital to every child. But our children are being left unloved, whilst our nurses support a war which is crushing our freedom. We need to stay on message, despite this politics of fear, and save them all."

Cleo agrees and so she leaves her job and walks through this snow, before she helps the Suffragist run the show; here in this maternity-ward. Where she offers words of peace-purity-and-prayer, gives comfort-compassion-and-care; and finds new nurses to bring on board.

This surgery soon becomes a headquarters for campaigning, a recruitment-office which is full of talking-teaching-and-training; feminist-stories and pro-peace tales. A place from which to march for *'Equal pay for equal work'*, convince patients that wars are berserk; and promote *'Votes for females'*.

"Oh darling child, the latest peace-conference was just fantastic," the Suffragist says, with her eyes ablaze, after she travelled to Europe without further delays. "One felt privileged to unite with so many peacemakers, who are now going cap-in-hand to leaders all across the continent.

"I even met some German peacemakers. There are thousands of them! German syndicalists are evading service, German Christians are going to prison for their beliefs, and German intellectuals are being taken to asylums. But they're not fighting, they're not killing, and they're not going to war! So we're not alone! There's been a paradigm shift; people in every single European country are sick to the back teeth of war, and they're demanding a better future."

People in this country are demanding peace all the time, because young-men are still dying before their prime; each morning and each afternoon. As Germany finds new countries to march on through, and Bulgaria commits her children too; whilst the British kill in the Falklands and kill in Cameroon.

And with the death-toll at war persisting, whilst the peacemakers discourage the public from enlisting; the government goes in search of new draftees. They allow older-men to fight in their disputes, and reduce the minimum-height for new recruits; as they search over land and search over seas.

The warmakers' fight-back takes to the street, where it sows weeds amongst Alfred's wheat; whilst newspapers corrupt his sermons. Whilst Barbers refuse to cut his hair, Butchers swear; and Gossips say he has impregnated Germans.

But Alfred has the strength to carry on, because he is sure-sturdy-and-strong; and incredibly resolute. So he ignores the warmakers' threats, and faces rejection without regrets; or any sort of dispute.

"You cannot have two masters," he starts to hoot. "Please understand! You cannot love both war-and-peace. Those who oppose war do so because they love peace, and those who support war do so because they hate peace."

"We must not eat German flesh or drink German blood," he tells the people on this seating, at this *UDC* meeting, where there is no sort of heating. "For like different rooms which all share the same roof, the Germans-and-Brits may have different nationalities, but we all share the same humanity!"

"Fight and you'll become the servant of war!" He starts repeating.

"Kill and you'll become the servant of death! Sin and you'll become the servant of evil!

"So don't be afraid of war, or rumours of war. Don't be afraid of nation rising against nation, or kingdom rising against kingdom. And don't be led by false-prophets. Resist the warmakers' temptations, and save your soul. I'd be ever so grateful. I'd be very much obliged."

This is a dangerous feat, because most of his forays end in defeat; slander-suffering-and-stress. Whilst *Dora* prohibits bonfires, out in the shires; and censors the mainstream-press. Which does not report on the peacemakers' gains, the soldiers' pains; or warfare's bloody-mess.

But returning-soldiers have started to speak their mind, so the public is no longer blind; it is aware of trench-foot and trench-fever. It is aware of the slug-infested bogs which soldiers call home, the corpses which are left to rot alone; and the smell which is a constant feature.

The smell of rotten-cadavers covered in poppies, unwashed-bodies; and overflowing-loos. The smell of poisonous-gas which makes men choke, gritty-smoke; and sour-ooze.

Peacemakers spread the truth across this land, as they pass journals from hand-to-hand; in total silence. Whilst the *UDC* host meetings in many locations, shops-stores-and-stations; which all oppose the violence.

But the jingoistic-cranks at the *National Service League*, fight back against the war-fatigue; and call for conscription again. They disrupt pro-peace meetings, with vicious-beatings; which are full of vicious-pain.

The Philosopher King is banned from movement, for '*Prejudicing military recruitment*'; as he tries to spread the good-word. And people who hide deserters, get called '*Traitors*'; '*Agents*'-'*Apostates*'-and-'*Absurd*'.

So as Alfred wears this jacket and the Suffragist wears that dress, on their way to the *Labour Printing Press*; they know they cannot afford to fail. They know that if they are caught with pro-peace composition, to use as ammunition; they will get locked inside a jail.

A parliamentary-statement has gained notoriety, after a politician said '*The UDC dupes society*'; by making false-accusations. And a peacemaker was imprisoned last week, but refused to speak; or reveal these presses' locations.

So Alfred and the Suffragist are filled with ill-ease as they enter this underground-den, where this silence deafens them; and fuels their fears. Because these pressers do not press, these printers do not progress; and these machines do not pass through their gears. There are no noisy-bumps, noisy-pumps; noisy-jeers or noisy-cheers.

Alfred and the Suffragist sneak in on the tips of their toes, and spy on these figures who are dressed in plain-clothes; behind that scrambled-metal. Behind these threads which dangle, and these frames which jangle; where Alfred squats down to settle.

"I'll be hanged! Damn peacenik-niks," a Crabby Censor says in fine-fettle.

This man has purple-blots, scars-scratches-and-spots; all over his moon-shaped face. He touches this ink-scraper, and this paper; which flutters around this place.

"Damn peaceniks no more!" This Cranky Censor replies, whilst he rolls his eyes; with very little grace. "Oi-oi! We've 'it the jackpot 'ere! We'll close this cesspool down, flush those gutter-rat peace-cranks into the open, and catch 'em all."

Alfred and the Suffragist scuttle around this wheel, which is made of steel; and then hide with trepidation. Whilst the Crabby Censor gathers evidence for a prosecution, stirs this solution; and mutters *peacenik-niks* without cessation. He touches this can of ink, and this rusty-sink; without noticing Alfred's location.

The Cranky Censor calls him over which fills Alfred with relief, before these two shining-eyes fill Alfred with grief; and make Alfred jump out of his skin. Alfred fills with fright, and turns white; with his head in a dizzy-spin.

Because he sees this old Typesetter, who is wearing this patterned-sweater; and is bound by this long white-string. He looks red-ruddy-and-raw, with a ball jammed into his jaw; and his knees jammed into his chin.

"Let's get this filth out of here," the Crabby Censor says with distress, near the *Labour Leaders* which are still in this press; and near that rubbish-bin. "We'll destroy it ourselves rather than go through the courts. I'll be hanged if I'm going to let some lame-duck magistrate deal with these peacenik-niks. Not after all the lengths we've gone to!"

"Oi-oi! Sounds like a plan to me," the Cranky Censor replies, whilst he rolls his eyes, and rubs his inky-thighs. "Grab 'em invoices first; we'll catch a few gutter-rats with those. And I'll call for some 'elp with this machinery; we'd be 'ere all week trying to break it up ourselves."

And so with their backs held bent at five-degrees, with bent-elbows and bent-knees; these censors ascend those stairs. Whilst Alfred and the Suffragist undo each fetter, to untie this Typesetter; behind a pile of chairs.

But the censors soon return with stomping-feet which tap, swishing-hands which clap; and swaying-legs which twist-tramp-and-turn. Alfred waits for them to disappear before he repeats this process, and makes slow-progress; which stops each time the censors return.

These three peacemakers begin to flee, once the Typesetter is free; with the ball removed from his mouth. They flee past these soap-dispensers, away from these censors; up these stairs and towards the south.

"Oi gutter-rats! Oi-oi!" The Cranky Censor shouts as he gives chase, with feet which race, and shoot him across this space.

"You go-go-go that way, we'll go this," Alfred tells the Suffragist, as he tries to assist; with the Typesetter's slow-pace.

So the Suffragist leads the Cranky Censor in that direction, beyond that busy-intersection; and beyond that busy summer-fete. The Typesetter hides in this alley, whilst Alfred leads the Crabby Censor into this valley; and into this council-estate.

"I'll be hanged if you think you're getting away from me, you damn peacenik-nik!" He begins to bark, as he chases Alfred through this park; and through this open-gate. "Damn peacenik-nik! Peacenik-nik!"

Alfred zigzags between these flowers-foxgloves-and-thickets, zooms past these centipedes-cockroaches-and-crickets; and enters this travelling-fair. He passes this mishmash of tents which host vaudeville-shows, these Belgian Boxers who exchange their blows; and this Clown with rainbow-hair.

Until the howls of 'Peacenik-niks' become delayed, and fade, when Alfred sees the Suffragist sat down in the shade.

"We have another printer," she says, sounding unmoved-untroubled-and-unswayed. "We can still get the truth out there. Yes we can! No matter how many presses they capture, we can always call on our reservists. Yes we can! We're as small as David, but we can beat this Goliath of a government. Yes we can! We can ensure that the sound of peace is heard!"

With a ring on her finger and a bangle on her wrist, the Suffragist; is completely right. The *Labour Leader* is not delayed, and reports on the raid; from which they just took flight.

"Oh darling child," she continues with fright. "We came mighty close to getting captured by those rotters, so to speak. At the end of the day, we're walking a thin-line now. We should be more careful, because our big-ideas won't do us any good in prison."

"So what if we go to jail?" Alfred replies, as he takes in these sunny-skies; aware of the risks he is taking. He expects to be arrested, for the way he has protested; and for the speeches he has been making.

"Please! They can lock me up and throw away the key; they'll never cage my resolve! Not whilst folk are dying as a result of our wars, concentration-camps and blockades. Not whilst our government, thanks to *Dora*, won't even let us melt down our own gold, or feed wild-animals. Not without arresting us for it."

"You're either brave or stupid!" The Suffragist replies.

"A bit of both," Alfred cries. "A bit of both-both-both!"

But Alfred does listen to the Suffragist's advice, he keeps his speeches concise; he does not scream-screech-or-shout. He spends months at home, on his own; before the *NCF* entice him out.

The *No Conscription Fellowship* was born after an appeal in the *Labour Leader*, inspired many a subscriber and many a reader; to write in the very next day. Those peacemakers took their chances, and established a national network of branches; with a head-office which is painted grey.

'Refuse to bear arms, because all human-life is sacred', they say.

In just a few months this illegal-organisation, has grown with acceleration; to oppose the government's brutality. To oppose conscription and support free will, to oppose the *'Military Service Bill'*; and support neutrality.

The *NCF* promotes its pro-peace positions, pickets prisons; and unites the peacemakers. It produces pro-peace petitions, presses politicians; and gives flyers to any takers.

'National service must not be degraded into national slavery', it says in their papers. *'Freedom of conscience must not be sacrificed to military necessity, nor British liberty to political expedience. Men's deepest convictions must not be swept aside!'*

This flyer encourages Alfred and his comrades to walk down these narrow-streets and narrow-alleys, past these traffic-jams and car-rallies; towards the *NCF*'s first ever national convention. It encourages them to walk past this market which only sells meat, this green-square which is full of green-peat; and this lawyers'-chamber which is full of legal-tension.

They walk past this funeral home, this nursing home; and this stock exchange. This eating house, public house; and rifle range.

This bicycle shop, curiosity shop; and whitewashed-drapery. This pork shop, hat shop; and rustic-bakery.

They walk past this Librarian, this Belgian and this Bulgarian; before they arrive at *The Nonconformist's Hall*. Where they see the Suffragist disguised as a maid, with her hair in a braid; in a scarf and in a shawl.

This building's tower pierces the sky, with four rows of windows which rise up high; and a row of statues which can be seen for miles. Inside these whitewashed-walls, a multitude of people fill these stalls; they sit on these seats and stand in these aisles. These Artisans are individualists at their core, and these Socialists hog this floor; with yellow-folders and yellow-files. Whilst these Liberals and these Tories, tell funny-jokes and funny-stories; with funny-winks and funny-smiles. And these Russellites, Methodists-Marcionists-and-Mennonites; lean against these tiles. Wearing different suits, boots; and hairstyles.

There are memorable-sentiments and memorable-quotes, peaceful-speeches and peaceful-votes; as these peacemakers all unite. As this Foreman calls for wars to cease, and that Teamster calls for peace; with delirium-devotion-and-delight.

In order not to incite the mob which waits outside, this crowd does not clap-cheer-or-chide; or make any sort of sound. But this handkerchief-swirling, and this handkerchief-whirling; definitely do abound.

These handkerchiefs are waved when the Philosopher King talks about his missions, his petitions, and his talks with politicians.

"Inspired by faith and freed from the dominion of fear, you'll be unconquerable," he says without suspicions. "Because war does not determine who is right, only who is left!

"So with love in our hearts and knowledge in our heads, we must put an end to war-and-conscription forever. Because if we don't, they will put an end to us!"

These handkerchiefs are waved at this well respected, and well connected; engine of the *NCF* machine. This suffragist Organiser who talks about the peacemakers, and the Quakers; who she has personally seen.

And these handkerchiefs are twirled, and they are swirled; at this fresh-faced Chairman. This boy who has just left university, who calls for diversity; as he introduces each sermon.

But before another word is spoken, this silence is broken; by these Sailors who crash through that window. They crash into these pews, and into those Jews; which creates a noisy-crescendo.

The undercover policemen who are here to spy on this conference, and the peacemakers who are here to follow their conscience; all begin to stare. Their feet all shuffle, their papers all rustle; and their eyes all begin to glare.

Before this Pensioner scuttles across the floor, and pacifies these men of war; by giving them some sugary-teas. She sits them down, without a frown; and pats their uniformed-knees.

"We believe in serving our nation," the Chairman shouts into this breeze. "But service can come in many forms.

"We consider our opposition to conscription to be a service. A service for life, for liberty, and for the divinity in every human-being. It's a service which we're performing in the name of Great Britain!"

The Chairman finishes before Alfred walks forward to speak, he passes the strong and he passes the weak; whilst his heart begins to beat. He begins his sermon from up on this mount, whilst his Disciples move in to hear his account; and sit down by his hairy-feet.

"Please!" He begins to tweet. "Mourn every soldier who is struck down in battle, whatever their side; you'll be comforted.

"Please be merciful; you'll receive mercy.

"Please be pure in your heart; you'll see a purer world.

"Please be a peacemaker; you'll attain peace.

"Be persecuted for your beliefs; you'll find release.

"Be insulted, be oppressed, be libelled, and rejoice! Be glad! For tough is the road to peace, and you're walking it well.

"You're the light of the world! So go out onto the streets and illuminate your countrymen. Help them to fulfil the law of nature, let them know that murder is wrong, but don't judge those who kill.

"And if conscription is enforced, and you're struck into prison for one year for refusing to fight, do not be hostile. Act with joy amongst the spiteful. Turn your mouth to the judge and tell him that you'd be happy to be imprisoned for two years!

"Love the judge who imprisons you, kiss the soldier who curses you, and pray for the white-feather lady who persecutes you. They're your brothers-and-sisters too. Yes thanky-you!

"So don't gloat about the good which you do; it's enough that you do good. Act in secret, act at night, and act in disguise. The consequences of your actions will be felt by all.

"Please! Be happy in your resistance to the warmakers who force you into their army, force you into their uniform, and force their muskets into your palms. Please-please-please! Their spoils of war will rust and become moth-eaten. Thieves will break-and-steal them.

"For whilst princes-politicians-and-priests may have claimed to have fought holy-wars in the name of the Lord, this is false. Please! Please-please-please! The warmaker is a false prophet; a ferocious-wolf who masquerades in the sheep's clothing of white-feathers, celebrations and propaganda. But his is a bad-tree that can only bear bad-fruit; bullets-and-bombs, gas-and-grenades, cannons-and-cavalry. Yes thanky-you! Only good-trees can bear good-fruit, and only the tree of peace can bring forth peace.

"So don't follow the soldier. Great-and-broad is his road, but it leads to death-and-destruction. Walk your narrow path of peace and, like a bird flying through the sky, you'll find life-and-light. You'll be grateful. You'll be very much obliged.

"You won't need to worry about what you have to eat-or-drink, what you have to wear, or about your health. Please! The soldiers fight for these things. But you'll act with love, and you'll find a far greater reward. You'll find peace. Peace-peace-peace! And it'll fill your soul with light.

"So look around at all the people in this room. These people are your brethren. Ask each other for strength, and you shall receive it. Seek each other, and you shall find allies across this land. Knock, and doors will open for you. Because there are more of us than you can ever imagine, we're a massive-family, and we're growing all the time.

"We're the gravy to this nation's mashed-potatoes! We're a whole bucket of awesome! We're simply the best! We're better than all the rest! We're better than anyone I've ever met!

"And so I say this! The warmakers have built their British Empire on a foundation of sand; rains will descend upon it, floods will rise, and winds will blow it away. But we're building on the rock of peace; a strong-foundation which is capable of withstanding rains-floods-and-winds. We can't be washed away, we won't be blown over, and we'll never be beaten down! No-no-no. No-thanky-you! Thank-you, thank-you, thank-you!"

This room floods with a sea of handkerchiefs, before these Speakers share their beliefs; as soon as they are all called. Even the Sailors, dressed in uniforms which were made by tailors; seem to be enthralled.

The Chairman reads from a page of his scribbled-notes, and leads this series of votes; which close this pro-peace meeting. This crowd vote to send flyers to a million addresses, and fundraise for new presses; before they vacate this wooden-seating. But Alfred soon feels out of sorts, when he reads the false-reports; which say there was a vicious-beating.

'Brave sailors, who infiltrated the hall, were beaten back by a hoard of so called pacifists', the mainstream-papers write.

"Our government," Alfred mutters with spite. "Thanks to *Dora*, won't even let you ring a church-bell these days. Not without arresting you for it. What have they done to the country I love?"

They have acted in disguise, to spread their lies; and destroy every piece of the truth. They are taking control, swallowing peacemakers whole; as they begin to conscript the youth...

THE BOY

Once upon a time there was a Boy. An honest Boy, with oneness-and-serenity which made him sure.

Boy embraced every tree-animal-and-bird in his forest. He embraced Fir who was the tallest tree, Eagle who was the strongest bird, and Cow who was the holiest animal.

And Boy used his oneness to embrace his forest, because oneness is peace, and Boy used his peace to become one with his fellow creatures.

Dog, meanwhile, was still full of love-loyalty-and-passion. But she was no longer loving enough to fall for the trees, loyal enough to visit the animals, or passionate enough to sing with the birds.

"I loved Owl so much," she told Boy. "But I've been sad ever since he died. Why, when I am full of love-loyalty-and-passion, do I still have to suffer?"

Boy looked at Dog and smiled.

"Come with me," he said, before he took Dog to see Fir.

"Hello Fir," Boy said to that knowledgeable tree. "You must see many things from up there in the sky. Please tell me, can you see love?"

"Oh yes," Fir replied. "I see Fox, the hunter who loves meat so much, that he kills other animals whenever he is hungry. And I see Bee, the florist who loves flowers so much, that she tears them from the earth."

Boy looked at Dog and smiled.

"Come with me," he said, before he took Dog to see Eagle.

"Hello Eagle," Boy said to that powerful bird. "You must see many things from your throne. Please tell me, can you see loyalty?"

"Oh yes," Eagle replied. "I see Army Ant, the soldier who's so loyal to his nation, that he creates wars to glorify it. And I see Shrew, the lawmaker who's so loyal to her laws, that she punishes anyone who breaks them."

Boy looked at Dog and smiled.

"Come with me," he said, before he took Dog to see Cow.

"Hello Cow," Boy said to that holy animal. "You must see many things inside your temple. Please tell me, can you see passion?"

"Oh yes," Cow replied. "I see Jay, the lover with so much passion for his wife, that he'd kill her if she ever betrayed him. And I see Praying

Mantis, the devotee with so much passion for God, that she'd be happy to die in his name."

Dog saw that love-loyalty-and-passion could all lead to suffering.

"I've tried to be kind," she said. "But when I see other creatures in pain it hurts me, their distress makes me stressed, and their tears make me cry. Is there anything greater than love?"

"Oneness-serenity-and-peace," Boy replied. "Because oneness can supersede love, serenity can supersede loyalty, and peace can supersede passion."

1916

The *UDC*'s pro-peace troops, and the *NCF*'s pro-peace groups; have embarked on a crusade as valiant as any before. With fewer resources than their state-sponsored foes, they have cushioned the blows; and reduced enlistment for war.

But Britain's leaders-lawyers-and-lawmakers, have allied with the warmakers; who have started to strike back. With control over power-property-and-publications, in many locations; they do not plan to backtrack.

They write a pro-war prescription, and introduce military-conscription; by passing the *Military Service Act* into law. Which compels the innocent, and the dissident; to fight in their vicious-war.

The year is 1916.

A Russian Communist is writing a book which calls for income-distribution to be more fair, an American Oil Baron is becoming the first ever US-dollar billionaire; and a Swedish Engineer is patenting a device to tune in radios too. In Ireland a city is being submerged beneath the insurgents' flames, in Germany they are cancelling this year's Olympic Games; and in America they are opening their first ever birth-control venue. Whilst the British win control over Qatar, to expand their empire near-and-far; without any need for a coup.

Alfred follows this and he follows the *National Service League*'s pro-conscription orations, which used to be met with denunciations; and a flurry of libertarian-tirades. For whilst the *National Service League* has added drill to the school-syllabus, without much fuss; they have failed with five pro-conscription bills in the last two decades.

This is because compulsory military service, the very thought of which makes Alfred feel nervous; has never been considered appropriate in Britain before. Although it has become a rite of passage for boys, in countries without Britain's poise; even in times without war.

But as the peacemakers get out of hand, the warmakers feel that they need to make a stand; before the flow of new recruits gets too slow. The Lord Of War has promised France seventy new divisions, and cannot get them without legal-revisions; so his despair begins to show.

"This war cannot be won if we insist on clinging to old-fashioned civil liberties," he says sounding strong, wrong; and gung-ho. "A thousand times no!

"We must force unskilled-workers to enter the fray, so that skilled-labourers can return from the front to produce munitions. These are desperate times, and desperate times call for desperate measures!"

The Lancastrian says that the Lord of War '*Acts without reason*', and accuses him of '*Treason*'; which earns him support in the press. Before two-million workers make a stand for free-will, and vote against the bill; with support from the *Trade Union Congress*.

They do not get their way, but they do have a say; and earn exemptions for police-inspectors. They earn exemptions for family-men, the bedridden; and '*Conscientious Objectors*'.

Which means Alfred could claim an exemption on moral-grounds, but scepticism abounds; with regards this classification. So peacemakers hide away, self-harm each day; and flee from this British nation.

"What will you do?" Cleo asks with exasperation. "I don't mean to push. Oh, I am sorry, but I do worry about you sometimes."

With this smell of herbs-housework-and-hair, Cleo sits down on this chair, and chops this conference-pear.

"Please! I'll face the fire," Alfred replies with flair. "You once said, '*I'm prepared to face the bullets for this cause. I'm prepared to serve my class-and-caste, gender-and-generation, with quintessentially British resistance*'.

"Well now it's my turn to face those bullets. Please understand! Conscription, along with the gagging of the press, is leading us towards totalitarianism. I mean, our government, thanks to *Dora*, won't even allow us to fly a kite these days. Not without arresting us for it. And now they want to stop us from choosing where we work. Our freedoms are disappearing as we speak.

"Well I'm going to combat this despotism from within. It's the greatest threat our nation faces, and I'm ready to go toe-to-toe with it.

"The *NCF* has trained me for my tribunal, my resolve is strong-strong-strong, and I'm up for the fight. Yes-yes-yes! We will win our war-on-war!"

"Is there anything I can do to help?" Cleo asks as she makes some piccalilli, near this water-lily, and this bowl of vegetable-chilli. "Oh, I am so sorry I haven't done more already. Do tell me what the *NCF* told you?"

"They told me what questions to expect, and how to answer them. They told me how to stand, how to speak, and how to behave.

"They're doing a grand job. Simply smashing! Being awesome is hard, but they're managing it. They've got so many peacemakers to help, and so little time to help them. But they're doing it! Yes they are!"

They help peacemakers to prepare for their trials, with bulging-hearts and bulging-smiles; each morning and each afternoon. And they help Alfred to prepare his defence, before he waits for his trial to commence; here in the town hall's main-room.

This place is still full of sloping-brickwork, rambling-turrets which seem to smirk; and merlons like those on a castle. With gothic-lines above purple-paint, wooden-panels with a varnished-taint; and curtains which each have a tassel.

A couple of chubby Lamplighters, and a couple of skinny Firefighters; sit together down there in the stalls. They face that stage, where seven men are earning a wage; for enforcing their country's new rules.

The Retired Captain has been sent by a War Office decree, with orders to launch a recruiting spree; and ensnare each potential recruit. He acts as judge-jurisprudent-and-jury, with fever-frenzy-and-fury; dressed up in his khaki-suit.

With a jacket which is full of dark-thread, and a beard which is a dark shade of red; the Councillor is also onstage. But he lacks his colleague's height, spite; and rage.

This Mayor with brown-hair, spurts insults without a care; wearing a robe with a fake-fur trim. Whilst this Don sits stony faced, and straight laced; without ever saying a thing.

Here to represent the working classes, this Trade Unionist wears this pair of red-glasses; and this shiny red-coat. This Gentleman Farmer who is rather smelly, has a rather substantial belly; and a habit of clearing his throat. Whilst this Banker who wears a shirt made of flannel, completes this panel; and looks like a billy-goat.

Sat in front of these Waiters-Watchmakers-and-Welders, this

motley-mix of assorted elders; follow a fairly predictable-routine. They dismiss lawyers who try to earn a shilling, and they separate the unable from the unwilling; like a well-oiled machine.

They rush through this Draper with a giant-nose, this Haberdasher with brand new clothes; and this Gardener whose scabs are covered in gauze. They rush through this youthful Scamp, this dirty Tramp; and these Butlers with protruding-jaws.

Alfred particularly enjoys watching these Christians, ardent followers of their religions; who all fill him with a sense of awe. Such as this red-faced Charity Worker, who the Mayor calls a *'Moral shirker'*; when he repeats his favourite law.

"What's your name?" The Retired Captain asks with joy in his voice, as if to rejoice; before he starts to guffaw.

"Thou shalt not kill!" The Charity Worker always replies, with narrow-eyes; and a narrow-jaw.

"Right-o! How old are you?"

"Thou shalt not kill!"

"Jolly-o! What's your defence?"

"Thou shall not kill!"

"You belong in the loony-bin!" The Mayor adds his insult.

"Thou shalt not kill!" The Charity Worker says as a result.

"What does a judge tell someone who's been found guilty of murder?" The Banker wonders.

"Thou shalt not kill!" The Charity Worker thunders.

The Retired Captain fills his pipe with fresh-molasses, and adjusts his crooked-glasses; before he repeats his only decree. Because even though tribunals have the seniority, and the authority; to set these defendants free. They have only ever given acquittals to brewers, wrongdoers; and a hunt based near the sea.

"Let's not mince matters," the Retired Captain always repeats with glee. "We've bestowed you with the privilege of speaking here today, and listened patiently to the whimsical ribaldry which you've had the gall to dish up. 'Tis clear that you've got no case whatsoever, and so you'll join the *Non Combatant Corps* forthwith. For your country! For your country! Cheerio."

The Retired Captain sucks on his ivory-pipe, gives his glasses a wipe;

and bangs his heavy-gavel. Before he continues with his questions, and his pro-war suggestions; as these trials all unravel.

"Jesus would support this war and you know it. You can count on it! Sure-o!" He says as this Christadelphian takes the stand.

"Christ in khaki?" The Christadelphian shoots back, on the counterattack; whilst he waves his podgy-hand. "Our Lord in France, thrusting his bayonet into the children of God? The Messiah with a machine-gun, ambushing a column of German infantry, and mowing them down in their helplessness? Jesus in a cavalry charge; cutting, hacking, thrusting, crushing, cheering? No! No! No! It'd never happen and *you* know it!"

Alfred cheers out loud, as does this crowd; which supports the next Christian in line. This Metalsmith who has wrinkled-skin, a topsy-turvy chin; and a topsy-turvy spine.

"If the Boche invaded your town," the Retired Captain asks in this jovial-whine. "And if they raped all the women there, wouldn't you consider it your duty to stand up to them? Strong-o!"

"Let me quote Romans twelve," the Metalsmith replies. "It tells us not to take revenge or succumb to wrath, because the Lord will avenge us. It tells us that if the Germans invade our towns, we should overcome their evil with good."

"Frowzy cad," the Mayor mutters. "This man may know his bible, but he only knows it narrowly. This jumping-jesus knows nothing about the real world. This juggins is a muddled-imbecile! An apish-buffoon! A crazy hoot-owl!"

"At all events, academic anarchism aside," the Retired Captain resumes. "Do you seriously think you could stop Hindenburg from bayoneting your dear mother, simply by giving him a cup of tea? Hot-o!"

"Perhaps not," the Metalsmith says. "But I wouldn't be able to protect her if you send me to France either, would I? And even if I could, there still wouldn't be any reason to hurt a fellow human-being.

"Because, as Matthew ten tells us, force may save our earthly-life, but love will save our soul. If I protected my mother down here on earth, I'd be able to hold her in my blood-soaked arms for now. But if the Germans were to kill her, she'd find peace in the arms of God forevermore.

"Matthew ten tells us to flee from persecution, not to fight it, and that's exactly what I plan to do."

The Retired Captain scratches his bushy-beard, because he is flatfooted by an opinion which he finds so weird; crazy-cuckoo-and-creepy. And he takes a different approach with this smoker, this Insurance Broker; who is wiry-waxy-and-weepy.

"Revelations nineteen does encourage a little judicious-severity," he says in a voice which is slightly creaky. "It tells us that God himself wages war; leading the armies of heaven, dripping with human-blood, to strike down evil-nations. The Lord, I tell ye, is a man of war. True-o!"

"He may very well be," the Insurance Broker replies. "He may make as many wars as he likes, but that doesn't mean we humans should."

"By hook or by crook, the bible does tell us humans to take an eye for an eye! Revenge-o!"

"The old-testament tells us to take an 'eye for an eye', but Jesus tells us to turn the other cheek; that an 'eye for an eye' makes the whole world blind, that you can't put out a fire by adding fuel to the flames, and you can't fight your way to peace."

"Well, I'm damned! What a funny thing. Ha-ha-ha! Such comfortable middle-class sentimentality. Right-o! But you must admit that the new testament does tell us to serve the state; to render unto Caesar everything which is his."

"That's also true," the Insurance Broker agrees. "But so few things are Caesar's; just the coins he mints, the palaces he builds, and the land he seizes. My life belongs to God; neither Caesar nor the state has any right to it."

"Profanity! Profanity! Profanity! You've turned the bible on its head," the Mayor begins to call, as he stands up tall, whilst the Don stares ahead at the opposite wall. "God is British to the bone, and every fellow here knows it. You can't exploit him to save yourself, you blaspheming cadaverous-prig; you disgusting shambles of porcelain-skin, unwholesome-fat and puny-bones. Your blatant disregard for God's word shan't earn you any favours here!"

"That's five minutes. Let's wrap this up. Chop-chop!" The Gentleman Farmer blurts impatiently, and shamelessly, whilst he clears his throat outrageously. '*Ahem. Harrumph. Cough-cough*'.

The Retired Captain continues to smoke, and begins to choke; before he empties his mermaid-shaped pipe. Before he looks at this potential-conscript, and reads from his script; whilst he gives his glasses a wipe.

"Let's not mince matters," he says with a joyous sort of hype. "We've bestowed you with the privilege of speaking here today, and listened patiently to the whimsical ribaldry which you've had the gall to dish up. 'Tis clear that you've got no case whatsoever, and so you'll join the *Non Combatant Corps* forthwith. For your country! For your country! Cheerio."

But most defendants do not have the Insurance Broker's eloquence, his intelligence, or his sense.

Alfred watches these peacemakers, approach the lawmakers; like pupils who have been sent to their headmaster. What they lack for in poise, they make up for with noise; as they speaker louder and as they speak faster. Uneducated-unprepared-and-unrepresented, they are discontented; as they march towards disaster.

Until this Docker who wears a hearing-aid, runs like a soldier who is on a military-raid; looking delirious-demented-and-deranged. He is mad at the Mayor who has just called him a '*Refusenik*', a '*Lily-livered tulip*'; and '*Short changed*'.

And so he slams his palm on the panel's bench, ignores the Gentleman Farmer's suilline-stench; and knocks over this three-legged chair. He removes this knife from his pocket, and launches it like a rocket; which flies through this stuffy-air. He stabs his own hand, and pins himself to this stand; before he begins to swear.

"Jizz! Sperm! Spunk!" He yells whilst blood pours over his knuckles, the Banker chuckles; and the Don continues to stare. "I'm no coward; I'm happy to suffer. See! I'd even be happy to sweep for mines. But there aren't any causes which I'd ever kill for. Not one! Never! No way!"

After a brief adjournment to unpin the Docker, Alfred watches this Moral Objector walk past that locker; after his medical records are torn into bits. Before he watches this Independent Objector with skinny-fingers, and a cologne which lingers; who slobbers-salivates-and-spits.

"I done got no defence against the letter of your here law," he admits. "Me comes only in the spirit of peace. I done volunteered in a temperance café, to help refugees in the Balkans, and to house the homeless. But I'll never go volunteer for you!"

"It's only because of a twist of fate that I'm British," a billowy Pharmacist says, with eyes which are ablaze, as they glare-grimace-and-gaze. "If I'd been born in Germany, I'd be refusing to fight for the Germans too.

"But you, who put your country first, would be conscripting people to fight against us, if you'd been born over there. You're just a bunch of hypocrites!"

'*Peckerhead! Slummock! Gundygut! You ought to be shot! You ought to be hung! You ought to be put across my knee and spanked*', the Mayor tells the Moral Objector with bitter scorn.

'*You're muddled! Criminally muddled!*' he tells the Independent Objector whilst he blows like a horn. '*The only way you'll get a discharge is by dying. There's no such thing as a conscience*'.

'*Confound your fooling!*' He tells the Pharmacist who looks forlorn. '*You ninnyhammer! You noddypole! Go create a potion for your cowardice*'.

This Youngster is told; '*You're too young to have a conscience*'.

This Atheist is told; '*We can't give your opinions credence*'.

And this Socialist is told; '*Stop your blasted impedance*'.

"That's five minutes," the Gentleman Farmer interrupts them all, whilst this Child bounces a ball, and the Don stares ahead at the opposite wall. "*Ahem. Harrumph. Cough-cough.* Let's wrap this up. Chop-chop!"

Before these Businessmen seek exemptions to continue their careers, and these Brewers seek exemptions to make more beers; whilst they act like frauds-forgers-and-fakers. But since they are unconcerned with airing their views, these slackers in shiny-shoes; seem more astute than all the peacemakers.

This Pauper who is frail and this Peasant who is thin, with scratches on his tongue and scratches on his skin; both lie about their age. This stubbly Transvestite in a floral-dress, pretends to be a female without much success; as he prances across the stage. Before this talkative Bore, takes to the floor; and feigns a broken-ribcage.

The panel dismisses this Elderly Man who will suffer without his son at home, and this Cripple with a bent-backbone; who they all call '*weak*'. They dismiss this Collier who looks demure, and this Farmhand who smells of manure; before he can even speak.

"Don't you ever wash yourself?" The Mayor begins to shriek. "You don't look like you do. You fopdoodle! You humgruffin! You milksop! Yours' is a case of an unhealthy-mind in an unwholesome-body. Off to war with you!"

"You shall join the *Non Combatant Corps* forthwith," the Retired Captain agrees. "For your country! For your country! Cheerio."

The panel scurries off to eat some lunch, which leaves Alfred with some thoughts to crunch; as he wanders down these streets. A prisoner of war whose prospects are thin, he prepares to face the army which has captured him; and want him to march to their beats.

When he returns he sees Cleo holding these telegrams, and this sack of fresh-yams; which she recently stole. For Cleo still steals cots-cabbages-and-carrots, pots-pens-and-parrots; cocoa-cream-and-coal.

"These telegrams came for you," she says as she drops this stolen-bowl. "From people who couldn't be here in person. Oh, I am sorry they couldn't be here in person. I am a good girl though, aren't I?"

"The best! You're simply smashing!" Alfred replies.

Before he looks around this hall where he sees the birds he once freed, during his first good-deed; who all begin to sing. He sees the cat he re-housed, who is unaroused; as she purrs away like a king.

He sees the Orphans who are sitting on the balcony, where they have been full of giggles-gladness-and-glee; ever since they all turned up. He sees the Fishermen he saved from a storm, who seem witty-whimsical-and-warm; near the Mute Boy who is holding a cup.

The Groom who Alfred provided wine for, sits near this open door; and near this Rheumatic who no longer has a fever. Near the Paralytic who sits in her new wheelchair, and the Fishmonger who sits over there; near that chirpy Cotton Weaver.

The Children who Alfred gives presents to, are sat on this pew; wearing a mix of golds-greys-and-greens. They chat with Alfred's Customers, these Costumers; and this group of skinny Deans.

The Disciples who Alfred has preached to on the streets, squeeze into the good-seats; next to this Nun who starts to pray. Next to the

Deserter who looks upbeat, and the Suffragist who looks sweet; disguised by a floral-bouquet.

They chant for Alfred's release, they chant for peace; and they chant with devotion. They create this symbol-smashing, drum-bashing, guitar-thrashing; commotion.

Which causes the Gentleman Farmer to sway, before his shiny-toupee; falls from his shiny-head. He coughs-convulses-and-chokes, cries-cackles-and-croaks; which makes him turn dark-red.

'*Ahem. Harrumph. Cough-cough.*'

Those Orphans stamp their feet on the floor, and the panel guffaw; whilst Alfred takes the stand. But the Don does not move at all, he just stares at a wall; whilst the Mayor just waves his hand.

"On the basis of what beef-witted scruples are you claiming exemption, my son? What one of our lily-livered government's two-cent rules are you here to abuse?" The Retired Captain pries.

"I'm claiming exemption on the basis that I have a conscience," Alfred replies. "Which makes me a conscientious objector. Yes-yes-yes!"

"Right-o. Are you a *Political Objector* or a *Religious Objector*?"

"I've sympathy for all those chaps. Yes thanky-you. I think they're smashing! Fantastic! Top notch! But I myself am a *Patriotic Objector*."

"And what on earth and the high-heavens is a '*Patriotic Objector*'? Blimey-o! It really is the small things which one bungles at."

"A *patriotic-objector* is someone who objects to anything, such as war, which sullies the good name of the country they love," Alfred explains. "Someone who truly loves their country, without needing to hate another country too.

"You see, I love Britain with all my brain, all my heart and all my soul. I love Britain with all my reason-emotion-and-spirit.

"I love our bubbling-brooks and hilly-fells, twisting-paths and stony-walls, trawling-towns and choppy-seas. Yes-yes-yes. Yes thanky-you!

"I love our ability to laugh at ourselves, mock our leaders, and lose at every sport we invent. I love our irresponsible consumption of alcohol, caustic sense of humour, and obsession with the weather. I love the Poet, the Bard and the Dandy. I love afternoon tea, Sunday roasts and crumpets.

"I love-love-love our school system, which educates even the poorest child. I love our democracy, and I love the liberties which we all enjoy.

"I'm thankful for this nation; it's the wind beneath my wings, it's the star of my daydreams, and it's made me the man I've become. I'm grateful for everything Britain has ever done for me.

"But I see the very things which make Britain great, coming under threat because of this war. I see a country's whose very identity is being destroyed.

"*Dora* is stealing our freedom of press, freedom of speech and freedom of thought. Our government won't even allow us to open our shops after eight o'clock these days. They'll even arrest us for sitting next to a bridge or a tunnel. And now conscription is enslaving our people. It's taking away our right to choose our profession, it's taking away our right to choose to live-or-die, and it's crushing British liberty beneath Prussian militarism. Please! Please-please-please!

"Our government is plunging this nation into tyranny-totalitarianism-and-terror, and I won't stand for it. I'll fight this fascism, I'll combat this coercion, and I'll destroy this despotism!

"I'll dissent because it is patriotic to dissent, because it's patriotic to mutiny, and because it's patriotic to oppose a war which is bringing our nation into disrepute.

"So I won't be conscripted. No-no-no. No thanky-you! I'll follow the tradition of British volunteerism to serve my country with random acts of kindness, not vicious acts of violence. '*Bene agere et laetari*'; rejoicing in the good which we do.

"And so I stand here as a *patriotic-objector*, opposed to conscription itself; in the name of liberty, in the name of freedom, and in the name of Great Britain!"

Peacemakers smack rolled-up papers against their sweaty-palms, and swing strangers by their sweaty-arms; whilst they howl-holler-and-hoot. They sing '*England Arise*', whilst the Groom stares into the Councillor's eyes; these Orphans shout '*Freedom*' and those Children salute.

Outnumbered-outthought-and-outplayed, distressed-disconcerted-and-dismayed; the Retired Captain changes his method of attack. To show that he is intelligent-respectable-and-strong, he interrupts Alfred when he speaks for too long; or tries to talk back.

"You believe in freedom, my son?" He jovially sings.

"I do," Alfred begins. "I do-do-do! I..."

"So you'd be prepared to protect European freedom then? For your country! For your country!"

"Of course! Yes please! I'd..."

"So you'll fight for it then? Freedom is bought by blood, after all. Freedom is slavery, ignorance is strength, and war is peace! We're fighting for peace, my son! We're fighting for peace!"

"No-no-no! That's just doublespeak. You can't fight for peace any more than you can fornicate for chastity, rape for love, or kill for life. Fighting crushes freedom. It..."

"Pooh! What a crummy little girl! I don't think you care a noodle for freedom, what with all your hair-splitting and selfish-fads," the Retired Captain begins to coax, as he smokes, and then chokes. "*Arrrk-gluck-chuck*. My son; I don't think you care a hang for Great Britain. Methinks you care more for those darn blasted Teutons, all covered in iron-crosses and red-eagles, than you do for us Brits. Boche-o!"

"I do care for the Germans," Alfred agrees. "I care for all humans. I..."

"A turncoat! A traitor! A prissy two-timer!" The Mayor nods.

"You even associate with a German, don't you? Sure-o!" The Retired Captain prods.

"Yes thanky-you," Alfred replies as he looks up to the gods. "A man who left Germany when conscription was introduced. Who..."

"Methinks 'tis safe to say that you're a German sympathiser then," the Retired Captain begins to fume.

"He hasn't, *cough*, offered Germany a jot of sympathy!" The Councillor interrupts, and erupts; because he is ambushed by a gaze from the mutilated Groom. "How, *hiccup*, absurdly befuddled you are. Aiding-assisting-accompanying-associating-and-agreeing with a, *sneeze*, person who opposes German militarism, an enemy-of-the-enemy, *sniff*, is no outrage-offence-crime-or-corruption. *Burp*. Far from it!"

The Councillor's statement is followed by this pause, which is followed by this noisy-applause; and this noisy-celebration. This crowd stamp their wellies, jiggle their bellies; and sway away in formation.

Which makes the Retired Captain feel agitated, frantic-flustered-and-frustrated; as he shakes behind his desk. Because he once loved Alfred as his own, so he feels battered-betrayed-and-blown; and he looks a little grotesque.

"I beg your pardon!" He shouts in a manner which is loud, proud; and Kafkaesque. "You're no more than an honest-idiot, full of damnable-lies. You're an ignorant foul-mouthed suffragette, even if I don't say so myself. It'd be false of you to deny it. True-o!"

"I'm a suffragist," Alfred corrects. "And I don't deny it. I'm grateful for it. I'm..."

"Terrorist! Thug! Princess!" The Mayor clicks, with sticky lips, which are covered in greasy-chips. "Scullion! Rampallion! Fustilarian! If ever a boy needed the army to toughen him up, 'tis this stewed-prune here. Blimey! Warfare would be just about impossible if everyone behaved like him."

"Don't play the fool," the Retired Captain continues, to proclaim his views, with a pen in his hand and some paper on his shoes. "Tell me son, are you scared of dying? Coward-o!"

"No," Alfred replies. "I'm scared of killing. I'm..."

"I shouldn't think you'd defend your very own sister from attack!"

"I don't have a sister; my Father was killed at war before he could sire one. So I'll not kill a German father, or..."

"Sister or no sister, what'd you do if I pushed you over? Violent-o!"

"I'd stand back up. Up-up-up! And..."

"And would you cuff me, once you were back on your feet?"

"No thanky-you; you can't overcome hatred with more hatred. Force can kill the liar but not the lie, the hater but not the hate, and the violent but not the violence. Hate begets hate, violence begets violence, and war begets war. If you attacked me, I'd run-run-run to the police. I'd..."

"And could the Belgians just run away?"

"One in five of them have! They've..."

"What naked lunacy!" The Mayor sputters. "This man is a smollygoster! A wallydrag! A jobbernowl!"

"That's five minutes!" The Gentleman Farmer utters. "Let's wrap this up. Chop-chop! *Ahem. Harrumph. Cough-cough.*"

"No, no," the Retired Captain mutters. "I've got more for this frowsy-ninny. He's one of the *No Conscription Fellowship's* fifty members. Yes-o!"

"There are over five-thousand of us," Alfred says as he smiles at his Supporters, these bookish Reporters, Interns-Investors-and-Importers. "And the *UDC* have six-hundred-and-fifty-thousand members too. We're..."

"You're a part of a rag-tag group which blasphemes against the state, and goes about in secret to spread twaddle amongst our people. Lies-o!"

"I've spoken openly to the world," Alfred replies. "I've made my views about war very-very-very clear; in church, door-to-door, and wherever people come together. I've never hidden away or spoken in secret. So why do you question me? Question those who've heard me speak. I'd be ever so grateful. I'd be very much obliged."

"Aarh! 'Tis true," these Fishermen growl.

"He's got you," these Supporters howl.

"Ooh! Ooh!" Those Orphans yowl.

The Gentleman Farmer begins to sneeze, wail-whimper-and-wheeze; before he throws this tarnished-coin. Which hits Alfred's cheek, and leaves this bloody-streak; which drips down onto Alfred's groin.

"Is that how your type speaks to a respectable military-man?" The Gentleman Farmer says whilst he scratches his loin. "It's damnable! Smarten yourself up boy. Chop-chop! Show some respect."

"If I've spoken wrongly, testify against me for it," Alfred answers. "But if I've spoken rightly. Please! Why do you strike me? Why-why-why?"

The Gentleman Farmer looks awry, because he is unable to reply; as he starts to cough. As people of every age, throw coins at the stage; which knock his toupée off.

After many noisy-chants and many noisy-cheers, many noisy-heckles and many noisy-jeers; this rumpus eventually dies down. Before the Retired Captain speaks in his jovial-tone, without starting to groan; or starting to frown.

"Alfred, your Pa was a strong soldier, an intelligent fellow and a respectable gentleman, even if I don't say so myself. This is your chance to follow in his footsteps and surpass his greatness. For your country! For your country!

"You know, I do recall being in your Pa's unit during the winter of 1900. He was out on patrol when a lion, a thundering big thing, came in from the bush and grabbed a Fusilier in its jaws. It was a damnably-horrific scene. Nasty-o!

"Well, your Pa chased after that lion. Just imagine it! When the lion rose up on its back-feet, your Pa pulled him down by his mane, and killed him with his bare-hands. It was a first-class show. Bloody-o!

"On another occasion, a Giant, a truly dreadful scoundrel, entered our camp in an almighty-fury; angry, well-armed and seeking blood. My son; all your Pa had to protect his men were some pebbles which he found in the dust, and a small-slingshot which he had made himself. Flimsy-o!

"His Comrade thought the Giant was so big, that he'd crush them both. Death-o! But your Pa thought the Giant was so big, that he couldn't miss!

"And so your Pa ran straight at the Giant, full of guts-and-glory, and floored him with the first stone he hurled. For his country! For his country! Your Pa beheaded the Giant with the Giant's own sword. Swish-o!

"Your Pa saved his whole camp from that invader. He saved life-after-life, just like our soldiers are doing in France.

"Don't you want to be a hero like him, my son? It'd be awfully-peculiar not to. Strange-o!"

"Not at all," Alfred replies. "No-no-no. No thanky-you! I'd never kill an animal who was following its instincts, or a man who was defending his homeland. It's disgusting, it's inhumane, it's..."

"It's rotten-buffoonery, that's what it is!" The Mayor begins to call, with gall, whilst the Don stares ahead at the opposite-wall. "All this drivel of yours; it's utter flimflam, codswallop and pish-posh."

"It is indeed," the Retired Captain resumes. "Nonetheless, I do believe there's a warrior inside you, my son; 'tis in your blood, and a spell in khaki should bring it out. For your country! For your country!

"My son; you'll thank me for it one day. Fancy! It'd be a wickedness for a fine young thing like you to bide time at home. Shame-o!

"So let's not mince matters. We've bestowed you with the privilege of speaking here today, and listened patiently to the whimsical ribaldry which you've had the gall to dish up. 'Tis clear that you've no case whatsoever, and so you'll join the *Non Combatant Corps* forthwith. For your country! For your country! Cheerio."

These Children hiss-holler-and-hoot, these birds tweet-twitter-and-toot; and this Child kicks a chair. This Customer throws a shoe, these Fishermen boo; and that Supporter starts to glare.

"I'll destroy your army from the inside!" Alfred starts to blare. "And in three years I'll rise up again. Yes-yes-yes. Thanking you!"

Alfred salutes this vociferous-crowd, who cheer out loud; and all salute him back. And he begins to smile, as he walks down this aisle; and down this central-track.

But as he leaves, his vision starts to freeze; which almost leaves him blind. Colours seem scuzzy, outlines seem fuzzy; and shapes seem less defined. Hellish hallucinations, and demonic divinations; begin to plague his mind.

He sees his Authoritative Teacher, this malicious-creature; who flashes rose-ruby-and-red. Who bends Alfred over, without composure; and fills Alfred with fearful-dread. As he crashes his cane through Alfred's skin, shin; and head.

He sees the Dominant Assailant begin to grab, jolt-jerk-and-jab; with these punches and with these kicks. Before he counts his spoils of war, throws Alfred onto the floor; and grinds him into these bricks.

And he sees his Father dressed up in an army-suit, acting like a vicious-brute; with fury on his face. As he floods Benin in a loutish-coup, and expels the Ashanti too; whilst his angry-hornets give chase.

He sees Dominant Assailants and Authoritative Teachers, people like his Father and similar creatures; who are waiting for him in the army. So sweat pours over his clothes, his temples-testicles-and-toes; as these visions drive Alfred barmy.

He feels glum-gloomy-and-grim, but no-one sees him; and no-one cares. Because everyone in this nation, in every location; is blinded by wartime-affairs.

As the war spreads from Russia to Australia, Turkey to Malaysia; and all across the east. From Mozambique to Angola, and Togo to Kenya;

like a ravenous sort of beast.

Portugal has just joined the fight, much to the Allies' delight; and Romania is about to step in. Brazil is ready, China is steady; and America will go when they know who will win.

But this news passes Alfred by, as articles call conchies '*Awry*', with headlines which cry.

Which screech; '*The Fellowship Of The Faint Hearters should all be ignored*'.

Which shriek; '*Send those weak-and-feeble souls abroad*'.

And which squeal; '*Homosexual hoard*'.

Streets turn into whirlpools of grey, and buildings seem to sway; as Alfred struggles for sanity. Sights seem to blur, and voices seem to slur; as he struggles with the warmaker's vanity.

And amidst this fuggy-haze, Alfred's call-up card arrives after three more days; but Alfred leaves it ignored. He insists on being taken militarily, so he refuses to register voluntarily; or of his own accord.

Which brings the Policeman here, with a scab on his ear; and orders to escort Alfred to his new battalion. The Policeman's truncheon hangs like a spike, and his lantern hangs from his bike; near his new medallion.

Cleo pretends to nap, dressed in her night-cap; her nightie and her night-ring. It saves Alfred from the frustration, that a separation; would probably bring.

For eight different dreams, with eight different themes; have given Cleo a psychic sort of foresight. So she has made Alfred get life-insurance before he forgets, settle his debts; and feel alright.

She has taken this battered-backpack, which is blue-beige-and-black; and filled it with the items suggested in her *NCF Guide*. She has packed a pencil, shirt-shaver-and-stencil; and she has hidden her frankincense-and-myrrh inside.

Alfred leaves her and walks past this unopened box of toothpicks, this stool and this crucifix; before he tiptoes down these stairs. Before he tiptoes past this gnome which Cleo broke, these stains from lamp-smoke; these apples and these pears.

He cuts off a lock of his hair, leaves it for Cleo on this chair; and steps out into his yard. Where he passes this olive-mountain, this broken-fountain; and this pile of folded-card.

"I'll walk behind, I shall," the Policeman says sounding harassed.

"No-no-no," Alfred starts to coo, sounding tickety-boo; and totally unembarrassed. "You've nothing to be ashamed of; you're a fine man. An upstanding member of society! A shining-light! We're lucky to have you."

So they walk together past this clock which rolls its eyes, this chippy which sells pies; and these chimneys which exhale grey-smoke. This Road Sweeper who earns a low-salary, this boarded-up gallery; and this majestic ancient-oak.

"Do what you got to do," the Policeman says as he hands Alfred to this Arresting Sergeant, who has a musty-scent; which makes Alfred want to choke. "Anyways, I respect you, I do. You're one of a kind, so you are!"

The Policeman waves goodbye, and the Arresting Sergeant starts to sigh; as he pushes Alfred's shoulders. As he pushes Alfred past this yellow-farm, this yellow-barn; and this pile of yellow-boulders.

"Keep in step like a soldier, boyo!" He demands somewhat formally.

"No-no-no '*please*'?" Alfred questions as he walks ahead normally.

"We don't do manners here boyo; you're in the army now, we demand blind-obedience here. And don't you think you can fight us. Stay in line and you'll profit, you've all the makings of a sergeant. But do be warned; we tame lions here!"

"I don't doubt it for a minute," Alfred replies. "But I do think you'll struggle to get this lamb to roar. Please!"

They walk down these misty-roads, past these mules who pull their loads; and these gas-lamps which glimmer in hidden-squares. Past this War Widow who mourns her spouse, this painted-townhouse; and these endless thoroughfares. These slouching-hills, crumbling-mills; and cottages which appear in pairs. Before they arrive in this remand cell, which has this fetid-smell; one table and three chairs.

Alfred sits near these Prisoners who look demure, this latrine which is full of manure; and this family of mangy-rats. He uses this moth-eaten rug to keep warm, whilst he ignores that storm; and those Drunks who engage in spats. Before dawn arrives, this Prisoner cries; and he is taken to this *Coastal Barracks*.

Where he is led into this cupboard by this Lanky Cadet who has a long-face, buckteeth which protrude into space; and eyes which are slightly grey. This equine-soldier tries to profit from this store, because he is bored of the war; and wants to supplement his meagre-pay.

"Put this on, ginger," he begins to neigh. "I can give you a uniform that fits for the *price of a pint*, if you like."

He throws this uniform with force, which releases this smell of damp-horse; as it falls to the ground in a ball. But Alfred just stands here looking forlorn, because he does not want a uniform; be it too large or be it too small. So he shrugs, looks at these rugs; and looks this crumbling-wall.

"You don't have to like it, you low life son of a bitch, you just have to do it," this Curt Cadet begins to drawl. "Because if you don't put this uniform on, right here, right now, right away, we'll force you into it ourselves. Just you wait and see! And may God have mercy on your soul if we do, scum bag, because I know I won't. I'll make you wish you'd never been born!"

This soldier's skin has the texture of candle-wax, it is covered in uneven-cracks; and it is misshapen by uneven-bone. The musty-smell in the air, mixes with the greasy-smell of his hair; and the stench of his cheap-cologne. But Alfred just stands here and shrugs, looks at those mugs; and refuses to be thrown.

"Be a doll, baby girl," the Lanky Cadet says with a sideways-shimmy, a whinny; and a moan. "It's only wool-and-webbing."

"Why should I?" Alfred questions with a groan. "Uniforms are for soldiers. I'll never be a soldier. No-no-no. No thanky-you! I abhor wars, the soldiers who fight in wars, and the uniforms which are worn for wars.

"You wouldn't make a German prisoner wear British khaki, so please don't make your British prisoners wear it. Please-please-please."

The Lanky Cadet starts to smile, whilst the Curt Cadet turns vile; and grabs hold of Alfred's collar. He tears Alfred's shirt apart, releases this fart; and starts to holler.

'*Ahh-Wooooo!*'

"Need I go on, oxygen thief? You half-baked moronic idealist! Yours is not to reason why, yours is to do-and-die. You swine! Drop and give me twenty."

Alfred just shrugs, looks at these bugs, and this row of slimy-slugs.

And like the assailants who mugged Alfred as a child, the Curt Cadet looks wild; as he stamps on Alfred's anklebone. As he punches Alfred's hairy-chin, and kicks Alfred's hairy-skin; which makes Alfred want to groan. Before he removes Alfred's trousers so quickly, that it makes him feel prickly; and makes him want to moan.

"Ready for your uniform, poltroon?" He asks is this nasty-tone. "We're gonna turn you into a lean mean fighting-machine. Just you wait-and-see!"

Alfred just shrugs, looks at these drugs, and this tray of empty-jugs.

"It's neigh good, cowboy," the Lanky Cadet snorts, whilst his horsey-face contorts; near that tray of mugs. "We should save our aggression for the Germans. The Staff Sergeant can deal with this foal."

And so the Curt Cadet mutters *'Blasted insurgent'*, and goes to find the Staff Sergeant; whilst the Lanky Cadet starts to smile. He laughs with so much force, that his throat turns hoarse; and he chokes on some snotty-bile.

"I can only apologize, bella," he blows in a horsey-style. "You've got your principles, dancer, and I've got mine. I don't agree with you, not one bit, but I sure do respect you for keeping hold of your reins."

The Lanky Cadet turns silent as soon as the Staff Sergeant enters this darkened-room, where he starts to flare-flutter-and-fume; simmer-seethe-and-snap. With a belly which sways with each of his motions, and a face which changes colour with each of his emotions; here is a bedevilled chap. A man who believes that everything is devilled-devilment-or-deviltry, calls people *'devils'* with devilish-revelry; and loves a devilish-scrap.

"Put that hat on this instant, you dirty-devil!" He bellows, whilst his face turns a mixture of yellows; and he hurls this khaki-cap. "Or we'll shoot you dead, just like the last peace-crank that came this way. Your devilish-pride shan't do you any favours here. Yours is the Devil's work! You damn degenerate."

But with only the hair on his chin, to cover his skin; Alfred just shrugs. He just rolls his eyes, sighs; and looks at that pile of rugs.

And he starts to sweat, because he is aware this is not an idle-threat; having heard of the Miner who was shot for insubordination. But

Alfred has promised to die for his beliefs, so he disobeys these army-chiefs; in spite of their intimidation.

"We all owe death a life, I suppose," he replies with resignation.

"Stupid-devil!" The Staff Sergeant replies with frustration. "Give the dirty-devil the water treatment! Throw the dreggy-devil in the horse-trough! Hose the dungy-devil down until he shivers so much that he stops his devil may care agenda and is grateful for the devilishly-warm uniform which he's being offered!"

The Curt Cadet follows this order with unquestioning-obedience, violent-subservience and violent-expedience; as he grabs at Alfred's arm. But the Lanky Cadet is so appalled by this experience, that he acts with perseverance; to protect Alfred from any sort of harm.

"This filly will come without force," he squeals with alarm.

And Alfred is indeed happy to walk past these munitions-stores, seashores; and stables. These redbrick-halls, redbrick-walls; and overhanging-cables.

He walks past these Recruits who parade militarily, before he enters this trough voluntarily; where this icy-cold water burns his skin. Where the Curt Cadet bounces him like a ball, bangs his head against this wall; and scratch his bloody-shin.

"Dank-devil," the Staff Sergeant shouts with this frown, which turns his face brown; near his chubby-chin. "Is this devil going to have to find more work for your idle-thumbs? Or are you ready for a devilishly-warm uniform?"

"It's ever so kind of you to offer," Alfred replies. "You're kinder than Santa and cooler than ice on the rocks. But I'd rather not. No thanky-you."

"What the devil? Don't be a fool man; it's cold enough without fools.

"Get this damned-devil out of here. Take him straight to the Devil!"

The Curt Cadet grabs Alfred's knees, drags him past these trees; to this cliff-top which is the colour of rust. Where Alfred is bashed by this icy-hale, beaten by this icy-gale; and battered by this icy-gust. Which splashes these waves, into those caves; and creates a cyclone of dust.

"Keep the little-devil here until he freezes or comes to his devilish-senses," the Staff Sergeant says with distrust. "And shoot the devil if he resists."

Alfred is still damp from the trough, so he feels rickety-wretched-and-rough; as his skin turns pale-blue. As his blood-pressure decreases, his heartbeat increases; and he starts to contract the flu.

"He's a wild-bronco, that Staff Sergeant," the Lanky Cadet snorts, and contorts; as he takes in this coastal-view. "An untamed-colt! That mare wouldn't allow me to return home on my day off.

"And I'm not the only one who detests him. So you'll earn some respect for sticking it to him, buttercup, that's for sure."

The Lanky Cadet flings Alfred over his back, and walks down this track; whilst Alfred's arms sway and Alfred's legs dangle. They arrive in this medical ward, near this calling-cord; and these drips which are all in a tangle. Near these Nurses in white-skirts, these Doctors in white-shirts; and these chains which start to jangle.

Alfred rests beneath this cotton-cover, and slowly starts to recover; over the course of the next few days. Before the Staff Sergeant enters this room, with this look of doom; and these eyes which are both ablaze.

"Doctor-devils, dentist-devils, dermatologist-devils; get the devil out of here!" He says as he removes his cap, puts it on his lap; and gives Alfred this devilish-gaze. "A devil of a fine show you put on out there!

"I only hope you'll come to see that what we're doing here is for your own good. We're not selling our souls to the Devil, but it sure is a devil's job we're doing.

"You see, when I was your age, men were men, women were women, and the world was all the better for it; we kept the Devil from the door. But these days, society has become full of effeminate-men and masculine-women. The devil is in the details.

"People have been in devilish-decline, physically-and-morally, for many years now. Working-class devils have become unclean-and-sickly, whilst upper-class devils have been corrupted by decadence-and-dandyism. The Devil sure has been taking care of his own.

"I see it every day! I see a whole stream of feeble-fainthearted-and-feminine conchies, with unwholesome-bodies and unhealthy-minds. I see our once great nation, and the British race itself, undergoing a process of reverse-evolution. Degeneration! It sure is a devil of a way to go. Most unsatisfactory.

"Too many defiant-devils are happy to live under our government without obeying it. Homosexual-devils! Nigger-devils! And you conchie-devils! You're as savage as the blacks, and as queer as the gays. You damn degenerates.

"But this war will sort you out. This war has been sent by the Devil as a punishment for your pursuit of luxury-and-vice. This war will fix you, and I'll fix you too. I'll fix every last conchie-devil out there, even if it's the last thing I ever do. Send me to the Devil if I don't!"

As he shouts and as he speaks, the Staff Sergeant puffs his cheeks; and changes colour with each of his emotions. He turns blue as he opposes insubordination, pink as he opposes degeneration; and red as he promotes his notions.

"Personally, I'm of the mind to line all you white-livered skunks up against the walls of hell, and shoot you out-of-hand," he says with these exaggerated-motions. "Your sort are so dreadfully slap-dash.

"But the commander-devils don't think you're worth the tuppence which the bullet would cost. Worse luck, I say. So I'm going to work you like the devil until your muscles turn to rock, drill you so hard you could run forever, and punish you with devil-fuelled fury if you ever cross me again. You damn degenerate!

"I'll build in you what you lack as a man, I'll make you obedient, and I'll make you serve. The devil I will!"

The Staff Sergeant brushes down his chubby-lap, and starts to clap; with the meaty part of his hand. His face turns red like chilli-powder, and his voice gets even louder; as he repeats his original demand.

"Put that uniform on this instant, you dirty-devil!"

"No-no-no. No thanky-you," Alfred replies.

"Tut-tut-tut," the Staff Sergeant sighs. "Yours is the Devil's work, and it shan't be tolerated here. This devil won't allow it. You're setting a devilishly-dangerous example to the other men."

Alfred shrugs his bony-shoulders, because he is happy to believe he might inspire some soldiers; to join his campaign for peace. He will think of these words whenever he feels rough, the going gets tough; and he needs to find release.

"I knew your Father," the Staff Sergeant says as his face turns bright-cerise. "The belligerent-devil was adopted, don't you know?"

This news rocks Alfred's senses, breaks through his defences; and leaves him totally mute. It leaves him feeling forlorn, tragic-torpid-and-torn; whilst he scowls at this chubby-brute.

"I knew your Grandpa too," the Staff Sergeant continues to shoot. "He was a devil of a first-class fellow, who fought in the New Zealand wars of the 1850s. He was the was the son of a soldier himself.

"Well, your Grandpa found your Father wrapped in a blanket, inside a papyrus-basket, which was nestled amongst some reeds. The little-devil was only three months old at the time.

"And your Grandpa thought, '*Better the devil you know*'. He took your Father home, raised him as if he was his own son, and turned him into a devilishly-fine soldier.

"But your Father's heart was never really committed the army, not like your Grandpa and those who have the army in their blood. There was no deviltry in that soldier-devil; the little-devil cared more about people than politics. He was a bit like you, when you come to think about it. The damn degenerate!

"So don't you think you could play devil's advocate, like your Father? Couldn't you make just one deal with the devil, and put this uniform on? I mean, you can't go on with this devil-may-careness forever; the Devil won't allow it!"

"Please," Alfred replies to this question, suggestion; and petition. As he questions his entire existence, consistence; and position. "Please-please-please."

"Please???" The Staff Sergeant replies with dismay, as his face turns grey; with this look of leery-suspicion. "Please? Please? What the devil do you mean?"

"You've never said '*please*'," Alfred explains with a grin, on his chin, as he tries to civilise this man who is trying to militarise him. "Or '*thank-you*', '*sorry*' or '*pardon*'. Your minions were happy to resort to violence, but they never thought to resort to manners.

"If they'd only been a bit more courteous we wouldn't be here now. No-no-no. Because if you want people to do something for you, you need to be nice to them, show them some respect, and explain your requests. People can't just be beaten into submission like sheep."

Unused to anything other than blind obedience, and unquestioning allegiance, the Staff Sergeant replies with uncomfortable expedience.

"Please be a decent-devil," he says, as he sways; because he is wary of Alfred's disobedience. "Please put a uniform on."

"I'd be delighted to! I'd be very much obliged. Yes-yes-yes. Yes thanky-you. You're as pretty as honeysuckle and as sweet as honey!" Alfred agrees, whilst he shakes his knees; now he has gotten what he asked for.

"What the devil?" The Staff Sergeant mutters, and splutters; as he walks through that door. "Why the devil? How the devil? Devil-devil-devil."

Alfred rests-recuperates-and-recovers before he is taken to this long-dorm, where he puts on this fifth-hand uniform; which smells of old blood. Which smells of *Old Spice*, is full of old lice; and bits of old mud.

This long dormitory-hall, which stretches towards that distant-wall; is full of these skinny-beds. Made from unpolished-wood, it is full of the misunderstood; who have skinny-bodies and skinny-heads.

Here are these long-faced Hustlers, these long-nosed Rustlers; and these long-winged flies. These pugnacious Punks, these dishevelled Drunks; and that brawny Delinquent who cries.

And sat between these criminals, are these two individuals; these conchies with ashen-eyes. This Clerk with ashen-cheeks, and this Nurse who speaks; whilst he slaps his ashen-thighs.

"One is a student," he tells his new allies. "A Quaker from a family of cotton-traders. And one did want to help, to be a volunteer in the good old-fashioned sense of the word.

"So one joined the *Friends' Ambulance Unit* as a nurse, travelled to France by oneself, willingly paid for one's own uniform, and was soon in the most frightful-place; a stonking big railway hanger which was full of thousands of unattended patients. The smell! Goodness gracious me! It just was not cricket.

"One loved one's position at first. It was ace, spiffing and top-drawer; one will swear upon it. We ran two hospital-ships, four hospital-trains, and a dozen hospitals. We administered tens-of-thousands of inoculations, fed-and-clothed refugees, and distributed milk-and-water without a single penny of government money. It was top notch, simply smashing, and really rather peachy. Rah-rah-rah!

"When conscription was introduced, one could have stayed where one was and been exempt from service. But one realised that if one resigned, a conscript would take one's place, and the sick would be cared for like before. Whilst if one stayed on, that conscript would be sent to murder the Germans.

"Well, darlings, one did not want to be responsible for that! It really was a beastly-fudge. One was not at all amused. It fair well brought one to the end of one's tether.

"But, it must be admitted, one had grown rather baffled by the role itself. Our unit had come under military-control, with orders to refit soldiers for war, and one was not inclined to aid-or-abet their killing. So one resigned one's commission and became a conchie. And fiddle-dee-dee; here one is!"

Whilst the Nurse's uniform fits his formal-stance, after wearing it for two years in France; the same cannot be said of the Clerk. This adolescent who has sandpaper-skin, a hairy-face and a hairy-chin; a stubbly-lip and a stubbly-smirk. This boy who is fiddling with this pillow, this piece of willow; and this model of a Turk.

"What about you? I think you've been a peacemaker from the start," he tells Alfred with a jerk. "Ghastly thing this war. Prefer work myself. Do you work? I bet you work. I worked in coloured-felt till I lost my job for not enlisting.

"Did your family kick you out? Of course they did.

"How did the soldiers get you into a uniform? Violence I bet. They wanted to assert their masculinity, no? Ouch! They tried to push both my legs down the same trouser-leg. The nitwits! I make them dress me every day. It's a pantomime! They don't like it. Not one bit. No-one likes a conchie."

"They beat me too," Alfred says. "But I got the Staff Sergeant to say '*please*' in the end. I did feel rather grateful to him for his manners. I felt rather obliged."

"He said '*please*'? No. I don't think he did," the Clerk says as he fiddles with these braces, these cases, and these brown-shoelaces. "Soldiers don't say '*please*'. Soldiers don't say '*thank-you*'. They consider it weak. They do respect for their seniors and scorn for their subordinates. That's all.

"They don't bother to think. The blighters would be fighting for Germany if they'd been born over there. But they just don't think about it.

"Have you ever seen a soldier do discussion? No. Soldiers don't do discussion. The more senior a soldier, the more right they are. That's how their minds work. If they have minds. And if they work.

"Understand? I think so. Understand the army-man and you can beat him."

"I couldn't have put-put-put it better myself," Alfred replies. "You sure do make me smile. Don't ever change. Thank-you, thank-you, thank-you. We'll turn this knowledge into game."

"A game? Is it a game? No! It's not a game."

"Maybe not," Alfred replies whilst the Clerk fiddles with these nails, and the Nurse holds onto those rails, before Alfred retells one of the Good German's tales. "Let me tell you about a disheartened young Ox who did all the hard-hard-hard work on his farm. That Ox pulled a cart, ploughed the land, and carried his farm's produce to market. But he was only ever given a measly-portion of grass-and-straw to eat.

"Ox lived with Pig, who didn't do any work at all. Please understand! Pig got given a feast every day. She ate apples-carrots-and-oats, parsnips-potatoes-and-plums, cabbages-broccoli-and-lettuce.

"So life didn't seem at all fair to Ox. He whinged-wined-and-whimpered, and complained to anyone who'd listen.

"Until one day, once she'd become as big as an elephant, Pig was taken away. She was killed, quartered, and turned into sausages!"

"Sausages!" The Clerk laughs. "Very good. Very good. But is it a game? No! No-one like a conchie."

"Please understand!" Alfred continues. "We're like Ox. The army will make us suffer-sweat-and-strain, and give us terrible food-and-conditions, but our hard-work in the name of peace will keep us alive. Whilst the soldiers who are enjoying the spoils of war today, will be slaughtered like pigs tomorrow. Yes-yes-yes. Yes thanky-you!"

"Have you told a story? Yes!" The Clerk responds. "Conchies are oxen. Soldiers are pigs. But is it a game? No! No-one likes a conchie."

"Perhaps I got sidetracked," Alfred apologizes. "I'm just so happy to be amongst like-minded souls. I'm ever so grateful for your company. I really like your style. You're full of youth!

"It's just that deep down, I don't think soldiers are pigs. We're all human after all, and if they're going to have their fun trying to militarise us, then we should have our fun trying to civilise them. We should try to turn soldiers into civilians, make them act civilly instead of militarily, and stand for civilisation instead of militarisation.

"This is the game. We'll ignore the warmakers whenever they don't say '*please*', and we'll correct their rudeness too. It'll help them to grow into fine oxen, and save them from being turned into sausages!"

"Make them say '*please*'? Yes," the Clerk agrees. "Make them explain their orders? I think so. Would it make them squirm? Yes. Would they like it? No! No-one likes a conchie. Ghastly thing this war."

The Clerk begins to chuckle-chortle-and-clap, and Alfred begins to tap; which improves the Nurse's disposition. Without a natural inclination for disobedience, he laughs without expedience; or any inhibition.

"By occupying soldiers here," Alfred concludes his tuition. "We can distract the warmakers from their killing. We can be a real menace! Yes please! Please-please-please. We can save hundreds of lives!"

But as he speaks the Curt Cadet enters this room, dressed in his khaki-costume; which has buckles which glow like the sun. He wears this khaki-backpack, these socks which are black; and these boots which are covered in dung.

"Zero dark thirty! Lights out ladies!" He bellows whilst he waves his gun.

"Please!" Alfred and the Clerk both reply as one.

"Shut your mouths, you toe-rags," the Curt Cadet responds with a bark, as he turns this room dark; and then leaves once he is done.

He leaves Alfred to sleep peacefully inside his coarse-sack, happy with his new plan of attack; and happy with his new peacemaker-regiment. Whilst the Clerk struggles to snooze, and fidgets with his shoes; which are covered in sooty-sediment.

But troubled by the prospect of nasty-punishments, and nasty-admonishments; the Nurse has ghoulish-premonitions. He dreams of a twenty-foot red-faced beast, who has gnashing metal-teeth; and many evil-missions. Who beats him down, and hangs him near town; in all sorts of tangled-positions.

So Alfred feels inspired, and the Clerk feels tired; as he stands on this parade-ground this morning. But the Nurse feels weak, blue-blighted-and-bleak; with a fiendish sense of forewarning.

"Att-ent-shon devils!" The Staff Sergeant bellows as he bounces on this crate.

"Please!" Alfred and the Clerk both berate.

"Lerrrft turn!" The Staff Sergeant commands, and demands; with horror-hostility-and-hate. "Quick march! Faw-waaard! Lerrrft, right, lerrrft, right, lerrrft, right! Devil-devil-devil!"

Most of the conscripts this *Non Combatant Corps* are happy to march around, across this ground; with lifted-elbows and lifted-knees. The Nurse marches without dissent-disagreement-or-delays, in a stuporific-daze; towards those leafy-trees. But Alfred and the Clerk stand still, and refuse to drill; until the Staff Sergeant says *'please'*.

"Halt!" The Staff Sergeant shouts, and pouts; feeling ill at ease.

"Please!" Alfred and the Clerk both tease.

"Right turn! Squad shin! Stand at ease! Devils!" The Staff Sergeant shouts at his corps, to turn them towards him once more, on the other side of this gritty-floor.

Alfred and the Clerk have been cast adrift, so the Staff Sergeant looks miffed; and a bit like a cartoon villain. His eyes are dilated, his lungs are inflated; and his face has turned vermilion.

He clambers down from his stand, and waves his podgy-hand; whilst his pedestal begins to squeak. He stumbles, and almost tumbles; whilst his joints begin to creak.

"You disobedient-devils are in the *No Courage Corps*," he begins to shriek. "Not to be trained. Oh no! You're here to be punished! You'll be punished for your deviltry, your deviance, and your insubordination. And you'll be sent to the Devil as an example for everyone else here to see. You damn degenerates."

So this Young Mercenary with a tattoo on his fist, grabs Alfred's wrist; and bends it behind his back. Whilst that Old Mercenary smirks, grabs the Clerk's; and gives his head a savage-whack.

Mud is squelched and gravel is churned, arms are twisted and wrists are turned; as these conchies are pushed ahead. As they are pushed past these drums, these guns; and this camouflaged army-shed.

Before they arrive in this gym where the odours of sweaty-feet, and rotten-peat; swirl around in this tepid-gust. Where these balance-beams, and these trampolines; are covered in orange-rust. And where these glossy-floors, and glossy-doors; are attracting this orange-dust.

"Now you puerile-devils shall march!" The Staff Sergeant says with orange-faced disgust. "We'll make you deadbeat-devils hoof it! We'll make you delinquent-devils drill! The devil we will!"

"I'd be happy to march," Alfred says. "If you'd only say 'please'. Please-please-please."

"Will I march? Yes," the Clerk says as he fiddles with his sleeves. "I'll march-and-march. Why? I don't know. Please just give me one good reason. Then I'll march. Yes I'll march. I'll march and I'll march again. Ghastly thing this war."

"Enough of this devil-talk!" The Staff Sergeant shouts as his face turns plum, near his gum, and pink around his tongue. "Why the devil do you think I'd let you dirty-devils tell me what to say? What a preposterous-notion! You damn degenerates will march when I say you'll march, and that's that. Don't you play the devil with me; there'll be the devil to pay!"

The Staff Sergeant's chubby-legs begin to hobble, his chubby-belly begins to wobble; and his chubby-hand slices through the air. The Young Mercenary kicks Alfred in his rib, which causes Alfred to fall into this crib; and into this wobbly-chair. He knocks this cabinet over, lands on the *White Cliffs Of Dover*; and gets blood in his ruffled-hair.

"Right turn! Devils!" The Staff Sergeant begins to blare.

And so the Young Mercenary stamps his welly, into Alfred's belly; until Alfred's hip goes '*crack*'. And he pushes right through, with the sole of his shoe; to roll Alfred onto his back. He completes this '*right turn*', but Alfred does not squirm; or respond to this attack.

"Quick march! Faw-waaard! Lerrrft, right, lerrrft, right, lerrrft, right! Devil-devil-devil!" The Staff Sergeant repeats his decree, with his hand on his knee; whilst his face turns pale-white. Whilst the Young Mercenary grips Alfred's ankles inside his fists, tenses-tightens-and-twists; with all of his feeble-might. Before he cycles Alfred's legs back-

and-forth, south-and-north; and left-and-right.

"Beautiful, beautiful-devils," the Staff Sergeant screams with delight. "You see, when I say you'll march, you'll march! The army is full of the devil, and it'll conquer you in the end. You damn degenerates."

In support of this statement, the Staff Sergeant continues his games without abatement; and with an impatient sort of haste. When Alfred refuses to swim in the sea, he is dragged through it with a rope round his knee; and a rope around his waist. When he refuses to jump over this vaulting-horse, he is thrown over it with force; and a fierce sort of distaste. And he is slapped in his chin, for not saluting; whilst he stands here stony-faced.

The slap covers Alfred's face in dimples, whilst the sea covers his body in pimples; and makes his body shake. The fall dislocates Alfred's shoulders, with pains which smoulders; and makes his body ache.

"I'd be happy to jump-swim-and-salute," Alfred says as his body starts to shake. "Please just ask politely, and I'll do it right away."

"Will I jump? Yes I'll jump," the Clerk says whilst he fiddles with this suede, this spade; and this rake. "Will I swim? Yes I'll swim. Will I salute? Yes I'll salute. Jump-swim-and-salute. Yes I will. Just explain why I should. No? No-one likes a conchie."

"Enough! Devils!" The Staff Sergeant shouts with dread, as his face turns red, whilst he shakes his chubby-head. "You disrespectful-devils shall face court-martials on the morrow, and shall be off to France soon after. Playing the devil shall get you shot quick-sharpish out in that devilish-hell. It sure is a devil of a way to go. You damn degenerates."

Alfred shivers as he takes a deep-breath, faces this threat of death; and this threat of France. Full of fright, he sees the Miner who was shot for refusing to fight; as he enters a hazy-trance.

He sees the alley in which he was once mugged, and the gun which his Father once slugged; which makes him feel wary-woozy-and-weak. He sees the alley in which he could be prosecuted, and the guns with which he could be executed; as images take over his sleep. Before he wakes from these fiendish-dreams, releases these fiendish-screams; and starts to weep.

His bruised-shoulder still aches, and his bruised-body still shakes; as he is escorted by the Curt Cadet. His sole legal representative, this man seems tentative; as he enters this office and starts to fret.

"Speak of the devil!" The Staff Sergeant says as he sits here dressed in a jumper which is fleecy, with hair which is greasy; and hands which are slightly wet.

He sits in front of the paintings which line these walls, this pile of cannonballs; and this pile of books. He sits behind this leather-desk, which looks grotesque; and is covered in brassy-hooks.

The Staff Sergeant is one of three soldiers who are ready for action, led by this Proud Captain; who is covered in shiny-pips. This elderly-soldier has a moustache which is pert, and a khaki-shirt; which is covered in shiny-clips.

"Please sit down," he says whilst he licks his shiny-lips. "This is a *District Court-Martial*. It hath the power to dish out any punishment, up to and including two-years of hard-labour. In my day it would've had the power to hang you.

"Staff Sergeant, read out the charges, if you please?"

"This defendant stands betwixt the Devil and the deep-blue-sea, if you ask me," the Staff Sergeant says as he reads from the *Manual Of Military Law*, sounding cocksure, stern-straight-and-sure. "This dissident-devil is accused of breaching section five of the *British Army Act*; spreading rumours designed to cause alarm. This disgusting-devil is charged with breaching section nine of the act; disobeying lawful-orders given to him by a superior-officer. Section forty of the act; prejudicing good-order and military-discipline. And section eighteen of the act; feigning an injury. The damn degenerate."

"Thank you, Staff Sergeant," the Proud Captain says whilst he looks up, holding his cup; with his back held perfectly-straight. Whilst Alfred smiles at the words '*thank-you*', and stamp his shoe; which perplexes this third-magistrate. This man who is pie-faced, mixed-raced; and slightly underweight.

This Legal Officer does not have any seniority, or any authority; so he calls his superiors '*Sir*'. His feet both tap, and his hands both clap; but he tries not to cause a stir.

"This court considers you to be a soldier, Private Freeman, and it expects you to behave like one," the Proud Captain continues to slur. "This court considers that you hath a duty to obey. And this court hath a duty itself; a duty to break the disobedient, and dish out extraordinary-punishments to extraordinary-criminals.

"For when you get to my age, you come to know how to swallow people whole. Well, this court is ready to gobble you down, chew you up, and spit you out in little pieces. This court will have its way!"

Behind this bravado the Proud Captain actually feels constricted, because he wishes that Alfred had never been conscripted; and was anywhere else but here. He considers conchies to be a plague, who are vain-vulgar-and-vague; and more alien than any foreign-foe he has faced in his career. A national danger who ignore his laws without regrets, ignore his threats; and fill him with untold fear.

"If you're really against all wars," the Legal Officer tests, and contests; in a voice which sounds cavalier. "Tell us! Yes sir! No sir! Right sir! Tell us!"

"If I tell you, you'll not believe me," Alfred begins to sneer.

"Tell us! Are you a conscientious objector? An absolutist; an extremist of peace? The Devil's own? Some sort of stupid-devil who's determined to disobey every bequest given to him?" The Staff Sergeant cries, as he looks at his two allies, with angry-red in his angry-eyes.

"You're right in saying that I am," Alfred replies.

"Well then, we don't need any more testimony; we've heard it from the devil's mouth!" The Staff Sergeant says in a self-congratulatory way, as he starts to sway, and put his papers away.

"This spineless-maggot punched me and spat at my men!" The Curt Cadet begins to say.

"What devilment!" The Staff Sergeant adds with dismay. "How devilish! Such devilry! That's a breach of section thirty-seven of the *British Army Act*; striking or ill-treating a soldier."

"And I heard that he's threatened to destroy the army and rebuild Britain without it, in just three years!" The Curt Cadet adds. "This one needs to be taken down a peg or two. Yessur!"

Alfred just shrugs, looks at these rugs, and that tray of china-jugs.

"Don't you have anything to say for yourself, deaf-devil?" The Staff Sergeant chugs. "Don't you have any response to this testimony? Aren't you going to give this devil his due? You damn degenerate."

Alfred just shrugs, looks at these slugs, and that line of busy-bugs.

"I demand you tell us, in the name of the Devil, whether or not you're some sort of peacenik who's hell bent on destroying the army? Do you or don't you sup with the Devil? Do you or don't you oppose all wars?"

"So you say," Alfred replies. "Nevertheless, I'll tell you this; after my time here you'll see civilians rather than soldiers in charge of our nation, and peace rather than bombs in our skies. Yes-yes-yes. Yes thanky-you!"

"What blasphemy! What slander! What deviltry!" The Staff Soldier starts to crow, boom-bellow-and-blow, whilst his face turns indigo. "What further need do we have of witness-devils? What invention of the Devil is this man? What the devil do you think?"

"He deserves death, sir," the Legal Officer answers with these hand-claps, foot-taps, and finger-snaps. "He deserves to die! Yes sir! No sir! Right sir! Death sir!"

"Death! Death before dishonour!" The Curt Cadet says as he spits at Alfred's face, pushes him past this bookcase, and into this fireplace. "Peace didn't save you from that, did it now? If you want to mess with the best, you'll die like all the rest. Just you wait-and-see!"

"Order! Order! Please!" The Proud Captain growls, and howls, as he twists his moustache and chomps his jowls. "I've seen some things, I've seen me some things, but I've never come across a blackguard like this.

"Upon my word Alfred. My heart and my liver! Please don't make a cat's paw out of me. I don't know what you think things are coming to.

"It's quite clear that you're guilty of grave-misconduct, and endeavouring to influence your fellow soldiers. It seems to me that you'll do just about anything you can to cause a nuisance, and aren't in any way conscientious. 'Twas different in my day; men were men back then.

"But, at all events, this court doesn't have the authority to issue the death sentence. That it should! That it should! It'd be good if a man like you died for the people."

As Alfred waits to be sentenced for his stance, to be given a spell in prison or a spell in France; he recalls his hellish-premonitions. He sees the alley in which he could be prosecuted, and the guns with which he could be executed; for all his pro-peace missions.

"This is your first offence," the Proud Captain says as he glances at those munitions. "And I still believe you can come good. Because when you get to my age you come to understand the need for patience.

"So I'm sentencing you to a month in the cells, on bread-and-water, under the rule of silence.

"You'll be released under court-martial and given one final opportunity to obey orders. If you behave like this again, I dare say you'll have a time. The military-machine will chew you up, swallow you down, and spit you out in little pieces! You've got thirty days to think it over. So don't say you haven't been warned. This is the only opportunity you'll have to conform!"

The Curt Cadet grips his buckle, tenses his knuckle; and escorts Alfred to this cell. Which is damp-dank-and-dark, stale-stagnant-and-stark; with a putrid sort of smell.

Once Alfred adjusts to these fumes, he can see that he is in one of three rooms; which are chiselled into the cliff-face. These rooms line up one behind the other, beneath a rocky-cover; and above that army-base. With mildew on these walls, and debris in these balls; which waft across this space.

Ghosts from the Napoleonic Wars, seem to shake these doors; and whistle on these winds. Whilst cockroaches scuttle, ants shuttle; and rats behave like kings.

"You'll be pushing up daisies before long!" The Curt Cadet stings. "Just you wait-and-see. Copy that, sucker? There're soldiers in France sweating blood to keep you fools snug. Don't you think you'll get away with this!"

He leaves Alfred and the Clerk to meet these prisoners who are barely alive, these Thieves who wallow and those Truants who thrive; whilst they all avoid the war. Before they meet these other conchies, who have started to freeze; sat here on this grungy-floor.

One is in this room and two are in further in, they look feeble-famished-and-thin; in straight-trousers and straitjackets. They are chained, and they are constrained; like sausages in paper-packets.

"Lord bless you, soldier of Christ," this Christian whispers in a hush, as he starts to blush; and tries to be chatty. With chubby-cheeks, this man would look at home in upper-class boutiques; if only he was not so tatty. His hair is tangled, his shirt is mangled; and his face looks slightly ratty.

"You'll be safe in here; God is your general, humanity your army, and the bible your weapon now. Let Jesus into your heart and you'll come to no harm. You *will never leave or forsake us*, will you my Lord? Just like you said in Hebrews thirteen."

"That's nice," Alfred says to strike a chord, with this man sits on a board, whilst he speaks directly to his Lord. "Thank-you-thank-you-thank-you. You're cooler than snow-and-ice combined!"

"You're not convinced?" The Christian pushes. "Dear God, this disciple of yours is not convinced!"

"I think your faith is beautiful; it's lit-lit-lit up my day. I really am obliged. I really am very grateful."

"Holy Mary," the Christian continues. "*Get rid of filthiness-and-naughtiness, suffer the injustices of this world, and save your soul.* That's James one, and it's exactly what we're doing here! *Don't do evil in return for the evil you suffer, but do good to all men.* That's Thessalonians five; it's the plain word of God!

"For it's hell without Jesus, but kneel in front of the Lord and you'll be able to stand up to anyone. He'll guide you, just like he guided me when I was thinking about becoming a soldier. I tossed a coin, and through heads beating tails, God told me to become a conchie."

"My Lord; you sure do move in mysterious ways!"

"He sure does," Alfred says as he turns to this Apprentice, who is slumped in the entrance; next to this plate of dry-bread. Here is a skinny sort, who is rather short; in a straitjacket which makes him look red. It makes his hands look black, it pins his shoulders back; and it draws lines across his head.

"I'm an atheist myself," he says as he stares straight ahead. "But I'll try not to convert you to it!

"I didn't need to toss a coin before I became a conchie either; resistance is in my blood. My Pa was a trade-unionist who stood up to the army during the *Miners' Strike* of 1910. He told me not to join the soldiers who tried to crush our community that day, and I listened to him.

"So I'll never be a soldier, I'll be a piano-tuner, and I don't care what anyone else says. Because when you have beliefs you've got to stick to them. And I do believe, even though we're as mild as curds-and-cream, we'll be too strong for the warmakers."

"I come from a family of peacemakers too," this gangly Tax Collector begins to say, sat on that clay, which is gooey-gravelly-and-grey. "My Grandpapa was a peace-campaigner during the Boer War; one was bullied for it at school. And my Pa thinks wars are a little bit silly too.

"God only knows what they'd say if they knew I was locked in here like some sort of common-criminal, with all these god-awful creatures. One did try to blend in when they conscripted me; cooking, cleaning, and such like. But one was court-martialled for refusing to carry munitions. Well, one really does have to draw the line somewhere!"

"You're a good Christian," the Christian whispers. "I was the same; I helped out in the kitchens because the Chef told me we were feeding the non-combatants. But I saw him give some of our food to soldiers, to buff them up for war. So I went on strike and, by the grace of God, here I am! You guided me Jesus! You're my hero!"

"Oh, you're a dashed stouthearted fellow, gee-whiz you're swell," the Apprentice says. "But chopping vegetables for soldiers? Fancy that!

"I haven't lifted a single finger for those blighters since they tore up my exemption to serve in the *Medical Corps*. They court-martialled me when I refused to clean the kitchen-floor with a toothbrush.

"But we'll be fine now we're all here together, I know we will! For sure we'll grumble about this crooked-deal, but we've got the patience of Job, the sand of a gamecock, and humour which tickles me to the bone. We'll have a lark and a jocund time. We'll stick it to those darned warmakers! Yes we will!"

"Stick it to them? Yes," the Clerk adds with a groan, as he fiddles with this stone, and this piece of ancient-bone. "Show 'em we're strong? Yes. They respect strength. But do they respect us? No! No-one likes a conchie."

They continue this conversation until they fall asleep on top of these bits of rock, and bits of block; which graze their sodden-skin. There is barely any food on which to feed, it is far too dark to read; and it is far too cold to sing.

So days-follow-nights before they adjust, to this soppy-water and this bready-crust; whilst they suffer from broken-sleep. Before the Nurse joins them, covered in phlegm; and smelling like a soggy-sheep.

"What happened to you old chum?" Alfred begins to cheep. "Please tell us. Please-please-please."

"Well, one was so awfully ashamed of oneself," the Nurse whispers as he tries not to weep. "One should never have marched, it was a ghastly thing to do, but the army had me on toast. One was wracked with nerves, without the courage to join in with your marvellous-stand.

"It took some time for one to pull oneself together, but one eventually came through. One told those blaggards, 'One is disinclined to acquiesce with your requests'. And so one did not march that day, the next day, or on any other day. The warmakers did consider one peculiar.

"Oh darlings! They dragged one through the gravel for an hour each day, wearing nothing but one's underwear, until one was red-raw all over. And they kicked-and-punched one too.

"But one just thought of you! I must say that you have been rather inspiring. A jolly good show you boys put on out there. Rah-rah-rah!"

These conchies soon become accustomed to the lice-locusts and-leaks, as days melt into weeks; whilst they eat stale-bread and drink muddy-tea. Before they meet this German Prisoner of war, who was washed ashore; after his ship was torpedoed at sea.

"I'm here for refusing to kill Germans," the Clerk says whilst he fiddles with his knee. "Why are we at war? Politicians! The British soldiers would be fighting for Germany if they'd been born over there. You'd be fighting for Britain if you'd been born here. Are you Germans any different to us? No! We're all the same. We're all human. Ghastly thing this war."

"You don't zink ziss is a goot conflict?" The German Prisoner asks as he wipes away this dust.

"No such thing as a good-conflict," the Clerk replies as he fiddles with this sock, this rock; and this rust. "No such thing as a bad-peace. Why are you fighting? Because you've never considered not fighting! Stop! Become a conchie. No-one likes a conchie."

"Huhuhu, hihihi, heeheehee, hahaha, HAHAHA!" The German Prisoner laughs. "Very goot, very goot. Yah, I'll oppose zee war like you, I zink, if I can. Very goot, very goot!"

These noisy-chuckles, encourage the Curt Cadet to use his bony-knuckles; to beat the silence back into these cells. But despite this treatment and despite his diet, Alfred enjoys the quiet; during these soundless-spells.

Because his life has been so fevered-frenzied-and-frenetic, so busy and so energetic; every day up till now. So Alfred appreciates this absence of prattle, tittle-tattle; and powwow.

He sits near these hairy-flies, closes his eyes; and exists in peaceful-contemplation. He feels like a king, as he unites with everything; in the whole of earthly-creation.

His breath travels from bronchiole-to-bronchi-to-larynx, up through his pharynx; and all the way out through his nose. He becomes calm, in each ankle-armpit-and-arm; as he frees his fingers and frees his toes.

'*Liberate your mind, Alfie!*' His mentor once told him, with a grin; whilst he wore his German clothes. '*Dear boy, you cannot become trapped by anger-jealousy-fear-or-desire. You must centre yourself, yah. You must become still in order to see beyond perceptions-ant-sensations.*'

So Alfred practices until he surpasses the Good German's abilities, despite the surrounding hostilities; and despite those noisy geese. He becomes a little bit introspective, and a little bit reflective; but achieves some inner-peace.

"Good God, what are you doing Alfred?" The Christian asks, aghast; because he thinks his friend might be going insane.

"Being," Alfred replies, with peace in his eyes; because he considers his behaviour mundane.

"Being?" The Christian questions again. "Bless your heart, we're all being. That doesn't explain why you're sat cross-legged on the floor, closing your eyes for hours on end."

"No," Alfred tries to explain. "Please! Most of us are too busy doing things, actions and whatnot, to simply be."

"My Lord! Pray whatever do you mean? I think you're suffering from truth-decay and need to brush up on your bible. God wants us to act first, don't you my Lord? Our actions make us who we are!"

"Kindness can make us kind, and love can make us loving," Alfred admits. "It's called *involution-and-evolution*; *involving* yourself in actions in order to *evolve* your being. But your actions never become your being. No-no-no. No thanky-you! There's always a divide.

"Please let me tell you a story to explain. It's about a busy Businessman was always doing this or doing that; buying-and-selling, hiring-and-firing, leading-and-lecturing. All day, every day, he was always on the go.

"Until he looked into a mirror one morning and realised that the person he saw wasn't actually himself; it was just a pale-pale-pale reflection of his body's image.

"The Businessman realised that his actions, like the image in the mirror, weren't his real self either; they were just a pale-pale-pale reflection of his inner-being.

"So he spent a weekend in the countryside. He didn't buy-or-sell, hire-or-fire, lead-or-lecture at all. He didn't do a single thing. And because he refrained from action, the phony-reflection of himself faded away. His actions could no longer define him!

"For the first time in his life, he was able to see himself for who he really was. He saw his real being. And he was ever so grateful. He was very much obliged."

"Why now though?" The Christian asks. "Why here?"

"Being imprisoned has set me free, I suppose," Alfred laughs. "I should be thankful for it really."

"Perhaps it's why you were arrested. God does everything for a reason, don't you my Lord? When you close a window you open a door. Yes, you will deliver us! You will *save us from the hands of the wicked, and deliver us from the grasp of the cruel*, like you said you would in Jeremiah fifteen."

"That's nice," Alfred nods. "Being arrested has certainly given me time to think. I'm grateful for that.

"I've been thinking about our defence of Belgium, our naval-blockade, and our African campaigns. Actions-actions-actions! Acts of war. But, please understand, actions which originate from the very nature of our nation, the very essence of our nation, and the very *being* of our nation. A nation who, after *involvement* in centuries of wars, has *evolved* into a warring nation; a nation with an innate propensity to fight.

"Please understand! This war won't end in peace. No-no-no! The nations fighting today will fight again tomorrow. Like a shark returning to an old hunting-ground, unable to resist the allure of fresh-blood, it's in their very nature.

"We'll return to the same battlefields, shoot the same soldiers, and fight the same nations again. Give it twenty years; you'll see.

"And then we'll turn our allies into foes, and fight them with new allies by our side. And then we'll turn our new allies into foes, and fight them too. It's a never ending cycle.

"We're always fighting with Germany-Ireland-and-France, Iraq-Palestine-and-Afghanistan. It's not about actions, or whether an individual war is right-or-wrong; it's a matter of being. It's become our nations' nature to fight-fight-fight, war-war-war and kill-kill-kill. Such that if an enemy didn't exist for us to fight, we'd be forced to invent one!"

"So," the Christian says. "In order to bring about peace, we must become peace!"

"Through *involution-and-evolution*," Alfred concurs. "Through *acting* peacefully and *becoming* peaceful. For peace cannot exist in actions alone. No-no-no. No thanky-you! It must be a part of our very being."

Alfred begins to smile, as he crosses his legs in the eastern-style; and close his peaceful-eyes. The Christian joins in, and begins to grin; as he tries to improvise.

After a few more days the Apprentice has his straitjacket replaced with a shawl, so he begins to engrave this wall; with this piece of shiny-rock. With this piece of crumbly-stone, crumbly-bone; and crumbly-block.

The Tax Collector draws images of his Lord, writes '*Don't live by the sword*'; and '*Men should brothers be*'. Whilst the Apprentice draws on this door, writes '*Fight the class war*'; and '*Peace-and-harmony*'.

Before the Lanky Cadet enters this room with force, and limps like an overworked-horse; as he carries this milky-brew. He approaches the Nurse, who starts to converse; before he removes this soldier's shoe.

The Nurse listens to the Lanky Cadet's description, gives him a medical-prescription; and starts to clean his shin. The Nurse stitches these ruts, and bandages these cuts; which makes this soldier grin.

"Do be a doll, old bean," he asks the next time the Lanky Cadet walks in. "Do help one to send a letter home to one's Ma and Pa? I fear they will be awfully worried."

And so a few days later, the Lanky Cadet brings this brown-paper; which he smuggles past that Guard. Who is distracted by this Goon, and that military-platoon; which is marching across that yard.

'*There are twenty-four of us in three small-cells*', the Nurse writes on this card. '*Including five other conchies who are also in irons for refusing to drill. But despite all the beatings-and-threats, we're still standing strong. Please do everything you can to let the public know*'.

"I'll send it at once, patch," the Lanky Cadet neighs, and brays, whilst he paws his feet and sways. "But I'll charge you the *price of a pint* if you ever want any help again. The other steeds in here wouldn't help you for all the money in the world, but I like you blaze, I think you're alright!"

Alfred starts to jiggle, grin-gurgle-and-giggle; because he loves this old-fashioned British enterprise. Which reminds him of the British hawkers, and British pavement-walkers; who sell papers-pasties-and-pies.

And he laughs at this black-eyed and red-nosed Scot, who is covered in green-snot; which drips down his purple-head. This man avoids the war in the east, by being abusive when he is released; in order to be locked here instead.

"I admire ye wee laddies!" He sloshes with his arms outspread. "Ye are cowards, but ye are outspoken cowards, an' that's ma favoureet kindee coward!"

The Scot's words fill Alfred with a joyous sort of cheer, as he is removed from here; and paraded through this military-base. Where he is deafened by these Soldiers who are learning to fight, dazzled by this natural-light; and overwhelmed by this open-space.

Alfred's ears are bombarded by this orchestra of firing-guns, these steely Marchers with steely-drums; and this Officer with a hairy-chest. Before he is weighed, and has his eyes prised open by this Opticians' Aide; during an official sight-test.

But Alfred refuses to dig the foundations for dormitory-floors, wash this cutlery here indoors, or tidy the clothes in those munitions-stores.

"Please understand," he explains as he stands near this chest of drawers. "Please-please-please. The dormitory will house soldiers before they fight-fight-fight, this cutlery will be used to feed them up to kill-kill-kill, and these uniforms will cover them in battle."

"Build this rifle range now, you peace-crank!" The Curt Cadet cries.

"No thanky-you. It'll be used to train soldiers to kill," Alfred replies.

"Clean this bus now, you Heinie lover!"

"No thanky-you. It'll be used to take soldiers to war."

"Load these supplies now, you pacifist-skunk!"

"No thanky-you. They'll be used to fuel the murder."

"If you don't do what I say right here, right now, right away," the Curt Cadet continues to moan, and groan, with a stench of cheap-cologne. "You'll be sent to France to lay barbed-wire in *No Man's Land*, where Jerry will shoot you down before you know it. And if you refuse to follow orders out there, you'll be shot by a firing-squad. Either way, you'll be coming home in a body-bag.

"So I suggest you suck up whatever misplaced pride is fuelling your stubbornness, and behave responsibly for once. For your good, not for mine, understand? Because a pint of sweat saves a gallon of blood, and those are your only options now; blood or sweat, life or death, be cured or be killed. It's the army way. Just you wait-and-see!"

Alfred had seen the alley in which he was mugged, and the gun which his Father once slugged; every time he had fallen asleep. He had seen the alley in which he could be prosecuted, and the guns with which he could be executed; which made him want to weep.

But not anymore! Not like before! Alfred is strong-steady-and-sure!

He does not speak, shriek; or shout. He begins to grin, breathes in; and breathes out.

His breath travels from bronchiole-to-bronchi-to-larynx, up through his pharynx; and all the way out through his nose. He follows this breathing-exercise, and starts to rise; as he frees his fingers and frees his toes. Before he is thrown back into this cell, where he is left to dwell; dressed in these dirty-clothes.

He is beaten-bullied-and-burned, released-reprimanded-and-returned; taken from prison and then put straight back. But like when the Suffragist experienced this *Cat And Mouse* treatment, he does not lament; or start to crack.

He gets imprisoned when he refuses to salute, looks astute; and remains silent. When he refuses to march, looks parched; and remains non-violent.

But this pantomime cannot last, the time for games has passed; and this charade has gotten old. So Alfred is shown into this office which is full of wooden-boards, hanging-cords; and fungal-mould.

"Please take a seat, Alfred," the Proud Captain says with manners which put Alfred at ease, before he begins to sneeze; because of his latest cold.

"*Aah-choo*!"

"Bless you!"

"Hmm. Yes. Well then. I've been bestowed with instructions to cancel your *District Court Martial*; a bond which, not to mince matters, galls both of us diabolically.

"Your *Non Combatant Corps* is being sent to France. Such things didn't happen when I was your age, but these are the times we're living in.

"Although I'm inclined to believe that you don't quite understand what this means, Private Freeman. In France you'll be under active service conditions; playing the hanky-panky jackass out there shall get you shot quick-sharpish. Your friends in parliament shan't be able to do anything to help you.

"Have I made myself clear?"

"Very clear, thank-you. Our politicians, elected to protect our people, have been usurped. Your army is staging a coup d'état!" Alfred says sarcastically.

"Upon my senses, you do talk lofty," the Proud Captain replies bombastically. "People wouldn't have had the gall to parley with their betters like that in my day. Really, Alfred! Pull yourself together.

"Now! Please take your pay, submit a list of your next of kin, and write your will in the army pay-book. Put yourself tidy, and off you go."

Alfred is able to rise above this threat, but he finds his comrades covered in sweat; with a variety of diverse-intentions. Some are seeking a fight, some are seeking flight; and some are seeking divine-interventions.

The Nurse is unable to speak through his wobbly-lips, as he rocks away on his wobbly-hips; quivers-quavers-and-quakes. Whilst the Tax Collector covers himself in ashes, plucks his eyelashes; shivers-shudders-and-shakes.

"Are we just going to let them kill us? No!" The Clerk says as he ups the stakes. "Stand up for our rights? Yes. Stick it to 'em? Yes. Take 'em down? Yes. Does anyone like a conchie? No! No-one likes a conchie."

"Bless you," the Christian replies. "But it's no good fighting the soldiers with our fists; they're well trained in violence, and so we wouldn't stand a chance. As Galatians five says; *if we bite-and-devour each other, we'll all be destroyed.* If you give the devil an inch, he'll become your ruler.

"No. We should hang out with Jesus; he hung for us after all. We should use our spiritual-force to overcome the warmaker's evil with good. We should let the army take us anywhere, do anything to us, at any time; just so long as we don't succumb to their tyranny. Because they may take our lives, but they'll never take our freedom!

"My Lord, you will *release us prisoners, give good news to the poor, and set the oppressed free!* Just like you said you would in Luke four."

"You'll let them shoot us? We're no good dead," the Clerk says whilst he fiddles with his head, this bread, and this led. "Ghastly thing this war. Do good? Do nothing! Overcome them? They'll overcome us!"

"No-no-no!" Alfred interjects. "We must be prepared to face the bullets for this cause.

"Please understand! If soldiers are prepared to die for their beliefs, then we must be prepared to die for ours as well. We must be as reckless as the warmakers in order to prove that we're not just cowards; it's the only way we'll win the hearts-and-minds of the people in our nation. It's the only way we'll convert the British people to peace.

"Please! Let's not fight the soldiers or lower ourselves to their level. Let's refute them, resist them, and repel them!

"We won't give them a list of our next of kin, take a wage, or write our wills. We won't fight like them, act like them, or be like them. We'll form a *Peace Unit*, a part of a *Peace Army*, on a crusade for peace-peace-peace. I'd be ever so grateful if you'd join me. I'd be much obliged."

"Peace Unit!" The Tax Collector cries as he overcomes his fear.

"Peace Unit!" Alfred replies as he smiles from ear-to-ear.

"Peace Unit!" The other conchies cheer.

Alfred gets slapped near his eye-socket, has his wages shoved into his pocket; and then throws it all away. Before his comrades stare at those hills, refuse to submit their wills; and ignore what these Soldiers say. Whilst they use the paper they are given, to write letters about being in prison; which they then hide out the way.

"Let's get a move on," the Curt Cadet begins to say. "Let's go!"

"Only if you push me first," the Apprentice replies without hesitation, procrastination; or delay. "We wouldn't want anyone to think that we've marched of our own accord."

So the Apprentice is pushed through this sludge which is brown and this debris which is black, whilst Alfred is given his old backpack; which hangs from his bony-shoulders. Figure-of-eight handcuffs pin his arms behind his spine, as he walks past this mine; which is surrounded by mossy-boulders.

The Peace Unit walk past these neatly-trimmed trees, which flutter in this breeze; which is full of delicious fresh-air. As these birds begin to sing, and those bees begin to sting; near this rabbit and near that hare.

They walk through pink-fields which are full of flies, and see these porcelain-skies; which turn leaves from green-to-yellow. They walk down these soppy-roads, and see these croaking-toads; who goad that elderly Fellow.

They walk past villages which are full of freshly-cut hay, horses which neigh; apple-trees and blackberry-hedges. These mossy church-spires, those burning-fires; and that row of painted-ledges.

These fields seem soundless, this sky seems boundless; and those rillets all seem to slither. As the Peace Unit walk past this exposed-pipe, this muddy-dike; and that overflowing-river.

As they cross this flooded-floor, separated from their *Non Combatant Corps*; who have been quarantined with measles. As they sing to these tunnelling moles, these hiding voles; and that pack of skinny-weasels.

As they sing '*I didn't raise my boy to be a soldier*' for the conchies without religions, '*Trusting every day*' for the Christians; and songs for peace. As they sing songs from the *Labour Songbook* for the socialists, *'God save the King'* for the nationalists; and songs for wars to cease.

And after a couple more hours, they pass these weather-beaten towers; with feet which are covered in blisters. Before they enter this station which is full of Servicemen, Firemen; Sentries-Servants-and-Sisters.

Where they see these Guards whistling at youths, and hanging from booths; whilst they check tickets-tokens-and-tracks. Whilst these Porters run this way and that, and stop to chat; before they move parcels-packets-and-packs. Before Coal Shovellers change trains, and carry grains; using these hessian-sacks.

"I'd watch out for them there soldiers returning home for leave," this Ticket Inspector says as he adjusts his cotton-slacks. "Bunch of drunkards the lot of 'em! You take care of yourselves."

And this Supervisor is considerate too, as he removes these handcuffs without much ado, and puts them down by his shoe.

"Please put them on again later," Alfred says whilst he sits on this wooden-pew. "Please-please-please. So it's clear that we're being taken by force."

"Err-hmm, err-hum, err-okay," the Supervisor replies, with surprise, and bemusement in both of his eyes.

And whilst their train starts to rumble with this gentle-vibration, Alfred looks out at this busy train-station; which is totally chockablock. He sees these Children who are going to the seaside, this Grieving Mother who is teary-eyed; and this dangling gothic-clock.

He sees this salty Sailor, this smartly-dressed Tailor; and this Sign Painter who carries his kit. This Cloth Merchant, this Servant; and this Miner who has been down a pit.

"Thank the heavens! That's our girl!" Alfred shouts through this slit. "She was at one of my pro-peace talks. Oh yes! Yes-yes-yes. Thank-you, thank-you, thank-you. She nodded along as I spoke!"

And so he rings this bell, starts to yell, and shouts out loud as well.

"Hey-hey-hey! Please-please-please! Friend-friend-friend!"

But this majestic old steam-train shouts *'choo-choo'*, starts to clunk-cackle-and-coo; wail-whoop-and-whistle. With the *clickety-clicks* of changing-tracks, the *cluckety-clucks* of engine-jacks; and coupling-rods which bristle.

"Comrade! Comrade! Comrade!" Alfred yowls.

"Sister! Sister! Sister!" He growls.

"Here! Here! Here!" He howls.

This Disciple who is dressed in a frilly white-shirt, and a frilly white-skirt; hears Alfred's cacophonous-voice. So her arms start to thrash, and her legs start to dash; more out of instinct than out of choice.

She jinks between these vending-machines, these jam-packed canteens; and these Boer War Survivors. These Telegraphers, these Stenographers; and that group of chatty Train Drivers.

But this rickety old steam-train, starts to hoot and starts to strain; as it starts to pull away. Alfred's Disciple is already at full-speed, on a stampede; which makes her shimmy-sidestep-and-sway.

"Please give me your letters," Alfred begins to say. "Please-please-please!"

He takes the letters which his friends just wrote, and removes his own note; whilst his heart begins to pound. Whilst his Disciple runs along, and seems sturdy-steady-and-strong; as she makes up all this ground. As this crowd thins out, her lips pout; and her bottom wiggles around.

But this train begins to accelerate, it passes this grille-gantry-and-gate; and it flexes its metal-muscle. It builds up a head of steam, passes this platform-ending beam; starts to clunk and starts to rustle.

"What on earth do you think you're doing?" The Escort questions with angry indignation, and pent-up frustration; as he tries to hold Alfred back. But Alfred escapes his grasp, and his crow-like clasp; to throw his letters down near that track.

"Thank-you for asking," he says in response to this attack. "Your teeth are as white as clouds, and your eyes are as blue as waterfalls!

"Well, I'm making sure-sure-sure that people know where we're being taken. That's all. Thanking you!"

Alfred cannot see if his Disciple has caught any report, any packet of any sort; or any of their cards. Because this train makes a deafening-blast, and starts to move fast; past that row of backyards.

It pulls him across these viaducts which are held by giant-arches, these squadrons who are embarking on military-marches; and these brown-streets which are full of brown-rain. These brown-fields which are full of brown-barns, this endless series of shimmering-tarns; and this animal covered plane.

In a state of constant vibration, this steam train rests at every station; to catch its smoky-breath. Soldiers board at these stations, fresh from their vacations; and set for disputes-dogfights-and-death.

They sit near this Pensioner with a golden-tooth, who is sprawled across his third-class booth; without any sort of grace. This Couple who kiss in the corridor, this blind Spinster with her labrador; and this Teenager who wears a brace. This overbearing Mother, with the pink Baby she loves to smother; and a smirk on her painted-face. And this lonesome Woman, who sits on a cushion; as she stares into empty-space.

And after many more hours, which are full of sleet-slush-and-showers; the Peace Unit board this boat. They pass this box of salmon, this soggy-cannon; and that soggy-coat.

Unused to being away from solid-ground, the Apprentice stumbles around; with legs which turn to jelly. He trips over his feet, over this seat; and over this Bonehead's belly.

"Jackass!" The Bonehead yaps.

"Jerk!" This Blockhead raps.

"Jagwacker!" This Belligerent screams, as he wakes from his garish-dreams; scared of a life full of bully-beef. Scared of a life full of blasting-shells, living-hells; and these waves which are causing him grief. He pees in his hat, chews his cravat; and gets drunk in search of relief.

England disappears from view, the sun disappears too; and the sky turns completely grey. It turns this dour-shade, whilst the smiles all fade; and the singing all goes away.

This is the Peace Unit's new world, it is cold; cramped-caliginous-and-confused. They are cut off from their nation, each relation; and each piece of the news.

The news that Russia has invaded Armenia with marching-bands, Bulgaria has invaded Macedonian lands; and Hungary has fallen to Romania. The news that food prices have increased by sixty percent in just two years, which has filled Brits with fears; and a hungry sort of mania.

The news that nineteen-thousand British soldiers were slaughtered by machinegun fire, in a boggy-mire; on just one horrendous day. Because life is cheap, now conscription can herd people like sheep; and replace the dead with men who do not want to enter the fray.

And the news of the Nurse's first letter, which was carried beneath the Lanky Cadet's sweater; before it was put on a postal express. Before it was passed to a Professor from the Nurse's degree, the relation of an esteemed MP; who ran to parliament in distress. Where he saw the Prime Minister, who he told that his army was being sinister; and making a real mess.

'*Abominable!*' The Prime Minister cried as he clutched his gown.

'*Abominable!*' He cried as he paced up-and-down.

'*Abominable!*' He cried with a frown.

For in spite of the politicians who resisted, the Prime Minister had personally insisted; on exemptions to avoid such abuses. So this news worried him, and put his head in a spin; as he ignored his Aides' excuses.

"The army will hear nothing of politics from me," he said as he drank some juices. "And in return, I expect to hear nothing of politics from the army. Abominable!"

But Alfred is completely unaware of this communication, the Professor's conversation; and the Aides' vociferous-debate. He is only aware of this Warrant Officer's rocking-head, his moustache which is red; and his hair which is unnaturally-straight.

"Welcome to France, mermen!" He yells whilst his lungs inflate. "Welcome to death-and-glory, gremlins! Welcome to war! Bish! Bash! Bosh!"

Alfred stands somewhat informally, and holds himself normally; as he looks at that new train-line. As he inhales this smell of garlic-gunfire-and-grass, brie-battles-and-brass; waffles-weapons-and-wine.

"Well, well, well!" The Warrant Officer continues to whine. "I'd heard of conscientious objectors, like I'd heard of giants-goblins-and-ghosts, but I never believed that you monsters were real. Not till now.

"Well, you may have your convictions, but I've got my convictions too. I've got a conviction that I can make you fairies work, make you fauns sweat, and make you fiends crack. Bish! Bash! Bosh!"

This Warrant Officer's head-nodding, finger-prodding; and *bish-*

bash-bosh-ism have no bounds. His feet '*bish*' as they stomp around, '*bash*' the ground; and '*bosh*' with these thunderous-sounds.

As he marches the Peace Unit up with a *bish-bash-bosh*, before he marches them down through these puddles which slosh; sending water everywhere. And when they are neither up nor down, they pass this Villager who has been to town; who gives them some scrumpy to share.

"Take a little for your stomach," she says as she eats this juicy-pear. "And take some more for your muscles, *mes amis. C'est trèes bon!*"

Even the Tax Collector, who is normally a teetotaller; drinks some of this pomaceous-brew. He looks bugged-bothered-and-brown, as he drinks it down; and becomes lightheaded too. Before the Clerk starts to flee, starts to pee; and starts to spew.

"Well, well, well! Did I say you could stop marching, golem?" The Warrant Officer shouts with a noisy sort of *bish*, as he *bashes* the Clerk with anguish; and *boshes* his stubbly-head. The Clerk pants for breath as he zips his fly, near that Passerby; wooden-fence and wooden-shed.

Before the Peace Unit walk past this church with a wooden-door, these sleeping Pensioners who start to snore; and this Maid who starts to mop. These peacocks who start to preen, this rustic village-green; and this rustic village-shop.

They reach this *Portside Encampment*, where they walk past the ill-injured-and-incompetent; who work hard and gamble even harder. This Southerner fashions a lighter from an empty-shell, whilst this Northerner stares at a gangly-bell; without much appetite-attachment-or-ardour.

They pass these Crooks with exposed-nipples, these Cripples; and this tangled barbed-wire. And they enter their new room, after they pass this tomb; and that rather swampy-mire.

Full of these bedspreads, blinds-blankets-and-beds; this place is nicer than the cells they were locked in before. Although it is spoilt by these smashed-windows, which drip glass onto these pillows; and all over this concrete-floor.

"The soldiers discovered we're conchies last night," this skew-whiff Watchmaker explains with a roar. "They threw us their stones to welcome us on board!"

With a skew-whiff ear, the Watchmaker is one of seven new

conchies in here; who have been classified as a threat to security. This Socialist-Schoolmaster-and-Engineer, all seem to be sincere; with Alfred's sort of purity. But this Athlete-Agitator-and-Coward, seem far less empowered; without Alfred's sort of maturity.

"We were shoved up against a wall and had blanks fired at us, didn't we?" The Schoolmaster says, as he looks both ways, and gives the Socialist a friendly-gaze. "It was as if we were modern-day Saint Sebastians, being shot at by Roman archers for clinging to our beliefs."

"It was the bloody capitalists what done it," the Socialist starts to speak, whilst his bed starts to creak, with legs which wobble and springs which squeak. "They're barmy, the whole lot of them. God gives them a power like the motor car, and what do they do? They go careering around in goggles killing children! And now the blighters want to kill us."

"They tore clumps out of my hair," the Engineer adds with this nervous-grin, as he tilts his head to show this skin, and this scar which covers his chin. "It hurt something chronic. Really, whatever have I done to deserve this? Have I been cruel to animals? Have I sinned in a past life? Have I dishonoured my parents? Oh my. Oh my. Oh my."

"I've been whipped, and rocked, and socked. But I'll get those suckers back; they don't know who they're messing with," the hairy Agitator competes, as he punches these sheets, and jumps on these seats. "Just you lemme at 'em! I'll kill the British King! I'll kill the German Kaiser! I'll kill 'em all!"

"They played hardball with me," the muscled Athlete tweets. "They tied my ankles to my wrists, behind my back, and left me until I was struck out; it was par for the course in my barracks."

"I was made to eat my own manure," the Coward cries, and sighs, with rainy-tears in his cloudy-eyes. "No-one gave me a bucket, so I relieved myself in a corner, and a soldier rubbed my face in it. I suppose he had to, hadn't he?"

"You win," the Watchmaker replies. "I thought they treated me badly when they locked me in a cubbyhole, which they rocked every hour to deprive me of sleep. But your story beats mine hands down!"

"Anyway," the Schoolmaster resumes. "We were thrown together in a medieval castle, which hadn't been used since the days of Viking invasions and Norman conquests. And we were packed off to France, weren't we?"

"Yeah! I sucked it to the warmakers when they made us march," the Agitator boasts. "I said; *'Lemme at 'em! I'll splat 'em, I'll rock 'em and I'll sock 'em'! Peace power!'* And I didn't move an inch."

"But it didn't do you any good, did it?" The Schoolmaster interjects. "They dragged you by your feet, didn't they? It was just like when Ganymede was punished for his homosexuality. And they made the rest of us march with bag-straps around our windpipes."

"That's awful," Alfred says. "We formed a *Peace Unit*, a part of a *Peace Army*, and we launched a crusade for peace-peace-peace!"

"I'll enlist in that," the Watchmaker chimes as he stands near this door. "All for one and one for all!"

"I like the cut of your jib!" The Athlete starts to roar. "All for one and one for all!"

"All for one and one for all!" The other conchies implore.

"All for one and one for all!" The Socialist says once more. "Us workers should unite! This is a capitalist war, made by the capitalists, and fought by us workers. The capitalists want to spin it out until we're too weak to fight back, but we won't let that happen. No way! The revolution starts here!"

So these outcasts unite, with delirium-delectation-and-delight, which makes them feel ballsy-brilliant-and-bright.

"We didn't resist our deportation at all," Alfred admits as he stands upright. "Please understand! We thought we could be more of a nuisance out here, a bit like the *Donkey In The Well*."

"The *Donkey In The Well*?" The Schoolmaster asks feeling enthused, confused, baffled-bewildered-and-bemused. "Like the donkey ridden by the Greek God *Dionysus*, the Hindu God *Kalaratri*, or *Jesus Christ* our Lord?"

"Maybe," Alfred replies. "It's a story from a long-long-long time ago, when a Donkey tripped hoof-over-heel and heel-over-hoof. The silly old thing fell down a deep-well!

"When Donkey didn't return home that night, his Master began to worry. So he launched a search to bring Donkey back within his ranks.

"And after many hours, he found Donkey neighing-and-braying, whinging-and-whining, and moaning-and-groaning. But he was unable to remove Donkey from his well. It was just too deep!

"Please understand! Donkey was so old that his Master didn't think he was worth saving. So his Master recruited some villagers, who helped him to shovel dirt into that well. They tried to bury Donkey alive!

"But Donkey just shrugged the dirt off his back, stamped it down, and created a hard-floor beneath his hooves.

"And as the well filled with debris, Donkey was lifted up. He gave his Master a nonchalant-glance, whinnied, and walked free.

"I bet he was rather grateful in the end. I bet he felt obliged."

Some of these conchies listen politely, some of them laugh lightly; and some of them start to clap. Twelve disciples face Alfred, twenty-four eyes stare at his head; and forty-eight limbs start to flap.

"So," the Schoolmaster starts to yap. "The Master is like the army-officers who are trying to bury our beliefs alive. The villagers are the British soldiers, the Master's willing accomplices, like the Egyptians who enslaved the Jews on behalf of their Pharaohs. And we're like Donkey, aren't we? We're the innocent-victims who are suffering today, in order to win our freedom tomorrow!"

"You've got it!" Alfred replies as he stamps down with his boots, amidst these slaps-smiles-and-salutes, howls-hollers-and-hoots. "Thank-you, thank-you, thank-you. I really am grateful to be in your presence. I like you more than homemade apple-pie!

"We allowed the army to deport us because it was like having dirt poured over our heads. Our passive resistance in France will lift us up, until the warmakers can't help but realise that we're not beneath them. In the heat of the battle, against all the odds, we'll achieve a greater victory out here. We'll win our freedom! We'll win freedom for the whole of humankind. Yes-yes-yes. Yes thanky-you!"

"Passive resistance," the Christian adds. "Lord bless you! It's just like when you, Jesus, were put on trial. *Offer no resistance to anyone evil*, you said in Matthew five. And we're listening!

"If the warmakers order us to cook we'll refuse, if they order us to clean we'll refuse, and if they order us to march we'll refuse as well. But we won't lash out, we won't strike back, and we won't fight them. We'll never sink to their level.

"We'll let you into our hearts, Jesus. We'll let you guide our lives, and we'll let you save our souls!"

The Peace Unit talks for a few more hours, before they are ordered to march past these flowers; which are planted along this groove. But as their company marches away, towards that golden-hay; they stand still and refuse to move.

"Well, well, well! I'll fine you your wages, you gorgons! Bish-Bash-Bosh!" The Warrant Officer shouts across this deck, as his head bobs away on his springy-neck; which shakes his khaki-gown.

"We're already refusing to take a penny, sucker! Peace power!" The Agitator shouts whilst he starts to frown.

"The poor don't profit from war anyway," the Socialist shouts whilst he bobs up-and-down. "Only the rich profit from war, the poor pay for it with their lives. You can keep your money; we can't be bought!"

This is a victory which is followed once more, as so often before; by a counterattack from the military-machine. Which tries to destroy the Peace Unit's solidarity, with military-barbarity; when it divides these thirteen.

But the Apprentice refuses to paint a door, the Agitator refuses to use a saw; and the Athlete refuses to mop. The Engineer cleans some handles, and carries some candles; but the Clerk gets him to stop.

Alfred is taken to this camp's boundary, and locked in this foundry; where injured soldiers are making fixings for a train-line. They dent-divide-and-drill, flex-forge-and-fill; sand-solder-and-shine.

By his side is this redheaded, bow-legged, and fear-imbedded; sort of a wimpish Coward. Unlike his fellow conchies, this boy has knocking-knees; and is unempowered. He feels queasy, uneasy; and devoured.

This boy is scared of flying, dentists-diseases-and-dying; doctors-deformity-and-drakes. He is scared of outsiders, sheep-swans-and-spiders; slugs-scorpions-and-snakes.

"I should probably be in the *Non Combatant Corps*, I suppose," he says as he shakes. "But in a moment of madness, I refused to polish some pebbles, and so they brought me here with you guys.

"It was most out of character. I mean, you must understand, that I shared a room with my three brothers as a child because I was too scared to sleep on my own. I've always feared the police, and I'm afraid of hospitals-exams-and-crowds; they all give me the heebie-jeebies!"

Even speaking makes the Coward shake, quiver-quaver-and-quake; so he stumbles towards this spade. Before the Warrant Officer shouts as loudly as he can, as if his volume makes him a man; and justifies this tirade.

"Stand to attention when I address you! You yetis! Bish-Bash-Bosh!"

The Coward stands up to salute, turns white and turns mute; because he feels weak without his other comrades. Whilst Alfred stands still, ignores this man's will; and ignores his childish charades.

So the Warrant Officer *bishes* Alfred's legs out straight, *bashes* Alfred's arms with all his weight; and *boshes* Alfred's bony-back. He makes the Coward sort some nails into packets, and sand some brackets; before he storms down that stony-track.

"They can't make you do that," Alfred says as he leans against this rack. "The rest of the Peace Unit will be refusing orders, like you did before. Please stop. Please-please-please. Do it for them."

"I suppose, I think, I guess," the Coward says as he gazes around.

"I'd follow orders if I were you," this Zealous Soldier starts to expound. "The other conchies who've come this way all done got conformed, done got hard labour, or done got shot. There's a list in the officer's canteen of their fates; death-or-conformity. You kiddies will be next!"

"Don't be listenin' to that eejit," this Sympathetic Soldier who is covered in cement, which has an earthy-scent, says in an Irish accent. "I expect they'll be takin' you boyos to the *Front Line Camp* if they want to shoot ya. Ta be sure! Ta be sure! They haven't ever shot anyone out here.

"Truth of the matter is no-one knows what they'll do to ya. The Hungarians do be slaughterin' Nazarenes for refusin' to fight, the Russians do be sendin' conchies to the front with bayonets tied to their necks, and the Americans do be tinkin' of imprisonin' peaceniks for tirty years, so they are.

"We wouldn't want that to befall ya! Especially when you don't even have to fight. The work us gammy dugout-hiders are doin', buildin' train-tracks here in the rear, hasn't ever got anyone killed. There's really no need to act the maggot or be a cod. It's only you I do be thinkin' of!"

This boy who is still in his teens, shares his Bovril-bread-and-beans;

and seems genuinely concerned for Alfred's wellbeing. So the Coward nods his ginger-head, with his arms outspread; as if he is agreeing.

"I'm only here to stand up for the small nations of Europe, the Belgiums and the Serbias, who aren't so different to Ireland. And because it could help us to win our independence back from you blackguardin' Brits!

"I couldn't join a firin' squad meself. Bejayzus! I'd sooner shoot the officer who was in charge, so I would. I came here to fight the Germans, not to be murderin' you guys. Ta be sure! Ta be sure!"

Similar scenes-situations-and-sentiments, with different actors from different regiments; repeat themselves each day. They take place in this prison-cell, in this workshop as well; and in this field which is full of hay.

Alfred does not work, nor do the Watchmaker-Schoolmaster-or-Clerk; but the Coward does gives in. There are some premonishments, some punishments; and some warmakers who make a din.

The Engineer is told *'You'll be killed'*, the Athlete that *'Your blood will be spilled'*; and the Nurse that *'Your protests will end in disaster'*. This Preachy Soldier talks to the Christian, and gets this Priest to visit him; who the Christian tells *'No minister is greater than his master'*. Before the Socialist gets hit, the Agitator gets bit; and the Apprentice gets covered in plaster.

Fast-forward through this show-reel at high-speed, pause-rewind-and-replay each generous-deed; and some highlights will come into view. This Frenchman tries to prostitute his sister without success, this Officer begins to stress; and this Maid brings some peaches too.

A casual approach towards sex seems to abound, in the army-sanctioned brothels which are all around; where soldiers can sleep with a whore. Where death-bound virgins can have the time of their lives, husbands can cheat on their wives; and soldiers can escape from the war.

"You should come and check them out, Freddie me lad," the Sympathetic Soldier says as they enter this store. "The crowds are like those at a footy match, and the rush to get in is a great craic. Girlies display themselves in dainty-lingerie, approach ya in the nip, and will take ya upstairs for a frank. It's a grand show, so it is. There are lassies with big-titties, little-titties and bouncy-titties. There are ones with legs which could choke ya, and ones who're shaven all over!"

"It's ever so kind of you to offer." Alfred replies. "You're a groovy dude. You're the cherries in my fruit salad. Yum! But it's really not our thing. Us conchies are on a moral crusade, so we have to be whiter than white. And anyway, I expect the girls are all full-full-full of diseases."

"Ta be sure! Ta be sure! The brassers with syphilis do be chargin' the most! Each dose is worth tirty days away from the trenches, so it is," the Sympathetic Soldier sings.

"They couldn't do that in Britain," Alfred rings. "I mean, our government, thanks to *Dora*, won't even allow you to possess a pigeon without a permit these days. Not without arresting you for it. They'd arrest anyone who gave a soldier a disease without thinking about it twice."

This proves to be the Peace Unit's last opportunity to go out, before the Warrant Officer starts to shout; and starts to fume. He adjusts his collar, starts to holler; and puts a curfew on the Peace Unit's room.

"Listen up you dirty bunch of trolls," he shouts with this look of doom. "I made you ogres one promise when you arrived, I promised that you'd work, and by God you'll work! Maybe not here, maybe not now, but mark my words; you manticores *will* comply!

"Because we turn lions into house-cats here, we turn wolves into puppies, and we turn sharks into goldfish too. Bish-bash-bosh! Every one of you dragons *will* be domesticated.

"Well, well, well! Tomorrow you'll be taken to the *Front Line Camp*. If you disobey orders there you'll be shot. Think about that, you dwarves! You wargs-werewolves-and-witches! Bish-bash-bosh!"

The Warrant Officer *bishes* his way across this grubby-floor, *boshes* his way through that grubby-door; and *bashes* his way outside. The Coward quakes, the Agitator shakes; and the Nurse looks horrified.

Alfred breathes in and breathes out, to escape his distress-discomfort-and-doubt; and to overcome his woes. His breath travels from bronchiole-to-bronchi-to-larynx, up through his pharynx; and all the way out through his nose. Before the Sympathetic Soldier arrives, smelling of chilli-cheese-and-chives; rum-relish-and-rose.

"Top-of-the-mornin' and a hundred-thousand welcomes to ya

laddies!" He sings whilst he taps his toes. "I heard ya do be goin' to the trenches. Well we've got a little tradition back where I come from; we give fellas headin' to war a rip-roaring send-off, so we do."

"A send-off? A party? A celebration? We can't do that. We're not allowed out. Can we afford it? No! No wages, no money, no gold. No-one likes a conchie." The Clerk replies whilst he fidgets with his chair, his hair, and his muddy-footwear.

"How much do ya be havin'?" The Sympathetic Soldier responds with his usual flair.

And so Alfred empties his pockets onto this bed, and nods his hairy-head; to lead by example. Before his comrades add these bronze-pieces, these notes which are full of creases; and this tatty linen-sample.

It is barely enough for some *Bisto*, and nowhere near enough for a party in a bistro; café-canteen-or-club. The Sympathetic Soldier leaves, the Agitator dusts his sleeves; and the Clerk looks out at a shrub.

"How's about ya?" The Sympathetic Soldier says when he returns with this massive amount of grub.

When he returns this rainy-evening, with this coffee which is steaming; and these fillets of fresh-hake. These pears-peaches-and-plums, bacon-burgers-and-buns; and this creamy chocolate-cake. Which has splashes of berries, sploshes of cherries; and sprinkles of chocolate-flake.

"We certainly backed the right horse here," the Athlete says as he eats a piece of steak. "We've hit the bull's eye! There's no way our money could've bought all this."

"Ya deserve it, so ya do," the Sympathetic Soldier says whilst he cuts the cake. "You've earned more respect than ya realise. Not from the slave-drivers, understand; they're all a bit arseways. But from plenty of footsloggers who think you're fierce brave, and wanted to be showin' ya their support. Ta be sure! Ta be sure!"

This sentiment makes the Watchmaker feel happy, the Nurse feel clappy; and the Agitator feel calmer too. He does not agitate tonight, he does not fight; and he welcomes these Soldiers without much ado.

He listens to their tales of filth-firearms-and-fears, tanks-trenches-and-tears; mustard-gas and warm-beers. About loopy-lieutenants who go berserk, mad-majors who make them work; and bonkers-brigadiers.

"We're not so different! Whenever they send me over the top I always shoot high. Just like you, I'll never kill anyone," this Tall Soldier says as he eats some berries.

"Shoot high?" This Short Soldier replies as he cuts some cheese. "I've never even loaded my gun! The ruperts never check the blasted thing."

"The Germans are in on it too," the Sympathetic Soldier agrees. "We be havin' a sort of agreement not to kill each other, so we do. They don't want to be here either."

This rag-tag group starts to sing like fishy-whalers, salty-sailors; and soldiers who are marching off to fight. They sing '*She Is Far From the Land*' feeling hunky-dory, and they sing '*Land Of Hope And Glory*'; with delirium-delectation-and-delight. They sing songs about being alone, about their home; and about their plight. And they feel great when they fall asleep here tonight.

They feel great when they walk through this rain, and when they board this sluggish-train; which is marked '*Forty Men and Thirteen Dogs Inside*'. They feel great when they are handcuffed, confined-contorted-and-crushed; torn-twisted-and-tied.

At first all is breezy and all is bright, without any sign of a feud-fracas-or-fight; trench-torpedo-or-tank. They pass fields full of grey stone-walls, markets full of farmer's stalls; and children playing petanque.

Red-and-white poppies infiltrate fields which are full of dry-wheat, horses-and-carts trot down a street; and soldiers share their *Bisto* cubes. This Private gets off the train to pick some apples, for these conchies who are still in shackles; and tied to these metal-tubes.

And so it seems to Alfred that soldiers become more considerate than ever before, the nearer they get to the war; and all of the war's afflictions. That the nearer they get to the war, the more soldiers understand what Alfred's campaign is for; and the more they understand his convictions.

But as the minutes turn into thirty long hours, these skies start to fill with acidic-showers; acidic-mist and acidic-rain. This thunder starts to crash, and this lightning starts to flash; over-and-over again.

So the Peace Unit's world is dank-dreary-and-damp, when they arrive at this *Front Line Camp*; which they walk through in pairs. They ride donkeys though this mud, and this flood; before they walk down these flooded-stairs.

They walk through this abandoned fish-market which smells of fish-brine, fish-spine; and fish-scales. And they walk past the these scraps of fish-skin, fish-fin; and fish-tails.

They walk past these wooden-poles, down through these wooden-holes; and into this underground wooden-box. Where they are unable to relax, with their arms behind their backs; and their feet in their crusty-socks.

"Listen-up cowfish! Listen-up hard!" This Commanding Officer screeches out like a fox.

Here is a man with a hairy-mole on one cheek, hairy-eyes which leak; and a solitary golden-tooth. With Alfred's Father's gait, he holds his back so straight; that his chin points up at the roof.

"This is a *Front Line Camp*, and not a domestic-barracks, and certainly not a holiday resort. Oh no! You're on active duty now. We demand blind-obedience here. Blind-obedience!

"If you don't comply with orders you'll be shot, and if you don't conform to army ways you'll be shot, and if you don't meet our standards you'll be shot as well. You've got your work cut out just to stay alive. Don't expect any sympathy, soldiers. Don't expect any sympathy!

"And don't expect to become martyrs, and heroes, and saints. Oh no! Your deaths shan't make the papers, and you shan't be talked about, and your stories shan't be told. Oh no!

"You'll disappear like dead fishes in the sea, and dirt underfoot, and water which has been flushed down the lavvy. Like the conchie who was shot for his lack of respect, and the conchie who was shot for his obstinance, and the conchie who was shot for his insubordination. Oh yes!"

The Commanding Officer stomps away and is replaced by this Goon who is hairy, this Goon who is scary; and this Goon who is stout. These Goons take the Peace Unit's packs, and their khaki-macks; which smell of stale-trout. But Alfred keeps his frankincense-and-myrrh, without causing a stir; or moving about.

"Sit doon," this Temperamental Soldier begins to shout. "We divn't tolerate girly-hair in the army; it isn't expedient.

"Whey aye man! There's nar place for effeminate homosexuals here. It's time for youse to act like a man, become a man, and look like a man. Aye. Nar. Aye. Nar. Aye. Youse do look nice."

He shoves Alfred onto this chair, and cuts Alfred's hair; with this pair of serrated-scissors. The Peace Unit are appalled, as he turns Alfred bald; with this pair of serrated-clippers.

"You think you're so strong, beating up a man who's tied up in chains," the Agitator begins to bleat, as his heart skips a beat, whilst he bobs his shoulders and stamps his feet. "I'd rock you and sock you if I was free. I'll kill the French President! I'll kill the Austrian Emperor! I'll kill you all! Lemme at ya! Lemme at ya!"

This Giggly Goon laughs, this Giddy Goon barfs; and that Grizzly Goon flashes his gun. He wants to hit the Agitator's gut; and kick his butt; because he thinks it would be fun.

"It's okay, I don't mind," Alfred says whilst the Clerk starts hum. "My hair *was* getting very-very-very long. I'm thankful for this haircut. I feel rather obliged to this man. This man is sweeter than a mouse, softer than a bunny, and smoother than a little kitten!"

Alfred says this because he does not consider the Temperamental Soldier to be vicious, malicious; or mean. As he loses his hair Alfred starts to feel light, bright; calm-cheerful-and-clean. Free from pride-passion-and-pain, he feels less vain; and more serene.

"Moustaches is for officers only, it's not expedient for conscripts like youse to have facial hair!" The Temperamental Soldier begins to say, as he shaves Alfred's face until it looks grey, and then leads his Goons away.

The Peace Unit breathe a collective sigh of relief, before they discuss their grief; and their current situation. Some are not sure what to feel, some think the threats are real; and others that they are a fabrication.

"I think it's all just bluff-and-bluster," the Apprentice says with elation. "They move us around and repeat the same old threats, but they never shoot us. They'd have done it already if they could. They're just trying to break us down, I'd bet my last penny on it. The sun will rise tomorrow, the tides will come-and-go, and peace will outmuscle war in the end. It always does!

"We're the bravest-boldest-and-best! We're awesome! We'll use the brains in our heads and the feet in our shoes to become unbeatable. I know we will! I just know we will!"

"I don't think I agree," the Coward counters. "I think they might mean it this time, I guess it's why they've brought us to France. Life is cheap here; no-one will think much of killing a few conchies like us. Oh, I can't even bear to think about it."

"You shouldn't throw the towel in just yet; it's too close to call," the Athlete says as he begins to stagger, and knocks this ladder, whilst he clenches his aching-bladder. "But right now I need the toilet, which is a bit of a sticky-wicket. I'm stuck behind the eight ball."

"There is a toilet over there," the Watchmaker cries, as he points at a bucket which is covered in flies, who all have bulbous-eyes.

"I know," the Athlete replies. "But I *need* the toilet, which is far from smooth-sailing in these chains. It's a whole new ball game now."

"Oh," the Schoolmaster tries to surmise. "You need help, don't you? Like when Bizhan needed Rustam to rescue her from a pit."

So the Schoolmaster reverses his skinny-loins, back into the Athlete's muscled-groins; until they connect like a stack of spoons. He grips the Athlete's breeches, undoes them near these leaches; and near those mouldy-prunes.

The Athlete shuffles to remove his khaki-pants, and squats down by these ants; with his hands tied behind his bum. His comrades close their eyes, and shake their thighs; because they know their turn will come.

This ritual bonds this group, and makes them a genuine troop; who are ready for the road ahead. Apart from the Coward, whose face has soured; and turned a bright shade of red.

The Peace Units' blazers become rumpled, their trousers become crumpled; and their shirts become creased. The Coward becomes stressed, the sun sets in the west; and then rises up in the east.

"Exercise daily," the Christian says whilst he paces like a caged-beast. "Run from Satan and walk with the Lord!"

"Let's level the playing field! Let's punch above our weight! Let's clear every hurdle!" The Athlete says, before he starts to graze; on this piece of stale-bread.

"Eat to stay strong," the Watchmaker says as a rat walks up that gutter, runs along that shutter; and falls on his skew-whiff head.

"Go to sleep," the Coward says with dread. *"Yawn-yawn-yawn."*

Before these Goons come to push them down these halls, past these seafood-stalls; and past these tables which are covered in dishes. Where they unshackle the Peace Unit's hands, near these seafood-stands; which were once used for gutting fishes.

"Crustaceans!" The Commanding Officer demands, commands; and screeches. As he points at this One Armed Bandit who has a hook for a hand, a khaki-headband; and a peg-leg beneath his breeches. "This man lost his arm fighting, and defending, and protecting you. Not so you can just live in peace, and lie about, and do nothing. Oh no! He did it so people would fight like him, and respect him, and salute him too. So salute him, soldiers. Salute him now!"

But with their resolve still intact, the Peace Unit do not react; and they do not salute. The Watchmaker giggles, the Coward wriggles; and the Athlete stamps his boot.

"I shall beseech you, and command you, and tell each one of you manatees in turn," the Commanding Officer begins to shoot. "And you shall salute, soldiers. You shall salute!

"Because if you don't, you'll be thrown in front of a military-panel, and face a trial, and be shot by a firing-squad before you know it. Oh yes!"

The Commanding Officer walks with a slippery-slide, and a graceless-glide; as he slithers across this ground. He holds his back as vertical as it can be, and locks his knee; which makes this clunky-sound.

"Salute, soldier. Salute!" He commands the Christian who refuses to obey.

"Salute, soldier. Salute!" He commands the Engineer who does not even sway.

"Salute, soldier. Salute!" He commands Alfred, the Athlete and the Apprentice.

"Salute, soldier. Salute!" He commands the Coward in a voice which sounds stupendous.

But the Coward has struggled to stick to his stance, ever since he arrived in France; and so he fills with faintheartedness. He struggles for air and he struggles for breath, as the thought of death; makes him stress. As it fills him with timidity, misery-misgiving-and-morbidity; and turns him into a mess.

He lifts his hand from by his side, lets it glide; and locks it into his brow. He drawls, blows-blubbers-and-bawls; and makes this sorry-bow.

"Sorry lads," he explains right now. "But you've all got religions-and-beliefs, I think, and I've got nothing; I'm just a coward. I'm just not brave enough to be a conchie, so I guess I'll have to be a soldier instead. Oh, I suppose it'd have been better if I'd never even been born."

"Judas! He's on the ropes and out for the count," the Athlete mutters with doom.

"Traitor! Turncoat! Treasonist!" The Agitator utters with gloom. "Lemme at 'im! I'll kill 'im! I'll kill the Japanese Emperor! I'll kill the Chinese President! I'll kill 'em all!"

"Good man!" the Commanding Officer splutters, and sputters; as he slides across this room. "Top hole! Go collect your uniform, and gun, and papers. You shall receive thirty silver-franks for signing on. Thirty silver-franks! And as for the rest of you; this fine gentleman should be an example, and a model, and an inspiration to every one of you. Oh yes!

"Salute or be shot, soldier. Salute or be shot!" He commands the Clerk-Schoolmaster-and-Agitator.

"Salute or be shot, soldier. Salute or be shot!" He commands the Nurse-Socialist-and-Watchmaker.

"Salute or be shot, soldier. Salute or be shot!" He commands the Tax Collector.

But with their resolve still intact, the rest of the Peace Unit do not react; they do not obey and they do not salute. The Coward stampedes away, like an elephant who has gone astray; and trips over himself en route. He tumbles like a boulder, hits his khaki-clad shoulder; and tears his khaki-suit.

"Very well, you cruddy sea-cucumbers," the Commanding Officer begins to hoot. "I do recognise, and respect, and admire your obstinance. You're rotten people but, to give you your due, your rottenness *is* truly magnificent. Oh yes!

"Don't be fooled though. Don't be fooled!

"You're like mice, and we're like cats. A mouse may run about, and hide, and manoeuvre. A mouse may believe that he's in charge of the game. But a cat can end his fun with a single swipe of his paw. Oh yes!

"Well, we've fenced with each other, and duelled, and had our fun. But the time for make-believe hath past. You're like mice in a steel-trap; whether you can see them or not, there are strong-springs, and heavy-levers, and mighty-bars gripping hold of you. We're in charge here, and we will get our way, privates. We will get our way!

"You'll start your punishments on the morrow. Until then you can consider yourselves free to leave this camp, and talk to soldiers, and consider your options. You've four-and-twenty hours to clear your head, and think about your actions, and succumb to rhyme-and-reason. It could be the last day of freedom you ever have, soldiers. Your last ever day of freedom!"

The Christian utters some religious-vows, the Clerk lifts his bushy-eyebrows; and the Agitator spits on the floor. They fill with dismay, as the Commanding Officer slides away; and exits through that door.

He leaves them on their own, whilst the Engineer starts to moan; and shells explode in the sky. Whilst trench-mortars bristle, whizzbangs whistle; and pom-poms fly right by.

The sound of exploding-munitions, and violent-missions; ring in the Peace Unit's ears. Whilst this smell of voided-bowels, and burning-fowls; float over these war-torn frontiers.

Alfred and the other teenagers walk past these French Villagers, these professional Pillagers; and those hairy-fleas. These Tommies who blow bubbles into the air, these French Maidens who brush their hair; and those buzzing-bees. Before they stop near these lakes, which are full of these drakes; and surrounded by those trees.

Where they wash for the first time in days, wallow in this smoky-haze; and recover from their incarceration. Where they swim front-crawl, and play football; until they are covered in perspiration.

"It seems to me," the Apprentice says with elation. "That the last lot of conchies must've given in to the army's demands; we wouldn't be here otherwise. But what the hell! We can be better than them! We can be the best! We can achieve whatever we want to achieve, and be whoever we want to be!"

"Please! Let's be strong-and-united," Alfred agrees. "Please-please-

please. Let's go toe-to-toe with the warmakers; it'll discourage them from sending any more peacemakers this way."

"If they don't kill us, they'll free us once they've won their war anyway," the Clerk adds as he fiddles with this weed, this reed, and this seed. "Will they want us on their hands? No! No-one likes a conchie."

"You think the Allies will win their war?" The Engineer asks in a voice which sounds unsure, demure, and obscure.

"We're all cooked," the Clerk replies, with fluttering-eyes; which have a certain allure. "It's a war. There are only ever losers in war. The last ones to realise that they've lost will declare themselves winners. That's all. Only our leaders will be too stupid to see that they've lost. They'll keep going whilst everyone else gives up. And then they'll say they've won."

Whilst they speak the older members of the Peace Unit sit at a promenade café, near the dock of a bay; and reach a similar conclusion too. They sup espressos which were bought by a Generous Soldier with veiny-eyes, veiny-thighs; and a uniform which is slightly askew.

And tonight they feel fine, they combine; and they unite. This morning they feel overjoyed, buoyed; and bright.

"All for one and one for all!" The Watchmaker cheers with delight.

"All for one and one for all!" The Peace Unit reply with might.

Before the Coward brings them their food, in a guilty-mood; and shakes with feeble-force. He cries, wipes his eyes; and speaks with feeble-remorse.

"I'm so sorry for abandoning you, I feel guilty beyond belief, I think," he says in a voice which is feebly-hoarse. "My nerves were on edge, my mind was hazy, and I was having nightmares every night. I just couldn't hack it, I suppose. Not when I only had to peel spuds to stay alive."

The Coward looks sullen-sombre-and-subdued, as he hands out the Peace Unit's food; which he has brought in this dented-can. He pours some water which contains chlorine, and looks a bit green; before he gives four biscuits to every man.

"They're a little bit stale, I suppose, but they're the best I could get," he says as he empties this toilet-pan. "I do want to help, I think."

"You don't have to eat them dry," Alfred says as he dips a biscuit in his water and gives it to the Coward to try.

"I suppose. I think. I guess. But I've abandoned you," the Coward says with a sigh. '*Aaaah*'.

"Please eat it. Please-please-please. What's mine is yours!" Alfred says in reply. "You were always doomed to destruction, but your heart is good; you just don't have the rebel passion. You did well to stick with us for so long. We're grateful for your efforts. We do feel obliged."

The Clerk fiddles with his sleeves, but no-one disagrees, before the Coward finally leaves.

"Please! Love one another as I love you," Alfred says as he begins to sneeze. "*Ah-chew*! Please-please-please. This is my only request. Because through love everyone will see that you're disciples of peace."

And before too long the Peace Unit are made to climb these sodden-stairs, prodded by these Goons who work in pairs; with malice on their faces. They are pushed next to this Grubby Soldier who is covered in grubby-dirt, with muck on his grubby-shirt; and dirt all over his laces.

"Gutless maggots," the Commanding Officer shouts as he clutches his shiny-braces. "You're all guilty of insubordination, and disobedience, and noncompliance. And you're all going to be punished for it. Oh yes! Starting with you, private. Starting with you!"

He approaches the Grubby Soldier with a slippery-slide, and a graceless-glide; whilst he slithers across this ground. He holds his back as vertical as it can be, and locks his knee; which makes this clunky-sound.

"You, private, are guilty of three counts of insubordinate-language, and two counts of threatening-language, and one count of disobeying a lawful-command. You've failed to march to army-standards, and annoyed your superiors, and distracted your fellow soldiers. Your actions have been deliberate, and public, and persistent, despite the second chances with which you've been bestowed.

"And so you shall be shot for your crimes at dawn. Oh yes! You've no right to appeal, private. No right to appeal!

"Get rid of this haddock," the Commanding Officer orders with furious-spite, and furious-might; now he has proven that his threats are not hollow. And so the Grubby Soldier is taken away, out of this fray; by these Goons who seem happy to follow.

"You're all as guilty as him, and have committed similar crimes, and face a similar punishment too," the Commanding Officer howls, and yowls; whilst Alfred starts to swallow. "Oh yes! You've had a day to consider your options, and change your ways, and you can be saved.

"All you have to do is salute. So salute, soldiers. Salute!"

But with their resolve still intact, the Peace Unit do not react; and they do not salute. The Apprentice glances, the Agitator advances; and the Athlete stamps his boot.

"Very well," the Commanding Officer begins to shoot. "I expected as much."

He stands with a posture with is perfectly erect, and pauses for maximum-effect; before he reveals the Peace Unit's fate. But despite seeing a soldier get sentenced, the Peace Unit wait without repentance; and do not take this officer's bait.

Because Alfred has told his friends to love one another, that they are all each other's brother; unified-undivided-and-united. This love makes them strong, it makes them feel like they belong; and it makes them feel delighted.

Alfred breathes in and breathes out, frees himself from doubt; and escapes from all his woes. His breath travels from bronchiole-to-bronchi-to-larynx, up through his pharynx; and all the way out through his nose.

"You'll be placed in solitary confinement," the Commanding Officer blows. "There'll be no more contact, and collusion, and camaraderie betwixt you any more. Oh no! You'll be thrown in the clink, and shackled, and subjected to *Field Punishment Number One*. You will fall in line, soldiers. You will fall in line!

"Get these puny-seaweeds out of here!"

The Temperamental Soldier whose skin is the colour of whey, and whose hair is the colour of hay; grabs both of Alfred's wrists. He drags Alfred down these sodden-stairs, and past those sodden-chairs; before he swings his sodden-fists. Before he chains Alfred to this pole, inside this underground-hole; with these knots and with these twists.

"Please tell me!" Alfred persists. "What is *Field Punishment Number One*?"

The Temperamental Soldier considers war expedient rather than right, so he despises conchies for their inexpedient refusal to fight; but he also respects their resolve. He flits between rancour-revulsion-and-rejection, awe-adulation-and-affection; as his emotions all revolve.

"Crucifixion!" He replies with this menacing-scowl, which looks fierce-feisty-and-foul, before he emits this teeth-gnashing growl.

This vocal-chord quivering, fear-delivering; yowl. This fist-smashing, limb-thrashing; howl.

This laugh which usurps linguistics, as he goes ballistic; and starts to ravage. As he becomes malicious, vicious; and savage.

Crash-bang-wallop! The Temperamental Soldier punches Alfred's breast. *Crash-bang-wallop!* This pain shoots across Alfred's chest. *Crash-bang-wallop!* Alfred falls to the ground to rest.

The Temperamental Soldier rolls up his khaki-sleeves, turns around and leaves; without making another suggestion. For *Field Punishment Number One* is crucifixion, a torturous sort of affliction; so he has answered Alfred's question.

Field Punishment Number One replaced lashing in 1881, because lashing had appalled everyone; in the whole of the British nation. People had considered army-life akin to penal-servitude, without any sort of gratitude; or any appreciation. So crucifixion took flogging's place, to help the army save face; and improve the image of their organisation.

Field Punishment Number One allows the warmakers to tie their victims to any standing-object, and leave them for two hours whilst their pain takes effect; clamped-confined-and-chained. Their victims are left amongst crickets-cockroaches-and-crows, in sleet-storms-and-snows; whilst they are slighted-slandered-and-shamed.

So Alfred has his chest stripped bare, his arms stretched square; and his palms strapped to these lines of spiky barbed-wire. These lines of twisted metal-strands, which pierce his hands; whilst his feet slip through this mire. Whilst blood pours over his fists, his wrists; and this discarded rubber-tire.

With *No Man's Land* and the Germans just out of touch, he faces the warfare he opposes so much; full of sickness-soreness-and-strain. He faces the reserve-lines and the frontline-trench, the Flemish-Fijians-and-French; the panic-plague-and-pain.

Mortar-shells fly this way, and splatter the sky with fiery-spray;

fiery-shrapnel and fiery-fire. It makes the Temperamental Soldier groan, before he leaves Alfred alone; here in this boggy-mire. The Temperamental Soldier smiles and then he scowls, he whispers and then he howls; he feels good and then he feels dire.

He is replaced by the corpses of people in the armed-forces, dead-mules and dead-horses; which pass Alfred by in a procession of gore. With bloody-limbs, bloody-skins; this smell of decay and this smell of war.

This ginger cat rubs Alfred's feet, whilst the smell of burnt human-meat; floats across this boggy-floor. Before this Provost Marshal walks down the street, with heavy-feet; and a voice which begins to roar.

His arrival reminds Alfred of the Nurse's ghoulish-dreams, ghoulish-screams; and ghoulish-premonitions. His premonitions about a twenty-foot red-faced beast, with gnashing metal-teeth; and many evil-missions. Who beat him down, and hung him near town; in all sorts of tangled-positions.

For here this beast stands, with this pair of knuckly-hands; and this pair of piecing-eyes. He has already had Alfred beaten down, and hung near town; using twine-twists-and-ties.

The Provost Marshal is tall-tanned-and-towering, with this stare which is overpowering; and this omnipotent sort of sheen. His face is impish-infernal-and-intrigued, frenzied-flustered-and-fatigued; maroon-magenta-and-mean.

But it is the Provost Marshal's teeth which look ridiculously-terrific, ridiculously-horrific; and fill Alfred with ridiculous-grief. For despite being a powerful man, the Provost Marshal cannot control a single fang; in his gnashing metal-teeth.

His teeth skew one way and then bend back the other, they lap up over one another; and they leave spaces where they are supposed to be. They sting when the Provost Marshal eats ice-creams, they bleed when he brushes their seams; and they triple up three-on-three.

So between the Provost Marshal's lips, is a line of metal-strips; with metal-pads pressed underneath. They form this metal-brace, which creates this metal-space; which is full of these metal-teeth.

"Hail the *King of the Conchies*," he says with disbelief. "You reckoned you could bring an end to war-and-armies, but you can't even save yourself. Bugger me! You knave, beggar, coward and pimp! You son and heir of a mongrel-bitch! Let peace free you from this.

"You wanted to save mankind. Son of a gun! What muddledom! You misshapen-dick! You profane-coxcomb! You can't even save yourself. The *King of the Conchies*! Tut-tut-tut."

And dressed in his military-attire, he speaks with spiteful-ire, as he coronates Alfred's head with this crown of barbed-wire.

"The *King of the Conchies*! Tut-tut-tut. You bean-fed horse! You piece of worm's meat! You empty-purse! Let peace free you from this."

"Peace will free me," Alfred replies. "For peace always overcomes war in the end. Yes-yes-yes. Yes thanky-you!"

But the very end, separated from each-and-every friend; does seem a long way away. As Alfred broods in his cell, this silent-hell; day-after-day-after-day.

As he spends weeks alone, missing home; whilst his muscles all start to pulse. Whilst they start to ache, break; and convulse.

He is left here whilst the mauled-mutilated-and-maimed, dead-dying-and-drained; all begin to cry. Whilst bullets beep, mortars weep; and missiles fill the sky. Before this Generous Soldier with veiny-eyes, and veiny-thighs; starts to walk on by.

"I think this crucifixion malarkey is disgusting-and-inhumane," he starts to sigh. "It makes you question why we're even fighting the Germans; I doubt they'd treat you any worse than this. Stick with it son! Stick to your guns!"

The Generous Soldier pats Alfred's hip, puts this cigarette on Alfred's lip, and lights its paper-tip.

"This should mix in some pleasure with your pain," he begins to quip. "Stick with it son! Stick to your guns!"

Alfred has never smoked before, and does not want to start here at war; even if it brings him rest-relaxation-or-relief. But this experience reminds Alfred that soldiers can be refined, cool-caring-and-kind; so his confidence starts to increase. He begins to grin, smile-swagger-and-spin; as he converts his jailor to peace.

"How are you doing?" He asks as he adjusts his fleece.

"Terrible," the Temperamental Soldier replies with caprice. "Well, champion actually. I've been eating the chocs my girl sent us."

"I've got a girl too," Alfred says with this empathetic-sway, which moves him this way, to look at this picture of his jailor's fiancée.

"Aye. A canny lass?"

Alfred uses this opportunity to speak about Cleo's spotty-nose, her jazzy-clothes; and her kindly-nursing. Whilst the Temperamental Soldier speaks about his Fiancée's curls, her pearls; and her cursing.

When the Temperamental Soldier is in a foul-mood, up for a fight-fracas-or-feud; Alfred stays mute. But when he seems alright, bubbly-buoyant-or-bright; they both have a hoot. They build a bond, correspond; and talk whilst they commute.

Alfred retells the Good German's old fables, explains how to make wooden-tables; and talks about Cleo's gnomes. Whilst the Temperamental Soldier talks about his town's timber-yards, boulevards; and working-class homes.

"Whey aye man! I'm a conscript like youse," he says as he brushes his hair with two combs. "And more than happy to be walking prison-corridors rather than muddy-trenches. Aye. Nar. Aye. Nar. Aye!

"I want to be fully-limbed for my girl when I get home. It's only expedient. I'm a plumba me; a man needs his arms in orda to plumb."

"Your heart's not really in this war is it?" Alfred asks as he ups the stakes.

"It's expedient," the Temperamental Soldier replies as he wobbles, hobbles; and shakes.

"Please tell me! Is it expedient to support those who kill-kill-kill, whilst you imprison those who refuse to?"

"It keeps us out of trouble."

"But is it right?"

"It's expedient."

"Right?"

"Expedient."

"Right?"

"Aye. Nar. Aye. Nar. Aye. Expedient!"

"Ha ha ha!

"Please can I have an extra biscuit to celebrate the King's birthday tomorrow? I'd be ever so grateful," Alfred concludes.

"Whey aye man!" The Temperamental Soldier replies in a confused mix of moods. "Are youse insane? Hmm. Aye. Nar. Aye. Nar. Aye. Nar. Mebbies. But only if it's expedient."

And so the Temperamental Soldier brings this vegetable-bake, and this carrot-cake; as he enters this cell today. He gives Alfred a slap, with this leather-strap; and then takes these handcuffs away.

He does this because the warmakers have realised that their punishments have not had an effect, earned them respect; or overcome the conchie's convictions. They have realised that their crucifixions need refinement, as does their solitary-confinement; because the peacemakers have coped with their afflictions.

So the Peace Unit return to their original-cell, get crucified together as well; and feel like they have been freed. Mouths which have been shut for weeks now jibber-jabber, chit-chat and blibber-blabber; at high-speed. They talk about beatitude, serenity-salvation-and-servitude; gluttony-generosity-and-greed.

"It's alright for you, you're tall," the stumpy Engineer begins to plead. "You'll excuse my bluntness, but I've had to stand on tiptoes for two hours a day. You think your arms hurt? Well my legs hurt more.

"Oh, whatever have I done? Have I stepped on a crack? Have I seen a magpie? Have I sung at the table? Oh, I don't see why the warmakers don't just hurry up and shoot us."

"They daren't; they're too scared-scared-scared," Alfred replies as he scratches his shoulder, looks at this boulder, and thinks of the Temperamental Soldier. "Please understand! The warmakers aren't the lions they pretend to be; once you get to know them you realise that they're more like mules than lions."

"Mules?" The Engineer asks, whilst the Agitator laughs, and the Clerk barfs. "Mules? I don't understand. Me? I understand nothing. Oh, whatever have I done?"

"Mules indeed," Alfred blasts. "Like the Mule who a penny-pinching Salesman once used to carry his wares.

"Please understand! That Mule worked really-really-really hard for his miserly master, and pulled his cart for many miles each day. But the Salesman never bought Mule any food. No-no-no. Not one bit.

"You see, the Salesman had a lion's skin; a really grandiose thing which had a lion's head, a lion's mane, and a hide covered in lion's fur.

He'd dress Mule in that skin so he looked just like a lion, and leave Mule in a field whenever he was hungry.

"No-one was ever brave enough to approach what they thought was a lion, so Mule was able to eat whatever he wanted.

"Until one day a brave-brave-brave Farmer felt compelled to act. He was worried that a lion might come into his village and attack a child. So he rounded up some villagers, and ran at Mule with them by his side. Please! Just imagine it! They screamed, they shouted, they hollered and they howled!

"Mule was scared. He galloped away so quickly that the lion's hide fell from his back, and he galloped so far that the Salesman never saw him again. He had to pull his cart himself! Yes-yes-yes. Thanking you!"

"So," the Schoolmaster explains once more, like before, whilst he sits cross-legged on this concrete-floor. "The Salesman is our government, isn't he? He sends Mule (our army) into fields (distant-lands) where he shouldn't really be. He does it day-after-day (war-after-war), until Mule finally flees, like when Spartacus fled for Mount Vesuvius in ancient Rome."

"That's right," Alfred agrees. "Thank-you, thank-you, thank-you. I love what you've done there. You're so smart!

"Mule does whatever the Salesman wants, just like a soldier who does whatever he is told. It doesn't make him intelligent-respectable-or-strong. No-no-no! It only makes him obedient.

"And it takes someone truly-truly-truly brave to stop his wrongdoing. Someone loving-loyal-and-passionate. Someone like the Farmer. Someone like us!

"Like Mule, the warmakers only appear to be scary; deep down they're harmless. Mule wouldn't attack the village, and the soldiers won't attack us. Please understand! Killing thousands of peacemakers would be a public-relations disaster for them.

"Which is why after many threats, and many-many-many opportunities, they still haven't shot us.

"They're only punishing us because they think it'll make us conform. And we, in turn, must continue to resist. We must make the warmakers realise that we'll never submit. Never-ever-ever!"

"I wish I had your confidence," the Engineer says with arms which ache, hands which quake, and legs which shake. "I expect they'll shoot us once they get bored of playing their games. I'm tremendously sorry to say it, but I fear we're hanging on by our eyelids now. Oh, whatever have I done? Have I not kept a guard of my heart? Have I supped with Satan? Have I kept a skeleton in my closet? Oh shoot. Oh my."

"Now-now darling," the Nurse calms, with open-arms, and open-palms. "Alfred is spot-on. His story was lovely; simply screaming. We are doing famously! Rah-rah-rah!

"I dare say, if people only knew about the ghastly-things the warmakers are doing to us, their shenanigans would soon stop. The warmakers have invested millions of pounds in propaganda; they would not want to risk all the goodwill which they have bought.

"We just need to get a message home."

Alfred listens and he understands, so he grabs this wood with both his hands; as he returns from today's crucifixion. He uses it to make a model of the Temperamental Soldier's amour, using the sharp-edges on this door; and some force-finesse-and-friction. And using the sharp-edges on Agitator's handcuffs, which he has worn since he made a fuss; and spoke out with abrasive-diction.

'I'm more patriotic than you, sucker!' He recently told a Grouchy Goon.

'I'm more patriotic than you, shirker!' That soldier replied in front of his whole platoon.

'Conchies are braver than soldiers!'

'Soldiers are braver than conchies!'

'Peace will kick war's arse!'

'War will kick peace's arse!'

'Morality before authority!'

'Authority before morality!'

'Civility over the military!'

'The military over civility!'

And the Agitator continues to talk, as he sits on this chalk; which covers this grubby-floor. With his wrists in these chains, which pinch his veins; and make him incredibly sore.

"I don't see why we don't just take 'em on," he begins to roar. "Those suckers wouldn't stand a chance! I'll kill the privates! I'll kill the officers! I'll kill 'em all!

"Ta dadada ta daaa! Peace power!

"In fact, the more I think about it, the more I think we should've joined the army in the first place. We could've wreaked some real havoc on the inside; poisoning troops, destroying weapons, and alerting the Germans to upcoming attacks. We could've splatted 'em, rocked 'em and socked 'em. We could've saved thousands of lives!"

The other conchies all begin to stare, swear; and sigh. Whilst the Schoolmaster begins to groan, moan; and cry.

"It was that kind of behaviour which got you tied up, wasn't it?" He tests.

"And I'd have gotten away with it too," the Agitator protests. "If it wasn't for you meddling kids! Peace power!"

"But you'd have been wrong to," the Socialist blares whilst he jiggles his gut, his butt; and his breasts. "The soldiers aren't our enemies; they're only here as a result of unemployment-and-conscription. They're working-class, just like us. And they're socialists too; we're all socialists, everyone's a socialist, we've always been socialists and we'll always be socialists.

"So we should be uniting with the British soldiers, the Austrian soldiers and the German soldiers. We should be fighting the capitalists with them by our side. This war is already pitting worker against worker; it doesn't need you to increase the infighting."

"You're right, I suppose," the Agitator agrees. "I'll kill the Russian Emperor instead! I'll kill the Ottoman Sultan! I'll kill them all!"

The Temperamental Soldier brings this conversation to a halt, as he storms into this underground-vault; in a fairly malicious-mood. Because after a day spent carrying bunks, and a night spent restraining drunks; he feels crabby and has started to brood.

"I made you this," Alfred says as he puts down his food.

Before he passes the Temperamental Soldier this wooden-sculpture, this piece of conchie-culture; which makes his jailor smirk. His jailor feels elated, chirpy-cheerful-and-captivated; as he inspects Alfred's handiwork.

"Sometimes when I'm out being crucified," Alfred says whilst he winks at the Clerk. "I see soldiers writing postcards. Please could we send one too? Please-please-please."

"Whey aye man! It's my job to control prisonas, not to provide services for them," the Temperamental Soldier replies as he shakes his head, kicks this bed, and throws this bread. "Aye. Nar. Aye. Nar. Aye. Mebbies. I'll see what I can do. But only if it's expedient."

And so after another long day and another long night, the Temperamental Soldier returns with this light; and this *Field Service Postcard*. It is pre-printed with pre-approved lines, and a premonishment that people who write messages will be punished with fines; imposed by an army-guard.

These lines say '*I have been sent to the base*', '*I am enjoying France/Italy/Other-Place*', and '*I have received your cigarettes/sweets/case*'.

"Well this is mortally useless," the Engineer whinges, whilst he cringes; with fear all over his face. "My eye! I knew they wouldn't let us write about our treatment. We're about as right side up as a billiard-ball. Oh, whatever have we done? Have we crossed knives? Have we sung before breakfast? Have we opened our umbrellas indoors? Oh my."

The Agitator simpers, the Socialist whimpers; and the Athlete whines. The Engineer's forehead, turns ruby-red; with all these furrowed-lines.

"Holy smoke!" The Nurse says with a face which glimmers, shimmers; and shines. "Righty ho! Yah! Rah! Hip hip hooray! One does believe one has got it. Do be a good-egg, do be a jolly fine-fellow, and pass one that card."

The Nurse covers this card with inky-scribbles, oily-squiggles; and splodgy-lines. He crosses through slashes, dashes; and signs:

'*I have been sent to ~~the base', 'I am enjoying~~ France ~~/ Italy / Other-Place', 'I have~~ received ~~your~~ bully-beef ~~/ sweets / case~~*'.

"There you go! Everything is just tickety-boo! Simply divine! Rah-rah-rah!" He says with this smile which bulges.

'*I have been sent to... France... I receive bull... ets*', this card now divulges.

"One's parents will forward it to one's connections, and chocks away; they will mobilise in our defence. We will soon be leaving this rotten place, saying '*Toodle-Pip*', '*Home James*' and '*Do not spare the horses'*. It is awfully top notch stuff. Rah-rah-rah!"

The Temperamental Soldier returns to take this postcard, which he carries past that courtyard; that office and those dormitory-blocks. Whilst the Peace Unit pray that he does not change his mind when he passes stores full of tanks, wooden-planks; and military-stocks. Because whilst they are grateful for his assistance, they worry he will not go the distance; before he reaches the army's postbox. So they are full of positivity, full of negativity; and in a full flummox.

And Alfred is just as confused, baffled-bewildered-and-bemused; by his breathing-exercise. Which brings him some peace, but not total release; no matter how hard he tries.

It makes him recall one of the Good German's publications, in which he read about an ascetic who resisted temptations; in order to clear his mind. *'You can't start a fire with wet trees'*, he read whilst he delivered some peas; and his horse pulled his cart behind.

"I'm going stop eating," he says feeling liberated, emancipated; and refined. "Who needs food anyway? Please! A contented mind is a continual feast.

"You can consider it a hunger-strike if you like. The authorities may even release me when I become frail, like they did with the suffragists."

"I'll pray for you," the Christian replies. "And by the grace of God you'll do it. Dear Lord, look after this man; *guard him against the evil ones*, like you said you would in Thessalonians three. And *be with him till the end of time*, like in Matthew twenty."

"I'm in your corner," the Athlete adds. "At this stage of the game you've got to cover all your bases, jockey for position, and move the goalposts wherever you can."

"You're not going to eat a thing? Nothing? Not even a biscuit a day?" The Clerk asks as he fiddles this seat, this sheet, and this block of concrete. "You're not even going to drink? No water. No tea. No coffee. Really? No-one likes a conchie."

"Not a drop!" Alfred replies.

And he begins his new diet which makes him strain, full of pain; and full of uncomfortable-vibrations. Whilst his blurred-vision makes objects seem blurrier, swirlier; and like psychedelic-hallucinations.

Alfred's body turns into a scabby-mesh, made from a sheet of loose-flesh; which hangs from his protruding-bones. His hair falls out when it is rubbed, his skin breaks when it is scrubbed; and his organs jangle like stones.

So Alfred's knees both begin to quake, and his torso begins to shake; as he carries his cross up to today's crucifixion. As he stumbles over his feet, tumbles across this street; and falls into an unconscious-condition. Before he wakes in this ward which is full of men with gonorrhoea, men with pyorrhoea; and men in remission.

"I'm missing an earlobe, two fingers and three toes," a Plucky Patient says as he holds a firearm.

"I was ba-ba-blown up whilst I ate some cheese," a Peppy Patient stammers because of the nerve damage in his arm.

"My leg is full of all the old iron in the world!" A Poorly Patient says with a certain charm. "Any old iron, any old iron, any-any-any old iron!"

And stood between them all, is this Medic who is scabby-scarred-and-small; with a particularly hairy-nose. With toilet-paper in his gun-holder, a scab on his shoulder; and a scab on each of his toes.

"Abusing your body won't bring you peace, you know?" He says as he brushes his clothes. "You won't stop any wars whilst you're lying in a hospital-bed."

"You're one-hundred percent right," Alfred blows. "Thank-you, thank-you, thank-you. You sure are intelligent! You must've been first in line when they were handing out brains.

"I thought I could find enlightenment without nourishment, but I've realised that you need to feed your body before you can feed your soul."

"*Mmm hmm*," the Medic says with an indifferent-grief, as he force-feeds Alfred this bully-beef, and these bits of overcooked-leaf.

Alfred is attached to two drips, in a straitjacket which points his elbows towards his hips; and folds his wrists across his chest. So he spits out this beef, and these pieces of leaf; before he begins to protest.

"I'm vegetarian thank-you," he says as the beef comes to a rest.

But the Medic just stands by this wooden-chair, without appearing to care; and without appearing to hear. He forces this unwashed-tube up Alfred's nose, grips Alfred's clothes; and yanks Alfred's ear. He pumps liquid into Alfred's lung, which returns over Alfred's tongue; and sprays over everything here.

Alfred turns away to inhale, feeling feeble-forlorn-and-frail; whilst the Medic pours water down his throat. Before the Medic gives Alfred this bread, and this fruit instead; whilst he pats his long white-coat.

Alfred is left here inside this straitjacket's strings, as strength returns to each of his limbs; and his health begins to improve. Before the One Armed Bandit starts to trip, fall-flounder-and-flip; and lands where he is unable to move.

"Help-ee me! I be frail-and-slow. Do help-ee me!" He whimpers as he stretches his arm towards Alfred.

"I'd love to!" Alfred replies as he sits up in bed. "Yes please! Please-please-please. But I can't, I'm afraid; I'm in a straitjacket."

"Desh! Just look-ee at this man!" The One Armed Bandit says as he nods his head. "He won't even do summat' to help an injured-soldier back 'pon his feet. Worse luck, I suppose.

"But that's a typical conchie for you, I'm afraid; with his head screwed on t'other way. Hearken to me youse; they're worse than the Germans. They're weak-wimpish-and-wicked, I tell-ee thee. Don't you good soldiers be associating with rubbidge like 'im."

"They're missing a backbone, two balls and three metres of guts," the Plucky Patient says as he rolls his eyes.

"He's in a straitjacket for Gods' sake!" The Poorly Patient replies.

"I'd like to eat some cheese," the Peppy Patient adds whilst he stares at some pies.

Alfred speaks to them about peace-and-war, before he is taken to be crucified near this munitions-store; here on this muddy-land. Where the Engineer complains, the Schoolmaster strains; and the Apprentice kicks this sand. Whilst the Agitator slumps, the Socialist jumps; and the Clerk just waves his hand.

They are bent-buckled-and-bound, atop this muddy-ground; where they are tied up every two yards. Where they are tied to these posts-platforms-and-planks, near this row of tanks; and that row of Guards.

"I can't handle any more *Field Punishment*. Please believe me. I haven't recovered from my hunger-strike; I just don't have the strength in my arms," Alfred tells the Nurse tonight in this poorly-drawl.

"Oh I say, darling. Dash!" The Nurse replies as he passes Alfred this bitter-vinegar and gall. "Drink it before tomorrow's crucifixion; it will knock you unconscious.

"One managed to smuggle a thing or two through, old chap. Just do not ask me how. Daze my eyes! One will not speak of such unpleasantness."

So Alfred drinks this potion before today's crucifixion, to overcome his affliction; injury-infirmity-and-illness. He lets out this deathly-scream, slips into an unconscious-dream; and a state of total stillness.

"Heavens above!" He shouts out with shrillness. "Please! Why have you forsaken me?"

Immersed-inebriated-and-intoxicated, Alfred feels emancipated; he feels limitless and totally free. With a smile on his face, he sees Cleo in this imaginary-place; and he sees his favourite tree. He sees his town's winding-streets, wooden-seats; and wavy-sea.

But back in the real world the Provost Marshal looks red-faced, disgraced; and at a total loss. He looks somewhat shoddy, as he inspects Alfred's limp-body; which hangs from this wooden-cross. His eyes are flashing, and his teeth are gnashing; full of metal-teeth and metal-floss.

"Bloody hell! Darned giglet-wench! In all my years on this here planet, I've never seen a bugger pass out so fast!" he hisses like a snake in a tin-can, like the officious-policeman, he was before the war began.

Swish! Swoosh! Stab!

Jerk! Jag! Jab!

The Provost Marshal grabs the knife in his pocket, swings it faster than a launching-rocket; and stabs it into Alfred's side with real violence. Red-blood and gooey-sweat pour out, squirt-spray-and-spout; whilst Alfred just hangs here in silence.

"Aha!" The Provost Marshal yowls like a kitten, playing with a mitten, who is sated-satisfied-and-smitten. "This rug-headed ronyon is still alive! Damn this tomfoolery; the dead don't bleed! Take this queen of curds-and-cream down. Take this doughy-youth down. Take the bugger down.

"And you, cullion, you're a Nurse so I'm told. Care for him afore I have a crack myself; this canker-blossom has had enough time in our hospitals already.

"Gawd damn this folly! What a dreadful bad business."

So this Grizzled Goon unstraps the Nurse in an impatient-hurry, before he unstraps Alfred with an impatient-flurry; and discharges this globule of phlegm. He marches them past the beaten-battered-and-bruised, and this donkey who has been abused; whilst the Nurse picks an aloe-vera stem.

He mixes Alfred's myrrh with its gum, stirs it in with his thumb; and coats Alfred's wounds with its sticky-broth. He watches Alfred till he wakes, comforts Alfred when he shakes; and wraps Alfred in a white linen-cloth.

"Thank goodness that's all over with. I'd be very much obliged if I never had to go through it again," Alfred exclaims.

"Oh darling; you are a regular sunbeam!" The Nurse claims. "This crucifixion malarkey is rot! Rot! Balderdash! Utter piffle! Although I dare say you *will* shine through it. Rah-rah-rah!"

But Alfred will not have to shine, bound by ties-twists-and-twine; and he will not have to endure another crucifixion. Because the Commanding Officer enters this cell with a slippery-slide, and a graceless-glide; like the king of this jurisdiction. He glares with a wandering-eye, lifts his chin to the sky; and speaks with heartfelt-conviction.

"Pigfish!" He shouts with rumbling-diction. "We've had enough of your insolence, and insubordination, and insubjection. And so we're bestowing you with one final opportunity to follow orders. One final opportunity!

"If you refuse, and protest, and rebel, you'll all face court-martials. And they shan't be like those namby-pamby *District Court Martials* you all sailed through afore. Oh no! *Field Court Martials* aren't nearly as lily-livered as those queer affairs. You'd be fools, and buffoons, and nitwits to labour under such a delusion. We can dish out the death-penalty here. Oh yes we can!"

This is not a false-prophecy which these peacemakers can just forget, or some sort of hollow-threat; it is a promise which brings them to these tracks. Where these carriages have their sides exposed, to reveal the crates enclosed; which are marked with words like 'artillery'-'ammunition'-and-'axe'.

Here are some trees with horseshoes nailed to their branches, around those cattle-ranches; which are covered in drops of rain. These birds in the sky, these hares hopping by; and those rabbits skipping down that lane.

And here is this fairly wobbly-soldier, who holds this fairly tatty-folder; with red-hair which is a beacon of fire-fuel-and-flame. With shoulders which are too wide for his chest, a waist which is too wide for his vest; and too wide for his gangly-frame.

Having been put together somewhat loosely, this boy used to sweat profusely; as he stumbled with wobbly-danger. He used to sway from right-to-left, with all his heft; as he searched for steady-behaviour.

He once played tag-tiddlywinks-and-troops, house-hopscotch-and-hoops; cricket-chopsticks-and-conkers. He once engraved 'Alfred and Bernie - friends for ever - A. B. See', into a tree; before he went slightly bonkers.

"Slimy slithery eels! Slithery eels!" The Commanding Officer chides, as he slides, and as he glides. "If you want to stay alive you'll empty this carriage, and carry these crates, and load this mule. Oh yes!"

But with his usual dissension, Alfred does not pay attention; or hear what that man has to say. He looks into Bernie's eyes, and he cries; as his legs begin to give way. As he struggles not to stumble, tumble; or sway.

"You charged me not to kill anyone when I enlisted," Bernie begins to say. "'Please don't kill anyone', you said. 'Not even to save yourself'. Not really, no, not at all. And I listened! No matter how rum it might seem, I haven't killed a single German since. Not one!

"Well now it's my turn to ask you for something. Please take this box, for my sake, not for the army. Just carry it a few metres and put it down over there. Good God man! You'd be mad not to. Bonkers! Doolally! Cuckoo!"

"For you, Bernie, I'd unload a million boxes," Alfred replies. "Please believe me! Please-please-please. I think you're smashing. I think you're better than strawberry ice-cream on a sunny-afternoon.

"But there are eleven other Bernies here, and they all want me to refuse. Well, for eleven Bernies I'd do anything; I'd give my life a million times or more!"

Alfred looks at the Peace Unit who are stood on this grubby-ground, and walks towards them feeling duty-bound; with a sense of real belief. Whilst Bernie hangs his head in shame, and walks away feeling rather lame; full of gripes-grievances-and-grief. Before the Commanding Officer escorts Alfred with the Schoolmaster-Christian-and-Nurse, starts to curse; and starts to debrief.

"Molluscs!" He shouts out like a tribal-chief. "We'll not have you ringleaders encouraging, and influencing, and educating t'others. Oh no! You'll not be able to help them from in here, privates. Not from in here!"

But these conchies do not even mention their upcoming trial, they just smile; and begin to play. They play *marbles* with these bits of asbestos-wall, *catch* with this shabby-ball; and *hopscotch* in that clay.

"I say old chap," the Nurse begins to say. "A Quaker Journalist visited us whilst you were in the infirmary. It *was* rather singular. One admits willingly that we should question his reports, as to their correctness; no doubt they will be full of some sort of poppycock-hogwash-or-bunkum. But he knew all about our situation, and he did seem jolly spiffing on the whole. We felt rather obliged to him, if the truth is to be told.

"Oh darling! A Reverend came with him too. He said that even the Lord Of War was interested to hear about our predicament.

"It is a blooming fine thing! Perfectly delightful! Oh Alfred; the message has made its way home. Rah-rah-rah."

The message might have made it back, in a postman's sack; or it might have not. After a stormy-night, Alfred has a trial to fight; so he is led on past this pot.

"Fall in line! Right turn! Quick march!" The Provost Marshal moos like a cow, as he leads the Peace Unit past this plough; Serb-Sergeant-and-Scot. "You're under bond to obey, I tell you. You sanctimonious-scroyles! You shotten-herrings! You whoremongers! March, Gawd damn you, march!"

The Peace Unit walk through this market without delay, inhale this smell of fishy-decay; and this smell of sweaty-cheese. They walk down these aisles, past these tables-toilets-and-tiles; and through this copse of trees.

Alfred is taken past this broom, and enters this room; which can only be described as '*piecemeal*'. It is full of pieces of fish-market paraphernalia, pieces of military-regalia; and pieces of rusted-steel.

It is full of these spiky-hooks, fishmongery-books; and saline-scalers. These bayonet-blades, grenades; and dusty loud-halers.

And it is full of people like this Colonel who tries to be impartial, as he sits next to the Provost Marshal; up here on this creaky-stage. The eldest soldier on site, with eyes which are black and hair which is white; he should be retired because of his age. His skin is shrunken-shrivelled-and-saggy, creased-crumpled-and-craggy; blanched-bloodless-and-beige.

"Stand to attention, salute, and *whatnot*. For God's sake man!" He begins to chastise.

"No thanky-you," Alfred replies. "That stuff is for soldiers, not for folk like me. No-no-no."

This statement makes the Commanding Officer look downcast, it makes the Colonel look aghast, and it makes the Provost Marshal blast.

"Damn you! What Gawd damn impertinence!" He says with a squawk, as he starts to talk, like a hungry-hawk. "Confound your nonsense. You sanguine-coward! You lanky mountain of rubbery-flesh! You creamy-faced loon! You watery-pumpkin! This court considers you to be a soldier, and it shall try you as one.

"We don't give a tinker's damn what you call yourself; that sort of froth is blown away quick-sharpish here. You really ought to be glad we haven't shot you already.

"Now look here man, I'm in no mood for your brand of tomfoolery. You stand accused of multiple-breaches of the *British Army Act*. Of breaching section seven; leading and taking part in a mutiny. Section eleven; refusing to obey orders. And section thirty-eight; attempting suicide by starvation.

"My Gawd, you've got something coming to you, you poor useless little boy. You dull-eyed fool! You dish of skimmed-milk! You puttock! Bugger. You'd be better orf dead; it'd be a blessing for us all.

"Why you've even been accused of breaching section twelve of the act; encouraging soldiers to desert their posts."

As he says this the Provost Marshal gives the Temperamental Soldier a knowing-glance, with his eyes askance; and a smile which is slightly tentative. This man whose skin is the colour of whey, and whose hair is the colour of hay; is Alfred's sole legal-representative.

But he looks for concord as well as for conflict, so he supports his superiors as well as his convict; and he retreats to sit before he advances to stand. He sways from kindness-to-cruelness, calidity-to-coolness; and bright-to-bland. Before he faces south, and covers his mouth; with the palm of his veiny-hand.

"Don't forget," the Provost Marshal starts to bleat, like a cat in heat; who is stood on some scorching-sand. "That this is a *Field Court Martial*. This court shall decide whether you'll live, or whether you'll die.

"We have laws here, and if found guilty of the charges against you, they state that you must die. Gawd damn you must die! You must die because you've opposed the customs-and-rites which the government has bestowed upon the army. You must die because you've attempted to mislead the nation, and opposed the will of the King. And you must die because you've claimed to be the *King Of The Conchies* yourself.

"Make no mistake! We consider your brand of buffoonery a damned menace; a threat which must be crushed afore it spreads. You caterpillar! You old crab-tree! You overweening traitor!

"Your frightful attempts to overthrow the army shall go no further. Bugger that! There's no place for your sort in our society. I dare say this war shall cleanse our streets of degenerate-parasites like you. You peevish-brat! You pernicious-caitiff! You poisonous hunchbacked-toad!

"Your days of agitation, troublemaking, and threatening the empire are coming to an end. This is your last chance to make amends. You shan't be bestowed with another Gawd damn opportunity ever again!"

"Thank-you," the Colonel bellows with force. "Have you any questions for this *Mister What's-his-name*?"

"Yes sir!" the Provost Marshal whinnies like a horse. "Tell me, you dissembling-harlot; is it true that they call you the '*King Of The Conchies*'?"

"You call me that," Alfred replies without remorse. "I just try-try-try to speak the truth."

"Damn you! You starveling, you elf-skin, you dried ox's tongue, you bull's pizzle, you salted-cod, you brazen-faced varlet! Have you heard what's been testified against you?"

"Yes, I have. I was very much obliged."

"And have you anything to say?"

"No thank-you."

"Bugger me; it's like drawing teeth! Drat-damn-and-blast-it; what a wanton-mind. You don't have a defence? None whatsoever? My Gawd! Do you take me for a sponge?"

Alfred just stands here and shrugs, looks at these mugs, and that box of assorted-drugs.

"Amazing," the Provost Master howls, like a group of horny-owls; or a group of horny-pugs. "Gawd damn amazing. Bugger me! How you gyp us. And how you shall be made sorry for it, you darned artful-hussy.

"You don't deny disobeying orders at all?"

"Not at all. I've never been in your army, I've never respected your rules, and I've never obeyed your orders. Not once. No-no-no. No thanky-you!"

"What a sea of tosh! It bears out everything I've been saying," the Provost Marshal cries. "You *are* in the army whether you like it or not. Disobeying from the orf is no defence. Damn you, you mouldy-rogue! You worthless gooseberry! You rat without a tail! Disobeying from the orf is twice as bad as only starting later."

"Well then," Alfred agrees. "You'll have to kill me twice then!"

Alfred inhales, flicks his fingernails; and laughs at his own remark. Before the Colonel starts to wheeze, sneeze; and bark.

"I beg your pardon, *Mister What's-your-name*; this is no *what-do-you-call-it*, *whosey-whatsit*, laughing matter. I've seen your *thingies*, your *doodahs*, your papers. And I dare say that they're marked quite clearly with the word '*death*'. I don't think you realise the extreme-seriousness of this situation."

"I understand," Alfred answers with a sense of obligation, and appreciation, because he is grateful for this man's consideration. "But there are men dying in the trenches as we speak, and I wouldn't want to be any less brave than them. No thanky-you! I *am* prepared to die for my principles. Yes-yes-yes. I'm just not prepared to die like a soldier; because of a lack of principles."

And much to Alfred's surprise, the Colonel smiles with his eyes, without beginning to chastise.

"Have you any statement at all?" He sighs. "To give yourself a *what-do-you-call-it*, a *whatsit*, a fair sporting chance?"

JOSS SHELDON | 263

"Yes please! Please-please-please," Alfred replies. "I'd like to tell the story of the *Guilty Dogs*.

"It happened a long-long-long time ago, when the King left his chariot outside overnight. He thought his fortified-wall would protect it from interlopers.

"Well, it rained cats-and-dogs that night, and the rainwater softened the leather which adorned the King's chariot.

"The royal-dogs couldn't help themselves. They growled, they pounced, and they tore at that meaty-leather. They chewed it up, swallowed it down, and filled their bellies with the spoils of their conquest.

"Please understand! The King was furious; his beloved-carriage had been torn to pieces. And so he flew into an almighty-rage, and sought revenge. He ordered his soldiers to round up all the street-dogs in his kingdom, send them to a distant-land, and shoot them dead.

"So thousands of street-dogs were taken abroad, where they were shot by firing-squads for a crime they'd never committed.

"Until a Brave Servant confronted the King. Yes thanky-you! He was a stout fellow. Top brass! A real good-egg!

"'*Your honour*', he said. '*The street-dogs can't have ruined your carriage, they were on the other side of your fortified-wall*'.

"The courtesans, obedient folk, were shocked by the Brave Servant's insubordination. But the King considered what he had to say.

"'*If you can find the guilty-dogs*', he replied. '*I'll spare the others*'.

"And so the Brave Servant rounded up the royal-dogs, gave them massive amounts of buttermilk-and-grass, and took them to see the King. Their bellies were so full that the royal-dogs were sick, and vomited pieces of the King's chariot all over the palace-floor.

"'*Your Honour*', the Brave Servant explained. '*These are the dogs who destroyed your chariot*'.

"The King saw that the Brave Servant was right, and so he reversed his order to kill the street-dogs. The Brave Servant was ever so grateful. The street-dogs were rather obliged."

This story makes the Commanding Officer look down, whilst the Colonel starts to frown; and look a bit confused. The Temperamental Soldier stares, whilst the Provost Marshal glares; and looks a bit bemused.

"Please understand," Alfred says sounding animated, captivated; and amused. "The King refused to judge his own dogs, but he was happy to blame the street-dogs for their crimes. And your army is much the same.

"Like the royal-dogs, your soldiers are all very-very-very guilty. They've stolen whole countries, mowed down men with machineguns, and killed women-and-children through blockades and concentration-camps. Our government, like the King in the story, has encouraged them. And now you want to kill us, like the King killed the street-dogs, even though we're the innocent ones.

"So please judge your own soldiers, your own army, and your own consciences, before you judge us peacemakers. Please-please-please!"

The Provost Marshal's face turns red with dismay, and his metal-teeth gnash away; which makes his saliva froth. The Commanding Officer does not seem to care, as he rocks in his chair; and stares at a frenzied-moth.

"How queer!" The Colonel replies whilst he wipes his brow with a cloth. "You do talk like a gibbering-monkey; playing the deuce with extreme-insolence. A bit like your Father, really; he was as mad as a hatter too.

"I met him at the *what's-its-name*, the *thingamabob*, the concentration-camp whence he was killed. Oh Alfred, I dare say you don't even know why he was there?"

"No, I don't" Alfred replies. "I'd be ever so grateful to hear. I'd be very much obliged."

"Well your Father was with his unit, back in 1901, when he came across a Trooper who was beating a *what-do-you-call-it*, a *gubbins*, a Pauper," the Colonel explains. "That little runt was cabbaging the army's food. He was suffering from extreme-starvation, with gaunt-eyes and ribs which poked out through his skin.

"Your Father wanted to protect that dismal little Pauper, and so he embarked on a deuce of a frightful dust-up with the Trooper. He tonked the Trooper's head, kicked him over, and pinned him down in the sand. Your Father hurt his own shoulder in the process.

"The Pauper filled his pockets with grub and slung his hook, whilst our General, filled with extreme-infuriation, gave order for your Father to be shot.

"So your Father disappeared, and ran astir for several hours afore resting by a well.

"I dare say he was rather tired, when the seven Daughters of a *whatsit*, a *deelybob*, a Tribal Priest came by to draw water for their livestock.

"All was good until some Shepherds, with extreme-bluntness, tried to drive those Daughters away. Your Father confronted those Shepherds, and left them in a blind-funk. He helped the Daughters to take all the water they needed.

"And so the Tribal Priest, with extreme-gratitude, cared for your Father until he was fit enough to rejoin the army. For your Father, with extreme-patriotism, was still driven by his duty to serve.

"But he was also keen to avoid the General. So he decided not to return to his original-unit, and went to a *doohickey*, a *doojigger*, a concentration-camp instead. That was whence I met him.

"His eyes weren't weak, and his muscles were still strong. But he was killed by a Zulu whose farm had been burnt by British troops, as part of our scorched-earth policy.

"After he'd spent many months running messages for the British army, that Zulu had returned to our camp, where he discovered that his wife had been raped. I dare say he was enraged, and seeking some sort of extreme-vengeance.

"And so, mistaking your Father for the man who'd abused his wife, he shouted, '*Your descendants may walk this land, but you'll never cross it again*'! He grabbed a rock, smashed it through your Father's skull, and killed your Father in an instant.

"Well, *Mr What's-your-name*, I dare say you think you're acting like he did; making a stand for humanity, no matter how much you might have to *whatsit, whatnot,* suffer for it."

Alfred starts to smirk-snicker-and-smile, because he is grateful for the Colonel's kind-style; and he is grateful to learn why his Father ended up in that ghastly-place. Having already seen that soldiers can be kind, and refined; he realises that his Father was not such a big disgrace.

"It's most important to consider," the Colonel says as he scratches the moles, and the holes; which cover his craggy-face. "That your Father, when you come to think of it, only died *after* he left the army. Most important! He never got hurt whilst he was *what-do-you-call-it, whatsit,* following orders; putting his country first.

"Because the army is here to protect you, *Mister What-do-you-call-yourself.* I dare say, like your Father, you'll only die if you skedaddle off alone.

"So don't be too clever; it's the clever ones who come to the worst grief. If, with extreme-dignity, you fall in line, you shan't come to a sticky-end like your Father."

Alfred just smiles, looks at these files, and this wall which is covered in tiles.

"Okay then," the Colonel negotiates, with his two associates; who are officiating these military-trials. "As is the custom, we can *what-do-you-call-it, what-cha-ma-jigger,* commute the sentence of one prisoner. Shall I release this *Mister What's-his-name*; this *King Of The Conchies*?"

"Damn that! Don't pardon this lump of foul-deformity! This bottled-spider! This burly-boned clown! Pardon a real soldier instead," the Provost Marshal squeaks like a mouse in a funk.

"Release the Barbaric Rebel," the Commanding Officer says, in a daze; referring to a soldier who rioted whilst drunk.

"Then what should I do with this *deelie*, this *dingus*, this man you call the *King Of The Conchies*?" The Colonel asks his flunky.

"Kill him!" The Provost Marshal screams out like a manic-monkey. "This puppy-headed monster doesn't care a rush for his country. The bugger has claimed to be the *King Of The Conchies*; he's guilty of treason! We have no king but the British King! Kill him! Kill him! Kill him!"

"Kill the jellyfish!" The Commanding Officer concurs. "He's tried to destroy the state which brought him into the world, and nurtured him, and educated him. Oh yes! He's failed to fulfil his duty."

"But why," the Colonel asks. "What crime hath he committed? This trial malarkey does fill me with extreme-shudders."

"Kill him! Kill him! Kill him! Kill this ugly-and-venomous toad! Kill this man of falsehood! Kill this sheep-whistling rogue! And damn the bugger too!" The Provost Marshal snarls like a coyote.

"Kill him," the Commanding Officer echoes in a voice which is throaty. "Kill him, and kill him, and kill him! Kill the mermaid!"

The Temperamental Soldier is about to shout '*Death*', but he stops for breath; and begins to sigh. He is about to swing his fists, but he desists; and begins to cry.

"*Mister What's-your-name*, you'll be sentenced on the morrow," the Colonel begins his reply. "But off the record, I dare say I'll have nothing to do with your *hoozy-what*, your *whatsit*, your death. I can't find any fault with you myself."

"Piffle! I'd be happy to shoulder the responsibility," the Provost Marshal barks like a seal, before he starts to squeal, whilst he stamps down on his heel. "Eeeeee! 'Tis my duty!

"I'll drink my cup to the dregs if it damns this whoreson, this senseless-villain, and this mildewed-ear; in the name of my children, my grandchildren, and my great-grandchildren too. Bugger the bugger! Bugger me!"

The Temperamental Soldier leads Alfred out of this store, through this door; and through this open-gate. He wears a wide-smile, as he shoves Alfred down this wide-aisle; and down this wide-straight. Before they arrive in this cell, with this fetid-smell; where Alfred sits down to wait.

He waits until his friends return with faces which are covered in fears, covered in tears; and covered in sweat. The Agitator looks meek, the Christian looks bleak; and the Socialist looks rather wet.

"Come, come," Alfred says whilst the Athlete starts to fret. "Please-please-please! We'll be fine. The Colonel is a good man; he has the biggest heart I've ever known. He has amazing energy for a man his age. For sure, the other soldiers may want us shot, but he'll look out for us. Yes thanky-you!"

"If only it were up to him," the Engineer whinges. "I fear the decision will come from above. Our trials didn't mean a jot. Oh, whatever have we done? Have we offended the heavens? Have we walked under a ladder? Have we broken a mirror? Oh my."

The Apprentice twists and the Nurse turns, before the Tax Collector returns; and the Schoolmaster follows him too. Their trials soon finish, with durations which diminish; as the army rush them all through.

"My trial only lasted seven minutes," the Watchmaker says whilst he taps his shoe. "But the Major did say '*It'd be monstrous to shoot us*'! We've split them like a banana, I tell you. Some of those fruits are on our side!"

"Have we split them? Yes!" The Clerk proclaims, as he fiddles with these chains, and those windowpanes. "Are some of them on our side? Yes. Would they be fighting for Germany if they'd been born over there? Yes. Will they set us free? No. No one likes a conchie."

"Perhaps," the Apprentice says. "But I did get the Generous Soldier to send a letter back to my parents. He's a good sort that one; he sure is first-class.

"I wrote, '*The military has absolute-power here, and our disobedience may very well get us shot. But don't be downhearted; if the worst comes to the worst, many have died for a lesser cause*'.

"Puff! It's a very nice bit! Jolly tippy!"

"That's the spirit!" Alfred tweets, as he discovers these sweets, between his folded bed-sheets. "This could be our last night together; it could be our last night on earth. Please! Let's make sure it's a good one!"

So amidst the monstrous-sound of this angry-battle, these stuttering-riffles with their rapid-rattle; and these demented-bombs which scupper. The Peace Unit sit down for one final time, near this grit-gravel-and-grime; to enjoy their last ever supper.

"My friends," Alfred begins to utter. "Please understand! We've been placed on this earth for a reason; we're here to bring an end to the bloodshed-and-slaughter of war. Yes-yes-yes!

"Tomorrow we'll walk in the name of peace, we'll stand for peace, and it will bring us peace. Peace-peace-peace! But first, please let us be cleansed."

Alfred walks around this underground wooden-box, gets his disciples to remove their socks; and washes their cheesy-feet. Unsure what is happening, his disciples do not say a thing; before the Engineer falls off his seat.

"You'll be fine," Alfred tells him in a voice which is blaring, caring; and sweet. "You'll be fine-fine-fine. You're rad! You're more fun than a barrel of monkeys!"

And before they eat their feast, Alfred lights the frankincense which came from the east; through Syria-Sudan-and-Spain. Having travelled with Alfred throughout his life, it helps the Peace Unit to conquer their strife; pangs-problems-and-pain. So Alfred's confidence increases, as he breaks this bread into twelve even pieces; and speaks out once again.

"Please eat this. Please-please-please. This is the body of our earth, the fields of home, and the ground beneath our feet!"

These conchies all follow, they all swallow; and they all digest this food. Before Alfred takes this jug, and fills this mug; in a particularly joyous-mood.

"Please!" He starts to conclude. "Let's drink from the same cup. This water has travelled down every river, filled every lake, and washed over every shore on earth. It'll unite us! It'll make us one with the world!"

"All-for-one, and one-for-all!" The Watchmaker cheers as he holds these things.

"All-for-one, and one-for-all!" His comrades reply like kings.

"All-for-one, and one-for-all!" Alfred sings. "I've been eager to eat with you before we're all made to suffer. You're special, I respect you, and I love you all.

"And so I won't eat-or-drink until we've been killed-or-freed. No thanky-you! Because peace is our sustenance now; it's the bread of our lives. With it we'll never be hungry-or-thirsty again; we'll be the living-earth, the water of the world, and we'll never experience death.

"For we are the way, the truth and the life. We've acted with peace, lived in peace, and become peace. Peace-peace-peace!

"And peace will protect us tomorrow! Yes-yes-yes. Yes thanky-you!"

Alfred's pomp-pageantry-and-pretences, assaults his disciples' five-senses; and prepares them for the road ahead. With the *smell* of frankincense which fills each lung, the *sight* of conchies uniting as one; and the *taste* of hardened-bread. With the *sound* of Alfred's powwow, and the *feeling* of water on feet just now; which splashed the Schoolmaster's bed.

Alfred has prepared his disciples for this morning's walk, during which they are told not to talk; as they climb through this boggy-flood. As they climb past these molehills in crimson-fields, these Farmers who are bundling their yields; and this boot which is buried in mud. These trees which have been bitten by pigs, these knobbly-twigs; and this tomb which is covered in blood.

The Peace Unit climb up to this great-height, where Britain is almost in sight; as it hides in the misty-distance. They think about being alone, their home; and their somewhat frail-existence.

These kestrels-kingfishers-and-kites, perch in many different sites; on each side of this massive parade-ground. They sit in these trees, near those bees; and watch these Soldiers who start to abound.

These Soldiers who are dressed in blue-trousers, buff-blazers; and khaki-suits. In crumpled-caps, leather-straps; and polished-boots.

Who line up with theatrical-precision, under authoritative-supervision; in perfectly-square blocks. Who line three sides of this square, with putty in their hair; and starch in their bright white-socks.

They sway in this breeze, and face these conchies; who are led like sheep to the slaughter. Who are prodded by these Goons, with these sharp-harpoons; and who are splashed with this murky-water.

Like a pearly-white dove, they make a stand for love; and they make a stand for peace. They hold their breath, wait to be sentenced to death; or given some sort of release.

They stand still whilst they wait to hear their sentence, without any sort of repentance; but lots of scorn-suspicion-and-suspense. Whilst this Bugler plays a song which he learnt in a concert-hall, this military-call; and this ballad which sounds immense.

Slow-tick follows slow-tock, as hands go round this clock; and these chickens begin to cluck. As these notes are chimed, these rhythms are rhymed; and these chords are struck.

The Peace Unit feel under threat, and begin to sweat; with hearts which begin to pound. Before that clock strikes noon, and the Bugler plays his final tune; which ends with a glorious-sound.

Silence descends, and stillness ascends; as the Commanding Officer faces this square. As he slides, glides; and gives a medal to this Goon with blonde-hair.

"Sea urchins!" He begins to blare. "This man should be an example, and a role-model, and an inspiration to every one of you. Every one of you! His bravery in battle is to be lauded, and commended, and celebrated. He has earned, and deserves, and merits this medal.

"But not everyone here appreciates the glory of war, and the army's honour, and their duty to serve. Oh no!"

The Commanding Officer continues to lecture, spouting his creeds-canons-and-conjecture; but Alfred's mind is already elsewhere. He sees Cleo's bleeding, and the time she started receding; before she approached him in the town-square. And he sees himself covered in blood, being shot down in the mud; which forms rivers everywhere.

He sees the time when the Mute Boy almost drowned, as he sees himself sink through this ground; surrounded by mud without any air. And he sees the papers in the Colonel's hands, from where he stands; on which the word '*death*' fills him with despair.

With shaking-knees, his vision starts to freeze; which almost leaves him blind. Colours seem scuzzy, outlines seem fuzzy; and shapes seem less defined. Hellish-hallucinations, and demonic-divinations; begin to plague his mind.

Gravel turns into whirlpools of grey, and trees begin to sway; as Alfred struggles for sanity. Sights seem to blur, and voices seem to slur; as he struggles with these soldiers' vanity.

But he breathes in and breathes out, to escape his distress-discomfort-and-doubt; and free his teeth-tummy-and-toes. His breath travels from bronchiole-to-bronchi-to-larynx, up through his pharynx; and all the way out through his nose. Before he watches the Provost Marshal, who seems far from impartial; as he spouts his pro-war prose.

"Friends, Brits, countrymen; lend me your ears," he cries, like a rabbit with shaky-thighs; and shaky-toes. "You represent a fine institution, with a proud history, and the highest Gawd damn standards known to mankind. Standards which must be maintained!

"Insubordination, free-thought and disobedience, are a threat to this establishment. Bugger me! They'll not be tolerated here. Fleshmongers-fools-and-cowards will not be tolerated here! Foul defacers of God's handiwork will not be tolerated here! Knaves who smell of stale-sweat will not be tolerated here!

"So let the sentence which you're about to hear be a lesson to you. Let it teach you to remain disciplined, forgo your individuality, and stay in line at all times. Gawd help you if you don't! Damn you if you don't!"

The Provost Marshal lifts his right-knee, storms off through this scree; and sits down on that portable-chair. Before the Colonel emerges from the shadows, passes these gallows; and addresses this enormous-square.

"Mister What's-your-name, what-cha-ma-bob, Alfred Freeman," he begins to blare. "Sally forth."

Alfred stands here still, and looks out at that hill; before he is pushed on into position. In his prime, this is his time; and the culmination of his mission.

"Private," the Colonel reads with a formal-disposition. "You've been found guilty of *whatsit,* of *whatnot,* of refusing to obey lawful-commands, extreme-disobedience whilst undergoing *Field Punishment,* and taking part in a mutiny."

This verdict was never in question, this introduction was just a procession; before Alfred is sentenced here. Where unlike each previous threat, which Alfred has been able to forget; this time he is full of fear.

Because this is war and this is France, where these Soldiers lead a merry-dance; with their *kabangs-kadangs-and-kablows.* This is war and this is active-duty, where these Soldiers kill with indifferent-cruelty; to deliver their deadly-blows. This is a show of intent, where these Soldiers are being taught not to dissent; by this Colonel's pro-war prose.

"The sentence of this court is for you to suffer death by being shot," he says whilst he scratches his nose. "This extreme-sentence hath been confirmed by the *what-do-you-call-him,* the *thingamabob,* the Field Marshal; the man in charge of the British Army."

"It's no more than these blobfishes had coming to them, and warrant, and deserve. Oh yes!" The Commanding Officer says with his mouth agape.

"Quite right too!" The Provost Marshal gibbers like an angry-ape. "Spot on! Damn hit the nail on the head! Damn this knotty-pated fool, this king of codpieces, and this old love-monger! Damn the bugger! Damn all the damned conchies!"

Bodies freeze and stomachs drop, hearts stop; and lungs forget to inhale. The Peace Unit feel bad, menaced-moribund-and-mad; fraught-feeble-and-frail.

The Engineer thinks about his health, the Athlete thinks about himself; and the Clerk thinks about his friends. They feel ethereal, shaky-spellbound-and-surreal; as their lives approach their ends.

"Tut-tut-tut. I'll kill those suckers! They're making Alfred die for their sins," the Agitator mutters after some moments have passed.

"One would think so," the Nurse slurs, and concurs; whilst he feels incredibly aghast. "Oh darling! Golly gosh! And to think; we will be receiving the same sentence in half a jiff. Crikey! Crumbs! Cripes! How very ghastly! I dare say our letters cannot have made it home."

But the Quaker Journalist *has* published his report, peacemakers *have* written to newspapers to show their support; and the Peace Unit's story *has* begun to spread. The Philosopher King *has* written articles about their plight, and their commitment not to fight; which *have* all been well-read.

Peacemakers *have* campaigned for them outside buildings-businesses-and-banks, warmakers *have* tried to rid them from the army's ranks, and three politicians *have* agitated from parliament's flanks.

"I say. Will the *Right Honourable Gentleman* either confirm or deny that my constituent, the Schoolmaster, has been sent to France against his will?" A wide-eyed Quaker Politician inquired with a lisp, on a night which was so cold-chilly-and-crisp; that fires had to be lit in parliament. His question had inspired a flurry of '*Hear-hears*', a flurry of jeers; and a flurry of argument.

"I can assure the *Right Honourable Member*, that the conscientious objectors in France are doing a splendid job. They're serving their country admirably," the War Secretary had replied, and lied, as he brushed the truth aside. "The fellow in question is not really declining to obey orders at all; he is going on quite happily."

"One has been led to believe by a certain gentleman in the lobby, that four conscientious objectors have been sentenced to death for refusing to follow orders. Will my *Right Honourable Friend* please reassure the house that this is not the case?" A Scottish Politician with a receding-hairline, and a crooked-spine; had quizzed just two days later. And the War Secretary denied it again, with fiercely earnest-disdain; as his lies grew ever greater.

"It is indubitable," he screamed like a crazed-dictator. "That this government has no intention of dealing with conscientious objectors in any way harshly. Aforesaid, there shall be no question of them being sentenced to death."

"We know that you've sent men committed to peace into the arena of war, high-handedly, with a resolve to kill them," a Liberal Politician accused after one more week.

"Order! Order! Order!" The War Secretary began to shriek, as he rose to speak, on the third-leg of his dishonest-streak. "What utter rot-flummery-and-balderdash! *Mr Speaker*; this gentleman is sorely misinformed. As far as I'm concerned, and as far as the War Office is concerned, no man shall be sent to France who we have good reason to believe is a genuine contentious objector. Not over my dead body!"

But before the War Secretary could find his flow, a rooster had flown in and begun to crow; it had clucked-cackled-and-cried. So despite the peacemakers lobbying, and jockeying; the Peace Unit's existence had been denied. They had been neglected, refuted-revoked-and-rejected; and nonchalantly brushed aside.

This was the case in the public-domain at least, but in private the peacemakers' efforts had begun to increase; across every British territory-township-and-town. Peacemakers had even influenced the Prime Minister, a man who considers conscription to be sinister; and once muttered '*Abominable*' whilst he paced up-and-down.

In the days which had followed, the Prime Minister had wallowed; because the Peace Unit's plight had driven him to distraction. Before he came to the conchies' defence, and sounded immense; when he condemned the army's action.

'*Under no circumstances*', he wrote with satisfaction. '*May the army conduct any executions which have not been approved by the War Cabinet first. Do not be abominable!*'

Yet wherever the Peace Unit have gone, for however long, the death-threats have continued on.

'*You disrespectful-devils shall face court-martials on the morrow, and shall be off to France soon after.*' The Staff Sergeant had shouted with dread, whilst he shook his chubby-head, and his face turned red. '*Playing the devil shall get you shot quick-sharpish out in that devilish-hell. It sure is a devil of a way to go. You damn degenerates*'.

'*The other conchies who've come this way all done got conformed, done got hard-labour, or done got shot. There's a list in the officer's canteen of their fates; death-or-conformity. You kiddies will be next!*' The Zealous Soldier had warned.

'*If you don't comply with orders you'll be shot,*' the Commanding Officer had said sounding scorned. '*And if you don't conform to army-ways you'll be shot, and if you don't meet our standards you'll be shot as well. You've got your work cut out just to stay alive. Don't expect any sympathy, soldiers. Don't expect any sympathy!*'

But those threats did have any sort of clout, because the warmakers did not have the authority to carry them out; and proceed with their other war. So they left the Peace Unit afflicted-annoyed-and-abused, bullied-beaten-and-bruised; because they could not do anything more.

Yet as thousands of soldiers line up on this enormous-square, with shiny-putty in their shiny-hair; it appears that their efforts has borne fruit. It appears that the warmakers have won a victory to savour, that decisions have gone in their favour; and they now have permission to shoot.

Things in Britain have indeed moved along, but it has been the peacemakers who have moved them on; with their non-stop braying-bellowing-and-bleating. They have moved things along in the Prime Minister's own study, where the Philosopher King looked ruddy; as he sat on some green leather-seating. Because the Organiser had spoken out in many directions, and used her many connections; to arrange a crucial-meeting.

"Good afternoon, Prime Minister," she had said by way of a greeting. "I think you should know that people, good people, peaceful people, have been thrown into a war which they abhor, and face being shot for refusing to support it. It's illegal, it's immoral, and it's irresponsible.

"If we don't do something to stop this awful deuce, if *you* Prime Minister don't do something to stop it, we can kiss goodbye to liberty, we can kiss goodbye to equality, and we can kiss goodbye fraternity. We can kiss goodbye to everything good about this country which we all adore. It's damnable! It really is the limit.

"So remember this! History shan't judge you for the way you act in the name of war, Prime Minister, but for how you act in the name of peace. History shan't judge you for your might, it shall judge you for your compassion. It shall judge you for this very moment; it shall judge you for how you act here, and for how you act now!"

The Prime Minister had already been forced into a war which he opposed, and he had already been forced to introduce conscription despite not wanting it imposed; as he marched to the army's beat. So as he sat amongst friends, he decided to make amends; without being detached-disconnected-or-discrete.

"You're right," he began to bleat. "It'd be monstrous for people to be shot for refusing to kill. Abominable! It'll never happen on my watch. Never!"

And yet Alfred finds himself surrounded by these Soldiers who are dressed in blue-trousers, buff-blazers; and khaki-suits. In crumpled-caps, leather-straps; and polished-boots.

He finds himself surrounded by these Soldiers who line up with theatrical-precision, under authoritative-supervision; in perfectly-square blocks. Who line three sides of this square, with putty in their hair; and starch in their bright white-socks.

'The sentence of this court,' the Colonel just said, staring ahead; whilst he kicked some bright white-rocks. 'Is for you to suffer death by being shot. This extreme-sentence hath been confirmed by the what-do-you-call-him, the thingamabob, the Field Marshal; the man in charge of the British Army.'

And so bodies have frozen and stomachs have dropped, hearts have stopped; and lungs have forgotten to inhale. The Peace Unit feel bad, menaced-moribund-and-mad; fraught-feeble-and-frail.

The Agitator mutters 'Lemme at 'em! Lowlife scum', the Socialist twiddles his thumb; and the Apprentice begins to scowl. Alfred sees his life pass before his eyes, the Nurse sighs; and the Engineer begins to howl.

But the Colonel seems blue, as he takes in this view, and continues his sentencing too.

"Your sentence hath subsequently been commuted," he says whilst he taps his shoe. "To ten years of penal-servitude with hard-labour.

You're extreme *whatsit, whatnot*, lucky; *Mister What's-your-name*."

This reprieve means that the Peace Unit's helplessness, and their speechlessness; do not last for long. The Watchmaker giggles, the Clerk wriggles; and the Apprentice breaks out into song.

"We're going home!" He says as he starts to feel strong. "What's ten years? Nothing! They'll never beat us! Wahoo! Yippee! Woop-woop!"

"Back of the net!" The Athlete says as he turns pale. "We've hit them for six!"

"Bring on the revolution!" The Socialist begins to wail. "Long live the workers!"

"I don't believe it," the Engineer says as he bites his nail. "I don't understand. Me? I understand nothing."

"Have we told them? Yes!" The Clerk says as he fidgets with his shirttail. "First they ignore you. Then they laugh at you. Then they fight you. Then you win. Ghastly thing this war. No one likes a conchie."

"Ta dadada ta daaa! Peace power!" The Agitator shouts like a buccaneer, without any fear, so that all these Soldiers can hear. "Lemme at 'em! Lemme at 'em! You suckers never stood a chance! We've splatted you, rocked you and socked you! You'll never keep us down."

"Hallelujah, praise the Lord!" The Christian cheers, in floods of tears, as he looks around at his peers. "Two minutes ago we were dead, but now we've been resurrected. We've become martyrs for peace!

"Praise you Jesus; you've saved us all. We've been condemned to death, crucified, and entombed in prison. But you'll help us to rise up again!"

STREET SPIRIT

Dog went to visit Boy, because she wanted to learn more about his oneness-serenity-and-peace, without which she had started to suffer.

And, after she had skipped through the forest, she found Boy meditating. He had an embracing-posture, two serene-eyes, and a peaceful-glow.

"In all my years," Dog said. "Whilst watering Apple Tree's roots, sowing Berry Bush's seeds and feeding Poplar's Bees, I've never been as content as you are now. When I see other creatures in pain it hurts me, their distress makes me stressed, and their tears make me cry. Please tell me; what is serenity?"

Boy looked at Dog and smiled.

"Serenity," he said. "Is watering Apple Tree without wanting her apples, sowing Berry Bush's seeds without wanting his berries, and feeding the Bees without wanting their honey. It's doing the right thing, and embracing the consequences, whatever they may be.

"And so I embrace Apple Tree, Berry Bush and Pine, no matter what they do to me. I embrace them as if they are an extension of myself, and a part of my very own being. As if we are one and the same."

Boy looked at Dog and smiled.

"Come with me," he said, before he led Dog through the forest. They soon reached Dog's favourite lake, dived in, and swum towards Carp, who was hiding in the reeds.

"We're looking for water," Boy said. "Can you help us to find it?"

Dog was confused. She knew that the lake was full of water, because when she was on dry land it was easy to see. But she kept quiet and allowed Carp to speak.

"Hmm," she said. "I've heard of this thing which you call 'water'. We should ask Crab about it; he might know where to look."

So they swum towards Crab, who was scuttling across the lake's sandy-floor.

"We're looking for water," Boy said. "Can you help us to find it?"

"I would have helped you before," Crab said as he scurried left and scurried right. "But I'm too busy trying to walk forwards right now, and so I don't have the time help you."

Dog realised that Crab could not see the water around him, because he could not embrace the way he walked. He could not embrace his body.

"Clam doesn't bother with such things," Carp continued. "She doesn't walk at all. We should ask her where to find water."

So they swum towards Clam, who was sitting in a pile of shale.

"We're looking for water," Boy said. "Can you help us to find it?"

"I would have helped you before," Clam said as she jumped up, and then fell back down again. "I used to be able to swim, and knew about everything in this lake. But Chub split my shell in two, because he thought it would help me to breathe. And so now I can't swim, I can't float, and I can't help you to find water. I only wish Chub had let me be."

Dog realised that Clam could not see the water around her, because she could not embrace how others acted. She could not embrace her society.

"Neither Crab nor Clam could help us," Boy said to Carp. "Perhaps you could?"

"Me? Oh no," Carp replied as she swum between the reeds. "I daren't leave these reeds; it's far too dangerous for a defenceless fish like me, out there in the open-water."

Dog realised that Carp could not see the water around her, because she could not embrace her environment. She could not embrace her universe.

"Thank-you for your help," Boy said, before he swum back to the shore.

"Do you see the water around you here?" He asked Dog.

"There isn't any water here," Dog replied. "It's all in the lake."

"You need to embrace," Boy said. "Be the world child; form a circle!"

But Dog could not think of a single thing to do or feel. And so after many moments of thought, she finally gave in. She hung her head in shame, looked down into her being, and deeper down into her soul.

No longer relying on her love-loyalty-and-passion, Dog used her spirit instead of her emotions, and her soul instead of her heart. It helped her to see that she had become a prisoner of action.

She saw that, like Crab-Clam-and-Carp, she had been blind to the world around her. And like them, she had never found peace; she had *never embraced herself, her society or her universe.*

"It's the air!" She exclaimed. "I've ignored the air which surrounds me, just like Crab-Clam-and-Carp ignore the water which surrounds them.

"For just as each fish swims in the same water, so each animal breathes in the same air. Each breath we take unites us! The universe becomes us when we inhale, and we become the universe when we exhale!

"We're all connected! We're all the same! We're all one!"

1918

After all his travails two years ago, when breathing-exercises and a hunger-strike had left him low; whilst crucifixions were enforced by soldiers on assignment. Alfred becomes one with the universe in this tomb-like cell, this cave in which he has been forced to dwell; throughout months of solitary-confinement.

This tomb-like cell is sooty-sunless-and-small, with a bed of wooden-planks propped against this wall; and a stone-door rolled across that divide. Without a chest-cabinet-or-chair, some bread-and-water is on the floor just there; and a garden is hidden outside.

The year is 1918.

A Canadian Sportsman is winning the first ever *National Hockey League* without making many mistakes, an American Inventor is installing the first ever set of hydraulic-brakes; and a South African Rebel is being born. In Latvia-Lithuania-and-Czechoslovakia the people are declaring their independence, in Russia the Communists are rising up in ascendance; and in Spain an influenza-pandemic is spreading with scorn. Whilst the British pass a bill to give some women the vote, as their army travel to Palestine by boat; where they dock during a tumultuous-storm.

But Alfred is unaware of these tales-tidings-and-tricks, now he is 'Prisoner Fifty-Four Forty-Six'; here in this reformatory. Having heard his death-knell, and descended into hell; this is his purgatory. Left here neglected, he waits to be resurrected; and rise again in glory.

Although if he was more of a prude, he could have better bedding and much better food; in a much better sort of a cell. He could have some paper on which to write, some natural-daylight; and a couple of pictures as well.

And at first he *was* happy to fix the postal-sacks, full of cuts-creases-and-cracks; with which he was supplied. Because he was told that those broken-rags, and broken-bags; would be used to send post worldwide.

After a month of good behaviour, which his guards were happy to savour; Alfred was rewarded with a *merit-stripe*. He received a mattress made of straw, a book about the law; and a photo of Cleo which he stuck to a pipe.

He received a second *stripe* and was allowed a visit, as long as he did not say anything explicit; whilst he sat in a wooden-cage. So the Suffragist disguised herself as an auctioneer, and Cleo wore her finest gear; as they sat on a wooden-stage.

They spoke whilst Alfred was hidden behind a sheet of dark-gauze, bent over on all-fours; unfed-unshaven-and-unkempt. His prison-issue trousers were covered in dirt, whilst his prison-issue shirt; hid his sense of contempt.

It hid him from the Suffragist who was on a mission to boost prisoners' dispositions, and document their conditions; as she tried to enlighten her nation. Because when she was not in prison for her crimes, for which she had been arrested twelve times; she was publishing new information.

'*Oh darling child,*' she began her oration. '*Thousands of conchies all over the land are fixing those sacks. This is the big picture. It makes one wonder why we need so many postbags all of a sudden. One does suspect a hidden agenda.*'

Her words made Alfred recall the bags of coal he saw in France, purely by chance; which were used during the army's attacks. And he found a coal-like residue, with a greasy-hue; on the frayed-fringes of some of his sacks.

His suspicions had been ignited, which made him feel blighted; so he asked the other conchies for their views. And he deduced that those sacks were helping the war, which he could not ignore; endorse-encourage-or-excuse.

He felt riled, duped-deceived-and-defiled; so he refused to work on another consignment. Which was why he was left to languish, full of angst-agony-and-anguish; here in solitary-confinement.

He was left here in 1916 when Germany issued a peace-note, and America issued a peace-note; which both called for peace-negotiations. But the Allies rejected those offers out of hand, because they were suspicious of their enemies' command; and wanted to crush their enemies' nations.

A senior Russian Minister, sounded sinister; when he said '*Peace! How will that appease the Dead? We want retributions!*'

The French Premier, began sneer; when he said '*Peace! We don't want peace! We want restitutions!*'

And Britain's Leader shook his head, when he said; '*Peace! Don't get on my nerves! We want reparations!*'

So Britain's blockade killed its three-hundred-thousandth civilian of the affair, which inspired Germany to engage in submarine-warfare; which inspired America to step onto the scene. They joined an Allied counterattack, which forced her enemies back; in the summer of 1918.

People's lifestyles suffered a rapid-descent, as taxes rose from six to thirty percent; during four years of ubiquitous-war. Policemen went on strike in the Big City, soldiers began to mutiny; and munitions-workers abandoned their factory-floor.

They fought against the doubling in food-prices, which was caused by a food-crisis; and they became members of socialist-groups. They joined famous reformers, and famous performers; who had also signed up with their troupes.

But Alfred is blissfully-unaware of this as he sits here in solitary-confinement, where he uses this stale-bread to find spiritual-refinement, and soulful-alignment.

For even though he has become a leathery-bag of skinny-bones, coated in chilblains in a mixture of tones; Alfred is accustomed to his diet. So unlike one in six conchies in this jail, who are suffering on a massive-scale; he has not gone to hospital on the quiet. His skin is not tired-tender-or-tight, his eyes are not affected by the lack of light; and his ears can ignore this riot.

This riot of German Gothas which dive down, towards this town; and rain bombs onto the urban-jungle below. These bombs which are dazzling-deafening-and-dark, with shells which are stark; and shrapnel which is aglow.

Those Criminals become manic, and they panic; whilst Alfred finds inner-peace. Whilst he contemplates this piece of bread, frees his head; and finds spiritual-release.

He *sees* its every hue, speck-shade-and-skew; and becomes each manifestation.

He *feels* its every angle, turn-twist-and-tangle; and becomes each materialisation.

He *hears* its every hollow, split-shred-and-swallow; and becomes each intonation.

He *smells* its every scent, scar-slice-and-segment; and becomes each emanation.

He *tastes* its every slice, salt-seasoning-and-spice; and becomes each palpation.

He escapes his torment, and exists in the present; without looking to the future or thinking of the past. He finds emancipation, life-liberty-and-liberation; as he achieves enlightenment at last.

He becomes the fields which grew this bread's wheat, the reapers who removed that crop from its peat; and the mills in which it was ground. The trees which lined those expansive-ranches, the birds who sat on their gnarly-branches; and the animals who meandered around. The farmer who cared for his crop, the baker who baked it in her shop; and the merchant who sold it by the pound.

He becomes the *fire* which burns the godly-grand-and-good, and rotten-wood; with equal-damnation. He becomes the *wind* which carries scented-perfumes, and putrid-fumes; across every single nation. He becomes the *earth* which holds a pretty-tree, and putrid-debris; without any discrimination. And he becomes the *water* which can be pure, or mixed in with manure; in any combination.

He becomes the earth-wind-water-and-fire in every dog, fox-fish-and-frog; deputy-drummer-and-draftee. In every cow-camel-and-cat, bee-bird-and-bat; and piece of artillery.

He becomes them all, embraces them all; and escapes from false-perceptions. He becomes part of a greater whole in which all things are connected, and subjected; without any exceptions. As all things unite, fill him with light; and free him from misconceptions.

And so Alfred embraces life, soldiers-struggle-and-strife; his society and himself. Serenity fills his heart, to start; before it improves his spiritual-health. Before he rises above strain, above pain; and above stealth.

Alfred is delivered, and he is transfigured; as he ascends his spiritual-mountain. Whilst bombs continue to spray, in every way; like water in a fountain.

His clothes glow with light, his face turns white; and these figures all start to appear. He sees his Father walk the earth, his own birth; and the Good German who whispers in his ear.

"You're like a son to me Alfie!" He says with revelry, glee; and cheer. "Viz you I am vell pleased!"

So Alfred's journey through understanding-love-and-oneness, has brought him to this state of wholeness; which is his final-destination. After being *involved* in many mistakes in his youth, he has *evolved* towards the truth; and achieved his soul's salvation.

The first leg of Alfred's journey *involved* using his *knowledge*, as he *evolved* his *understanding* at college; where his studies made him strain. His Father's stories taught him about action, and his school taught him about abstraction; as he struggled to use his *brain*. Before the Good German's fables, showed him what understanding enables; which helped him to truly gain.

But Alfred's understanding was only ever finite, because even with hindsight; there was always more information for him to discover. A matter of gradation, his knowledge relied upon education; with an infinity of facts to uncover.

So the second leg of Alfred's journey *involved* using his *emotions*, as he *evolved* his *love* for many notions; during experiences which tore him apart. His Sunday School Teacher brought him lust, and his Authoritative Teacher brought him disgust; as he struggled to use his *heart*. Before his good-deeds for the community, unlocked love's opportunity; which helped his life to start.

But Alfred's love was only ever finite, it brought him despair as well as delight; because there were always more sensations for him to discover. Based on desire-possession-and-need, love was never guaranteed; with an infinity of feelings to uncover.

He treated the cadets with a rebellious sort of scorn, refused to wear the army's uniform; and argued with his Mother. He challenged the *White Feather Brigade*, protested against the naval-blockade; and rebuffed the requests of others.

So the third leg of Alfred's journey *involved* using his *spirituality*, as he *evolved* his *being* towards immortality; and proceeded towards his goal. His breathing-exercise made him introverted, and his hunger-strike made him disconcerted; as he struggled to use his *soul*. But as he practices mindfulness, he finds oneness; and finally becomes whole.

He uses compassion to overcome brutality, detachment to overcome modality; and love to overcome hate. And he embraces this one-legged Jailor without going berserk, refusing to work; or starting a new debate. He smiles during this random cell-inspection, acts with affection; and holds himself perfectly-straight.

"Can I work on behalf of the other prisoners please?" He asks as he passes this empty-plate. "Please-please-please. To cook-or-clean for them, perhaps?"

This request would have been rejected before, but the warmakers are not so rash anymore; now the *NCF* report on their inhumanity. On force-feeding hunger-strikers to stop their starvation, leaving the sick without medication; and driving conchies to insanity. On the peacemakers who have died in prison, and lost their vision; due to the warmakers' vanity.

"See what can be done, me hearty," the Jailor replies with mundanity. "Ahrrrr. But don't talk to me again, Fifty-Four Forty-Six. The rule of silence!"

The Jailor leaves Alfred behind these immutable metal-bars, where his cheeks glow like moons and his eyes shine like stars; in a manner which is serene. And because of these characterisations, or the government's communications; Alfred wins over this former-marine.

"Ye can work vampin' the clink's furniture," he says, after some delays; which were caused by a leak in the canteen.

So Alfred gets to know this man whose muscled-triceps, and muscled-biceps; bulge after years spent sailing the oceans. Who wears his uniform with a chest which is puffed, a face which is chuffed; and pride in all of his motions. In all of his stumbles, and all of his tumbles; as he struggles to use his wooden-leg without taking any potions.

"They needed me hither. They were understaffed. The war!" He says, as he sways; because of his heady-emotions. "Couldn't return to the navy, even though me be a veteran of more conflicts than most. Gammy leg! Ahrrrr. The war!

"Got it enforcin' the blockade, me tells ye. Was loadin' ammunition in the bow of our ship, as we chased a swashbucklin' Jaeger squadron away. Every Hohenzollern ship fleein' yonder was firin' back on our craft, and spoilin' for a fight. Shot the fuel store! Shattered a turret! Smashed the boiler!

"One of Fritz's shells landed nearby and broke asunder into several chunks, which flew through the air, and flew through me leg. Fair well sliced-and-diced it. Ahrrrr. The war!"

"That's awful," Alfred sympathises, and empathises; as he offers to shake his Jailor's hand.

"What the deuce?" His Jailor replies with this sound which is marvellous, vainglorious; and grand. "Don't ye speak, Fifty-Four Forty-Six. The rule of silence! And don't ye offer yer hand. Don't shake hands with scurvy-dogs, squiffies or scallywags, me.

"Fought hard for the land under yer feet with this here hand. These fingers! This palm! The war! Ahrrrr.

"Shiver me timbers! Don't get ye, really don't. Ye either be precious-peculiar or uncommon-shameful, cannot be sure. But mine's been an honourable life. Ahrrrr. Lost a leg! Not gonna be shakin' hands with yer type. No thanky! Ye've been quodded for a reason, me tells ye. Don't ye be thinkin' ye can make a game of me, sonny-jim. Ahrrrr. Me bees of a good mind to clip ye 'round yer earhole; ye may lay to that!"

The Jailor is neither feisty-foul-nor-fair, without cruelty-charity-or-care; but he is disturbed by the conchies' morality. He controls other inmates with force, and shouts till he is hoarse; but cannot affect the conchies with such brutality. Because they meet his threats with fraternity, his hatred with humanity; and his gloom with geniality.

"You're getting much-much-much better at using that leg," Alfred says as he works away steadily.

"Silence, Fifty-Four Forty-Six! The rule of silence!" The Jailor replies as he breathes in heavily. 'Oooh-ahrrrr, oooh-ahrrrr, oooh-ahrrrr '.

"You're looking good-good-good today," Alfred tries after two more weeks.

"Silence, Fifty-Four Forty-Six. The rule of silence!" The Jailor snorts, and contorts; whilst he speaks.

"I'm loving that new haircut; it makes you look like a film-star!" Alfred continues as he stands by this tap which leaks.

"Silence, Fifty-Four Forty-Six. The rule of silence!" The Jailor says as he gasps for air, rest on this chair; and puffs his scarlet-cheeks.

"Please tell me! Do you have a family? Pretty please. Pretty please with a cherry on top," Alfred asks as he sands this wood at various-speeds.

"Silence, Fifty-Four Forty-Six. The rule of silence!" The Jailor pleads. "Have a toddler who's in love with the bilge. Ahrrrr. A sailor, me tells ye. Ahrrrr. The war!"

So Alfred carves this seagull, and this wooden-hull; whilst he makes this wooden toy-boat. He makes some portholes, some poles; and some sails from a piece of his coat.

And with his oneness-serenity-and-peace transferred, he gives it to the Jailor without adding a word; or seeking profit-pleasure-or-praise. He does not act with expectation, exhortation; or malaise.

"Please tell me! What's sailing like?" He asks after a few more days.

"Silence, Fifty-Four Forty-Six. The rule of silence!" The Jailor says. "It's like home, landlubber. Ahrrrr. It's like fish-and-chips, warm-beer and Sunday-roasts. Bobbin' up-and-down, cradled in the frothy-waves; there's nothin' like it. Savvy?

"Seen it all me tells ye. Ahrrrr. The rise of the battleship! The birth of the torpedo! Submarines! The war!

"Sailed across every ocean. Served near-and-far. The navy! Merchant fleets! Private yachts! Ahrrrr."

Alfred waves-whistles-and-winks, beams-blushes-and-blinks; but does not add a single word. He helps the Jailor to rest his leg, sands his wooden-peg; and whistles like a bird.

"Please tell me! What's fighting like?" He asks after a few more weeks.

"Silence Fifty-Four Forty-Six! The rule of silence!" The Jailor snorts, and contorts; as he slobbers-salivates-and-speaks. "It's an honour to serve, me tells ye. Pride! Honour! Glory! Ahrrrr. The war!

"Victories! Battles! Success! Treasure-troves full of booty. It weren't so bad. Ahrrrr. Middlin', me tells ye.

"Canons! Mortars! Kabangs! Sinkin' ships. A sinful waste. Ahrrrr.

"Blood! Gore! Dead bodies! 'Twas a melancholy affair, me tells ye. Guts! Silver! Spleen!"

Alfred smiles before he makes a clock for the Jailor's club, and a birdhouse for the Jailor's pub; whilst he acts with peaceful-tranquillity.

He makes pots for the Jailor's plants, and vases for the Jailor's aunts; whilst he acts with peaceful-humility. But he does not manipulate, or stipulate; whilst he acts with peaceful-civility.

"Please tell me! Has your life brought you peace?" He pleads.

"Silence, Fifty-Four Forty-Six. The rule of silence!" The Jailor huffs, and puffs, before he proceeds. "No! No! No! Done what was expected. Ahrrrr. The war!"

But this talk ends abruptly as these German Gothas swarm overhead, rain down these bombs which are painted red; and which make this ground quake. They make these Christians pray, those Cowards sway; this cupboard fall and those floorboards shake. But Alfred stays calm, free from alarm; until the cupboard crushes his leg and makes it break.

The Jailor sees Alfred lying here like he had once done at sea, wounded in the same place just beneath his knee; with the same sort of hurt. With the same sort of blood which is as red as his own, which pours over this piece of Alfred's bone; and this piece Alfred's shirt.

Dynamite like that which the Jailor once detonated, against which Alfred once demonstrated; continues to explode outside. It destroys those properties, those trees; and that patch of countryside.

The destruction which the Jailor once adored, and Alfred once abhorred; now spreads itself all around. Over shops-spaces-and-stores, desks-drapes-and-doors; and this workshop's grubby-ground.

The death which the Jailor once imposed, and Alfred once opposed; fills every bloody-street. Blood covers every window-pane, winding-lane; and wooden-seat.

The Jailor starts wheezing, sighing-sniffing-and-sneezing; but he believes in Alfred right now. So he hobbles across this floorboard, removes this fallen-cupboard; and wipes down Alfred's brow. He dresses Alfred's leg in this wrap, which he ties with this strap; as well as conditions allow.

"We ain't so different, ye-and-me, matey," he says whilst he pants like a cow. "Ahrrrr. Yo-ho-ho. A bottle of rum! Ain't so different at all. The same! Ahrrrr. The war!"

Alfred glows with peaceful-serenity, and peaceful-tranquillity; without adding a single word. For with a leg which is broken, no words need be spoken; for him to be held-heeded-and-heard.

BURIED IN TEETH

Dog thought about how Owl was full of intelligence-respectability-and-strength, before he became full of love-loyalty-and-passion.

She thought about how she was full of love-loyalty-and-passion, before she became full of oneness-serenity-and-peace.

And she thought about Owl's delicate-bones and bird-wings, which would never fly again; buried beneath the earth, and swallowed down into the gut of centuries.

So she visited Owl's grave, where she saw a Young Pine who was holding a Young Owl in her branches. And she saw a Young Dog who had befriended a Young Boy.

"Form a circle!" Boy had said. And it made Dog feel good.

She walked past Wolf, who lived with Lamb, and Leopard who slept with Goat. She walked past Cow who ate with Bear, and Lion who shared with Ox. And she walked past Baby, who was playing near Cobra's den, with her hand in Viper's nest.

Baby was leading the other animals towards a mountain of shining-light.

1919

Having been entombed inside, after he was crucified; Alfred is resurrected anew. In clothes which are snow-white, and snow-bright; this gate rolls back and he walks on through. This ground shakes, that Guard quakes; and these Prisoners bid him adieu.

The year is 1919.

An American Mechanic is inventing the pop-up toaster whilst he drinks some tea, a German Locksmith is forming a fascist-party; and a Cuban Sportsman is becoming the first Latino to play in a *World Series*. In America some race-riots are spreading from town-to-town, in Portugal the first transatlantic-flight is touching down; and in Ireland some revolutionaries are promoting their theories. Whilst the British massacre some protestors in India, and then ignore their media; who have lots of queries.

The British also ignore Alfred when his sentence is cut short, by a magistrates-court; which admits that he should not in be here. Less than three years into a ten year spell, he is discharged from the army as well; and told not to volunteer.

The war has passed Alfred by, it has bled European civilisation dry; and it has been celebrated with a series of victory-parades. Four-hundred-and-fifty-thousand Germans, mainly children-commoners-and-civilians; have been killed by Britain's blockades. Tens of millions of soldiers have been tangled, maimed-mutilated-and-mangled; whilst they served in their armies' brigades. And millions of conscripts in the armed-forces, innocent-civilians and innocent-horses; have died in needless-crusades.

Thirty-one conchies have turned insane, and seventy-one conchies have died in pain; because of hepatitis. Because of frozen-pneumonia, stuporific-catatonia; and phlegmy-bronchitis.

Sixteen-thousand conchies have faced tribunals, and been threatened with funerals; because of laws passed down from above. Six-thousand conchies have been imprisoned in the name of peace, and been released; after they followed the law of love.

Fifty-Four Forty-Six was Alfred's number, but right now someone else has that number; because Alfred is being unfurled. He clutches his release-papers, inhales these smoggy-vapours; and steps into this brave new world. With clothes which are baggy, a beard which is shaggy; and hair which is slightly curled.

Alfred considers these tubular underground-trains, which snake through the Big City's veins; to be a miracle beneath the earth. These Street Traders who carry their knickknacks, and these Porters who carry their sacks; fill him with a sense of worth.

He is deafened by these double-decker trams, these noisy traffic-jams; and this Taxi Driver who calls-cusses-and-curses. These motorcars which start to brake, these Babies who start to shake; and this Trombonist who rehearses. These church-bells which ring, these Singers who sing; and this group of uniformed Nurses. These doors! These doors! These doors!

He is dazzled by these Ladies in short-skirts, and these Men in bright-shirts; as he walks down this stretch of grey-pavement. He finds them bright-brilliant-and-bold, and something to behold; as he fills with utter-amazement.

As he breathes in this fresh spring-air, and arrives in this old town-square; where he finds this gathered trio. Here is the Suffragist who looks healthy, here is the Deserter who looks stealthy; and here is Cleo. She is crying, sobbing-snivelling-and-sighing; in this dress which is pale-yellow.

"Woman, why are you crying?" Alfred asks in a voice which is mellow.

"Sorry," Cleo begins to reply, cry; and bellow. "I'm so very sorry. It's just that the government has taken my man away, and I don't where they've put him. Oh, don't I just look a state? Please don't judge me for it."

Cleo does not recognise Alfred after all his time in jail, which has made him look pasty-pallid-and-pale; with skin which has started to harden. His shoes are battered-blemished-and-broken, and he looks like he has just awoken; or been at work in a muddy-garden.

"Please tell me! Why are you crying? Who is it you're looking for?" Alfred asks as he points at his bruises.

"Where you've put him?" Cleo accuses. "What have you've done to him? Why have you done it?"

"Cleo! It's me!"

"Alfred! Alfred! Alfred!" Cleo sings in a joyous-rhythm, as she embraces her man for the first time since prison, now he has finally risen. "Oh do forgive me, I am so very sorry. Are you happy to see me? Have I done good?"

"You've been amazing," Alfred says. "Thank-you, thank-you, thank-you! I appreciate your efforts. I dig you! You're better than unicorns-and-pixies combined.

"Peace be with you! Down with the war!"

The Suffragist removes her maid's disguise, wipes her eyes; and looks overjoyed. Whilst the Deserter who is still big-headed, and bow-legged; starts to look annoyed.

"'Pon my word, who on earth are ye?" He asks as he stares across this void. "What on earth is all o' this? I ain't never seen nothing like it in my life."

"Please! Put your finger here. See my hands. Touch my side." Alfred tells him. "Please! Stop your doubting and believe. Please-please-please."

So the Deserter investigates Alfred's bearded-chin, and blemished-skin; which is still covered in the scars from his smallpox. He investigates the stigmata on Alfred's palms, ankles-armpits-and-arms; beneath his shirt and beneath his socks.

"My friend! My comrade! My leader!" He responds as he becomes aware.

"Oh darling child," the Suffragist responds with her usual flair. "It sure is good to see you. One does hope you're going on favourably, so to speak.

"Because all your sacrifices have been worth it! Your calls to mutiny have been heeded! British soldiers have mutinied, German sailors have mutinied, and German soldiers have deserted. British soldiers have marched on parliament, British sailors have marched on parliament, and Europeans soldiers have turned their guns on their leaders. The German people have revolted, they've established a republic, and the Russian people have revolted too. They've ended the war which you opposed, and they've delivered the peace which you supported.

"And the *UDC* are going great-guns too. Their campaign for a *League of United Nations* is going to bear fruit. They're crushing the gender-nationality-and-class divides.

"We're at a tipping-point! We're building bridges to the future!

"Say Alfred, new legislation has overpowered *Dora*; we've won back our freedom of speech. And we've crushed conscription too; we've defeated the military-machine. The green shoots of recovery have begun to sprout!

"Yes, the ninety-nine percent think the army won the war. They don't realise how miserable they are because they think they're successful. They don't realise that no-one wins in war; that the dead-orphaned-widowed-and-injured aren't winners.

"But there is hope; the times they are a-changing. People are looking for an alternative to the politics which created this mess; the membership of every socialist-group is on the rise, and the Labour Party is set to be elected for the first time too. It's taking over the middle-ground!"

The Suffragist pauses and then she sighs, rolls her eyes, looks down at the ground and up at the skies.

"But not everything is rosy, so to speak," she cries. "The Slave Emancipator, who has only just been released from prison, is protesting against the *Treaty Of Reparations*. He says that it's harsh enough to inspire another war.

"So we've won the peace, but ensuring it lasts won't be easy. We're neck-and-neck with the warmakers as it stands. Say, they're still horse-trading behind closed-doors, in their smoke-filled rooms."

"That's true; they're still hungry for blood," Cleo adds with scorn, whilst she looks forlorn, tense-troubled-and-torn. "They've already launched another war, fighting in Afghanistan for the third time in under a century. Oh, there's just no rest for the wicked.

"Darn! I am sorry to speak of it. Look at you, just out of prison for peacemaking, and here I am speaking about war. Please don't think me wrong, but it did need to be said. I am a good girl, deep down, aren't I?"

"You're fantastic," Alfred replies. "But surely no-one supports the soldiers anymore? Please! Not after they've caused so many-many-many deaths, destroyed so much land, and torn so much our nation apart.

Please! People must have realised that soldiers aren't heroes, and that conchies are, now that we've proved ourselves? Please! People must realise that peace is better than war?"

Cleo feels so embarrassed, that she starts to look harassed; as she hangs her head in shame. The Deserter shrugs-shivers-and-sighs, closes his eyes; and looks a little bit lame. Which leaves the Suffragist to explain.

"Oh darling child," she begins to exclaim. "You've beaten the military, that's for sure, but people will hate you all the more for it. It's the politics of envy, so to speak. Virtue, you see, is persecuted more by the wicked, than it is loved by the good.

"At the end of the day, you've beaten an army which people adore, challenged a government which they respect, and opposed their sons-brothers-and-lovers. You're in the proverbial toilet.

"Most job-listings are now marked '*Contentious Objectors need not apply*', most families have ostracised their pro-peace relatives, and most conchies have lost their right to vote.

"There aren't any pensions for crippled-conchies, or any maintenance-allowances for their widows. You'll be an outcast and a pariah. You'll be despised. You'll be a hero for sure, but no-one will say it here on British soil. You'll never get the respect you deserve. Never!"

"I can accept all this," Alfred replies. "I am happy to embrace all the hardships which come my way. Yes-yes-yes! My campaign was fought for humanity, not for personal-glory.

"But how can you be so sure? Please tell me. I'd be ever so grateful. I'd be very much obliged."

"Because one met a few of your comrades from France on one's prison-visits," the Suffragist explains. "One still writes to some of them.

"Say, the Schoolmaster has been searching high-and-low for work, but no school will employ him, even as a janitor. He could look till the cows come home if you ask me, for all the good it will do him. He's picking fruit for now, whilst the harvest is plentiful and the labourers are few, but he'll be out of work in under a month.

"The Apprentice has also moved to the countryside, to an area where there aren't any other piano tuners, and so the locals have to hire him. But he's been struggling to keep in touch with his family, and he can't find a wife. No-one will marry him, not with his history.

"And one has not heard from the Nurse, but rumour has it that he's become a bit of a big hitter, so to speak; healing people using the cloth he wrapped around you in France. It's been said that he's used that shroud to end a siege, deliver men from evil-spirits, and heal the terminally-ill!"

The Suffragist winks, she blinks; and she lightens the mood with this tale. Which makes Cleo wriggle, Alfred giggle; and the Deserter flick this shale.

"Say, we're at a crossroads, so to speak," the Suffragist continues to wail. "And it's up to us to get Britain moving again. For one always feels that any protest is better than none, and that a life without a cause is a life without effect. So one is still encouraging soldiers to mutiny.

"And our grassroots membership is cleaning up the warmaker's mess as we speak. The *Quakers* are sending apostles all across Europe; to rebuild villages, purify water-supplies, build hospitals, and care for starving children. They're sending conchies on holidays to lift their spirits, and training them so they can find new jobs.

"The *Brotherhood Church* is helping conchies to recover from their hunger-strikes at a commune in the country. And the *NCF* are campaigning against war, conscription, and military-training in schools.

"The fight continues, and one is proud to be a part of it!"

As the Suffragist finishes this speech, Cleo finishes her peach; and the Deserter is overcome by some pessimistic-predictions. Because he has been working in the greengrocery, with rhubarb-radishes-and-rosemary; and some peacemakers who were sacked for their convictions. The Good German's old-store, with unchanged-decor; has joined an *NCF* labour-exchange which combats such afflictions.

It has raised money for an *NCF* kitty, to support the families of conchies in the Big City; and it hired more staff after rationing was introduced. Because shopkeepers had got clubbed, and delivery-boys had got mugged; amidst the panic which that policy produced. But now Alfred is back, the Deserter worries about getting the sack; or having his hours reduced.

"So what d'ya plan to do?" He asks Alfred apprehensively.

"Please understand!" Alfred replies pensively. "I plan to reconcile with the people who I alienated during my pro-peace campaign. Because I've come to realise that the more you preach, the less you teach. Yes-yes-yes. Yes thanky-you!

"I should've been more embracing. I didn't need to be a warrior for peace; peace was already in me. The kingdom of God was already in me! The whole universe was already in me! It was above-and-below me, within-and-without, to the left and the right. It was before-and-behind me; in the great-and-small, male-and-female, and soldier-and-conchie alike.

"And so I plan to reconcile with the *White Feather Brigade*, the Cadets, Bernie and my Mother. And I plan to embrace them all. It's a matter of *involution-and-evolution*. Yes-yes-yes. Thanking-you!"

"But what are ye gonna do wi' the shop?" The Deserter asks because he cannot tell if he is still employed, which makes him feel annoyed, despondent-downhearted-and-destroyed.

"Please! Do you understand me?" Alfred asks, as he clutches this flask; feeling overjoyed.

"Yeah, ye know that I understand ye."

"Then tend to my fruit. Please! Do you love me?"

"Yeah, ye know that I love ye."

"Then tend to my vegetables. Please! Do you embrace me?"

"Alfred," the Deserter replies again, because he finds these questions inane, and verging on the insane. "Ye know all o' these things; ye know that I embrace ye!"

"Please! Guide my customers, shepherd my flock, and manage my shop. Make followers of everyone you meet, wash them in peace, and teach them what I've taught you. I'd be ever so grateful. I'd be very much obliged."

Alfred smiles with beauty-balance-and-bliss, and gives the Deserter a farewell-kiss; knowing they will never meet up again. He walks past this row of rickety-gutters, and this row of rickety-shutters; before he returns to his childhood-domain. This workshop which is full of taps-tools-and-tapes, saws-sanders-and-shapes; chisels-crayons-and-chain.

He unearths his feathers from beneath this board, under which they have all been stored; throughout days of sunshine-showers-and-snow. Hundreds of barbs jut out from each shaft, thousands of barbules extend with craft; and millions of hooklets still glow.

Alfred soaks-softens-and-shapes each feather, fills them with blue-ink together; and then dries them out in this sand. He places these quills in homemade-cases, with homemade-bases; which he engraves with a steady-hand.

'*The pen is mightier than the sword*', he writes in these letters which look artistic, majestic; and grand.

Before he skips down these winding-lanes, past these horses who are dressed in reins; and this Belgian who is dressed in brown. Past these Soldiers who are embarking on military-marches, these giant white-arches; and this Don who is wearing a gown. Past these Chefs-Costermongers-and-Caretakers, Builders-Butchers-and-Bakers; and this freaky-looking Clown. These Men with their Spouses, these workmen's houses; and that tomb which is falling down. Before he climbs the tallest hill in this town.

Where he sees the Blonde Bombshell who thinks he is a stranger, sat with the Sunday School Teacher and Moneychanger; beneath this leafy-tree. They are chattering, nattering; and drinking some tea.

"Please tell me! What are you talking about?" Alfred asks them as he walks through some scree.

"Oh honey bunny, aren't you funny?" The Blonde Bombshell replies, as she flutters her eyes; and strokes her slender-knee. "You must be the only person in town who doesn't know what's happened."

The Blonde Bombshell's beauty has waned with time, now she is past her prime; with blue-veins all over her face. With cheeks which are blue, as if she has the flu; and with her neck in a cervical-brace.

"What are you talking about?" Alfred cuts to the chase. "Please tell me. Please-please-please."

"What are we talking about? Talking about?" The Moneychanger replies, as she swats these flies; and ties a brown-shoelace. "Well about the contentious objectors of course. They claimed to be prophets of peace. Of peace! Our leaders sentenced them to death, and crucified them for it.

"But we heard that they'd been released from jail this morning, so we went to see for ourselves. And, low-and-behold, there wasn't a single conchie there.

"It's a disgrace. It doesn't do! It just doesn't do! They should have all been shot!"

Alfred sits down with these girls, who are wearing fake-pearls; and he starts to commune. He talks with tranquillity, and humility; until the sun is usurped by the moon.

When his Sunday School Teacher continues on with her foot-shuffling, hair-ruffling; and bottom-shaking. Her flirtatious-winking, unconscious-blinking; and dimple-making.

"Stay with us tonight, sweetheart," she says as her heart starts quaking. "It is getting late, my love."

"Thank-you," Alfred replies as he looks out at this town, takes this bread down, and shares it all around. "Thank-you, thank-you, thank-you! I do respect your white-feather campaign. You did what you considered was right; it was a good effort. Way to go! Your efforts deserve recognition.

"The peacemakers did what they thought was right too, so we're not so different. We're the same! Yes thanky-you.

"Although I did let my emotions overpower my spirit, and my heart overpower my soul. I'm sorry for that. Sorry-sorry-sorry. I do understand-love-and-embrace you now."

Alfred stands up to leave, touches the Moneychanger's sleeve; and wins over these ladies' hearts. He puts three feathers onto this bench, which is near that trench; and reveals his identity as he departs.

"I feel like there is a fire ablaze within me! I'm in love!" The Sunday School Teacher volunteers, as she falls for Alfred after all these years; near some horses who are pulling their carts.

She starts to cry as Alfred walks downwards, walks onwards; and walks into this old church-hall. Where he crosses these boards, and holds seven cords; in front of this painted-wall.

The Retired Captain leads this cadet-meeting, near this seating; where these Moneychangers count their gold. Whilst these Children get groomed for war, in this military-corps; where they do whatever they are told.

Bathed in shiny-light, Alfred ascends to this height; from where he spoke out once before. These Merchants turn his way, and those Cadets begin to sway; on that shiny-floor.

Their hearts stop, their bodies freeze and their stomachs drop; they cry-clamour-and-call. They recall Alfred's last speech in here, so they flee in fear; flop-faint-and-fall.

"What-o? Surely this is a spirit," the Retired Captain begins to drawl. "This man was crucified. For our country! For our country! Oh, boo hoo. Boo hoo hoo! He can't have risen from the dead. What a pickle! Golly-o."

Alfred walks across these tiles, smiles; and puts his rope on top of this chest. He nods keenly, smiles serenely; and looks like he has been blessed.

His breath travels from bronchiole-to-bronchi-to-larynx, up through his pharynx; and all the way out through his nose. He is held-heeded-and-heard, without adding a word; or trying to impose.

So he walks out of this grey-stone church, leaves the Retired Captain in the lurch; and ends his belligerent-reign. Whilst these Cadets run in many ways, with their hearts ablaze; alight-afire-and-aflame.

Alfred walks past these mansions which are surrounded by vines, these apartments which are surrounded by pines; and these Schoolgirls who all have the giggles. He walks past these houses which are rather tall, these cottages which are rather small; and this billboard which is covered in wiggles. This hut which is painted black, this ramshackle-shack; and this shopfront which is covered in squiggles. Before he enters his home, where Cleo is alone; with a curious case of the wriggles.

"Oh, I'm sorry to say it," she says whilst she jiggles. "But I just don't get all this reconciliation malarkey. Whatever happened to 'Live by the sword, die by the sword'? Oh, I am terrible, but I just don't get it. Does that make me bad? Oh, I am a good girl really, aren't I?"

"You're perfect." Alfred replies. "But please! Too many-many-many people have already died by the sword. It's time to start living.

"You see, there was once a Maid whose Mistress was the perfect boss. But then again, she had no reason not to be. She had everything she ever wanted, and her Maid did whatever she was told.

"So the Maid tested her Mistress to see if she was truly kind, by arriving late one morning. Well, her Mistress flew into a mighty-rage, and beat the Maid. The Maid turned up late the next day too, and her Mistress beat her again. Her Mistress beat her every day that week.

"Because whilst her Mistress's *actions* had always been kind, her *being* had never been pure. No-no-no. No thanky-you!

"And I was much the same. I performed many good-deeds when I was younger, and gave many gifts to poor children at Christmas time. They were really-really-really kind *actions*, but they only had a limited effect on my *being*. I did them because I had no reason not to.

"And when I made a gift for the Temperamental Soldier, it was only because I wanted him to send a postcard home. It was selfish.

"But last year, when I made gifts for my Jailor, I did *evolve* my soul. I understood-loved-and-embraced my Jailor, even though he slandered me and put me in solitary-confinement. I understood-loved-and-embraced him without ever wanting anything in return, which helped me to become a better person. Yes-yes-yes. Yes thanky-you!

"I embraced myself, our society, and our universe. I embraced the warmakers as a part of my very own being. And it helped me to rise. It helped me to transcend this world of suffering-and-pain.

"But it also helped me to see that I'd told people to love their enemies, the Germans, without ever following my advice. I'd never loved my own enemies, the warmakers. And for that I'm now making amends."

Alfred takes some brimstone-and-treacle before he shaves, before he bathes; and before he falls asleep tonight. Before he goes to see Bernie, feeling bright-bouncy-and-breezy; with a joyous sort of delight.

He walks past this Gardener who carries a rake, this Gypsy who charms a snake; and that unshaven Tiller. This large group of suited Solicitors, this small group of Belgian Exhibitors; and that lonesome Distiller. Before he arrives at this restaurant, where Bernie is sat near a plant; a fish-tank and a pillar.

Bernie works for the firm which employed him before, now he is a hero of war; and an archetypal-soldier. Now he has become a sergeant, and feels resurgent; with three chevrons on either shoulder. He has the fiancée he desired, and found it easy to get hired; now he is five years older.

"Good God man!" He says as he closes this folder. "You don't have to explain yourself to me. Not really, no, not at all. I only asked you to follow orders for your own good. We'll always be friends! *Alfred and*

Bernie - friends for ever - A. B. See!"

"That's just it!" Alfred replies. "We shouldn't let silly little things like wars get between us. Please!

"I'm sorry for the way I spoke to you when you enlisted, I should've embraced your decision to fight. I understand-love-and-embrace you now. What a fabulous person you are! My Mother always said I should be more like you. I'm so happy to see that you're happy."

These friends talk as if they had never been separated, which makes time feel accelerated; whilst they slurp their soup and chew their tart. Whilst Bernie talks about France without revision, and Alfred talks about his time in prison; with all his soul and all his heart.

"Please tell me! What happened to the Coward?" Alfred asks as they depart.

"He became introverted at first," Bernie replies, and cries; because this question tears him apart. "I think he must've gone mad. Bonkers! Doolally! Cuckoo! He didn't speak for days and, in the end, he just couldn't hack it anymore.

"'*I've sinned!*' He shouted. '*I've betrayed innocent blood!*'

"Oh blow man! No-one cared much for what the Coward thought.

"'*What's that to us, you lowlife prawn?*' The Commanding Officer taunted. '*That's your responsibility, and fault, and burden; not ours*'.

"And so the Coward threw down his thirty silver-franks, and stormed off. It was awfully rum. We didn't have an earthly what he was doing, until we found his corpse hanging from a tree in an empty-field. Good God man! The silly little boy had only gone and hung himself.

"The army used his silver-pieces to buy that field, and turned it into a mass-grave for foreigners-deserters-and-civilians, which they called '*The Field Of Blood*'."

"Oh gosh! I'd like to visit that field, to pay my respects. Yes please! Please-please-please!" Alfred says.

"For sure man. I'll show you where it is," Bernie replies before they go their separate ways.

Before Alfred goes to his childhood-home, where he sees this comb; and these biscuits which are slightly stale. This photograph which is faded, this painting which is jaded; and this pile of yesterday's mail.

And he sees his Mother who has become so thin, with wrinkled-fingers and wrinkled-skin; that she looks a little bit weird. Her clothes are fraying, her hair is greying; and she has started to sprout a beard.

Her spine shoots her back in awe, as Alfred walks through this door; with this look of peaceful-serenity. It swirls her around with dread, and wobbles her head; as she questions her own identity.

So Alfred pours her some water to drink, gives her some time to think; and acts with peaceful-tranquillity. He acts with peaceful-care, peaceful-flair; and peaceful-civility.

"You've brought shame upon me, this family and this nation," his Mother says with hostility. "Somewhere-somewhen-somehow, you-have-you-have-you-have.

"Look at me. How dare you show your face in here, Alfred Freeman? You're a disgrace, and every damn fool knows it. My little-soldier, you're just not respectable!"

"I know," Alfred confesses. "I know that I've hurt you. In life you often hurt the people who love you the most; it's a tragedy in which I've played a leading role. And so I've come to apologize. I am sorry. Please understand. Please-please-please."

With a smile on his clean-shaven face, Alfred looks around this place; and sees the memories which live on in this room. He sees the time when his Stepfather was introduced, the silence that moment produced; and his Aunts were doused in perfume. He sees the time when his Father died, when his Mother cried; and when she darned his Father's costume.

"Please tell me!" Alfred asks as he sits down near this tape, this drape; and that broom. "Do you know why gladiatorial fights were abolished in ancient Rome?"

Alfred's Mother is overcome with breathless-distress, and breathless-stress; so she is unable to reply. As she starts to shake, quake; and cry.

"It happened after an Ascetic jumped into the arena," Alfred explains, whilst his Mother strains; and clutches her wrinkled-thigh. "That Ascetic walked across the Coliseum, past many-many-many gladiators, and past some chariots too.

"Tens-of-thousands of Romans watched on from the stands as the Ascetic marched up to Caesar. Please! Just imagine it! The Ascetic looked a complete wreck compared to that magnificent leader. But he was brave. Yes thanky-you! He told Caesar that killing people for sport was barbaric. He told Caesar to end to it there-and-then.

"Once he'd finished speaking, the crowd threw rocks at the Ascetic. They were offended by the way that moral-upstart had challenged their culture.

"And beneath that storm of stones, a lion approached the Ascetic, and ate him whole. The Ascetic died in an instant, but as a result of his sacrifice, no-one was ever killed in that arena again. No thanky-you! So his actions, which were so unpopular at the time, saved countless lives.

"Well, when I refused to be a soldier, I was happy to be rejected by society too. I was happy to be eaten by the lion of war. Like the Ascetic, I believed my sacrifice would inspire a newfound respect for human-life.

"And like him, I can see that I'm dead to you now. And I can accept that, because I understand-love-and-embrace you Mother, I really do. There isn't a single thing about you which I don't like. There's not a single thing about you which I'd change. Not one! I'm grateful for everything you've ever done for me. Yes-yes-yes!"

Alfred smiles as he removes this homemade wooden-box, places it down by those wooden-clocks; that cotton-sock and that leather-shoe. So like the Private in the Admiral's book, he has proved that he is not a caitiff-coward-or-crook; and returned his four feathers too.

"I plan to leave this country," he says with his arms askew. "I plan to follow in the footsteps of the Good German.

"Through *involution-and-evolution*, by the descent of spirit into matter, and the ascent of matter into spirit, I shall rest. I shall find shelter in the hills, surrounded by bubbling-springs and blossoming-orchids.

"Please come with me, Mother? Pretty please. Pretty please with a cherry on top."

Alfred lifts his hands to bless his Mother, to show her that he loves her; before he gives her this gentle-kiss. He acts with peaceful-tranquillity, peaceful-humility; and peaceful-bliss.

"Never," his Mother begins to huff, rebuff; and dismiss. "Look at me. I'll never come with you, I'll never be like you, and I never want to see you again. My notion! There's just nothing to be done with you,

Alfred Freeman.

"Your family hates you, your country hates you, and I hate you too. Don't you ever come hither again. You and your mischity will never be welcome here!"

So ends this story about understanding overcoming compulsion, love overcoming revulsion; and oneness overcoming abuse. This story about the rare sort of kind-geniality, and brave-morality; which we all possess but seldom use.

For detractors have been defeated, challenges have been completed; and principles have been proclaimed. Acts of persecution, and threats of execution; have all been constrained.

This is the end of Alfred Freeman's story, the end of a life full of glory; and the end of Alfred himself. Because Alfred is about to depart, with a peaceful-heart; and perfect-health.

"You'll never be welcome here! There. That is all." His Mother says as her spine thrusts her into that shelf.

"I understand," Alfred replies with peaceful-tranquillity.

"I love you," he says with peaceful-humility.

"I am you," he says with civility.

He walks outwards, walks onwards; and walks free.

DEMOCRACY
A USER'S GUIDE

THEY SAY WE LIVE IN A DEMOCRACY. WE ARE FREE AND WE SHOULD BE GRATEFUL.

But just how "Free" are we? How democratic are our so-called "Democracies"?

Is it enough to simply elect our leaders and sit back, helpless, as they rule over us like dictators? What good is selecting our politicians, if we cannot control our media, police or soldiers? If we must blindly follow our teachers' and bosses' commands, whilst at school and in the workplace, is it not a little naïve to believe that we are the masters of our own destinies? And if our resources are controlled by a tiny cabal of plutocrats, bankers and corporations; can we honestly say that our economies are being run for us?

Could things not be a little bit more, well, democratic?

Indeed they can! "Democracy: A User's Guide" shows us how...

Within the pages of this story-filled book, we shall visit Summerhill, a democratic school in the east of England, before stopping off in Brazil to check out Semco, where workplace democracy is the name of the game. We will travel to Rojava, to explore life in a democratic army, and head to Spain, to see why Podemos is giving liquid democracy a go. We shall travel back in time, to see democracy at work in hunter-gatherer societies, tribal confederacies, the guilds and on the commons. We will consider the case for participatory budgeting, deliberative democracy, collaborative hiring, community currencies, peer-to-peer lending, and much much more.

The message is clear and concise: Democracy does not have to be a pipe dream. We have all the tools we need to rule ourselves.

INDIVIDUTOPIA

"One of the most important books of 2018"
The Canary
"One of those books you'll want to read again and again"
Medium
"A modern classic"
The Dallas Sun

Beloved friend,

The year is 2084, and that famous Margaret Thatcher quote has become a reality: There really is no such thing as society. No one speaks to anyone else. No one looks at anyone else. People don't collaborate, they only compete.

I hate to admit it, but this has had tragic consequences. Unable to satisfy their social urges, the population has fallen into a pit of depression and anxiety. Suicide has become the norm.

It all sounds rather morbid, does it not? But please don't despair, there is hope, and it comes in the form of our hero: Renee Ann Blanca. Wishing to fill the society-shaped hole in her life, our Renee does the unthinkable: She goes in search of human company! It's a radical act and an enormous challenge. But that, I suppose, is why her tale's worth recounting. It's as gripping as it is touching, and I think you're going to love it...

Your trusty narrator,

PP

MONEY
POWER
LOVE

"Breathtaking" – **The Huffington Post**
"Picaresque" – **Scottish Left Review**
"Unputdownable" – **The Avenger**
"Strangely kind" – **The Tribune**

Born on three adjacent beds, a mere three seconds apart, our three heroes are united by nature but divided by nurture. As a result of their different upbringings, they spend their lives chasing three very different things: Money, power and love.

This is a human story: A tale about people like ourselves, cajoled by the whimsy of circumstance, who find themselves performing the most beautiful acts as well as the most vulgar.

This is a historical story: A tale set in the early 1800s, which shines a light on how bankers, with the power to create money out of nothing, were able to shape the world we live in today.

And this is a love story: A tale about three men, who fall in love with the same woman, at the very same time...

ALSO BY JOSS SHELDON...

THE LITTLE VOICE

"The most thought-provoking novel of 2016"
Huffington Post

"Radical... A masterclass... Top notch..."
The Canary

"A pretty remarkable feat"
BuzzFeed

"Can you remember who you were before the world told you who you should be?"

Dear reader,

My character has been shaped by two opposing forces; the pressure to conform to social norms, and the pressure to be true to myself. To be honest with you, these forces have really torn me apart. They've pulled me one way and then the other. At times, they've left me questioning my whole entire existence.

But please don't think that I'm angry or morose. I'm not. Because through adversity comes knowledge. I've suffered, it's true. But I've learnt from my pain. I've become a better person.

Now, for the first time, I'm ready to tell my story. Perhaps it will inspire you. Perhaps it will encourage you to think in a whole new way. Perhaps it won't. There's only one way to find out...

Enjoy the book,

Yew Shodkin

OCCUPIED

"A unique piece of literary fiction"
The Examiner
"Darker than George Orwell's 1984"
AXS
"Genre-busting"
Pak Asia Times

SOME PEOPLE LIVE UNDER OCCUPATION.

SOME PEOPLE OCCUPY THEMSELVES.

NO ONE IS FREE.

Step into a world which is both magically fictitious and shockingly real, to follow the lives of Tamsin, Ellie, Arun and Charlie; a refugee, native, occupier and economic migrant. Watch them grow up during a halcyon past, everyday present and dystopian future. And be prepared to be amazed.

Inspired by the occupations of Palestine, Kurdistan and Tibet, and by the corporate occupation of the west, 'Occupied' is a haunting glance into a society which is a little too familiar for comfort. It truly is a unique piece of literary fiction…

www.joss-sheldon.com

If you enjoyed this book, please do leave a review online. Joss Sheldon does not have a professional marketing team behind him – he needs your help to spread the word about his books!!!